YOUR TRUTH
IS OUT THERE

Find Your Truth: Book One

by DAVID ALLEN KIMMEL

YOUR TRUTH IS OUT THERE

Find Your Truth: Book One

Copyright © 2016 by David Allen Kimmel

ISBN-13: 978-0692484562
ISBN-10: 0692484566

Cover art by Stephen Youll.
Cover design by Jamie Youll.

www.DavidAllenKimmel.com

Give feedback on the book at:
DavidAllenKimmel@gmail.com

Twitter: @dak1963

First Edition

Printed in the U.S.A

To Mom, Dad, Bill & Laura.

And to Rhonda—I could not have done this without you, nor would I have wanted to try.

CONTENTS

PART ONE: ENEMIES & FRIENDS

PART TWO: FRIENDS & ENEMIES

PART ONE:
ENEMIES & FRIENDS

Chapter 1

I Lost My Job Today

Henry glanced up at the clock behind the bar, saw that it was almost 2:30 in the afternoon, and realizing it was much too early in the day for his third shot of whiskey, proceeded to take the full glass in front of him and knock it back.

"Another one, please," he said to the bartender, "in fact, after what I've just been through, you should probably just leave the bottle."

"Look my friend," said the bartender, "I don't want to get into your business, but I can't leave the bottle unless you pay up front."

"No problem," said Henry, pulling out his wallet. He took out his one and only credit card, hoping through the buzz in his head that he had enough credit left to pay for the bottle, and slapped it down on the bar. "There ya go, put it on that."

"You sure about this, buddy?" said the bartender, giving Henry a once-over. "You're not one of my regulars, and you don't look like the kind of guy who polishes off a bottle of Jack in the middle of the afternoon."

Henry nodded. "Take it," he said.

"Suit yourself," said the bartender taking the card and turning back to the register. "It's your money ... and liver."

Henry looked at the clock again, and then chastised himself after seeing that it was now exactly 2:37. Why the hell should he care what time it was? It wasn't like he had anywhere to be. It wasn't like he still had a job or anything.

"What's your name?" he said to the bartender when the man turned back around with his credit card, the approval slip, and the nearly full bottle of Jack Daniels.

"Craig," said the man, who didn't seem much older than Henry's twenty-nine years. He took the slip back after Henry signed it, and looked at the generous tip Henry had left him. "Thanks for that, Mr. Backus."

"Mr. Backus ... hmmm ... almost makes me sound important when you say it like that. Call me Henry, please."

"Sure thing," said Craig absently, as he put the ticket into the cash register and went to check on another customer at the other end of the bar.

"Almost sounded important," said Henry quietly to himself as he poured another drink, "almost."

Henry downed the shot, then looked around the darkened room through eyes that, even though hazed by alcohol, were still perceptive enough to quickly understand the place. It was a bar, sure, that was easy enough to see. There were booths lining the far wall and tables in the middle of the room, all empty at this time of day. Then of course, there was the bar itself where he sat, along with the establishment's only other customer, the one Craig was tending to now. Yes, this was a bar, but it was more than that; it was a kind of resting place, a place where the wounded of spirit came to find a small modicum of respite from the pain that tortured them.

His counterpart at the end of the bar, for example, was clearly a regular. The man was quite comfortable with his surroundings, much more so than Henry. He clearly knew his way around the place, too, reaching behind the bar and grabbing a stack of cocktail napkins and stuffing them in his pocket while Craig had his back turned, then going for a can of peanuts the next time the bartender wasn't watching. Aside from his kleptomania, it was clear this man had an affliction of some sort, a disease upon his soul. Otherwise why would he be in here and not out amongst the living? As Henry began to wonder what his situation could be, the man turned toward Henry and made eye contact with him. It was brief, but it may as well have been an eternity, for in that moment, in those eyes, Henry saw a darkness, a level of broken despair he never thought possible, even knowing how deep his own pain went. Henry turned back to his bottle, poured another shot and downed it, deciding that the rest of the world was none of his damn business.

"You know, I'm not one to tell someone how they should drink their bottle," said Craig, as he returned to Henry's side of the bar carrying a glass filled with ice, "but shooting the whole thing is a pretty tough way to go. I might suggest taking it a little slower and trying some on the rocks. You might even think about mixing it with something."

Henry looked up at the bartender as the man set the glass down in front of him.

"Thanks, that's probably a good idea," he said, doing his level-best not to slur his words. He poured the whiskey over the ice, watching the two forces of golden liquid alcohol and frozen solid ice interact with one another. The liquid melting the solid, doing its best to tear it down, while the solid, not giving in without a fight, quietly diluted the liquid, leaving it less potent than it once was. He wanted to believe there was a lesson to be learned there, inside that glass, some parallel he could equate to his own life, but if there was, he couldn't find it. He picked up the glass and took a drink, but just a sip this time.

"So, what brings you into my corner of the world dressed in business casual in the middle of the work day?" asked Craig, breaking Henry's downwardly spiraling train of thought.

Henry looked up at the bartender, his eyes definitely hazier than they were a few minutes before. He was almost certain he wouldn't be able to answer this time without slurring.

"It's okay," said Craig, "you don't have to tell me, I just thought you might need someone to talk to. It's kinda what I do." He started to turn around, back toward the other end of the bar.

"I lost my job today," said Henry, suddenly not caring if he slurred or not. Someone had actually asked about him, had actually cared enough to ask why he was where he was, and not in a negative, angry way. He couldn't remember the last time that had happened. In fact, he couldn't remember that ever happening. Not his parents. They barely noticed him, much less cared about where he went or what he did. They were too busy with their own lives to be concerned with his. And certainly not Lucy. No, definitely not her. But Craig actually seemed interested in the answer. He couldn't let him walk away.

"I didn't actually lose my job," he said, correcting himself as Craig turned to face him, "I pretty much threw it away all by myself."

"I see," said Craig, "and how did you do that? More importantly, why? I can't imagine you just up and decided that you wanted a bottle of Jack more than you wanted your job."

"No," said Henry with a snicker, "nothing so simple. I was giving a presentation to my boss, the company's CEO, about a new ad campaign I was proposing. I've spent the last three months working my ass off putting this thing together and before I even got halfway through it, he cuts me off and tells me it's no good."

"Sounds pretty harsh," said Craig.

"You're telling me. But hey, I remained calm. I stayed professional. I restrained myself and politely, but firmly, I defended the campaign strategy."

"And?"

"And ... he didn't budge. He said he wanted me to start completely over and he wanted to see six new concepts, and he wanted them in two weeks. Six! In two weeks!"

"Wow, the guy sounds like a total ass. What'd you do?"

"I lost it. I mean, I completely lost it. I called him every name I could think of, and I know quite a few. I threw things, knocked other things over, and basically made a complete fool of myself."

"I don't know," said Craig, "it sounds like you were just standing up for what you believe in, right?"

Henry looked up from his drink. Someone was taking his side. That had never happened before. Never.

"Right," he said, "that's right. I put a lot of work into that campaign. The least he could have done is let me finish the presentation, but no, he had to stop me right in the middle, tell me I wasn't worth a crap right in front of everyone."

"Yeah, that's messed up, especially since other people had to have seen the campaign before he did, right? I mean they would have approved it before it got to him, so it's not all on you ... right ... Henry?"

Henry didn't answer, he was too busy taking a long drink from his glass and doing his best to avoid eye contact with the suddenly too-inquisitive bartender.

"You did let someone else review it before you showed it to the head of the entire company, right Henry?" Asked Craig again, as Henry lowered his glass.

"Well," said Henry, "not exactly. But it wasn't like I was hiding anything. That's the way it's always been, nobody sees my work until I'm ready to show it, and then I show everyone at once. I've been there for almost a year now and it's never been a problem."

He stopped to take another drink, and as he did so, the words the bartender could have said, but didn't, hit home, making him realize something he hadn't before.

"Then again," he said, looking back at Craig, "I've never had a project like this before. It's always been small, one-page flyers and stuff like that, never anything on this scale. Even so, it never crossed my mind to consult with anyone else."

"It couldn't have hurt," said Craig, "it's tough to go it alone all the time."

"That's all I know how to do," said Henry softly, staring into his now empty glass, "it's all I've ever known."

"People change, Henry. It's never too late."

Henry didn't respond, but continued staring at the empty glass. Something as small as asking someone for help might have changed everything. Understanding so simple of a social norm might have been the difference between achieving success within his company and the reality of what happened today.

But even as he said those words in his head, they rang hollow. A second, more insistent, inner voice said: *Who would you have asked for help? Which one of those philistines would you have trusted when it came to matters relating to creativity? The accountants? The lawyers? The engineers? The sales staff? Okay, maybe the sales staff, but even then it might be iffy. Besides,* the voice continued, *is success within the company what you really want? Do you really want to climb the corporate ladder, trading in ever larger pieces of your soul along the way? Is that what you really want, Henry? Henry? Henry?*

"Henry? Henry, are you still with me?" It was Craig.

"Oh, sorry," said Henry, stirring from his inner tug-o-war, "yes, I was just thinking. What is it you were saying?"

"I was asking about the campaign. Tell me about it, let me see if it's any good or not."

"Sure," said Henry, pouring himself another drink, "why not? Are you a fisherman?"

"Yeah, I like to fish every now and then."

"Ever heard of Telasco rods and reels?"

"Oh yeah, sure, that's what I use."

"Well, that's who I work ... used to work for."

"No kidding."

"Nope, no kidding. They wanted a whole new ad campaign, print, video, mobile, social media, the works, and they wanted to see what I could come up with. So, I spent several weeks developing a slogan, and then the next couple of months creating the art for all of the different media where the ads would be placed."

"So, let's hear it, what was the slogan?"

Henry took a deep breath. After what happened in the conference room with his former CEO, he wasn't sure he wanted to say the slogan out loud again. He took another sip of his drink.

"Ah, what the hell?" he said. "Here goes ... it was, 'Telasco Industries, We love fish, and fish love us!'"

Henry looked up at Craig, hoping for a better reaction than he received earlier in the day. He didn't get it. The bartender appeared to be doing everything he could not to laugh directly in Henry's face.

"I'm sorry, Henry," he said, unable to contain his laughter any longer, "that is terrible. I mean, it's really, really bad."

"Thanks," said Henry, "thanks a lot. Go ahead and kick a guy when he's down, why don't ya."

"Hey, Henry, I'm sorry buddy, but even you have to admit that it's really bad."

"No I don't. If I thought it was that bad, I wouldn't have presented it."

"We love fish, and fish love us? Come on, Henry, that's terrible."

Henry stopped and thought about it for a second.

"Okay," he said with a smirk, "I guess you're right, it is pretty bad. And yes, you were right, I should have let someone else review it before I presented it to the CEO of the company. But so what? It's too late now, I've already screwed up and I'm out of a job."

"Maybe not," said Craig with a nod of his head toward the door, "I think maybe someone's looking for you."

Henry turned to the door and saw his former boss, Jason Lesko, President and CEO of Telasco Industries.

"Oh crap," said Henry, half under his breath. "What the hell? Is he going to fire me again?"

"Henry," said Jason, walking over to where he was sitting, "I was hoping I could find you. It's taken a while, but I'm glad

I caught up with you." He looked at Craig. "I'll have whatever he's having."

"Here, sir," said Henry taking his bottle, "allow me." He took the glass that Craig handed him and poured his former boss a drink. "What are you doing here?"

Jason took a sip of the drink, then pulled an envelope out of his suit jacket pocket.

"I wanted to deliver this personally. It's your final paycheck."

Henry's heart sunk. Whatever chance he thought he might have had of getting his job back was gone now.

"I see," he said. "Thanks, I appreciate you delivering it, although I don't really understand why. I said some pretty awful things, called you some pretty awful things."

"Yeah," said Jason, smiling into his drink, "you did at that. But I know you didn't mean them. Look Henry, we've worked together for nearly a year, and in that time I've come to appreciate your ... let's call it, candor. Although, today's display was a bit too direct and, well, inappropriate."

"Jason, I'm really sorry about how I acted today. You're right, it was totally inappropriate and unprofessional. And, you know I didn't really mean any of it, I was just frustrated, that's all."

"I know, Henry. But that's not why I'm here."

"I'm not sure I understand," said Henry.

Jason picked up his glass and sloshed the whiskey around.

"Do you like to bowl, Henry?" he asked.

Between the buzz in his head from the alcohol and the bizarre conversation, Henry was confused as ever.

"I'm not following you, sir," he said.

"Bowl, Henry, you know, do you like to go bowling?"

"I can't really say for sure. I've never tried it."

"Ah well, there's nothing like it, Henry," said Jason as he downed his drink and slid his glass over for a refill. "Nothing like being in the groove and throwing strike after strike after strike."

Henry nodded his head, as if he understood what his former boss was talking about.

"I'm guessing you're pretty good at it then," he said, refilling the glass.

"I used to be," said Jason, a far-away look in his eyes. "I used to be very good." He turned back to look at Henry. "I was all set to turn pro ... had my sponsors lined up and everything. All I had to do was show up at the first tournament in Memphis nd compete."

"What happened?"

"My father died."

"Oh God. Oh Jason, I'm sorry."

Jason nodded and took another sip.

"Thanks," he said. "But that's not the tragedy of this story. When he died, I didn't go to Memphis to compete in that tournament. Understandably, I stayed home to handle the funeral and to wrap up his affairs. But, I didn't just miss the Memphis tournament, I missed them all. My father left Telasco to me, on the condition that I give up my "childish fantasy" as he put it and stay home to run the family business."

"Wow, sounds like your dad had some serious control issues," said Henry, not knowing what else to say or do. "Believe it or not, I can relate."

"I believe you can, Henry," said Jason, looking at Henry in a way Henry wasn't used to. "But, I'm not looking for sympathy or anything like that. My life turned out just fine. I'm likely a lot wealthier now than if I'd gone pro, but that's not the point either. I didn't chase my dream, Henry. Not many of us get the opportunity to go after our dreams, and when we actually do, even fewer of us actually take the risk to chase after it."

"Okay, but what does that have to do with me?"

"Henry, I was going over your presentation, you know, giving it a closer look to make sure I didn't miss anything."

"And ...?"

"And ... well, your artwork is ... is amazing."

"Excuse me, sir?"

"Henry, please don't call me sir, you don't work for me anymore. I'm here as a friend. You are a truly gifted artist, I mean beyond anything I've ever seen before and I have a pretty good eye for this kind of thing. Henry, if I can offer you this one piece of advice, don't think of the fact that you no longer work at Telasco as a setback, but as an opportunity for you to chase your dream as an artist. Do what I didn't. You weren't meant to work the eight-to-five shift in the corporate world; you're far too talented for that."

Jason reached over and put his hand on Henry's shoulder.

"You're going to be just fine," he said, "and to make sure, I added a little extra to your check. Think of it as an investment in your new future."

Henry felt a lump in his throat, but fought it down with another drink.

"Thank you, Jason," he said when he finally regained his composure. "I don't know what to say."

Jason got up and held his hand out.

"Say that you'll consider my advice and pursue your dream."

"I will," said Henry.

"Good luck to you."

"Thank you," said Henry, standing up as well. "I hope you find someone who can create the right campaign for you."

Jason nodded, then turned around and left.

Henry sat back down and looked at the glass in front of him, which a moment before seemed half-empty but was now clearly half-full.

"Everything okay?" asked Craig coming back from the other end of the bar.

"Yeah," replied Henry as he picked up the glass and downed the rest.

"Did he take you back?"

"Nope," said Henry. "Better. He told me to chase my dream."

"Is that a good thing?"

"It would be, except for one problem."

"What's that?"

"Not a that, but a who."

Not bothering with the glass, Henry grabbed the Jack and drank it straight from the bottle.

"My wife," he said as he set the bottle back down on the bar. "You'd best call me a cab."

Chapter 2

A Slow, Tedious Affair

"**W**e have a major snarl along Channel 1753, where a multi-vehicle wreck has completely blocked traffic. Clean-up crews are on their way, but those traveling along 1753 may want to consider alternate routes ..."

Gsefx turned the vidcon off. He'd heard enough.

"Great, just great," he said aloud, as his vehicle crawled forward, along with the rest of the inbound commuters. Like Gsefx, they were all making their way in from the thousands of outlying systems they called home, to their jobs on Laxor, the primary business hub for this sector.

He glanced at the console chronometer for the third time in the last five ebyts and slammed a fist into the top of the console.

"Gralt!" he shouted. "So much for getting to the juricking office early and catching up on my juricking work. At this rate, I'll be lucky just to arrive in time for my first meeting."

Even under the best of circumstances, the commute to Laxor from his home on Clangdor was a slow, tedious affair, and after nearly ten turns of slogging his way through heavy traffic, Gsefx had, for the most part, resigned himself to the fact that the commute was simply a part of the job. Sometimes, when he allowed himself to escape into the music he loved so dearly, that resignation worked. The trip to and from the office provided Gsefx with the perfect opportunity to turn the volume up as loud as he wanted and kick everything else out of his mind, if only briefly. As the amount of free time he had to simply sit and enjoy his music was such a rarity, the privacy of his vehicle could be a welcome sanctuary—when he allowed it to be. At times like this, however, when there was so much work piled up and waiting for him, even his favorite music wasn't enough to keep him from exploding in frustration.

"Gralt!" he shouted again, with another slam to the console.

He took a deep breath in an effort to compose himself before briefly considering taking the next exit to access an alternate route. There were numerous ways to get to the Galacticount offices, of course, and Gsefx knew them all. He discarded the idea as quickly as it crossed his mind.

Just be patient, Gsefx, and stay on course, he thought. *As slow as traffic is moving, alternates never work and usually end up taking longer.*

He took another deep breath and attempted to steer his thoughts away from the traffic, and the trouble it was currently causing him.

It's not like your life is going to come crashing down around you if you don't get there early, he told himself. *After all, you have it pretty juricking good—a great career with the single most prestigious accounting firm in the galaxy. And, lest you forget, you just got a promotion. You have a beautiful home—even if it is a bit far from the office. Best of all, you're married to Lhvunsa, the woman of your dreams. How much better do you think you can do than that? No better, that's how much, so quit pitching a fit. You're only ten turns out of Higher Learning, so I'd say you're doing pretty juricking good. Certainly good enough to not let this traffic ruin everything for you. What if someone from the office were in a vehicle close by and saw you cursing and slamming your fists into the console? How good for your career do you think that would be?*

This wasn't Gsefx's first attempt at talking himself through his frustrations. He'd recited this script many times before. Too many times, in fact, for it to have the intended effect of taking his mind off the traffic. No matter that it was all true, the facts simply didn't matter at the moment. What did matter was that he'd awoken early, which in and of itself was no easy task, then left home early, hoping to beat the traffic and get to the office ahead of everyone else. All so he could catch up on his work before the chaos of the rotation put him even further behind than he already was. That was out of the question now.

"Gralt!" He shouted again, this time refraining from hitting the console, or anything else. "I'm not asking for much! Just a little time to work without interruption so I can catch up a little. Now, thanks to this juricking traffic," he waved two of his arms around wildly, "that's not going to happen, and I'm probably going to have to stay late again ... or work through the break. Either way, Lhvunsa is not going to be happy about it."

He reached into his storage compartment and grabbed a snack bar, his fourth since leaving the house. He tore off the wrapper and tossed it to the floor with the others, then stuffed the entire bar into his mouth. As he did so, the console chronometer caught his attention once again.

"Graulgh!" he shouted, as best he could around a mouthful of junk food. According to his onboard timekeeper, getting to work early was no longer his biggest concern. At his current rate of travel, simply arriving on time was going to be a stretch. Gsefx wasn't sure how many times he'd been late this semi-turn, but he knew it was more than once. He also knew that his supervisor, a Dremin named Qilzar, definitely was keeping track of his tardies. After a quick calculation in his head, he decided he had time for at least one song, maybe two, before he'd have to call in and admit to Qilzar that he was going to be late again.

"Albalan, random, play," he said to the ship's computer. Moments later, the cockpit filled with the wonderfully discordant sounds of this new form of music from a little-known planet called Irt.

> *Night is day and day is night*
> *Don't say I won't 'cause you know I might.*
> *You are wrong and I am right*
> *Don't cross my path 'less ya wanna fight.*

As the music engulfed him, his thoughts drifted back to his wife. *Lhvunsa.*

They'd been together for twelve turns, married for ten, and their love was as strong as ever—at least he believed so. From the time they'd left Higher Learning and entered the work force together, their careers had demanded a lot of them both. That was just a given with their chosen professions. But as her career in architecture advanced, she'd found more freedom—and clients—by working independently out of their home. Gsefx, on the other hand, only seemed to devote more of his time and energy to his work at Galacticount, especially since his promotion. And he knew it had taken its toll on their relationship. Still, he also knew his love for Lhvunsa hadn't changed, and he felt confident that her feelings hadn't either. They just needed to find some time for each other—some time alone, without interruptions, to get their marriage back on track again.

"This break will be different," he had promised her, "we'll leave Clangdor and go to the fancy new resort on Alnost everyone's been talking about. We'll shut everything out and it will be just the two of us."

But once again, it looked like this break was going to end up just like all the others—with him working and Lhvunsa stuck at home, alone. She was not going to take the cancellation of their romantic getaway very well; she had been looking forward to it for quite some time. So had he. But they would work through it. She would be upset, no doubt about it, but Lhvunsa would understand. She always did.

Rock on my children!
Rock on my love!
Rock all day and rock all night,
Roll in the sounds from heaven above.

The song came to a resounding end just ebyts before Gsefx was supposed to have arrived at work. Unfortunately for him, the traffic had not moved one bit. Far from just being a little late, it was clear now that he was going to miss most of a very important client meeting. He took another deep breath to calm himself before entering his boss' dial-code into the vidcon. This was not going to be a pleasant conversation.

The vidcon lit up and the thin, pale-gray face of Qilzar appeared.

"My dear Gsefx," he said casually, "late again, I see." Strangely, he did not seem angry. In fact, he seemed quite pleased.

"I'm truly sorry, Et Qilzar," said Gsefx, "but it's not my fault. I left the house thirty ebyts early. It's this traffic, it's ..."

Qilzar interrupted before he could completely justify himself.

"Of course, traffic is always terrible at this time." He paused for a moment. "You do realize this is the fifth time you've been late this semi-turn?"

"Yes sir, and I am sorry. No matter what it takes, it won't happen again, I promise."

"No need to concern yourself, Gsefx."

Qilzar was actually smiling now, an action that concerned Gsefx immensely.

"In fact, there's no need for you to come into the office at all."

Gsefx looked puzzled.

"I'm not sure I understand."

"Of course you do." The smile left Qilzar's face. "Galacticount employment policy 462b-7, paragraph 18c, specifically defines tardiness as arrival at the Galacticount offices by more than ten ebyts past the beginning of the established work rotation. Further, an employee is allowed no more than four unexcused tardies per semi-turn. Additional tardies are grounds for immediate dismissal."

"Now wait just a minute, you can't possibly mean ..."

"The regulations are quite clear on the matter." Qilzar's expression remained blank and all emotion left his voice. "Et Gsefx, you are hereby terminated from the employ of Galacticount and your credentials revoked. Your final paycheck will be delivered to your home address within five working rotations. This transmission is ended."

"Wait! You can't do this!" yelled Gsefx.

His screaming had little effect, however, since the vidcon screen had already gone blank.

As he sat there in stunned silence, the traffic began to move.

Chapter 3

Do Your Worst

Henry counted the cash in his wallet, and then compared it to the amount due currently displayed by the cab's meter. They were still more than a mile from his house and the meter was already demanding twenty-four dollars and thirty-seven cents, while he had just twenty-six in his wallet, along with an untold amount of loose change in his pocket.

"Stop here," he said to the cabby. "I'll walk the rest of the way."

"You sure?" asked the cabby. "It's awful cold outside."

"Yeah," he said with a sigh, "yeah, just pull over."

Once the car had come to a stop, Henry handed the cabbie all of his cash, change included, got out of the cab, pulled his coat tight and began walking. As the cab pulled away, Henry focused all of his energy into walking a straight line, but he'd had a lot to drink and it was all he could do to defy gravity and remain upright, something he wasn't always successful at that. Weaving, stumbling, shuffling, and sometimes falling, Henry eventually made it to his block, where he leaned against the stop sign at the end of the street to rest for a moment and gather his strength before going the rest of the way. Before going home to face Lucy.

Lucy was going to be angry, that much was a given. It was simply a question of degree, and whether or not he was drunk enough to deal with whatever she threw his way. He had a sneaking suspicion he wouldn't be.

Henry took a deep breath and let it out. *How did I get here?* He thought. *How did I get to the point where I have no say over my own life?*

Deep down he already knew the answer. It was why he couldn't face Lucy without downing the better part of a bottle of whiskey first. If he had dug deeper, he'd have uncovered the realization that he'd never had any say over his own life. From a childhood marked by parental neglect and no real friends, to his loveless marriage with the controlling Lucy—a woman chosen more as a way out of his parent's house than out of any true affection for her—Henry had been overlooked for most of his life and bullied the rest of the time.

The only thing that had sustained him was his art. Through drawing, sketching and painting the world around him, he had found a temporary respite, a brief sense of relief from the constant pain that enveloped his soul. But when he'd married Lucy, she insisted he quit tinkering around with his "silly hobby" and get a real job, one that paid real money. Henry reluctantly agreed to put away his pencils and brushes and focus on finding, and keeping, a "real" job. Now, however, with Jason's encouragement, he was going to start again. He was going to stand up to Lucy and make her understand how important his art was to him. He had to make her understand.

"Well," he said aloud after a few minutes, "standing here isn't helping any, I'm only getting more sober. I might as well get on with it."

Henry took a step forward and released his grip on the stop sign. At that very moment, a horn sounded from behind, startling him, causing him to lose his balance and fall to the ground.

"Hey you drunken idiot," yelled a voice from the car that had sounded the horn, barely audible over the laughter coming from the same car, "what happened? Did they throw you out of the bar for being too damned ugly?"

More laughter from the car.

"Either that or they figured out that losers like him can't pay their bills."

The laughter turned raucous, followed by more jeers.

Henry turned to look at his admirers. It was a car full of college frat boys, out looking for an evening of trouble. He didn't recognize any of them, and he didn't want to be their source of fun for the evening. He got up and started walking toward his house.

"Hey," yelled a voice that quieted the others, "where are you going? We're not done talking with you."

Henry heard car doors open, then slam shut, and feet running after him. He did his best to start running, but in his state, he knew he wouldn't get far. It was only seconds before several pairs of hands grabbed him.

"That's far enough," said the leader, spinning Henry around. "It's time to have some fun." He grabbed a hold of Henry's shirt collar, picked him up by it, and slammed him against a nearby tree.

"Perhaps ...," said Henry, trying to hold back a nasty burp. "... if I might ... oh my ... I really think you should put me down now ..."

"Yeah, like that's gonna happen," said the frat-pack leader, pulling his fist back, "it's time to say goodnight, drunk, because I'm about to turn out your lights."

Henry didn't actually say anything at this point, but instead, like anyone who's had too much to drink and then been tossed around like a rag doll, he proceeded to spew the contents of his stomach all over his captor.

"Oh my God!" cried the leader. He threw Henry to the ground. "You sorry son-of-a-bitch ... you'll pay for this ... oh God, this is disgusting!"

"Hey, I told you to put me down," said Henry, still gasping. "I can't help it you're too stupid to understand English."

"You're a dead man! You're gonna die and no one will ever find what's left of you, if anyone even bothers to look."

Lying there on the ground, looking up at this hulk of a man-boy, a being bereft of everything except testosterone and muscle, Henry knew he was about to get the beating of his life. Glancing down, he realized how close he was to the man's knee, and without waiting to think about his actions, he pulled his leg back and kicked him with every bit of strength he could muster, then climbed to his feet and ran away as fast as his drunken state would allow.

The frat-pack leader let out a scream and dropped to the ground.

"Get him!"

Whether it was fear or adrenaline, Henry's senses seemed to be somewhat clearer now, and he was more stable as he ran toward his house, although he still wasn't moving that fast. He heard the footsteps of the frat boys chasing him and it wasn't long before he could hear them getting closer. Fortunately, he was almost home.

"Lucy!" he said as loud as he could muster as he closed in on his porch, the cold night air burning his lungs. "Open the door!"

At the same time he was attempting to get his keys from his pocket, but he was almost certain he wouldn't have time to use them once he reached the door. "Lucy!"

He reached the door, grabbed the handle, and tried to get his cold hands to work the keys.

"Lucy!"

He finally got the right key and tried to fit it into the lock, but he was too late. Hands grabbed him by the arms and shoulders, forcing him to drop his keys.

"Lucy!"

"I don't think Lucy's home, old boy. Too bad for you."

As they drug Henry off the porch, he saw the curtain to the front window slide open just enough for Lucy's face to appear. She looked at him with eyes as cold as the ocean depths. Just before they pulled him completely into the shadows, Lucy smiled and blew him a kiss.

"I hope your affairs are in order, drunk," said a voice in his ear, a voice that reeked of vomit. "This is going to be your last night on Earth."

Henry closed his eyes. "Do your worst," he said.

Chapter 4

What Could Happen?

... You are hereby terminated ...

The words reverberated in Gsefx's mind as he unconsciously steered his vehicle toward his former place of employment. He was too stunned to do anything else. Traffic was moving at what could almost be called a normal pace now, but Gsefx hardly noticed. He even went so far as to turn into the Galacticount entryway before he realized what he was doing.

This can't be happening, he thought, *this just cannot be happening. It's got to be a mistake or something. I need to talk to Xtlar. He'll straighten all of this out. He'll make Qilzar see reason.*

Before he could get into the parking structure, the guard at the entrance gate waved him to a stop.

"Your credentials have been revoked, Et Gsefx," the guard said as Gsefx opened his window. "I cannot let you in."

"It's all just a misunderstanding, Yklax," said Gsefx. "I just have to go in and talk with Et Xtlar and we'll get this all cleared up."

The guard's expression didn't change. "I'm sorry sir," he said, "I cannot let you in."

"Yklax, it's me, Gsefx. We've known each other for more than six turns!"

The guard's face softened a bit. "Sorry Gsefx. I'd lose my job if I were to let you in. I can't do it."

Yklax made a small, barely discernible gesture, signaling Gsefx to look over his shoulder. Gsefx saw the camera pointing at them and noted the brilliant green light. They were being watched.

Gsefx gave Yklax a reluctant smile.

"I understand, Yklax."

Yklax mouthed the word "sorry" as Gsefx closed his window, turned his vehicle around and headed out away from the Galacticount offices.

I need to speak to Xtlar, he thought, *but flying around aimlessly won't accomplish anything except frustrate me more. I need to find a place to park and think.* He thought for a moment before remembering the nearby shopping complex. *It's not open yet, so it should be a good place to wait until Xltar is out of his early rotation meetings.*

As he flew toward the shopping complex, Gsefx tried to figure out what had just happened. Until recently, Gsefx had gotten along reasonably well with Qilzar. He and his now former boss had worked together for nearly six turns with only a few minor run-ins. That changed during the last semi-turn when Gsefx received a promotion at the hands of Xtlar, Galacticount's Chief Financial Officer. The promotion came after the successful completion of a particularly grueling project caught the CFO's attention. Xtlar suggested to Gsefx's boss that a promotion was in order, but Qilzar believed the work was simply part of the job and not grounds for any special treatment. Qilzar expected excellence as a matter of course, not as something to be rewarded. Xtlar promoted Gsefx anyway, dismissing Qilzar's objections as nothing more than simple jealousy.

Appreciative of his new status and the significant raise in pay that came with it, Gsefx was completely unaware of the conflict between his bosses, although it didn't take him long to realize something was wrong. Qilzar's attitude toward him quickly took a dramatic change for the worse. Prior to the promotion, Qilzar had always been sure to point out even the smallest mistakes of his subordinates, but at least he had done so in a tactful way. Now, he delighted in crowing about every little error Gsefx made to everyone within earshot. Fortunately Gsefx was very good at his job and his mistakes were rare. The one area where Gsefx had difficulties was in getting to work on time.

Although he could partially blame his tardiness on the increasing traffic around Laxor, it was mainly his own fault, and he knew it. Gsefx rarely got enough sleep, often staying up late working, reading, or sometimes just piddling around with whatever his latest hobby happened to be. After a few rotations dominated by low levels of sleep, Gsefx would inevitably have difficulty waking up on time, ultimately leading to his being late for work. With all of the extra time he put in, his tardiness had never been an issue—until after the promotion. Now, just as with every other mistake Gsefx made, Qilzar was right there to let him have it.

Gsefx arrived at the shopping complex, parked and waited patiently until he felt comfortable Xtlar was out of his meetings. He punched in Galacticount's main code number into the vidcon. The communication was answered immediately by a young female he didn't recognize.

"Greetings, and welcome to Galacticount. How may I help you?"

"I need to speak to Et Xtlar, right away please!"

"I'm sorry, Et Gsefx," said the receptionist. "I'm showing your credentials have recently been revoked. I'll be unable to connect you. Goodbye."

Now, if he had been in a reasonable state of mind, Gsefx would not have been surprised at his inability to reach Xtlar. It was only logical that all terminated employees be denied access to company facilities and not be permitted to bother high-ranking executives with their disgruntled ravings.

Gsefx was not in a reasonable state of mind. He went into a total and complete rage. Shouting obscenities at the top of his lungs, he threw whatever objects he could get his four hands on, and beat his fists on top of the console. All-in-all, it was quite an entertaining display for the employees of the shopping complex, who were arriving to begin their shift.

As his outburst subsided and he began to regain some semblance of control, he considered what to do next.

I have to reach Xtlar, but how? I can't get to him physically, and any attempt to call him is automatically terminated. Perhaps I can reach him later.

He searched the Laxor database for Xtlar's residential communicator code, only to find that it was, of course, un-listed.

As he racked his brain in an attempt to figure out how to get his job back, he noticed his vehicle's energy levels were a bit on the low side, so he left the shopping complex for a refueling station not far away. As he locked into the fueling channel and began to recharge, it finally hit him.

"Planvc!" he said to the rather confused attendant. "Of course, Planvc will help me! Why didn't I think of him before?"

The attendant simply shrugged his shoulders.

"I wouldn't know," he said, as he finished the recharging process.

Planvc was Gsefx's closest friend and co-worker at Galacticount. He would be able to get a message to Xtlar.

Yes, that will work, thought Gsefx. *But he will be at the office now as well, and I won't be able to get through to him any more than I could get through to Xtlar. I'll have to wait until the end of the rotation and call Planvc at home.*

He took a deep breath and decided to go home and wait it out. Lhvunsa was there, but she would be locked in client meetings all day. She probably wouldn't even notice him.

A few additional deep breaths later, Gsefx pulled out of the refueling station and turned his music on again. He smiled as he thought of Lhvunsa's reaction when he first played albalan music for her. She had called it loud and obnoxious and told him not to ever play it again around her. He'd laughed at her reaction, and agreed to only play it when he was by himself in his vehicle. What made it all the more amusing was that he couldn't disagree with her description. Albalan was, in fact, loud and obnoxious, but that's what he liked about it. It was what made it, surprisingly enough, soothing and relaxing to him. So much so, that as his cockpit filled with with its discordant sounds, his mind quickly drifted away from his current predicament and onto the curious nature of this latest musical find.

Meaning "primitive" in Galactine Standard, albalan was defined by a stringed instrument known as an "elek trik git-arr" by the natives who played it. The git-arr was usually accompanied by a variety of other instruments just as primitive. All were played at exceptionally loud levels and what vocals there were often resembled primal screaming, rather than true singing. Albalan would likely have remained undiscovered for several more millennia, except for a small group of musical pioneers, who took it upon themselves to travel throughout the galaxy and search for musical compositions that were unique, interesting, and ultimately marketable, as an alternative to what they described as "the soulless, pre-packaged garbage the major galactic labels continually pushed on the general public." What these independent mavericks came back with wasn't always pleasant, but it was never boring, and on occasion it was actually quite good. As Gsefx sang along with words he didn't understand, the thought hit him that he didn't actually have much albalan in his collection.

Maybe I'll go back to the music store in the shopping complex and see what's new. Probably not the wisest thing to do, financially speaking, since I've just lost my job, but the rest of the rotation will be unbearable without some sort of distraction.

He was calculating just how much he could reasonably spend when a new thought struck him.

"Wait a minute," he said out loud. "I've got a whole rotation to kill. Instead of going shopping, maybe I'll just go to the source."

Checking his onboard computer, he found that the planet Irt could be reached in about three sars. He could go there, upload some music, and be back in time to call Planvc when his rotation ended. Nobody would be the wiser and he'd be able to expand his music collection significantly without it costing him a thing, except for a little fuel and some time—which he currently had in abundance. Plus, it would keep him out of the house, just in case Lhvunsa stepped out of her office for any unforeseeable reason. It wouldn't do for her to discover him sleeping on the couch or playing games and listening to music when he was supposed to be at work trying to catch up.

Besides, I deserve a bit of a break, he thought, his mood brightening considerably. *After all, what could happen?*

Chapter 5

It's Personal Now

A brightness filled Henry's field of vision, and he found himself being drawn toward it.

I'm dead, he thought, *and this must be the bright light everyone talks about.* His body shivered. *I thought the afterlife would be warmer …*

As if on cue, his entire body cried out in pain from the beating he'd received the night before.

"Oh God!" he said aloud. "I can't be dead. If I were, it wouldn't still hurt so damn much."

The brightness reached its zenith and his eyes involuntarily popped open to reveal a cold and bright morning sky. On any other day, this might have been a lovely sight, but today, it only served to make his skull throb as if it were a toy drum in the hands of a four-year-old child. The shivering didn't help either. Henry closed his eyes and attempted to grab his temples in agony, only to find he was wrapped up tight in an old sleeping bag. After a few moments of monumental effort, he freed his hands enough to move them to his temples where he was able to slow the throbbing to a dull ache.

Now, let's see if I can figure out where I am.

Henry fidgeted around within the sleeping bag enough to loosen it, being careful not to disturb the fragile noggin attached to his shoulders. When he was free enough, he took a long, slow, deep breath and let it out. He then counted to three, and in one rapid movement tried to sit up and look around. He made it halfway into the sitting position before realizing what a colossal mistake he'd made and fell back to the ground, but not before learning that he was, in fact, in his own back yard.

"Holy crap, that was stupid," said Henry as he lay there, head and body burning with pain. Through the pain, seemingly from out of nowhere, a memory flashed into his mind. It was Lucy, yelling at his attackers, which seemed odd, given the way she'd looked at him as they'd dragged him away the night before. Perhaps she hadn't completely deserted him after all. Henry could hear her voice in his mind, but couldn't quite make out what she was doing.

"Hey," she had said, getting the attention of the frat-pack leader. "Not so hard. I said to knock him around a little, but don't break anything. If he ends up in the hospital, it will end up costing me, and that will end up costing you."

"Why, yes ma'am," the leader had said back to her in a voice dripping with sarcasm. "The only problem is that it's personal now. The son-of-a-bitch ralphed on me, and I'll break whatever I damn well please."

"Is that so?" asked Lucy, her voice making it clear—to Henry at least—that she hadn't played her trump card yet. "In that case, I'd suggest you smile pretty for the cameras, because I have you, all of you, on record assaulting my poor defenseless husband."

There was a pause, in which Henry could only guess the frat pack leader was looking around for the cameras and weighing his options, only to realize he had no choice other than to do Lucy's bidding.

"Now," said Lucy, "do your damn job as instructed and you'll get paid. Do anything else and you'll go to jail. Any questions? Oh, and don't bother trying to destroy the cameras or come after me for the memory card, because there are more than one, and I've already put a failsafe in place. Anything happens to me, you'll be in jail before you know what hit you. Now finish up and get out of here, I have to work in the morning. And make sure you wrap him up in that sleeping bag like I told you, it's going to be a cold one tonight, and frostbite means doctor bills."

In spite of his pain, Henry couldn't help but smile just a little. Lucy was nothing if not predictable. She clearly hated him, so much so that she hired a group of fraternity thugs to beat him up last night. Be that as it may, there was a truth in her predictability, a consistency that was to be admired. To be sure, it was an ugly, vicious truth, but it was a truth just the same. And even though her viciousness was aimed at him, at least she was being true to herself. He laid there a while longer, oscillating between the physical pain in his body, the emotional despair in his heart, and the jealous rage he felt toward a despicable woman who was somehow more real, more honest, and truer to herself than he'd ever been to his own needs and desires. He had finally decided he could no longer remain prostrate in his back yard, when the full impact of last night's events hit him at last.

My God, he thought, *it's my fault. I'm the one to blame. Not for getting the crap beat out of me, of course, but for the way my life has turned out. All these years I've been telling myself I haven't* had a choice, that I've been forced one way and then another by the people around me. But I'm the one who let them. My parents, Lucy, they've been true to themselves, and I've blamed them for not allowing me to be true to my own self, but it's not their fault. I'm the only one who can decide whether I'm going to follow my truth, or allow myself to be pushed around by others.

With more than a few grunts and groans, Henry forced himself onto his feet.

That ends now.

He made his way to the back porch. As he reached for the door handle, he noticed a note taped to the window. It was from Lucy.

Henry,

I don't know how much you'll remember from last night, and honestly, I don't care. I'm sick and tired of your constant failures and they have to stop. I kept them from hurting you too badly, but only because I'm giving you one last chance. Get your job back at Telasco, or find another one that pays the same or better – I don't care which, but don't come back until you do.

He pulled the note from the door, crumpled it into a ball, tossed it into the yard, and went inside to get cleaned up.

He emerged from the house a couple of hours later, this time from the front door. He still carried the physical pain from the beating he'd taken, but even so, he felt better than he had in some time. He felt as though a fog had been lifted, and for the first time in his life he was able to see things clearly. Lucy's despicable example of wicked self-honesty had helped Henry make a decision about his own life and what he was going to do with it, though he didn't dare give voice to his intentions. Henry put his two suitcases into the cab he'd called; one filled with clothes, the other with pencils, brushes, and other art supplies that had been in storage far too long. He got into the cab and gave neither the house, nor his life with Lucy, so much as a backwards glance as the car drove away.

After a quick stop at the drive-through ATM, Henry had the cabbie drive him to the bar where he'd left his car the evening before. He paid the cabbie, put his suitcases in the trunk, and then paused to look at the bar's entrance. He thought about going in, just to say hi to Craig, or so he told himself, and maybe have a drink. Sure it was early, but one drink would be okay. Henry stood there a moment longer, then shook his head, got in his car, and drove away.

He went back to the bank first, cashed his paycheck and closed his checking account. Throughout their marriage, Lucy had insisted on keeping their money separate. As inconsistent as his working had been, he couldn't really blame her. Even though his work had been sporadic, Henry had managed to squirrel away nearly fifteen hundred dollars. Added to the eleven hundred from his last paycheck, it would be enough, considering the short-sightedness of his plans.

Next he found a hotel that was sufficiently inexpensive but not too seedy looking.

"I need to check in," said Henry to the desk clerk. "I'll be staying for two weeks, and will need a room on the first floor, in as quiet of a spot as possible."

"This is a busy hotel," said the clerk, giving him the once-over. "We don't have any rooms like that available. You're going to have to go somewhere else."

She started to turn away when Henry plopped down fourteen hundred dollars in cash on the counter.

"Two full weeks, in advance," he said. "Are you sure you don't have the room I'm looking for?"

The clerk looked at him again, counted the money and handed him a key.

"I'll need a receipt, too," said Henry with a smile.

When Henry got to the room, he pushed all of the furniture into one corner and set up his studio in the open space. He planned to spend the next two weeks painting to his heart's content. By the time he finished settling in, which included a trip to the art store to pick up canvasses, brushes, paints, and other supplies, it was too late to obtain the last item necessary to his plan. That would have to wait until morning. With nothing else to be done, he ordered a pizza, turned on the radio, and began painting.

Chapter 6

Zaras 7

At Qilzar sat at his desk, nervously sorting the same stack of files he'd already sorted seventeen times since he'd fired that miserable little show-off, Gsefx. He knew it had been seventeen times because he'd counted. Qilzar also knew it was only a matter of time before his boss, Et Xtlar, Galacticount's Chief Financial Officer, showed up at his office to shred him into little tiny pieces for firing that clelchin's ass. Gsefx may have made his life a waking nightmare, but he was one of Xtlar's favorite pets. As Qilzar began sorting the files for the eighteenth time, he realized his foot was bouncing up and down in time with his racing heart.

"No, no, no," he said aloud as he put the files back down. "This won't do. He'll be here any minute and I have to be ready. I have to focus."

He took a deep breath and then punched a code into his vidcon.

"You are Qilzar," said a voice from the vidcon, his own voice. "You are a Dremin, and as such you are a born bureaucrat. Whenever someone questions you, remember that no one knows or understands the rules, regulations, and policies better than you. It's who you are. It's what makes you special. Don't let anyone take that away from you. You can do anything ..."

The door to Qilzar's office burst open interrupting the recording, and Xtlar came in, not making the slightest attempt to hide his rage. It must be noted that Fweurlians were not a common site on Laxor, and even less so at Galacticount. In all of Qilzar's twenty turns there, Xtlar was the only being from the planet Fweurl that had ever worked at the firm. His five legs, four arms, enormous torso, and even more enormous head often caused quite a stir to the company's newer employees. Even so, after a while, most of the employees, including Qilzar, had grown accustomed to Xtlar's unique appearance. It was only on the rare occasions when he was in a foul mood, did he get those strange, "I don't believe what I'm seeing" kind of looks. When Galacticount's CFO was angry, like he was now, his normally smooth light-green complexion turned a very deep purple and the small patch of normally docile blonde hair on the top of his head stood straight up, turning a brilliant shade of red.

"How dare you fire the best up-and-coming accountant this firm has seen in turns without first discussing it with me," said Xtlar with a roar. "I ought to fire you immediately!"

Because he was seated, it was hard to tell that Qilzar was actually quite tall and thin, as were most Dremins. His pale gray skin and sharp features gave him a look of seriousness that matched his personality. At the same time, his nervous mannerisms tended to make others take him less seriously than he felt he deserved. Though belated, the recording had helped Qilzar prepare for his boss' outburst, enabling him to respond calmly, (the knots in his stomach notwithstanding). He reached over and turned the recording off, seemingly not at all disturbed by the rantings of his immediate superior.

"Et Xtlar," he said in a smooth voice that belied his nervousness, "you know I am as fond of young Gsefx as anyone, but this was his fifth unexcused tardy this semi-turn and company policies are quite clear on this matter. I hated to let him go, but he gave me no alternative."

Xtlar leaned closer, placing all four of his fists on Qilzar's desk and glared at the Dremin with eyes that had now turned a terrifying shade of crimson. He said nothing, but focused his gaze with an intensity so deep, he might have been trying to drill a hole straight through Qilzar's head. Qilzar was quite certain that was the intent.

"The Chief and I met with Pigawitts earlier," said Xtlar, "you remember Pigawitts, one of our oldest and most influential clients? His company is up for a GTCA review soon and you know what that means. I told him not to worry, that I had exactly the right individual in mind to handle the prep work. Now, tell me Qilzar, how do you suppose I felt when I tried to contact Gsefx to assign the job to him, only to find out that you fired him?"

Against his will, and all the resolve he had just built up, Qilzar began to shrink under the force of that stare. He had expected some anger, of course, but it was impossible to be completely prepared for something like this.

Then, almost as if someone had flipped a switch, Xtlar cleared his throat, straightened his jacket and tie, turned, and moved quietly to the corner opposite Qilzar's desk. A few moments later, when he turned back to face Qilzar, his skin colors had returned to normal and his hair was once again docile and blonde. It was, in every regard, an impressive transformation.

Qilzar had been too unsettled by the intensity of his boss' earlier outburst to notice. At the moment, confusion was the best he could manage.

"Sir," he began, "I know you're upset about this turn of events and I assure you my team can handle the Pigawitts ..."

"Shut up Qilzar," Xtlar said with a sigh. "Just shut up and listen."

Qilzar opened his mouth as if to speak, but thought better of it and closed it again. Then, unable to keep silent, he exploded, "I was completely within my authority as section supervisor! You can't fire me for doing my job!"

"Oh be quiet, will you. I'm not going to fire you." Xtlar paused for a moment, as if in deep thought. "In fact, you were correct in your actions."

He began pacing back and forth in front of Qilzar's desk.

"We can't have slackers like Gsefx setting a poor example for the others, can we? Why, if we let him get away with such insolence, others will follow suit and it will be chaos around here. Thank you, Et Qilzar, for pointing out my error in judgment."

Qilzar was speechless—this was not at all going as planned.

"Qilzar, you're an outstanding supervisor and long overdue for a promotion. A district directorship has just opened up and I believe you're the perfect candidate for the job."

"Really," said Qilzar slowly. A part of him had to believe this was some sort of cruel joke Xtlar was playing on him. Yet, he did deserve a promotion. Perhaps, just perhaps his actions this morning had nudged Xtlar into recognizing that fact. It would certainly be about time, even if the circumstances weren't the most ideal.

"May I ask what section and district it would be?"

"You'll remain in corporate tax accounting," said Xtlar, "just at a higher level and in a different location. Zaras 7, to be exact."

Qilzar's jaw dropped and what little color there was in his pale complexion drained away completely. His hands began to shake.

Zaras 7 was the single most undesirable location in the entire civilized galaxy. In fact, most questioned whether Zaras 7 could be considered civilized at all. The harsh conditions, and the exceptionally odd behavior of the natives, made it nearly impossible for anyone to maintain their sanity for long. As a direct result of these conditions, Zaras 7 also boasted an incredibly inexpensive cost of living. So inexpensive, in fact, Galacticount decided it would be the perfect location for a field office servicing that portion of the galaxy. It was difficult to keep employees there, but even considering the turnover and the additional costs of mental health insurance, it was the district with the lowest cost structure in the entire company.

"Zaras 7?" he stammered. "I thought Et Faspai was the director out there."

"He was, right up until they found him curled up under his desk a few rotations ago, rocking back and forth, and mumbling to himself. Something about giant squids, if I recall. He's now under full-time observation at a maximum security clinic on his home planet."

Xtlar turned to leave.

"Report there at the beginning of tomorrow's rotation. I'll take care of the paperwork immediately."

"NO!" Qilzar said with a cry. "You can't send me there. I don't want that kind of promotion. I won't go."

Xtlar looked Qilzar directly in the eyes.

"What did you say?"

Qilzar's shoulders slumped and he looked down at his desk as the realization set in that he'd been had. He paused, swallowing hard before responding.

"I ... I said I won't go ... I don't want a promotion if it means going to Zaras 7."

"Are you sure, Et Qilzar? I don't want there to be any confusion on this point. You do realize that refusing an assignment is grounds for immediate dismissal? Oh, who am I talking to? Of course, you do. You know the corporate policy handbook better than anyone."

"Surely we can work something out, sir. I mean, can't we work something out?"

Xtlar leaned over and placed all four of his fists on Qilzar's desk again.

"Have Gsefx in my office, ready to work, by the start of tomorrow's rotation, or you'll be on Zaras 7 before the rotation is over. That's the deal and it's not negotiable."

Xtlar turned and started out of the office. Qilzar didn't bother trying to hide the fact that he was shaking when his boss turned to look back at him in the doorway.

"Don't ever try to play me again, Qilzar," said Xtlar, his voice deathly serious. "I've been around too long and you're no good at it."

"But sir, what if Gsefx won't come back?" said Qilzar, "Or is late again? He was supposed to begin his break tomorrow."

Xtlar turned and left without answering.

Qilzar wasted no time in gathering his coat and case. He was out of his office before Xtlar rounded the hallway corner.

"Hold all of my calls," said Qilzar to his assistant as he passed by in a flash, "indefinitely."

Chapter 7

Get Me on the Ground

I t had been established long ago that emerging cultures, still in the primitive stages of development, are extraordinarily paranoid. Almost without exception, once they attain the technology, either on their own (preferable) or through the interference of an outside, more advanced culture (highly illegal, although it does happen), they begin exploring the space in the immediate vicinity of their planet, sometimes going further into the galaxy, sometimes not, depending on the inquisitiveness of their species. In the course of this exploration (and paranoia), they nearly always devise a way to detect any extraordinary activity in the space around their planet. A fascinating sociological study, these primitive cultures usually believe themselves to be the only sentient beings in the galaxy, yet they insist on building such detection devices, nonetheless.

It had also been established long ago that no matter what precautions the Galactic Community took, it could not seem to keep its citizens from passing too close to these various primitive planets and being detected, usually wreaking havoc in the process. So, after a particularly nasty incident on Carobashius Minor, where some misguided tourists nearly caused the complete annihilation of the planet's entire population, all vehicles were required to be equipped with standard tamper-proof anti-detection devices. This way, any vehicle, from the most inexpensive economy ship to the most luxurious jumbo cruiser, could pass through a planet's atmosphere, or indeed descend all the way to the surface, and be invisible to whatever type of detection equipment the inhabitants were using. The devices do not make the vehicle truly invisible, they can always be seen by the naked eye, but as long they stay out of visual range, the ship will remain hidden from detection.

So it was when Gsefx entered into a high orbit around Irt and began scanning for albalan music, and anything else of possible interest, he gave no thought to the possibility of being detected. Instead, he was relieved that he'd finally reached this backwater planet after one of the most boring trips he'd taken in some time. This entire section of the galaxy had only recently been explored and charted, and there were few habitable planets, even fewer with intelligent life on them, no established routes to travel, almost no other vehicles, and absolutely nothing in terms of interesting scenery. He'd never been more thankful for his music collection in his entire life.

Gsefx's first attempts to scan the planet's radio waves achieved only limited success. There was so much activity it was impossible to separate it into intelligible segments.

How can such a small planet, he thought, *with such a limited population, have so much to say to one another?*

He let out a deep sigh and started in for a closer orbit. This was not going to be as easy as he'd hoped. Just as he was about to lock into the lowest orbit possible, he heard a loud thud and nearly lost control of his vehicle. A warning light came on indicating his automatic attitude control had failed.

"Gralt!" he shouted, struggling to maintain control. "I know, I know! I should have taken you in for your juricking check-up today instead of coming out here." He knew the ship couldn't hear or understand him, but it didn't stop him from talking to it regularly. His ship was long overdue for a check-up—a check-up that would have detected any impending problems, such as a worn attitude control. But since it hadn't given him any problems, he'd put it off, telling himself he didn't have enough time to get it done. He was now paying the price for his procrastination.

Forget about the music now, thought Gsefx, *I'm in serious trouble. Without repairing, or somehow bypassing the attitude control, I won't be able to break out of orbit, much less make it home.*

The good news was that it wasn't a difficult repair. The bad news was that he'd have to land to make it, while avoiding any of the planet's inhabitants.

"Just hang in there and get me on the ground," he said to his ship. "I'll patch you up and then I'll get you a complete work-over when we get home, I promise."

He scanned for a location on the planet's surface that would be completely unpopulated and that had the best possibility of containing any materials he might need as well. It took a while, but he finally found a suitable spot and began his descent. The on-board computer directed him toward a location in the very center of a large landmass on the sunlit side of the planet. Landing on the darkened side would provide better cover from prying eyes, of course, but it would also force him to wait until the sun came around to make his repairs. He couldn't wait that long. Not if he wanted to get home in time for dinner—and avoid a long, uncomfortable conversation with Lhvunsa.

It has been said that ignorance is bliss. It has also been said that what you don't know can kill you. Gsefx knew enough about basic mechanics to make a relatively minor repair like this, but not enough to realize that his ship's anti-detection device was dependent on a properly functioning attitude control.

Chapter 8

A Happy Ending

What a turn my life has taken over the past two weeks, Henry thought as he stared at the greasy burger and even greasier fries sitting on the plate the waitress had set down in front of him. *I never dreamed I could ever be this content.*

He'd spent nearly every waking hour in his motel room-turned-makeshift studio, reaching an almost nirvana-like state as he sketched, drew, and painted. More than once, after falling exhausted into his bed, he had been tempted to ditch his plan and make another attempt at living a normal life. He knew if he could find this kind of happiness, even for just a small part of each day, it would make up for all of the rest of life's pain and drudgery.

But these thoughts were nothing more than illusions, pipe dreams that disappeared quickly when mixed with the harshness of reality. His money would not last forever (indeed, he had spent most of it already), which meant getting a job, which, in turn, meant devoting most of his time and energy to accomplishing rote tasks that meant absolutely nothing to him. By the end of each day, the life and heart would be sucked out of him, leaving nothing for his art.

His art.

If only he could make a living at painting, his heart would overflow with joy. The darkness in his soul would be kept at bay, if it didn't disappear altogether, replaced by an inextinguishable light rooted in his unwavering pursuit of truth and beauty. The very thought filled his eyes with tears.

Sadly, the stark reality was that there was no money in art, not for Henry anyway. Though a part of him always believed his talents were beyond ordinary measure—his former boss even confirming those suspicions recently—monetary compensation only comes when someone with money sees the beauty within the work and is willing to pay for it. In a world filled with so many things competing for attention, he simply couldn't find anyone to give him or his work a first glance, much less a second. Even though Jason's earlier encouragement had been comforting, it wasn't enough to base a career on. Failure would come and it would break his heart beyond what he could stand. The more he thought about it, the clearer it became that the balance between practicality and happiness necessary to survive in this world was something unattainable for him. He knew what he had to do. He had stayed in his little room and painted almost non-stop for two weeks straight. Not for money. Not for fame. Not for anyone or anything but himself. Rarely eating, and sleeping even less, it was the most joyous time he had ever experienced.

Up until two weeks ago, his life had been a miserable one. By leaving this world on a high note, it would at least have a happy ending.

After leaving the restaurant, Henry drove for almost an hour before exiting the freeway. A few twists, turns, and switchbacks later, he finally turned eastward onto a deserted two-lane country road. If he'd continued east for another twelve miles he would have ended up in the town of Blainesbury, a nice-enough community whose only true distinction was that of being the natural rival to Henry's hometown of Glenwood, located exactly twelve miles west.

It had been a long time since Henry had been home, and even longer since he'd been to the secluded spot he'd chosen as his final destination. Not since he was fourteen, in fact. During those painful years of late childhood and early adolescence, when the reality of his unimportance to those around him had become too strong to ignore, he would hop on his old red Schwinn, backpack loaded with all the essentials: a pad of paper, a dozen number two pencils, his trusty transistor radio, and a 32-ounce bottle of his favorite caffeine-laced soda and ride out to the middle of nowhere. The hours would fly by as he listened to the local rock station while creating page after page of magnificent penciled beauty. Finally, as the sun melted into the horizon and the paper became too hard to see, he would reluctantly get on his bike and pedal home, only to find his absence had gone virtually unnoticed.

In a sense, coming here was more of a homecoming for Henry than any visit to his parent's house had ever been. It was a return to the only part of his childhood that ever felt like home. This time, he wasn't coming to draw, sketch, or paint. The time for his art was over.

Henry turned off on to a nondescript dirt path leading away from the paved road and from nearly all civilization. He drove along the path for almost two miles, descending slightly into a narrow ravine. The ravine was bordered on both sides by boulders that continued to increase in size, until they passed the point where they could no longer be considered boulders, but instead had to be referred to as small hills of rock. He rounded a final corner and stopped in a flat open area about the size of two football fields placed side-by-side. He shifted the car into "park," turned off the engine, leaned back in his seat, closed his eyes and took a deep breath.

He was scared; there was no doubt about that. But he was also strangely calm. He had come to terms with the action he was about to take and was glad it would all soon be over. His plan was quite simple. He would remove his paintings from the car and set them up on display, hidden from view of all but the most prying eyes. It would be his first, last and only true gallery exhibit.

Then he would have one last meal: a peanut butter and jelly sandwich, a small bag of tortilla chips, and a bottle of the same caffeine-laced soda he'd favored in his youth. After that, he would end it. One shot, upward through the chin and into the brain. It would be over quickly and would be virtually painless. Who knew what would happen after that? Maybe nothing at all. In any case, his miserable excuse for a life would finally be over. Steeling himself for what was about to happen, he got out of the car, put his coat on and looked around.

"So, this is it," he said quietly and started unloading the car.

Chapter 9

This Was a Bad Idea

Qilzar was visibly shaking by the time he reached his vehicle.

Zaras 7!

Even with all his careful planning and preparation for this day, the day when he would finally be rid of Gsefx, that disloyal cretin, he had not seen this coming. He would rather be unemployed and living in a cave than go to Zaras 7. Of course, he'd rather not be unemployed, either. He had to find that miserable creature and convince him to come back.

Qilzar's initial attempts to contact Gsefx through his vehicle communicator proved unsuccessful, so he decided to break protocol and call Gsefx's home. Though the home was considered a sanctuary from all unsolicited contact, under the circumstances he was sure Gsefx would overlook this small transgression.

"Hello?" said a voice on the other end of the communicator (the receiver was currently blocking the video feed). The voice was female; Gsefx's wife, perhaps?

"Ah, hello Madame," said Qilzar, "may I speak to Gsefx?"

"He's not here, he's at work. Who's calling?"

Oh no, thought Qilzar, *this was a bad idea.*

"Uh ... this is Gsefx's supervisor, Et Qilzar." His voice was shaking. "Unfortunately, Gsefx is not at work this morning. I was hoping he had returned home."

Qilzar's screen flickered momentarily before the image of a quite attractive Relnarian female appeared.

"What's happened? Is Gsefx all right? He's not hurt is he? What's going on?"

"Madame, I assure you, Gsefx is fine. There was just a bit of a misunderstanding, that's all."

The woman's expression changed from concern to cold wariness.

"What has happened, Et Qilzar? Yes, I know all about you. Gsefx has told me how you treat him."

"I assure you, Madam, nothing has happened ... well, not nothing ..." Qilzar was barely holding it together under the force of her glare. "... you see, to be precise ... uh ... ahem ... oh dear ... ah ... it ... it seems Gsefx mistakenly got the impression that I ... umm ... fired him this morning."

"YOU WHAT? YOU FIRED HIM?"

"Well, you see ... it was like I said ... I didn't actually fire him ... well, yes I did ... but, you see, it was just a terrible misunderstanding ..."

"Why would you do such a thing? Gsefx is the top accountant in your department; he's saved your pale gray hide more times than I can count! What's wrong with you? And more importantly, where is my husband?"

"Madam, please calm yourself, I don't know where he is, which is why I'm contacting you ... I just ..."

The screen went blank. She hung up on him. Qilzar sat for a moment in stunned silence. With each passing moment and new encounter, this rotation's events continued to stray further away from what he had expected. He had certainly not been prepared for an encounter with Gsefx's wife, especially one that had gone so horribly wrong. He collected himself and began considering his alternatives, only to realize that he didn't have any. The woman who had just hung up on him was his only hope and he had to find a way to convince her to help him.

"Gralt!" he said under his breath, as he reached for the vidcon again. But before he could punch in the code, it lit up with an incoming call. It was her again and her mood hadn't improved any.

"I just spoke with Et Xtlar and he confirmed your idiocy," she said. "Meet me in the parking lot of the Pigawitts building on Lecturn and Semler in twenty ebyts."

"Madam," said Qilzar, "I don't understand why we have to meet. Can't we just discuss this now?"

"Just be there, unless you want to spend the rest of your career on Zaras 7!" The vidcon went blank once again.

His anxiety rising to a whole new level, Qilzar started his vehicle and left the Galacticount parking structure, for what he hoped was not the last time.

Chapter 10

Not From Anywhere on Earth

enry washed down the last bite of his sandwich with a final swig of his soda, then reached over and turned off the radio, which had been blasting rock music from his favorite childhood station. He reached into the glove compartment, removed the .357 magnum and the single box of bullets he'd purchased specifically for this occasion. A slight smile crossed his face as he checked to make sure the safety was on before loading each of the gun's six chambers.

No sense in blowing a hole in my leg before I'm ready to put one through my head, he thought.

He got out of the car and walked over to his paintings. There were nineteen large and twelve smaller works; he'd been busy over the last two weeks, no doubt about that. He slowly reviewed each painting, inspecting them in much the same way he imagined a military commander might inspect his troops before sending them into battle. By the time he'd looked them all over, a sense of detached satisfaction came over him. He knew they were good, better than anything he'd ever done before. Certainly as good as anything he'd seen at a gallery or museum.

In another time and place, Henry's satisfaction would have been tainted with the sorrow and resentment that came from knowing his work, as good as it was, would never be seen by those who might appreciate it. Knowing that if he'd only had the right connections, he could possibly have had a real exhibit somewhere, perhaps even have sold some of his work, maybe even enough to make a living. But his current state of calm would not allow him to step back into such sadness. Thoughts of this kind no longer mattered. A few minutes from now nothing would ever matter again.

Standing in the midst of his works, Henry took a deep breath and let it out slowly. He lifted the revolver to click the safety off, but before he could do so, a high-pitched whining sound from above caught his attention. He looked up, but failed to locate its source at first. After several minutes, in which the sound grew continually louder, he saw a small object descending rapidly and coming directly toward him.

As it got closer, Henry could see that the object was a ship of some sort. A craft unlike anything he'd ever seen before. He tried to dismiss the crazy notion of this being some sort of alien spaceship—it was probably just some new airplane the military was testing. But as it got closer, all doubt left his mind; this ship was not from anywhere on Earth.

Chapter 11

A Single Irtling

Gsefx watched his screen intently as he struggled to control his ship. Descending through the planet's atmosphere without a functioning attitude control was difficult enough, but he also had to avoid any encounters with native air traffic. Considering he had no idea what their air ships looked like, or how fast they might travel, he had to stay sharp all the way to the ground. Thankfully, Irt's small population meant relatively clear skyways. All things considered, things were going pretty well so far, but as he got closer to the ground and the planet's gravitational forces grew increasingly stronger, he found it even more difficult to maintain control of his vehicle.

As he guided his ship downward, he also scanned for sentient life-forms on the ground. From what he could tell, it appeared there were no natives close enough to observe his landing, which was a good thing. A very good thing. Like Gsefx, most of this planet's inhabitants seemed to prefer living close together in large urban settings. This location had been as far away from those population centers as he could find, while still offering a reasonable possibility of having the materials he needed to fix his ship.

He was nearly to the ground, ready to breathe a sigh of relief at his good fortune, when his console lit up with a warning, and the screen zoomed in on the lone figure of what Gsefx assumed to be a single Irtling staring up at him.

"Gralt!" he spat, his heart sinking and stomach twisting into a knot. Panic, mixed with feelings of self-pity and despair, began to set in.

Why did I ever come here? He thought. *Whatever possessed me to attempt such a stupid stunt? I should have just gone home and waited for Planvc, or better yet, taken the ship in for a check-up like a responsible adult. That's what Lhvunsa would say, anyway. By the Gods, Lhvunsa! How am I going to explain this to her?*

He was about to vow that if he made it out of this in one piece, he'd pay more attention to his wife in the future, when the ship lurched heavily to the left and he nearly lost control, snapping his focus back to the task at hand.

No time for vows, self-recrimination or second guessing now! I can do that once I'm safely out of here. For now, it looks like I'm just going to have to deal with what's in front of me.

Struggling to control the ship, he glanced out of the front window.

"Gralt!" he shouted frantically, seeing his bad situation turning disastrous. He was about to land right on top of the Irtling!

Pulling back on the controls and frantically pushing buttons, Gsefx maneuvered the ship up slightly and over just enough to clear the Irtling and set the vehicle down in a clear spot without doing any further damage to the ship or the native on the ground. He shut the engines down and took a few deep breaths to compose himself before unbuckling his safety restraint and opening the door.

"Thank the Gods there's only one of them," he said, as he stepped out to meet the lone representative of planet Irt.

Chapter 12

Something to Live For

As it descended, the ship lurched from side-to-side with ever-increasing frequency, never leaving its track directly toward Henry.

It's going to crash for sure, and take me and my paintings with it! Thought Henry after a particularly violent surge. A part of him wanted to get out of the way of the rapidly descending ship, a part of him wanted to save his paintings, and still another part of him wanted to raise the gun in his hand and start firing on the intruder. In the end, he could do nothing but watch, transfixed by the strange craft bearing down on him.

The ship stopped suddenly, barely fifty feet above his head, bounced around for a few seconds and then moved off, missing Henry and safely setting down in an open space about thirty yards away. Henry clicked the safety off on his revolver and walked toward the new arrival.

As he approached it, he could see that the ship was about twice the size of his car—about forty feet long and ten feet high, with a strange looking tent-shaped appendage on top of the hull that added another four feet to its height. The ship was off-white, with a rounded front, a dark tinted windshield and dark windows on the side where he suspected the passenger seat would be located. Outlines for the doors were set midway between the front and rear of the craft.

Henry stopped about ten feet away from the now silent ship and waited to see what would happen next. To say he was scared would be putting it mildly. Just a few minutes earlier, he'd been ready to take his own life, but the arrival of this uninvited guest to his farewell party brought on a new feeling that overrode all other considerations. Regardless of the circumstances that brought him here, Henry was now the only thing standing between an alien of unknown intentions and the rest of humanity. For the moment, at least, it seemed he had something to live for.

Without warning, the dark windows cleared and the doors slid silently open. Its pilot stepped out onto the dirt and faced Henry.

Chapter 13

The Irtling

What he saw when he stepped out of his vehicle was more foreign to Gsefx than he had expected. The landscape was like nothing he'd ever seen before. He and his Irtling counterpart were standing in a large open area, covered with dirt and large rocks. They were surrounded by hills clearly made of the same material as the rocks scattered about on the ground and except for the two of them, it was completely uninhabited. Of course, that was why he had chosen this spot to land and make repairs, but to actually experience such a large empty space was very new to him. He was the product of an urban metropolis and had never before been anywhere this bereft of life, aside from travelling through space, and even then there were usually other ships passing by.

The Irtling who stood before him was not nearly as strange as he had expected someone from a world this primitive. Its dimensions were not too unlike Gsefx, himself, except for the fact that it had only two arms and two legs. It was similar in height, although much thinner. Its face and head were also of similar size and shape and the hair on the top of its head was fuller than Gsefx's, and of a light brownish color.

Wanting to get a closer look at the creature, Gsefx momentarily forgot the potential danger and started walking toward the Irtling. As soon as he did so, the creature raised one of its two arms, pointed something at him and yelled something completely incomprehensible. Gsefx froze, cursing himself for once again being so careless.

Chapter 14

The Alien

Fear and fascination mixed together in Henry's mind as the alien emerged from the ship. His first reaction was that this creature was not totally unlike him, it was humanoid at least, similar in height but a bit larger around. What fascinated him the most was the creature's four arms and four legs. He wondered how so many limbs could work in concert with one another. It seemed impossibly inefficient.

The creature's face was rounder than the average human, but it contained the same basic features, two eyes, two ears, a nose and a mouth. The skin was very smooth, seemingly incapable of growing facial hair and had a light bluish hue to it. Aside from a small ring of short, straight blonde hair around the top of its head, it seemed completely hairless. It also wore clothes not unlike those found on Earth. They were obviously made of different materials and were dramatically more colorful than anything Henry had ever seen before, but the basic pants and shirt concept were still the same. Its feet were large and leathery and seemed to require no shoes.

The creature, who had been staring at Henry in much the same way he had been staring at it, began walking toward him. Fear took over and without thinking Henry raised the gun and pointed it toward the creature.

"Stop right there or I'll shoot. Don't come any closer!" he shouted, fighting to keep the gun and his voice steady.

Chapter 15

Bang!

topped dead in his tracks, fear making an impression on him at last, Gsefx slowly raised all four of his arms with his hands open wide in a gesture meant to show he was unarmed and posed no threat. He didn't recognize the specific item being pointed at him, but knew what it was just the same. *Primitive Cultures* was a required course in school and he remembered learning just how paranoid and violent beings of lesser evolvement could be. Whatever it was being pointed at him was undoubtedly a weapon of some sort. Primitive perhaps, but dangerous nevertheless, possibly even deadly.

"Please, put down your weapon," he said, "I'm just here to repair my vehicle. I don't want any trouble."

The Irtling again said something unintelligible and continued pointing the weapon at him.

"Please, just let me fix my vehicle," he said as he gestured toward his ship, "and I'll ..."

He was interrupted by a loud "bang" and the whirring sound of a small projectile as it passed by his ear. The Irtling had just fired at him!

Gsefx jumped at the near-death experience and began backing up toward his ship, hands still in the air. The Irtling remained where it was, but surprisingly had lowered its weapon. Gsefx stopped and looked closer at the creature. It was clearly shaken and seemed to be just as scared as he was. Perhaps it hadn't meant to fire on him.

Gsefx was about to repeat his appeal to be left alone, when a thought struck him. He didn't know if it would work, but it was worth a try and he was out of alternatives.

Chapter 16

"Night is Day and Day is Night"

Although his hands were steady as he aimed the .357 magnum, Henry was a complete wreck inside. His heart was pounding, his mouth was dry, and he could feel the sweat pouring down his face.

The alien's four hands were raised as if it was trying to show it wasn't a threat. When the creature spoke again and made a movement toward the ship, Henry's shaky nerves could take no more. It wasn't until he heard the sound of the gun firing and felt the recoil that he realized he had actually pulled the trigger. Fortunately for the alien, this was the first time Henry had ever fired a gun. The shot missed and glanced off of the ship's tent-shaped appendage.

Henry was as surprised as his alien counterpart. He certainly hadn't meant to fire. Stunned, he lowered the weapon and tried to think about what to do next. He thought about simply dropping the gun completely and running away. Let the alien kill him if it wanted to, he was prepared to die. The only thing stopping him was the tiny voice in his head that insisted on reminding Henry there were things worse than death, and that turning his back on this creature before knowing what it had in mind was a very bad idea.

The alien began backing away toward its ship, hands still in the air. It opened its mouth to speak, then closed it again as if considering another option. When it opened its mouth again, Henry was shocked to realize he understood what the creature was saying.

"Night is day and day is night," it said in a high-pitched, but clear voice, "don't say I won't 'cause you know I might."

Henry stood in stunned silence, trying to process what he had just heard. The creature repeated the words, and as it did so, Henry realized he recognized the words as lyrics from one of his favorite songs. As his mind tried to come up with a logical explanation as to why an eight-limbed being from outer space would know the words to a late 70's rock song, he failed to notice the gun slipping from his hand and falling harmlessly to the ground.

Chapter 17

A Man of Action

Where is it now?" yelled the General into the ear of his assistant. His helicopter was fully powered-up and waiting just a few feet away, but he needed one last check before he lifted off.

"Ops says they've lost coverage, sir," replied the assistant. "They say the craft appears to have continued along its projected path and landed."

"All right, Major, we're a go. Have all units proceed to those coordinates. Keep me posted of their progress."

"Yes, sir. Good luck, sir."

The General nodded, climbed aboard the chopper, and shut the door.

Along with the four stars on his shoulders, General Theodore Eustace Alcorn carried a full set of mixed emotions as well. When he was assigned this command, he had known contact with a non-terrestrial race was a possibility and had, in fact, spent the last three years preparing for this day. Even so, he never really believed it would happen. He never actually believed non-terrestrials even existed. But now, it seemed one had actually arrived and touched down within the borders of the continental United States, and he found that he was actually excited.

Still, a part of him had hoped this day would never come. With less than eighteen months until retirement, he had settled into an acceptable, even comfortable routine. Throughout his career, Alcorn had always been a man of action, preferring to see his plans and strategies enacted in real-world situations, rather than endless drills and simulations. In this case, however, he would have been content with running drills and conducting exercises designed to simulate all the potential ways first contact could occur until it was time for him to retire. At this point in his life, he and his wife had begun doing many of the things they'd been unable to do while Alcorn had been climbing the ladder, and their son, Theo, had been at home. But that was all over now. Theo had long since moved out, and there were no more rungs on the ladder left to climb. Contentment was no longer a dream for General Alcorn, it was an attained reality.

Even before graduating at the top of his class in high school, Teddy, as he was known by those closest to him, knew he would be a career soldier. His friends and family all urged him to reconsider his application to West Point and his choice of a military career. The civilian sector is where it's at, they said. With your intelligence, instincts, and ability to read people, you can write your own ticket, they said. And they were right, of course. He could have done anything he wanted, which was why he pursued a career as a military officer. It was exactly what he wanted; it was exactly what he was meant to do.

For nearly thirty-nine years now, he had served proudly and been well rewarded. Few ever made it as far as he had. There had even been talk of a possible appointment to the Joint Chiefs, but he knew how that game was played. The powers that be might dangle the possibility of an appointment in front of him, like they did with all of his four-star peers, but he would never have been assigned First Contact Command if they were truly serious about a seat at the Joint Chiefs' table. Around the Pentagon, First Contact Command was better known as Last Stand Command. Being assigned to it meant it was your last stand as a commander. Although he'd played the political game well enough to make it as far as he had, sitting on the JCS was the last place Alcorn wanted to be anyway, so he accepted his assignment to Last Stand with the same vitality and vigor he had every other command. He told himself he would give it everything he had until he reached the forty-year mark and it was time to retire. It was only lately that he'd caught himself starting to look forward to the day when he could spend the rest of his life golfing, fishing or just plain lounging around the house in blissful ignorance, instead of poring over troop levels and readiness exercises.

Today's events could change all of that. It now appeared he would be required to fulfill his assigned mission. To make first contact with a species not of human origin. His plans for retirement could very well be delayed, if not canceled altogether. The needs of the Army came first. They always came first.

Adding to the mix of emotions was the additional aspect of his mission. Simply making first contact might not be good enough. He and his men might have to forcibly detain, or even eliminate the aliens if he determined them to be a threat. He hoped it would not come to that. Alcorn always believed his mission was to find a peaceful resolution to conflict, whenever possible. But that wasn't always an option. Sometimes military action was required and it was his job to be ready when force became necessary. In this case, securing the safety of the United States, and perhaps the entire planet, was priority number one. Everything else was secondary.

Besides, he thought to himself with a smile, *all of those other four-star bastards who actually want a seat at the Joint Chiefs table have enjoyed the hell out of seeing me assigned to this crap command.*

He strapped in and put on his headset.

"Pilot, what's our ETA?" he asked.

"17 minutes," came the response.

"Let's go."

Last Stand Command, my ass, thought Alcorn, as the chopper lifted off. *Who's laughing now?*

Chapter 18

Have You Lost Your Mind?

Qilzar was miserable. He had experienced many uncomfortable moments in his lifetime, including the recent encounter with his boss just a couple of sars earlier. But, compared to his current situation, his confrontation with Xtlar seemed almost pleasant. Traveling with the belligerent wife of an ex-employee to some backwater planet named Irt was easily the worst experience of his entire existence.

As planned, they met in the parking lot of the Pigawitts building, at which point Gsefx's wife immediately insisted on demonstrating her penchant for verbal assault. Unpleasant as it was, it was not totally unexpected, and Qilzar weathered the barrage as best he could. Through the various obscenities and other choice words she flung his way, he discovered her name was Lhvunsa and that she and Gsefx had been married for ten turns. Only when her tirade ended and she paused to catch her breath, did she reveal she knew where her husband was and that he was very likely in serious trouble.

"I've tracked his vehicle to a remote sector of the galaxy about three sars from here," she said. "It appears he's gone to a tiny, recently-charted planet called Irt."

"Irt? Never heard of it," said Qilzar, doing his best to act as casual as possible. It wasn't working. "Whatever would possess him to go there?"

Lhvunsa's thick eyebrows bunched together as her eyes narrowed to barely-open slits. "He wouldn't have had the opportunity to even consider such a foolish idea if he hadn't been fired! You would both be sitting comfortably in your offices doing whatever it is you do there. And I would be wrapping up my contract for the new addition to the Klarock Museum instead of ..."

She paused and sighed deeply.

"All right, enough of that," she said with a wave of one of her three hands. "Apparently, since he had some unexpected free time, Gsefx went to Irt to obtain some music straight from the source. Albalan originates from Irt, you know."

"Alavan? What's that?" asked Qilzar.

"Al-ba-lan. It's a newly discovered form of music. Quite primitive and all the rage lately. I don't care much for it, but Gsefx just can't seem to get enough. He's obsessed with it. I'm sure that's why he went there. He may be a great accountant, but there are times when his common sense leaves a lot to be desired. It's doubtful he considered any of the potential consequences before taking off like that."

Qilzar was about to ask another question, but Lhvunsa stopped him with another wave of the same hand. "Before you ask any more questions, get in your vehicle; we have to go and find him."

Qilzar stepped back as if he'd been slapped. "Have you lost your mind, Madam?" he cried. "I'm not going to Irt, or whatever it's called. Gsefx is an adult, and quite capable of taking care of himself. If you feel like chasing after him, please do so, but you'll not drag me along."

He paused for a moment, reminding himself of his tenuous employment situation. "When you do see him," he said gently, "please tell him the whole firing business was a terribly unfortunate mistake, and to please contact me immediately."

He turned as if to get back in his vehicle, only to feel a rather determined hand grab his arm and spin him back around.

"Don't even think about walking away from me!" said Lhvunsa, one hand gripping his arm, another sternly planted on her hip, and the third shaking a delicate green finger in his face. "Gsefx's vehicle has stopped responding, which means he's in trouble. Not only are you going with me, you're piloting. This entire turn of events is your fault and if anything happens to my husband, I will hold you personally responsible."

In all of his forty-seven turns, Qilzar had never been married, had never, in fact, even had a serious romantic relationship. He liked the female form well enough, but found the corresponding psyche completely impossible to fathom, not to mention rather frightening. So it wasn't at all out of character when he shrank in the face of Lhvunsa's demands. To his credit, he did try to object—three separate times, in fact. Each time he got no further than opening his mouth before realizing anything he might say would only serve to diminish his already poor standing with this woman, whose help he desperately needed if he was going to avoid exile on Zaras 7. In the end, he simply closed his mouth and opened the passenger door for Gsefx's wife.

From that high point, things went downhill rather quickly. There were no further outbursts of anger, only a cold, harsh silence, as Lhvunsa sat quietly staring out the window. It wasn't long before Qilzar hoped she would start yelling again. He twice attempted to start conversations, asking about her family first, then her career. He was abruptly cut off both times with glares that cut right through him, which were followed by even more intense silence. Shortly thereafter, he switched the vehicle over to manual control and focused on piloting. According to his on-board navigational computer, they were about thirty ebyts from Irt when Lhvunsa finally broke the silence.

"Why do you hate my husband so much?"

The suddenness of her question startled Qilzar out of his dark thoughts, which mostly centered around the disaster awaiting him on Zaras 7.

"Ahh ... excuse me? What did you say?"

She surprised Qilzar further by reaching over and engaging the auto-pilot.

"I want to know why you despise Gsefx so much."

Her tone was conversational, but there was nothing casual about the question.

"He's done nothing to you except make you and your department look good time and again by meeting impossible deadlines with unmatched accuracy. He works so much, especially since his promotion, I hardly see him anymore. Yet you treat him like a criminal."

"And speaking of the promotion," she continued, her voice rising again, "why in the galaxy would you promote him, only to hound him mercilessly and make his life miserable afterwards, then fire him on a minor technicality? That doesn't make any sense! What do you have against him?"

"Whatever do you mean?" asked Qilzar, slipping into the smooth voice he used on troublesome clients. "Gsefx has always been my top employee and I am actually quite fond of him. As I tried to explain earlier, this whole thing was just a simple misunderstanding. I was merely trying to point out that he needed to do something about his consistent tardiness and somehow it got blown out of proportion. You must believe me, I would never intentionally do anything to hurt your husband."

"Ha!" she cried. "You don't really expect me to believe that, do you? I don't know who you think I am, but I assure you ..."

Qilzar watched as an expression of shocked disbelief overtook her face.

"Unbelievable," she said shaking her head. "As far as you're concerned, you're telling the truth. You actually believe what you're saying, don't you? You've convinced yourself that none of this is your fault, that it really was just a misunderstanding. You've probably even convinced yourself that somehow this is all Gsefx's fault."

Qilzar opened his mouth as if to speak, but he wasn't given the chance.

"You fired him, Qilzar!" continued Lhvunsa. "For some reason, ever since his promotion, you've been looking for ways to hurt him and today you succeeded in the worst way imaginable. You fired your best employee for nothing more than spite. You might be able to convince yourself this was a simple misunderstanding and that you're not the cause of it, but you won't get me to buy into that lie."

She reached over and switched the ship back to manual mode.

"Forget I said anything and just pilot." She turned her back to him and looked out the window again.

Qilzar was stunned. Too stunned to do anything except what he was told. As he piloted the ship, his thoughts were no longer on Zaras 7, or even Irt for that matter. He had never encountered anyone like the woman sitting next to him. He was used to getting what he wanted, either by bullying or manipulating those around him. Lhvunsa would allow him to do neither. She had, in fact, done a pretty good job of bullying him since the moment he first contacted her.

Moreover, she was right. He really had started to convince himself that none of this was his fault. That Gsefx was, in fact, the miserable show-off he made him out to be. But why? What had Gsefx actually done to him to deserve such treatment? The answer was simple. Admitting it wasn't.

"I don't hate Gsefx," he said quietly.

"What?"

He reengaged the auto-pilot and turned to face Lhvunsa.

"I said, I don't hate Gsefx."

Lhvunsa turned from the window to face him.

"I don't dislike him at all. It's just that ..." he looked down at his hands, unable to meet her eyes.

"Yes? I'm waiting."

"I'm jealous of him," he said softly. "I know how juvenile that must sound, but it's the truth. He's successful because he's smart, talented, and good with people in a way I'll never be. He's a natural leader."

He took a deep breath and summoned the courage to look at Lhvunsa directly.

"His success isn't limited to the workplace, either. He's happily married to a beautiful woman who clearly loves him very much. I, on the other hand, have never even been on a third date."

He turned away from her and looked out his window, silence enveloping the cockpit once again. When Lhvunsa finally spoke again, her voice was gentle, but firm.

"Qilzar," she said, "you are a selfish, bitter, heartless bully who punishes everyone around you to make up for your own failings. But I have to give you credit, it took a lot of courage to say what you did just now."

He turned back to face her.

"I think it was more difficult to hear the words than it was to say them."

"There may be hope for you, yet," she said with a smile.

He returned her smile, but before he could say anything, the navigational computer signaled their arrival at Irt.

Lhvunsa removed a small device from her purse.

"This device allows us to know where our vehicles are at all times. It also lets us know the status of each vehicle. We each have one. Gsefx invented them about a turn ago. He took a couple of basic vehicle analyzers and reprogrammed them so they'd not only analyze each vehicle's status, but they'd also talk to each other and alert us if either vehicle traveled outside of a one hundred parsec range. I thought they were just a part of his ridiculous hobby and a waste of time. When I see him again, I'm going to tell him just how wrong I was, right after I strangle him for being so stupid!"

"That's quite impressive," said Qilzar, marveling over the device in his passenger's hands. "I had no idea Gsefx was such an electronics wizard."

"I wouldn't call him a wizard," said Lhvunsa, flatly. "All it really amounts to is a lot of excess junk laying around the house. It's mostly just a big mess."

"Perhaps," said Qilzar, "but Lhvunsa, that device you're holding in your hand is not something just anyone can throw together. Gsefx's talents are clearly not limited to accounting."

"I suppose you're right. It still doesn't get him off the hook. He's still in deep trouble."

"Of that, we're in solid agreement. Any sign of him, yet?"

"Not yet, you'll have to move into a lower orbit. Depending on what side of the planet he's over right now, this may take a while."

Qilzar moved the ship into the lowest possible orbit and accelerated to maximum speed in hopes that wherever Gsefx was, they could overtake him soon.

Chapter 19

I Will Never Be Helpless Again

hvunsa stared at the device in her hand, willing it to reveal the location of her husband's vehicle. As angry as she'd been at Qilzar earlier, she was now more frightened than anything. After all she had been through recently, the thought of losing her beloved Gsefx was too much to bear, especially over something as trivial as his ridiculous music. Even if things weren't all that wonderful between them right now, she never doubted their love for one another, not for a moment.

She shook the device, then tapped its side, hoping in vain that such actions would somehow make it find Gsefx faster. It didn't.

She knew he'd been looking forward to going away to Alnost this break and relaxing at that new resort. It was all Gsefx talked about, when they talked at all. She supposed getting away would be good for them, but honestly, she didn't care where they went, or if they went anywhere at all. She just wanted to spend some time together, time where he was really with her and not working. She needed it. They needed it. It had been so long since they had talked, really talked. Not since "the incident," which is how she'd come to refer to it lately. She couldn't seem to bring herself to verbalize what had really happened. She focused on the device again, but still no sign of her husband.

"May I ask you a question?" asked Qilzar softly, breaking her concentration before she could sink any deeper into her thoughts.

"Of course," she said, pulling herself away from the device, grateful for the distraction, "ask me whatever you'd like."

Qilzar hesitated for a moment, as if he were summoning the courage to ask a question he knew would be better left unasked. Perhaps he was just too frightened to hear the answer.

"Go ahead, Qilzar," said Lhvunsa, her curiosity piqued. "I promise I won't bite ... or yell. What's on your mind?"

"When we first met," he said slowly, without turning to face her, "you were angry with me for firing Gsefx, correct?"

"Yes, and understandably so," she said, caution now overtaking her former curiosity. "What about it? I thought we just resolved all of that."

"Well, yes and no."

Qilzar turned suddenly to face her.

"Lhvunsa, you attacked me quite viciously back in the Pigawitts parking lot," he said, holding up his hand to ward off any objection before it had a chance to start. "Now, I understand you were angry, and I was deserving of your anger, but I can't help but think there's something more going on than mere anger toward me. I think I should know if there's anything else, any deeper issues that might be going on."

Lhvunsa felt as if she'd been slapped across the face. How could he have known? How could this ridiculous Dremin read her so well? She felt her blood begin to boil and before she knew what was happening, she was unleashing on her escort once again.

"How dare you accuse me of such a thing! You are unbelievable, even after all I've ..."

She fell silent as she watched Qilzar start to shrink backward in his seat. Before she could decide what to say or do next, she noticed the tears streaming down her cheeks. Moments later, she was crying so uncontrollably that she failed to notice her head falling onto Qilzar's shoulder, as his arms gently embraced her. When the tears finally subsided, she pulled herself back into a sitting position.

"By the Gods," she said softly, "I am so sorry, Qilzar, not to mention terribly embarrassed. I've put you in a very awkward position, I ... I don't know what to say."

"Lhvunsa," said Qilzar in the gentlest voice she had ever heard, "please don't apologize. When we first met and you began yelling at me as you did, I honestly didn't know what to think other than you were a horrible person. As much as I disliked Gsefx at that moment, I simply couldn't imagine him being with someone like you."

"Thank you, Qilzar, you're making me feel SO much better," she said, managing a sarcastic frown as she wiped more tears from her face.

"But then, as we began talking, you seemed like a completely different person than the one I first met in the Pigawitts parking lot. Something just didn't seem right, and so it seems that something isn't right. Lhvunsa, I don't mean to pry, but if there's anything I can do to help, please allow me to do so."

Lhvunsa looked at the Dremin who was looking back at her. Dremins were notorious for being skilled bureaucrats who knew every detail of every law, rule and guideline, and who also knew how to bend those very laws, rules and guidelines to their advantage. What they weren't known for was their empathy, or even patience, toward other beings. But Qilzar was different. There was something about him, something about the way he was looking at her—not in a creepy, lustful way—but in a very un-Dremin-like, empathetic way. It was clear that, even though he didn't really know her, he cared about her and her well-being, and that was something she really needed right now.

"Thank you Qilzar, but I honestly don't think there's anything anyone can do to help. Don't worry, I'll be fine."

"I see," said Qilzar. "So why don't I believe you?"

"What do you mean by that?"

"Lhvunsa, in case you forgot, you were nearly inconsolable just a few ..."

"I remember," said Lhvunsa, interrupting before he said something that would cause her to breakdown again. "All right, all right, I'll tell you. But you have to swear that you won't tell anyone, not even Gsefx."

"Gsefx doesn't know?"

"He knows some of it, but not all."

"I see. Go on."

"Swear to me, Qilzar, not a word leaves this vehicle."

"Of course, not a word. I swear it on my life."

Lhvunsa watched Qilzar as he swore to keep her secret. When she was fully convinced she could trust him, she turned away, took a deep breath and let it out slowly. The thought of reliving that horrible "incident" again made her want to scream at the top of her lungs, curl up into a little ball, and disappear, all at the same time.

But haven't I been reliving it over and over ever since it happened anyway? she thought. *Perhaps it would be better to tell someone than to keep it all bottled up inside.*

"Lhvunsa? Are you okay?"

"Yes. Yes, I'm fine, Qilzar." She looked back at the gray-skinned Dremin, who was watching her with more genuine concern than she'd felt anyone show her in a long time, including her husband. "No, Qilzar, I'm not. I'm not fine at all. Our home was broken into a while ago. Gsefx was at work, but I ... I was there."

"By the Gods! Who did it? Did they hurt you? What happened?"

Lhvunsa held up a hand to ward off further questions or outbursts of compassion. She knew it wouldn't take much for her to break down again.

"I was working from home, as I usually do, and was on the vidcon discussing my proposal for the Klarock Museum when the call was cut off and my vidcon went dead. As I was trying to figure out what was going on, I heard a loud crashing noise, which turned out to be two Bralian thugs breaking down my front door."

Qilzar gasped.

"Bralians?" he said. "On Clangdor? I've read that the Bralian gangs were getting bolder and expanding their territories, but I'd never have thought they'd venture as far in as Clangdor?"

"I wouldn't have thought so either, but there they were, kicking in my front door and coming into my home."

"What did you do?

"Fortunately, they didn't see me and didn't realize anyone was home. I was able to find a place to hide and call the police. But Qilzar, you have no idea how scared I was."

"No," said Qilzar thoughtfully, "I can't even imagine. How long before the GCP arrived?"

"Nearly too long," said Lhvunsa, who was now staring forward, almost in a daze as she replayed the "incident" in her mind and described it to Qilzar. "I watched as they ransacked our home, taking everything of value and stuffing it into these large cases, then destroying everything else." She felt tears slip from her eyes and roll down her cheeks. "Then ..."

"Yes, what happened then? Lhvunsa?"

"Then ... they found me."

"Oh Gods!"

"Yes." She shivered as a sudden chill overtook her body and she couldn't go on. She lowered her head and sobbed quietly.

"Lhvunsa, I don't know what to say," said Qilzar in as gentle a voice as she'd heard in a very long time. "I'm so sorry. I cannot begin to ..."

Lhvunsa raised her hand to stop Qilzar from going any further, although she couldn't seem to stop crying or even look up, she certainly couldn't take any more sympathy. She just needed to be able to let it out. With the hand she raised, she reached out for comfort and was relieved when Qilzar took it, and held it silently while she regained her composure. Even so, she silently cursed herself for not being strong enough to deal with this on her own.

When she was finally able to talk again, she sat up, took her hand from Qilzar, and wiped the tears from her eyes.

"From the way I've acted you probably think they attacked me," she said, "but the truth is, they didn't actually do anything to me. They didn't have time."

Qilzar nodded his head but didn't say anything.

"One of them wanted to, he kept saying that they should take me with them, that they could 'have some fun' before they killed me. But the other one, who was clearly in charge, said no, they needed to kill me right away and then get out of there. That was when the GCP arrived."

"Thank the Gods! They arrested them, right?"

"Not exactly. The Bralians took me hostage, or at least tried to. I must give the GCP credit, their snipers are very good. While the Bralians were negotiating their demands, the GCP killed both of them, with me standing right between them. It all happened so quickly, I didn't even have time to react."

She waited for Qilzar to say something as he digested this last bit of information, but he just stared at her, mouth agape.

"Qilzar? Are you going to say anything?"

"I don't know what to say. You're fortunate to even be alive, yet you sit there telling me this story as calmly as if you were telling me nothing more than that you had lunch with a friend."

As she watched her husband's boss stare at her in shock, mouth still open, she found herself once again fighting back tears.

"Qilzar, I am far from calm. You know I'm not calm. I've already fallen apart twice and it's taking everything within me to hold it together right now."

"Of course, Lhvunsa, I only meant ..."

"Wait!" said Lhvunsa, cutting him off as she realized that the device in her hand was now flashing red. "I think I've ... yes, I've found him. That's his vehicle. Oh Gods, no! The engines are off and it's parked on the planet surface! It appears to need repairs. Come on, we have to go down and help him."

"We can't go down there!" cried Qilzar, suddenly the whiny bureaucrat she'd met in the Pigawitts parking lot once again, and not the gentle, kind soul he'd become over the last couple of sars. "What if there are natives around? These primitive cultures are often quite paranoid and almost always terribly dangerous. Besides, I hardly think you're in any condition ..."

"We can deal with my problems later," said Lhvunsa. "He may be in serious trouble."

"Lhvunsa, this is a luxury passenger vehicle and while it's the best on the market, it's not a military ship. We do not have the capability to rescue Gsefx or even defend ourselves. If we go down there, the only thing we'll be successful at is getting ourselves caught, right along with Gsefx. Then who will notify the authorities of our whereabouts?"

Lhvunsa turned to face Qilzar squarely.

"Qilzar, my husband is down there and he's in trouble. You know as well as I do the authorities are not going to do anything to help. They can't even if they wanted to; this planet is outside the Galactic Community."

She reached over and took Qilzar's hand. "I told you that Gsefx knew some of what happened, but not all of it. He knows everything I've told you up to this point, but what he doesn't know is just how scared and traumatized I was. So much so, that I started taking self-defense classes."

"That's understandable, under the circumstances," said Qilzar, appearing a bit uneasy at this turn in the conversation.

"Including how to handle and fire various weapons."

Qilzar's head snapped back as if he'd been slapped.

"But ... but ... but, Lhvunsa, no! I mean, you can't, can you? If I'm not mistaken, you're a Relnarian, and Relnarians have very strict beliefs about violence, and killing in particular."

"You're not mistaken Qilzar," said Lhvunsa softly. "Our beliefs are very strict and leave no room for interpretation. As a Relnarian female, the consequences for going against our beliefs are even greater."

Qilzar was nodding his head in understanding.

"If you take a life," he said, "you will never be able to bring life into the universe."

"That is correct," said Lhvunsa, her words barely a whisper.

"So why do so?"

"I hope I will never have to take a life," she said, looking up at Qilzar, fighting back more tears, "but regardless of the consequences, I will never be helpless again."

She watched as Qilzar turned back to the controls, a stunned look on his face.

"I understand, my dear," he said. "Here's to hoping you never have to take a life." He pointed the nose of the ship toward the planet and reached over to squeeze her hand. "You'd better buckle yourself in. We don't know what their primitive atmosphere might be like."

"Thank you, Qilzar," said Lhvunsa with a smile. *There really is more to this Dremin than meets the eye,* she thought as she watched him work the controls.

"Don't thank me yet," he said. "Thank me when we are all safely away from this horrible place."

Chapter 20

Rokandrole

Gsefx had clearly gotten through to the Irtling. It was staring at him, mouth open, in what could only be interpreted as surprise or shock, regardless of what planet one was from. More importantly, it had dropped its weapon.

It started speaking rapidly, and although Gsefx couldn't understand a word, it was gesturing in a manner that suggested it wanted Gsefx to repeat the words again.

"Night is day and day is night, don't say I won't 'cause you know I might."

Not wanting to go through the bother of learning a new language just for the sake of a few songs, Gsefx had practiced the bizarre-sounding words over and over until he could easily sing along with the music. Now, speaking them slowly, without the benefit of musical accompaniment, the words felt stranger than ever.

The Irtling whispered something that sounded like "rokandrole" and took a step toward Gsefx. After a brief hesitation, during which the Irtling gave the appearance of being deep in thought, he took another step.

"Night is day and day is night," said the Irtling, motioning for Gsefx to join in, "don't say I won't 'cause you know I might."

They spoke the next line together. "You are wrong and I am right, don't cross my path 'less ya wanna fight."

The Irtling was smiling when they finished and Gsefx was a bit surprised to realize he was too. They still had no idea of one another's intentions, but at the very least, they had discovered a small patch of common ground.

Now we just need to figure out what to do next.

Chapter 21

Sunset Over An Empty Life

Henry would later reflect on the surrealism of this particular moment in time. He would explore the ramifications of how, just minutes after his attempted suicide had been interrupted by a four-armed, blue-skinned visitor from outer space, he would be standing face-to-face with that same visitor quoting lyrics from one of his favorite rock songs. But that would come later. Right now as he stood there grinning uncontrollably at this being from somewhere out in the great beyond, standing not ten feet from him, there was no time to grapple with the deeper meaning and implications of this close encounter. They had found common ground and needed to find a way to build on it, before a misstep on either of their parts sent things uncontrollably in the opposite direction.

Before he could come up with any ideas, the creature raised one of its hands and pointed at the ship. Apparently it was thinking the same thing and had come up with an idea of its own. Henry nodded and it stepped back, turned, and reached into its ship. A few moments passed and just as he was beginning to think he had made a big mistake, Henry heard the music start.

Night is day and day is night,
Don't say I won't 'cause you know I might.

Henry suddenly had an idea of his own.

"Stay here," he said, even though he knew it didn't understand. He raised his hands, palms out, hoping the alien would know he wanted it to wait there. Pausing just long enough to grab the gun, click the safety on, and stuff it into the back of his pants, Henry ran back to his car, started it up and pulled it over next to the ship. He loaded the same song into his stereo and synchronized it just in time for the chorus.

Rock on, my children!
Rock on, my love!
Rock all day and rock all night,
Roll in the sounds, from heaven above.

After the music stopped, Henry watched as his new alien friend appeared to be trying to tell him its name. Although he didn't understand much of what was said, he did catch the word "Zef" repeatedly as it pointed to itself.

Following suit, Henry said his name as he pointed to his chest. Zef nodded understanding and repeated Henry's name in near perfect English.

Henry smiled and tried to think about what to say next. He was about to try some different music, when he noticed Zef was looking very intently at something over his shoulder. Henry turned around and realized Zef was staring at his paintings, which were still arranged in the clearing behind him.

"What? You want to look at those?"

Clearly he did, as he had already started walking toward them. Henry followed his new eight-limbed friend, who appeared to be totally captivated by his latest works.

Zef started started with the painting closest to them and slowly progressed from painting to painting, paying no attention to Henry or anything he was saying. The alien stopped at one painting in particular, clearly moved by what it saw on the canvas.

"You like that one, huh?" said Henry, not really expecting an answer. "I have to admit it's my favorite too. It has ... um, special meaning."

Indeed it did. It was the last one he had painted and depicted a sun, which had almost completely set behind a gorgeous, snow-capped mountain range. In the foreground was a single figure, sitting on the ground with head in hands. All around the figure lay blank canvases.

"I call it 'Sunset Over an Empty Life,'" said Henry quietly.

When Zef looked up at him, Henry noticed a single tear flowing down the alien's light blue cheek and wondered how this being could relate so closely to Henry's most intimate work. He hoped he might find out someday. Zef pointed to the figure in the painting, then pointed to Henry.

Henry nodded. "Yes, that's me," he said.

Zef looked at the painting again, then turned suddenly and started back toward his ship.

"Wait!" Henry said. He picked up the painting and handed it to Zef. "I want you to have this."

Their eyes met and without further words, there was understanding. Zef accepted the painting with a low bow. As he arose, Henry saw another tear rolling down his face. It was all he could do to not break down himself. They walked back toward the ship in silence, each deep in their own thoughts.

Without warning the peace of the moment was torn apart by a loud voice, which seemed to come at once from everywhere and nowhere.

"ALIEN BEINGS, REMAIN WHERE YOU ARE, WE MEAN YOU NO HARM, BUT YOU MUST COMPLY WITH OUR COMMANDS."

Chapter 22

Secure the Human

"Are all units in place?" asked the General.

"Yes, sir," came the answer from the other end of the line.

"Continue with stage one greeting, all known languages and dialects."

His command was clear and sure, with no indication of the mixed emotions he felt inside. This was no place for any of the personal concerns he might have about their mission. The ramifications this mission would have on his life could be dealt with later. With so much at stake, first contact with an alien race of unknown intentions, there was no room for uncertainty. He hoped the non-terrestrials would be peaceful and they would understand the necessary precautions he had to take, but that was a lot to hope for. Friendly or not, understanding or not, he and his troops would do what was necessary.

The first step, of course, was to try and establish verbal communications, which is why the initial greeting was broadcast in every possible language known to man, including ones based on mathematics and other sciences. This was a long shot, of course, but it had to be tried. The next step would be much simpler and more straightforward; they would take the non-terrestrials into custody, using force if necessary. It would then be up to the linguists and diplomats to sort things out.

"Within visual range, sir," said the voice in his ear.

The general looked out the window of his chopper and saw a rather tiny spacecraft, with an automobile parked next to it and what appeared to be an alien and a human male in the middle of the clearing.

"Damn," he said. "It looks like we're not the first to arrive. Major, be sure to secure the human, as well."

"Yes sir," said the voice on the other end of the line.

Chapter 23

Take the Gun

"ALIEN BEINGS, REMAIN WHERE YOU ARE, WE MEAN YOU NO HARM, BUT YOU MUST COMPLY WITH OUR COMMANDS."

The message was getting louder and was being repeated over and over in English, French, German, and hundreds of other languages Henry couldn't make out. As he looked around, he could see military choppers moving in. In the distance, dust was rising from the dozens of ground vehicles heading their way. They were being surrounded.

Henry had watched too many sci-fi movies to believe any military or government, particularly his own, would actually mean no harm to Zef.

It's more likely they'll take him to some secret location like Area 51, or something like that, thought Henry, *and perform unspeakable experiments on him. I can't let that happen. Zef has to escape, and it's up to me to help him.*

"Zef, take the gun," he said, as he raised his hands and jerked his head toward his back.

He looked at Zef, who didn't appear to comprehend. Looking around to see how close their captors were, he risked reaching back with his right hand, keeping his left raised, to point at the gun and then at Zef. He raised his hand again and turned his back completely to Zef.

He glanced back at Zef, who now appeared to understand. Henry felt the gun being removed and they made their way slowly back to the ship.

Chapter 24

The Hostage Alternative

"Sir, it appears the human has been taken hostage," said the voice in the General's ear.

"I can see that Major," he replied. Alcorn thought for a moment, leaning heavily on his instinctual abilities to read people and situations. "I'm not sure I buy it, but proceed with the hostage alternative."

There was hesitation on the other end of the line.

"Major Wellston, do you copy?"

"Uh, yes sir. Pardon my asking sir, but what makes you think it may not be a hostage situation?"

"Call it a hunch, if you want to. Proceed with the hostage alternative, but be prepared for anything, and that means taking down the human, if necessary. Is that clear, Major?"

"Yes, sir." No hesitation this time.

Chapter 25

I've Got to Get Out of Here

For not speaking the same language, Gsefx believed Henree and he were actually communicating quite well. When Henree raised his hands and pointed to the weapon, it was clear to Gsefx that Henree wanted him to act as though he were taking him hostage. Apparently Henree didn't trust his fellow Irtlings very much. All the more reason why he shouldn't trust them either. He was glad he'd met Henree first.

Their ploy seemed to be working; the incoming air and land vehicles had slowed and were currently holding their positions. Gsefx wasn't sure how long the act would keep the other Irtlings away, but if this planet's militia was anything like it was on the worlds Gsefx was familiar with, it wouldn't be long.

Once they made it back to his ship, all he would have to do is get in and take off. He wouldn't be able to make it home. He wouldn't even be able to get out of orbit, but he could easily outrun their primitive airships and make it to another location on the planet's surface. Perhaps one a little less active.

Gsefx kept the weapon pointed at Henree with one hand, opened the door with another, and gently put the painting in the back seat with the remaining two before slipping into the pilot's seat. Henree remained in front of the doorway, doing his best to block Gsefx from the view of the encroaching military. Gsefx set the weapon down and began strapping himself in, thinking about how nice it would be to take his new friend with him when he left. Languages were easy enough to learn, and after the events of the last few ebyts, he knew they would always be friends.

He shook his head roughly.

By the Gods! This is no time for sentimentality, he thought. *I've got to get out of here!*

He reached over to start the engines, but was struck by the shape of the primitive weapon sitting on the seat. Picking it up again, he gave it a closer look and noticed something he'd missed before.

Chapter 26

Don't Come Any Closer

his is getting serious, Henry thought as he stood in front of the doors of the alien ship. He knew his own capture was inevitable, even if Zef got away. He wasn't exactly sure what the military would do to him, and though he wasn't looking forward to finding out, it would be worth it if he could help his new friend escape. Perhaps he could get his gun back before Zef took off. Then he could still complete his original plan. Suicide might be preferable to the nightmare of being a military prisoner.

Even as he thought this, he shook it away. After all that had just transpired, and after seeing the impression his work had made on a being from an entirely different world, he knew he could no longer voluntarily end his own life. He had to continue painting. He had to find a way to live for his art, even if it meant finding and holding down a mind-numbing day job.

If I get out of this in one piece, he thought.

When the jeeps, tanks, and other vehicles were within a hundred yards, they stopped and held their position. It appeared they were waiting for something, or someone. If Zef was going to escape, he had better do it now. Whatever they were holding for, it was doubtful they'd wait long. Henry chanced a quick look inside the ship to see what was taking so long. On an afternoon filled with shocking surprises, what he saw offered yet another.

Zef was nowhere to be seen, though Henry could hear him doing something below the ship's floorboards. What he did see was his .357 magnum, or what was left of it, and five bullets scattered on the floor. The gun had been completely disassembled and the cylinder was missing.

"What are you doing?" he said in the loudest whisper he could manage.

Zef didn't reappear, so Henry turned back to face the siege party. A jeep was now coming up the road, likely carrying what or who everyone was waiting on. Zef was nearly out of time.

He turned back to the ship's cockpit. "Whatever you're doing, you'd better hurry it up!"

From below the floor, Zef appeared, his face all smiles. In one hand he held the missing cylinder to Henry's .357, and in two of his other hands he held pieces of a strange looking metal that, when pushed together were almost identical to the cylinder of the revolver. Zef showed him the different pieces and pointed down to the area he'd been working.

"What are you trying to tell me," said Henry, shrugging his shoulders. "I don't understand."

Undeterred, Zef pulled the two pieces from his ship apart and with his remaining free hand made a downward motion. He then dropped the broken pieces, held up the gun's cylinder, and moved his hand upward.

"Aha!" said Henry, a light switching on inside his brain. "I get it. That's why you're here. Your ship broke down. That's why it looked so out of control when you landed. It all makes sense

now. Okay, get back to work and I'll do what I can to stall them."
He made a shooing gesture to his new friend.

"STOP WHATEVER IT IS YOU'RE DOING, TURN AROUND
WITH YOUR HANDS UP, AND STEP FORWARD!"

A frightened look came over Zef's face. He said something
Henry didn't understand and disappeared under the floor.

Henry raised his hands again, turned around, and saw a large
man walking toward him, decked out in full desert camouflage,
and four stars on his shoulder.

"Stop! Don't come any closer," shouted Henry, trying to sound
frightened, which at this point wasn't difficult. "This thing means
business. It won't hesitate to kill me if you come any closer."

The General didn't appear to be concerned with the threat,
but slowed to a stop about twenty feet from Henry.

"Just take it easy, son," said the General. "Everything is going
to be fine. We have the situation under complete control."

"Please don't come any closer," said Henry. "It's already shot
at me once and I don't think it'll miss the next time!"

The General paused for a moment.

"I can tell you're scared son," he said finally. "But I don't
believe it's the alien you're afraid of, nor do I believe you're
really being held hostage. No, the way you've been fidgeting
and turning around, it looks more like you're trying to protect
whatever is inside that ship, maybe even trying to help it escape.
Trust me when I tell you, son, you wouldn't want to do that."

Henry kept his hands up in the air. The hostage idea wasn't
working and Zef needed more time. His mind raced frantically
trying to come up with something that would delay things as
long as possible.

"Okay, okay, you're right," he said finally. He kept his hands raised and glanced quickly back toward the inside of the ship. "I guess we can talk openly. The alien doesn't seem to understand English very well. I sure don't understand anything it has said. I'm playing along with it, trying to convince it I'm his friend, so I can get a look inside the ship. It's working too. It seems to trust me. I've had a chance to look around the cockpit. If you keep playing along with me, I might get a chance to learn something more important about it and its intentions."

The General's face remained calm and expressionless.

"What's your name, son?"

"Henry."

"Henry, listen to me very carefully. I'm General Theodore Alcorn and the soldiers you see around you are an elite division of the United States Army. They have all been hand-picked and extensively trained for a contingency just like this. We are in total control of this situation. I can assure you the non-terrestrial is not going anywhere. I can also assure you we'll have plenty of time to learn all about it and its intentions. Now just come on over here and let us do our jobs."

Henry was in trouble and he knew it. He was fresh out of ideas and he was sure Zef needed more time.

"But ... but what if there are more of them coming?" he stuttered. "If we provoke it, it might signal others and speed up their arrival or something. We wouldn't want to do that, would we?"

He wasn't making any sense and he knew it, but he kept going anyway.

"If ... if we can get some insight into what it is and what it wants, without raising its suspicions, that would be better, wouldn't it?"

General Alcorn paused, but only briefly. "Perhaps it would, but we're prepared for that and any other scenario that might arise. Now come on out of there, Henry, and tell your friend to do the same."

The General nodded to one of his subordinates and several large, heavily armed soldiers began walking toward Henry.

Chapter 27

I Said Hold On!

We're getting close, Qilzar," said Lhvunsa watching her homemade tracking device. "Once we break through these clouds, we should be able to see him."

"All right then," replied Qilzar. "We'll take a look, but hold on to something because it's going to be a very quick look."

They broke through the clouds not far above the ground and immediately saw the huge crowd of soldiers and weaponry surrounding Gsefx's ship.

"Gods!" gasped Lhvunsa. "The Irtlings have captured him! Qilzar, we've got to do something!"

"We are doing something," Qilzar said, a bit too loudly for the small confines of the ship's cockpit. It seemed the excitement of the situation had gotten the better of him. "I said hold on!" He scolded, looking over at Lhvunsa.

The ship jumped forward as Qilzar increased the ship's speed and headed straight for the surface.

Lhvunsa said nothing, but grabbed the armrests and held on.

Chapter 28

A Klurdine Glakton

Finished with his repairs, Gsefx lifted himself from below the deck plates and was immediately met by a weapon much larger than the model Henree had carried. It was being held by an Irtling who was also a much larger model than Henree. Its clothes were obviously designed to help it blend into the local environment. The expressionless face was painted in similar colors, completing the look.

Gsefx raised his hands slowly and tried to remain calm. As unfamiliar as he was with Irt's society and customs, it was easy enough to recognize this creature as a foot soldier, and a rather large one at that.

Best to be careful with these types, he thought. *They're usually trained for only one purpose and there's no need to give it a reason to act on that training.*

A voice from outside the ship bellowed unintelligibly and the soldier stepped back. He motioned with his weapon for Gsefx to get out of the vehicle.

Gsefx nodded his understanding and carefully exited his ship. Looking around, he saw Henree off to one side, with three soldiers detaining him. Several hundred additional soldiers filled the clearing, all with weapons pointed directly at him.

He stood there silently, his four arms high in the air, and tried not to think about how close he had been to getting away. His vehicle was fixed and ready to go. Another ebyt or two and he would have been beyond the Irtling's ability to catch him.

A large soldier, who appeared to be significantly older than those around him, but dressed in the same manner, stood a short distance away. As it spoke to the others standing close by, several of them began walking toward Gsefx.

Henree yelled something and tried in vain to break free from the soldiers holding him. One of the soldiers punched Henree in the stomach dropping him to his knees. When he looked up again, Gsefx caught his attention and shook his head from side-to-side. He knew this whole situation was his own doing and the last thing he wanted now was for his newest friend to get hurt because of his own foolishness.

The soldiers had nearly reached him when a loud humming noise from above interrupted them. They, along with everyone else in the clearing, looked up to see another ship coming straight at them.

His vision being much stronger than his Irtling counterparts, Gsefx recognized the vehicle coming toward them long before anyone else. It was a Klurdine Glakton, one of the finest luxury vehicles on the market. He remembered when its current operator, his former boss, Et Qilzar, first flew it to the office. Qilzar had taken great pains to show it off, without trying to look like he was showing it off, of course. As he recalled, that Glakton had created quite a stir among his coworkers.

But what was Qilzar doing here? And who was that in the passenger seat?

As the ship drew closer, he was shocked to see that Qilzar's passenger was none other than his beautiful wife, Lhvunsa. The sight of her always brought joy to his heart, now even more so. Although this time, his joy was accompanied by puzzlement.

What in the galaxy was she doing with Qilzar, here on Irt?

Exactly what had brought his wife and his former boss to Irt together was a mystery to Gsefx, but what they were about to do was not. He planted all four of his feet solidly in the ground and braced himself.

Chapter 29

Romeo Alpha! Romeo Alpha!

Having never before seen a Klurdine Glakton, General Alcorn didn't recognize the vehicle headed his way, but like his non-terrestrial counterpart, he too knew what it was planning. It was a contingency he and his troops were supposed to be prepared for.

"Romeo Alpha! Romeo Alpha! Move! Move!" he shouted.

The soldiers sprang into action, but were too late. The approaching ship was moving too fast and was on top of them before they could get into position. A few of the soldiers, including the General, were able to open fire, but none were able to do anything to the incoming ship but perhaps chip its finish. Within seconds, the ship flew by, less than twenty feet over the tops of their heads, knocking everyone in the clearing to the ground. Everyone except the four-legged alien.

Chapter 30

He Saved My Life

Henry raised his head to look around. The soldiers who had been holding him had been knocked several feet away and were still lying face down. He jumped to his feet, and as he did so, he noticed the General had risen as well. He glanced toward Zef's ship and saw his friend had already gotten back inside and was firing up the engines.

A shot rang out, ricocheting off the ship. It was Alcorn.

"Get up! Get up!" the General screamed at his troops. "The alien's getting away!"

Without thinking, Henry took off across the clearing and launched himself at the man with the stars on his shoulders. The General cursed loudly as they both hit the ground hard.

"Leave it alone!" shouted Henry, his rage overcoming his fear. "It didn't do anything to you! It just needed to repair its ship. That's all it wanted!"

"Get off of me ..." the General tried to shout back. But his words were lost in the din created by the ship's departure. Louder still was the music that suddenly filled the air.

Night is day and day is night,
Don't say I won't 'cause you know I might.

Henry looked up, just in time to see his friend smile and wave. Then the ship, along with Zef, was gone.

Henry was about to return the wave when he was grabbed and thrown face down into the dirt. His hands were yanked behind his back and handcuffs were placed none too gently around his wrists. A moment later he was jerked back to his feet, and was standing face-to-face with a dusty and very unhappy-looking General.

Alcorn glared at him without saying a word, jaws flexing in an obvious effort to control his rage. After a few tense moments, in which Henry felt his fear return, the General stepped back and appeared to relax a bit. He reached into his pocket and pulled out a pack of chewing gum.

"Henry," he said as he unwrapped a stick and popped it into his mouth, "do you have any idea just how much trouble you're in?"

"I think I have a pretty good idea."

"No, son, I don't think you do. Interfering with a federal military operation, aiding in the escape of an non-terrestrial being, and an assault on a government official. There's probably more, but those charges alone will be enough to put you behind bars for the rest of your life."

The General chewed his gum slowly, eyes never leaving Henry's. Finding a confidence he never thought possible, Henry held the General's gaze.

"I don't get it, son," continued Alcorn. "You seem relatively bright; you had to know there would be consequences. What made you pull a stunt like that? Whatever possessed you to throw your life away like that? And for what? So a creature you'd never met before and couldn't even communicate with, whose intentions you didn't know, could escape. Thanks to you, we may never know its intentions. For all we know, it could've been a scout, here on a reconnaissance mission. An invasion fleet might already be on its way."

Henry never wavered, his earlier fear a thing of the past. He had helped Zef escape and that's all that mattered to him now. Let them take him to prison. He was ready.

"General Alcorn, just because you've chosen a military life, why would you automatically assume the alien has done the same? Couldn't it just as easily have been an explorer on a scientific mission, or an ambassador here to establish peaceful relations? Hell, General, for all you know, it wasn't interested in Earth at all, but was nothing more than a wayward traveler with car trouble and this planet was the closest thing to civilization it could find. How would you like to be surrounded by an army of strangers pointing weapons at you the next time you have a flat tire?"

The General was unmoved.

"Interesting theories, but we'll never know now, will we? I'm still waiting on an answer as to why you defied your own countrymen to aid an alien being of unknown intentions."

"He saved my life," said Henry defiantly. "It was only fair I should try and do the same for him. Isn't that what friends do for one another?"

The General stared at Henry for a moment, then shook his head and looked away. He spit out his gum, then motioned for his troops to take the prisoner away.

Henry knew the General had not been bluffing. He would spend a long time in prison, perhaps even the rest of his life. Even so, he felt an inner peace he'd never felt before. After all the years of pain over not being accepted by those around him, he had finally found a being who understood him. Not his language perhaps, but him, as a person. Zef had done more than foil his suicide attempt. In the ways that mattered, he had truly saved Henry's life.

PART TWO:
FRIENDS & ENEMIES

Chapter 31

I Need to Go Back

I t didn't take long to break out of Irt's atmosphere, and as soon as he did, Gsefx almost turned right back around to go and rescue Henree. The only thing that stopped him was that he couldn't be sure how long his makeshift attitude control would last, and it wouldn't do either of them any good to go right back down and get caught again. He had just decided to go back and try anyway when his vidcon lit up with Lhvunsa's image. All thoughts of returning to Irt's surface immediately melted away with the appearance of his beautiful wife.

"Gsefx, thank the Gods you're all right!" she said. "You scared me nearly to death!"

"I'm fine, my love. Thanks to you and ... to Qilzar. Although, I'm a bit fuzzy on that part, since the last time I spoke to him ..."

"All in good time, my dear boy," said Qilzar, sticking his head into view, "but first let's get out of here and to a safe location, where we can discuss things more comfortably."

"Of course, Et Qilzar. Lead the way. I'm right behind you."

They made their way back to more civilized parts of the galaxy and found a refueling hub with what passed for a restaurant. After Gsefx was properly reunited with his wife, and then subsequently scolded by her, he turned to Qilzar. He was stopped by his former boss before he could ask the obvious question that was on his mind.

"Gsefx," said Qilzar, "I owe you an apology, a long overdue one at that. I have treated you unfairly and, well, thanks to your lovely wife, I have had a chance to not only see you in a different light, but to see myself differently as well. I am genuinely sorry for all the difficulties I have caused you."

Gsefx was stunned. He couldn't think of what to say, so he stammered out the only thing that came to mind.

"So, I'm not fired, then?"

"Most certainly not! In fact, Et Xtlar has a new assignment ..."

Qilzar's voice trailed off as his eyes wandered toward the back seat of Gsefx's vehicle.

"What is that magnificent work of art in your back seat?" he asked.

"What?" said Gsefx, turning around. "Oh that. One of the Irtlings helped me escape. He painted it. At least I think it was him. He gave it to me as a gift."

Lhvunsa was now staring at the painting too. "You didn't mention that you had made contact with any of the Irtlings individually, my dear."

"We haven't really had time to tell each other's whole stories yet, have we, my darling?"

Gsefx watched his wife as she struggled to tear her gaze from the painting. When she was finally able to look at him, her eyes were filled with something he'd never seen in her before, something he recognized as desire, but on a scale he was completely unfamiliar with.

"Perhaps we should do so now, and let's not leave out any details," she said, her eyes wandering back to the painting.

"Yes, I agree," said Gsefx. "But let's get out of the parking lot and into the restaurant."

When neither his wife nor boss moved a muscle, he pressed a button on his shirt and the door to his vehicle closed and locked, and the windows turned completely opaque. Lhvunsa and Qilzar jumped as if they'd been slapped.

"What did you do that for?" asked Qilzar.

"That wasn't necessary," said Lhvunsa.

"I'm afraid it was," said Gsefx. "Now inside, both of you. This is a side of you I haven't seen before and I'm not sure I like it."

"Who are you talking to, darling, him or me?" asked Lhvunsa.

"Both of you. Now come on, let's go."

Once inside and seated, they each told the other all that had happened since parting ways earlier that rotation. Gsefx told of his poorly thought out trip to Irt to pick up some music after being fired by Qilzar, for which Qilzar apologized again. He told of his malfunctioning attitude control, subsequent landing, and fortuitous meeting of Henree. He told them of the painting, purposely skipping over the fact that there were others beside the one in his back seat, and of how Henree tried to protect him when the other Irtlings tried to capture him. He finished the tale of his adventure by recounting how he used Henree's primitive weapon to fix his broken attitude control.

"But even then," he continued, "I wouldn't have escaped without your help. How in the Galaxy did you get together in the first place, and then find me?"

"Well, you see," said Qilzar, uncomfortably, "shortly after our, ahem, conversation, Xtlar came ..."

"I contacted him, Gsefx," interrupted Lhvunsa, much to Qilzar's apparent relief. "Remember those devices you invented for the vehicles a turn ago?"

Gsefx nodded.

"Well, I got a notification that said your vehicle had gone outside the one hundred parsec perimeter we set up when you first installed them, which made me wonder what was going on. I tried contacting you but couldn't get a response, so I called Qilzar. He explained what had happened and suggested that since I could track you with the device, we should go look for you."

Qilzar gave Lhvunsa a surprised look, but Gsefx pretended not to notice. He also pretended not to notice his wife kick Qilzar gently in the shin. She was up to something, but it was on his behalf, so he wasn't going to spoil it.

"By the time we reached Irt," said Lhvunsa without missing a beat, "we realized you were on the surface and in trouble, and knew we had to do something. So, we did about the only thing we could do, fly low enough and fast enough to hopefully give you enough time to escape. We were going to come around for another pass but saw that you were already lifting off, so we headed out of the atmosphere."

"It was fortunate the first primitive you ran into was a friendly one," said Qilzar. "Otherwise, things might have turned out quite differently, my boy."

"Yes, quite differently, I'm sure," said Gsefx. "The worst part of it is that while I escaped, I'm afraid he didn't."

"What do you mean?"

"I mean his fellow Irtlings took him into custody. I'm certain they'll imprison him, or worse, and it's all my fault. I need to go back and help him."

"No, Gsefx!" said Lhvunsa, becoming uncharacteristically frantic. "You can't!"

Gsefx looked at his wife with concern. He knew she was right, of course, but her sudden outburst was completely unlike her.

"Lhvunsa, are you all right?" he asked. "You don't seem yourself."

"I'm fine," she said. "Just promise me you won't go back to Irt."

"I won't," he said quietly. "I promise."

Lhvunsa wrapped one of her arms gently around one of his and laid her head on his shoulder.

"Even so," said Gsefx, "I can't help but feel responsible. I ruined Henree's life."

"I understand how you feel, Gsefx," said Qilzar, quietly. "I once had a pet Clelchin when I was a boy. Clydon was his name. We were inseparable. We went everywhere together. One rotation we were out fooling around in an area outside of the city that was off limits. It was an abandoned construction site with lots of old equipment and such. I was climbing up an old staircase that had no wall on one side and was completely open to the air. On the way up, one of the steps broke through and I lost my balance. I surely would have fallen over the side, but Clydon grabbed me by the shirt and pulled me back over. In the process of saving me, though, Clydon lost his balance and went over the side himself. I've never forgiven myself, Gsefx, but there was nothing I could do. His blind affection cost him his life, even though it saved me in the process."

"I'm sorry, Qilzar," said Gsefx. "That must have been devastating."

"It was, but I was just a child, only eleven turns. As I grew, I learned that lesser creatures sometime act on instinct, rather than intellect. There was nothing I could do. Just like there was nothing you could do for the Irtling."

"Excuse me? Qilzar, Irtlings may be primitives, but they are hardly lesser creatures."

"Oh, my dear boy, of course they are. Perhaps in a few thousand years, when and if they've evolved far enough along, they won't be so far beneath us. But as someone who's flown by and seen for myself, they are nothing more than wild animals. Quite dangerous ones, at that."

"How dare you ..." said Gsefx rising from his chair, his temper exploding like a stack of Plurian gas mines. Qilzar was talking about Henree, and that was crossing the line. Lhvunsa took hold of his arm, gently pulling him back into his chair. Soft green fingers rubbed his neck, calming him in a way only she was capable. At the same time, she shook her head and softly shushed the Dremin on the other side of the table.

"My darling," she said, looking Gsefx in the eyes, "you saw for yourself what they were going to do to you. But even if, as a species, the Irtlings are not what you'd like them to be, we can all agree that we owe a debt of gratitude and friendship to Henree." The last she directed toward Qilzar.

"Quite right," said Qilzar, catching her look. "We owe Henree a great debt for helping save your life."

"Yes, we do," said Gsefx, sadly. "A debt that can't be repaid, I'm afraid."

"The way to repay him is to live your life the best way you know how," said Lhvunsa, continuing to rub his neck.

"You talk as if he's already dead. What if he's not? What if he's imprisoned somewhere, waiting for us to rescue him?"

"Gsefx, we are not going back, and that's final," said Lhvunsa, the neck rub coming to an abrupt end "None of us are going back. Not you, not me, and not Qilzar."

Qilzar interrupted Gsefx before he could object.

"I know this isn't what you want to hear," he said, "but Henree had to know he wasn't going to survive. Otherwise, why would he give you that stunning painting you have in your vehicle. Anyone who thought they might live would have never given up a work of that magnitude. It had to have been a treasure to him. Especially since he likely couldn't have painted many more of its equal, probably none, would be my guess."

"Many more of its equal?" asked Gsefx incredulously. "Qilzar, Henree had thirty more paintings in that clearing, all equally as good. Some probably better. The one in my ship happened to be my favorite and I think he saw how much I liked it, so he gave it to me. You have no idea what you're talking about."

He looked at his wife.

"Either of you. Yes, I will grant you that perhaps Irtlings are not as advanced technologically, intellectually, or socially as we are, but that's just the stage of evolution they're in. It's not like each of our species weren't there at some point ourselves. The determining factor about whether a species is considered a lower form of life is not how evolved they currently are, it's whether or not they will always stay that way. Qilzar, your pet Clydon, for example. He was a Clelchin, and Clelchins have always been Clelchins and will always be Clelchins. Regardless of what point in history you choose, they will always be the same lovable pets they have always been. Not so with the Dremin race, eh Qilzar? While your pale gray skin and sharp features have always been characteristic of your species, you haven't always been as civilized as you are presently. No different with my Clangdorian ancestors, or Lhvunsa's long-distant Relnarian relatives. We're all descended, at some point, from a Primitive Cultures class case-study, but we all evolved out of it because we all have the innate ability to grow beyond ourselves. So do the Irtlings, especially Henree."

"Be that as it may, Gsefx," said his wife in a growl he was all too familiar with, "you, are not going back there to rescue him. None of us are."

"Let's not be too hasty on that subject," said Qilzar suddenly, his eyes somewhat glassy, as if he was in deep thought. "You said Henree had thirty more paintings? Perhaps Irt might be worth a second visit after all."

"What?" said Lhvunsa, clearly amazed at what she was hearing from her former ally. "Qilzar, have you lost your mind?"

"My dear Lhvunsa, you saw the painting in Gsefx's vehicle for yourself, how mesmerizing it is, or was, until Gsefx hid it from us. Think how much a work of art like that is worth. Think how much thirty more of them would be worth."

Lhvunsa stopped to consider Qilzar's proposal for a moment.

"No, it's not worth the risk," she said. "We're not doing it."

"Not worth the risk?" asked Qilzar. "They could literally be worth millions. I'd say that's worth the risk. Besides, with a little bit of planning, we can be in and out before anyone even knows we were there."

"No Qilzar," said Lhvunsa. "We just got Gsefx back safely and we barely managed that. After all we've been through,

I'm not going to risk losing him again. I would think you'd understand that."

Gsefx could see that his wife was on the verge of tears, but he remained silent. Something had happened between Lhvunsa and Qilzar on their way to Irt, something he needed to figure out. He looked over at Qilzar, who seemed to be taken aback by Lhvunsa's reproach.

"Of course I understand, my dear Lhvunsa," said Qilzar softly. "But I also understand that this would be a very simple operation. We go in, rescue Gsefx's friend, make sure he's safe, and in the process, we make sure the paintings are safe as well. He'll be free and we'll be rich. I don't see the problem."

"You don't see the problem?" said Lhvunsa. "The problem is that we could all get caught and killed by the Irtlings, that's the problem, Qilzar."

"Furthermore," said Gsefx, jumping in to back up his wife, "even if we didn't get caught, it's called stealing, and I wouldn't be a part of it in any case, but in this case I absolutely will not allow it. You're talking about taking someone who literally saved my life and repaying him by stealing the one thing that makes him feel important, the one thing that makes him feel different from everyone else on that despicable little planet. We may not have spoken the same languages, but what little we were able to communicate, I know that Henree would rather rot away as a prisoner, or die, than have his artwork ripped away from him, especially by someone he trusted. We are not going back to steal his art and that's final."

"Nice speech," said Qilzar, "but isn't that why you went to Irt in the first place, to steal that music you like? That albalan?"

"That's different and you know it."

"How Gsefx?" pressed the Dremin. "How is it different?

"First off, I was going to download a copy, not the one and only version of the music. With Henree's painting, once the original is gone, it's gone forever. Secondly, it's for my own personal use, I wouldn't have sold it for a profit."

"It's still stealing."

"Yes Qilzar, you are correct," said Gsefx, raising his voice in an effort to retake the moral high ground. "It is stealing and it's wrong. I admit that I have been wrong on many accounts during this rotation, chief among them was the idea that going to Irt and stealing music that didn't belong to me was acceptable. I almost paid for that mistake with my life, and in the process I put your lives in danger as well. I'll not do that again. Qilzar, you must promise me that you'll not go back to Irt for Henree or his art, or even discuss it again. We all have to close this chapter and just go forward."

"Gsefx, my dear boy, I will make no such promise," said Qilzar, breaking the mood completely. "I am your direct supervisor as you know and ..."

"Et Qilzar, within the confines of Galacticount, you are my supervisor. That is true. Beyond that, I also owe you a debt of gratitude for the part you played in my rescue. But in this, I will not be swayed and I insist that you swear your allegiance to me."

"My allegiance? The mere thought is ridiculous!"

"Ridiculous is it?" Gsefx was losing his temper. "Qilzar, you flew by the ground at a high rate of speed, which means you got nothing but the quickest of glances of the Irtlings and their capabilities. I was there, on the ground, with their weapons in my face. You call them dangerous, but you don't begin to know the half of it. To be honest, I don't begin to know the half of it, and I know a lot more than you do. To go back and attempt a rescue of Henree would be foolhardy, and even as I talked about it before, I knew it was nothing more than idle talk. But you are serious about trying to get those paintings and I can tell you that it's impossible. If you're lucky, they would simply kill you and be done with it. But I honestly don't think you would be that fortunate. I believe it would be much worse than a quick and simple death. Qilzar, you must swear to me that you will not take this notion any farther."

"And if I don't?"

"Then I will not return to Galacticount and Et Xtlar may do with you as he will. I believe I heard something about Zaras 7?"

At the mention of Zaras 7, Qilzar's once brave facade melted completely, and Gsefx knew he had won.

"Gods, will I be forever cursed with that horrendous place? So be it. I promise."

Gsefx knew better than to accept an open-ended promise from his boss.

"Promise what, exactly?"

"I promise," sighed Qilzar, "to never ever again speak of Irt, Henree, or his artwork. There, are you satisfied."

"That's half of it, now let's hear the other half."

"Oh very well. I also promise not to go to Irt and attempt to gain control of the paintings or rescue Henree or anything else that might upset Et Gsefx." He was in a full pout now and Lhvunsa had to duck her head to not be caught laughing.

"Thank you, Qilzar. Now, shall we go home?"

Chapter 32

You Like Being
the Hero, Right?

"And that concludes the formal portion of my report," said General Alcorn. "If someone will get the lights, I'll be happy to answer any further questions you may have."

The General did his best to put forth a positive demeanor, but he was far from happy. Nor did his audience resemble anything close to a receptive, or even impartial group. In attendance within the secure walls of the Pentagon briefing room were several of his O-Ten colleagues, all of whom shared a mutual disdain for him, a feeling that did not go unrequited.

His direct supervisor, General Frank Allen, was there as well. Though they rarely agreed on anything, and sat on opposite sides of the philosophical fence, Allen was one of the few men at this level of the armed forces that Alcorn actually respected and trusted. The Joint Chiefs of Staff, whose only opinion of Alcorn came from what they read in his files and heard from the suck-ups who sought their favor, were also in the room. He was certain they would not be friendly to anything he had to say.

The only one in the room he believed might be reasoned with would be Secretary of Defense, Langhorne herself, but he had to tread lightly. She was a politician, which meant she would be looking for a scapegoat, and he had no doubts about whose name was at the top of her list. The sad truth of the matter was that, in this case at least, his name belonged there.

"General Alcorn," said Secretary Langhorne, slowly and deliberately, "it's been nearly two weeks since this incident took place and we received our initial briefing. Why has it taken so long for us to receive the full report?"

Good, thought Alcorn, *she's patient. She's willing to give me enough rope to either save or hang myself. Either way, her hands stay clean. That gives me a chance at least.*

"Madame Secretary," he said, "you'll notice that even though we opened fire, neither of the non-terrestrial ships took aggressive actions toward us. Between that and my initial interrogation of the prisoner, I believed then, as I do now, that there is no immediate threat, and therefore felt the wiser course of action was to pursue a more detailed investigation in order to provide you with better intel, even at the risk of a slight delay."

"I see," said the Secretary. "What I find interesting is that you don't seem to have any more information now than you did after the incident happened, which tells me you wasted two weeks for no good reason."

Alcorn smiled at the Secretary. Not a smirk, not a fearful grin, but a smile that was warm and sincere.

"With respect, that's where we disagree, Madame Secretary," he said, being careful not to tell her she was flat-out wrong in front of the entire room. "Had I called everyone together immediately and given this same briefing, it would have been based on intuition and conjecture, not on proof. I have personally reviewed and analyzed every single piece of evidence, every frame of film, and every word of transcript from this event in order to come to the conclusions I've presented today. That takes time, Madame Secretary, and could not have happened if I came to you immediately after the incident occurred."

"For the love of God, he's just playing semantics," said a voice from the other side of the room. It was General Samuel Walker, U.S. Air Force and Chairman of the Joint Chiefs of Staff. He looked straight at Alcorn. "General Alcorn, let's cut the crap and get to what all of us here really want to know."

"Yes sir, what's that?"

"How in the hell did you, a highly decorated commander, hand-picked for this assignment, leading the most elite unit in the entire armed forces, let one alien in one tiny little unarmed ship, get away?"

And now we come to it. Alcorn held Walker's gaze without wavering. He desperately wanted to glance over at the Secretary to see her reaction to the Chairman's outburst, but this was a game, one where a single flinch meant certain defeat. Fortunately, he was prepared.

"General Walker," he said, finally breaking the stalemate, "with all due respect, there's not one individual in this room who's unaware of how one is 'hand-picked' for this assignment." He held up his hand to ward off Walker's attempted interruption. "But, for clarity's sake, let's just say that this assignment is where Generals are sent to retire when there is nowhere else to send them."

"You'd do well to watch your tone, General," said Walker indignantly, leaping from his seat amid the shocked murmurs that filled the room. "Not only are you wrong in your assessment, you're dangerously close to insubordination."

"That's enough Sam. Sit down and let the man talk." It was Secretary Langhorne. Once the room quieted, she continued. "It's not as if General Alcorn is telling us anything we don't already know. The truth about First Contact Command, or should I say Last Stand Command, is the worst kept secret in the Pentagon."

The Secretary looked back at Alcorn, not specifically to give the floor back to him, but as if she was still thinking about whether or not she was finished speaking. Alcorn decided to wait until he knew for sure.

"You know," she said a few moments later, "I've always enjoyed TV shows and movies about aliens and such—at least as much as everyone else, I suppose, but can anyone in this room look me in the eye and tell me that prior to two weeks ago, they believed intelligent non-terrestrial life actually existed?" She paused while waiting for an answer. "I didn't think so. General Alcorn, please continue."

"Thank you, Madame Secretary," said a relieved Alcorn.

"Don't thank me yet, General," said Langhorne, no hint of sympathy in her voice, "you're not off the hook by any means. Don't think that being given a lousy command excuses you from your obligations. You were expected to capture and hold that non-terrestrial, were you not?"

"Yes ma'am, I was, and as commanding officer, I fully accept the consequences of my failure to do so. Be that as it may, Madame Secretary, there is a much larger issue at stake than whether or not I'm an effective commander."

Alcorn paused for effect, expecting the Secretary, or someone else, to ask what that issue was, but hoping they wouldn't. When nobody asked, he pressed on, directing his attention solely at the Secretary herself.

"The issue that concerns me, Madame Secretary, is that, as you've noted, up until two weeks ago, nobody has given a second thought to the idea that non-terrestrials might actually exist, and therefore, we're simply not prepared, regardless of how many exercises or drills we run. You saw for yourself how quickly, agilely, and unpredictably those ships moved. Do we have anything that can match them? Certainly nothing I had in the field on the day of the incident. Judge my performance, then do with me what you will, I gladly accept whatever punishment is deemed appropriate, but for the sake of our country—for the sake of our planet—don't overlook the larger issue. Without a better understanding of what we're dealing with, and more focused, dedicated resources to get our defense capabilities ..."

"Stop right there, General Alcorn," said the Secretary as she rose to her feet. "That's enough. This meeting is adjourned." She turned and left the room without another word.

Alcorn was stunned. He had been prepared to argue his case and had even been prepared to lose, but to be cut off like this in mid-sentence was, well, it was just plain weird.

The rest of the room must have thought so too, as the chatter amongst Alcorn's colleagues showed that they were as confused by the Secretary's behavior as they were angered by this entire situation.

"You still know how to stir up a crowd, Teddy, that's for damn sure," said Frank Allen as he walked up and patted Alcorn on the back.

"I suppose so," said Alcorn. "Frank, what the hell was that?"

"Beats the hell outta me. Come on, let's get outta here before you get cornered by someone less friendly."

"Good idea. Lead the way."

Alcorn followed his supervising officer toward a side door, but was stopped before he reached it.

"General Alcorn, a moment, please."

Alcorn turned to find a rather unremarkable young civilian man standing before him, wearing an ill-fitting suit and looking as if he felt extremely uncomfortable.

"Yes, what is it?" said Alcorn.

"Sir, Secretary Langhorne wants to see you in her office immediately."

Alcorn started to say something, then thought better of it. He looked back at General Allen.

"It was a nice attempt anyway, Frank," he said. "Give my best to Karla and the boys."

Frank nodded and left the room. Alcorn turned back to Langhorne's assistant and motioned for him to lead the way.

Am I walking toward my salvation or my doom? He thought as he followed the Secretary's lackey down the Pentagon's seemingly endless hallways. *There won't be any middle ground, that's for damn sure. I suppose she could demand my resignation, but if that's all she was looking for, she wouldn't have ended the meeting like that and asked for a private meeting. She would have humiliated me right then and there in front of God and everybody. No, she's got something else in mind, something that could make getting fired look like a walk in the park.*

When they finally reached her office, the handful of assistants parked at their desks in the reception area didn't even bother to look up. Four-star generals might rate some excitement in certain parts of the world, but this wasn't one of them.

"The Secretary is waiting General," said the unremarkable lackey. "Go on in."

Alcorn nodded his head in acknowledgement, but couldn't quite find it within himself to actually say "thank you" to the man. He thought briefly about why as he walked toward the Secretary's door, but couldn't come up with anything except that perhaps he was just an arrogant ass. He shrugged inwardly and thought, *I can live with that.*

Unable to simply walk in on the Secretary of Defense of the United States of America, Alcorn knocked on the door, one loud knock, just as he'd been taught from the very the beginning of his military training.

"Come!" came the answer from the other side of the door. It gave no indication of irritation or welcome, it was simply a command.

Alcorn opened the door, entered the room and turned toward the desk, only to find Secretary Langhorne not in her seat but instead pouring herself a drink at the bar by the window.

"General," she said before he could speak, "on the wall, to the left of the door, you'll find a retinal scanner and security control panel. Please submit to a scan and follow the instructions accordingly."

Alcorn turned toward the scanner, ready to comply, but hesitated when he saw that it was unlike any retinal scanner he'd ever seen before. For one thing, it had a full visor, covering both eyes, whereas every other scanner he'd seen only had optics for one, which is all that was necessary for identification. It also had a handprint and voice recognition system built into it. Whatever was behind this firewall, it was only meant for the select few. He paused for a moment as he considered asking more about what was going on.

"Please General, we have much to discuss and I have a full day ahead of me."

"Yes ma'am, of course."

I guess I've been selected.

Once he completed the retinal scan, hand and voiceprint ID, the system made a locking sound, and a computerized voice announced "Identification authorization complete. Room will be secure in 5 ... 4 ... 3 ... 2 ... 1 ... Room secure."

"Pardon my asking, ma'am, but would you mind explaining just what the hell that was all about?"

"The latest in secure technology," said the Secretary, as she poured herself another drink. She poured Alcorn one as well and motioned for him to sit down. "And for the moment, let's dispense with the formalities. I'll leave my title in my desk drawer, if you leave your stars at the door. Whad'ya say Teddy?"

Alcorn took the drink she offered as she sat down across from him. "Fine by me, Natalie. Now, would you mind telling me what in the Sam Hill is going on? I don't know if I'm supposed to be packing my bags for an early retirement, or leading the next Charge of the Light Brigade."

Natalie smiled.

"I understand your concern, and your confusion. Your encounter has put our entire DOD philosophy into a state of utter chaos. The boys back in the briefing room were ready to roast you over an open flame, but that was the only thing they could agree on. They simply couldn't come to terms with the idea that advanced non-terrestrial life exists and that we're not prepared for it. For the sake of their own careers, they're ready to hand you over as the one who made sure America wasn't prepared."

"I assumed as much, even before I went in," said Alcorn, nodding in agreement. "But you didn't let them do it. You stopped me, and them, before it could go that far. Why?"

"Because what none of them seem to understand is that neither their careers, nor ours, such as they are, will amount to a damn thing if we're overrun by hostile alien forces. I don't know if it was your encounter, or if you're just wired differently, but you seem to get that, which is why we're here talking now."

Alcorn smiled and nodded.

"I'd like to think I'm wired differently than those jackals, but that's something only time and results can prove." He glanced back at the retina scanner by the door. "I'm sorry, but I can't take my mind off of that security thingamajig hanging on the wall over there. What's that all about?"

Now it was Natalie's turn to smile.

"It's called a 'secure room.' It allows us to talk in complete freedom without any concerns of being overheard, spied upon, etc. We are totally isolated from the outside world."

"Interesting. But why did I have to submit to the ID scans?"

"As the room's owner, I can initiate the call for a secure room, but if there is anyone in the room besides me, they have to consent, which is why you were scanned. The idea is to keep me from locking you or anyone else in here against their will, taking you hostage, as it were."

"Nice tech," Alcorn paused for a moment, thinking. "I understand how it knew who I was, I'm in the DOD system, but what if it was someone who wasn't in the system? How would the computer know who they were?"

"Everyone's in the system, Teddy," said Natalie, casually sipping her drink. "Whether they know it or not. I thought someone in your position would have realized that by now."

Alcorn felt a slight chill at the Secretary's casual big brother-like implication, but said nothing.

"But enough about that. I've looked through your files and tend to believe that you're wired differently too, for the most part."

"For the most part?"

"Like all kids who play soldier, you like being the hero, right? So, here's your chance. Let's see if you can actually shed some light on the non-terrestrial situation and help us formulate a plan. Do that, and we all win. Fail, well, I think we both know what happens then."

Alcorn didn't have to think long about Natalie's offer. He'd been given a reprieve and he knew it.

"What kind of resources will I have access to?" he said.

"What do you need?"

"I need more and better ... well, everything. This project has received the least of nearly every resource, troops, equipment, logistical and tactical support. You name it, we need it."

Natalie smiled again.

"Have your list of requirements to me by 0800 tomorrow morning and my staff will get started on it before lunch. But, and this is important, Teddy, I expect results and I expect them sooner, rather than later."

Alcorn shifted in his seat.

Madame Secretary is definitely a politician.

"Yes, well, I guess that's what we should discuss next, isn't, it ma'am? Expectations?"

"Indeed," said Natalie. "The Security Council meets in four weeks. What can you have for me in three?"

Three weeks! Alcorn stood up and paced as he thought. *What can I do for you in three weeks? Almost nothing, that's what!*

"I tell you what, Natalie," he said, turning back toward the Secretary of Defense. "I'll make that list of requirements and you have your team start preparing, but let's wait until after your meeting before we attempt any implementation. To do so would disrupt things too much, virtually guaranteeing failure."

"Agreed," said Natalie.

"Good. For the Security Council meeting, I will have a brand new full-scale contingency plan, based on our recent encounter and any new intelligence we extract from the eyewitness. I will also deliver a detailed report from the eyewitness of his role and any details from, and of, his encounter."

"Really?" said Natalie, with mock surprise. "We're talking about the eyewitness named Henry Backus, correct?"

Alcorn nodded. "Yes, that's right. Why?"

"It's been my understanding that he's been, well, let's just say, less than cooperative so far."

"That will change, Madame Secretary, I promise you," said Alcorn with a grimace. "That will change."

Chapter 33

My Name is Henry Backus

"On your feet, maggot!" said a voice over the loudspeaker as the door to Henry's cell flew open and two armed guards, pistols drawn, stepped inside and took up positions by the door. Two more guards ran in immediately behind them, grabbed Henry from his bunk, and threw him up against the wall. If Henry hadn't been so shocked by this surprisingly uncharacteristic action, he might have noticed that the guards were actually being quite careful to ensure his chest took the full force of the impact with the wall, while also making sure his face remained unscathed. As it was, Henry was doing all he could just to try and catch his breath.

"The man said UP, maggot!" said the guard on Henry's right arm, the smell of barbeque sauce and jalapeños on his breath making Henry gag on what little air he was able to pull in. The guard snickered as Henry coughed and sputtered, but only briefly. The other guard swept Henry's legs out from underneath him and he dropped to the floor like a marionette whose strings had just been cut.

The guards wasted no time rolling Henry onto his back, as two more guards came in with shackles and chains, and bound his legs and arms so tight that he could hardly move. When they were satisfied with their work, the guards lifted Henry to his feet and pointed him toward the door.

"March!" Came the harsh command from jalapeño-breath.

Henry had mostly recovered his breath by now and did his best to move, but his best was nothing more than a slight shuffle.

"There's no time for this," came the voice over the loudspeaker. "Pick him up."

Without a word, four sets of hands grabbed, lifted, and carried him from his cell and down the hall. As his captors carried him to God-only-knew-where, Henry recovered enough of his wits to realize two things: first, this clearly wasn't normal protocol. For the past however many days or weeks he'd been a guest of the United States Army, it hadn't been particularly pleasant, but it had at least been relatively civilized. When not being actively questioned, he'd been in his cell, under constant observation, of course, with no visitors and only sparse amounts of food and water. When it was time for his interrogations, he'd been led out of his cell peacefully. Nothing at all like what was happening now. Something had definitely changed, something seriously detrimental to Henry's well-being. The second thing he noticed was, that even though the guards jumped at the sound of the voice on the loudspeaker, just like they did whenever they heard his dear old friend, General Alcorn, the voice clearly wasn't the General's. In fact, it was a voice he had come to recognize and loath. A voice that confirmed just how deep of a predicament he was really in.

"Sergeant Hickam," said Henry, deciding it best to take the initiative, as his armed escort stood him upright in the middle of what was normally a prisoner day room. "I should've figured you'd be behind something like this. This is rather bold, even for you. Does the General know what you're up to?"

Sergeant Hickam nodded to the guard on Henry's left, the one with barbecue and jalapeño breath. Before he knew it, Henry was doubled over, moaning in pain, as the butt of an M-4 was rammed into his mid-section.

"You were saying?" said Sergeant Hickam.

Henry coughed and sputtered as he tried, for the second time in the last ten minutes, to catch his breath. Something inside told him it wouldn't be the last time he would be practicing that exercise this night.

"That's what I thought," said Sergeant Hickam. "Now, let's get down to business, shall we?"

He nodded again to the guards, who forced Henry back against the wall, where they chained him in place.

"Prisoner Two-One-Seven-Three-Three-Nine-Seven-Six-Three, you are hereby charged with …"

"My name is Henry Backus," said Henry, interrupting the Sergeant as loudly as he could. "You should try getting it right at least once." This time, the guard with the bad breath didn't wait for any signals from Hickam before using the butt of his rifle to silence the prisoner.

"You no longer have a name," said Hickam as Henry once again gasped for air. "You gave it up, along with everything else, when you aligned yourself with the non-terrestrial and against your countrymen. You are a number and nothing more."

Henry had been ready for the blow this time, and recovered more quickly.

"Apparently, a bit more than a number," he said. "A number with something you want. Otherwise, you wouldn't be this interested in me."

"Perhaps," said Hickam. "Or perhaps I'm just bored and looking for a little fun. Now, you can either shut your trap, or we'll shut it for you."

At that, he held up a roll of silver duct tape and smiled. Henry grimaced, but said nothing.

"Good," said Hickam. "It appears we understand one another. Now, as I was saying, Prisoner Two-One-Seven-Three-Three-Nine-Seven-Six-Three, you are hereby charged with aiding and abetting a non-terrestrial being escape custody of the United States Army, interfering in the lawful maneuvers of a United States Army unit, assault of an officer of the United States Army, and finally treason against the United States of America. What do you have to say for yourself?"

Henry would have been shocked by these charges, especially the last, if he hadn't already heard them several times before during previous interrogations. This was all part of the game, as was his response.

"What I have to say, is that not only are all of the charges against me completely false, it is the U.S. Army who has acted, and is continuing to act, illegally by holding an American citizen against their will without legal representation or due process of law."

Jalapeño-Breath pulled back his rifle and aimed it at Henry's midsection again, but was halted when Hickam cleared his throat.

"When asked," said Hickam, "the prisoner is allowed to state his opinion, even if it's incorrect."

Henry knew he was being baited and held his tongue.

"What? No response?" said Hickam. "Well then, allow me to elaborate on all of the ways you are incorrect, Prisoner Seven-Six-Three."

"By all means," said Henry. As long as they were talking, they weren't beating on him, although he felt pretty certain they couldn't talk forever.

"First, Prisoner Seven-Six-Three, your actions constituted a clear and specific terrorist threat to the United State of America, at which point, your so-called right to legal representation became forfeit. Second ..."

Henry had heard this all before, and it infuriated him each and every time. Except now. As he listened to Hickam dispel each of his arguments, and explain how the Army was not only legally obligated to take the action they did, but morally obligated as well, Henry sensed somehow that this wasn't Hickam speaking. It was his body and his voice, but it was someone else's words. Someone else had put him up to this.

That makes sense, thought Henry. Hickam never came across as someone who was capable of much on his own, certainly nothing as elaborate as this. But who was behind this? Alcorn? Perhaps, but that seemed unlikely. Henry didn't like Alcorn much. He was on the wrong side of the table, and he was kind of like a bull in a china shop, but he was an honest bull. At least that's the feeling Henry got from him. Another rifle butt to the gut snapped Henry back to the immediacy of his situation.

"Prisoner!" said Hickam at the top of his lungs. "Are you going to answer me or are you going to just stand there and stare into space like the freaking moron you are?"

Henry caught his breath, but instead of replying, he simply smiled at the Sergeant in quiet defiance.

"Fine," said Hickam regaining his self-control. "I was just trying to help you out. But since you insist on being uncooperative, have it your way."

He nodded to the guards on both sides of Henry, who began pelting him with blows—Jalapeño-Breath with the butt of his rifle, the other with his bare fists. They hit him on his sides, in his stomach, and on his arms and legs.

"Anywhere that doesn't show," said Hickam in a voice barely discernible over the commotion.

Another guard came in to join the fray and they continued working Henry over until he was on the verge of unconsciousness. Whether Hickam stopped them, or they pulled back on their own, Henry didn't know. He only knew it had finally stopped. He felt, rather than saw them, detach him from the wall and lay him on the ground, the lights from the ceiling shining bright into his eyes.

"You're headed back to your cell now, Prisoner Two-One-Seven-Three-Three-Nine-Seven-Six-Three, and I have one final thought before you go. What happens here, stays here. Any talk of this outside of these walls, and you will beg for the sweet release of death before I'm through with you."

Henry barely heard the Sergeant and his meaningless threat. His only thought was how the lights reminded him of the light he saw when he was laying in his backyard the morning after Lucy's fraternity thugs had beat him senseless. He thought then that maybe it was the light everyone talked about seeing after you died, that maybe he was finally dead and was headed into the light. He remembered how disappointed he'd been when he opened his eyes to find that it was merely the morning sunlight shining on his bruised and battered body. How, even as he had forced his physical self into motion that morning, his emotional self slipped into a state of unreachable despair. Now, as he lay here on the hard concrete floor, drifting away toward unconsciousness, he felt himself slipping back into that same level of despair.

Nothing had really changed, had it? Just the form of his prison.

His eyes closed involuntarily and the light gave way to darkness. Just before Henry fell into complete unconsciousness, a song began to play in his mind, just barely audible over the tedious barking of the overgrown man-child.

Night is day and day is night
Don't say I won't 'cause you know I might.
You are wrong and I am right
Don't cross my path 'less ya wanna fight.

The song brought memories of Zef, and how this being from another world had reacted when he first viewed Henry's paintings. Even as he lost total consciousness, the darkness lifted, replaced by the light of hope.

Henry would have been pleased to know just how angry the smile on the face of Prisoner Two-One-Seven-Three-Three-Nine-Seven-Six-Three's face made Sergeant Hickam as the guards carried the unconscious prisoner back to his cell.

Chapter 34

The Ricnor Gang

"Yes sir, Et Xtlar, I understand sir," said Gsefx into the vidcon. "I realize we're a little behind ..."

"You are more than seven rotations behind schedule," said the angry Fweurlian on the other side of the vidcon, his skin beginning to turn purple. "If I agreed that you were just a little behind, it would make me a big behind."

"... ah ... yes, well, you see, it's just that we've run into some areas within the client's account that require deeper analysis than we originally thought ..."

"Et Gsefx, please don't make a bigger fool of yourself by lying to me." Xtlar paused to take a deep breath. "Gsefx, I like you. You wouldn't still be here if I didn't. More than just liking you, I want to see you succeed. You have the rare gift of not only being an excellent accountant but a true leader, as well. Someone who could one day rise into the ranks of upper management, if your foolish impulses don't derail you first. Believe me when I tell you, Gsefx, I can't abide liars and if I ever catch you in a lie, you will see just how quickly your career can and will evaporate before your very eyes."

Gsefx tried to speak but was shut down before he could make a sound.

"Don't say anything, not a word." Through the vidcon screen, Gsefx could see his boss' boss lean back in his chair, his skin turning back into its normal light green. "I don't know what's gotten into you lately, since your last run-in with Qilzar, but you're not acting or performing like you were before, and frankly, I'm more than a bit concerned. Come to think of it, Qilzar hasn't been his miserable little self either. What happened between you two? No ... wait ... don't tell me. I just realized, I don't care."

Xtlar leaned forward again.

"Pigawitts is one of our oldest, wealthiest, and most influential clients, and his company is facing a GTCA audit in less than three multi-rotations. You and your team have barely scratched the surface of his accounts, which makes me wonder if I was wrong to have assigned this project to you. Was I wrong in doing so, Gsefx?"

"No sir, you weren't," said Gsefx, sufficiently shamed by Xtlar's admonition.

"Then do not disappoint me."

The vidcon went blank and Gsefx sat in stunned silence. What he had said about some of the Pigawitts accounts had been true, at least in part. They were requiring deeper scrutiny, but that wasn't the problem. Ever since his narrow escape from Irt, he'd been unable to focus on his work, or anything else for that matter.

He'd been obsessed with learning as much as he could about the primitive planet and its inhabitants, hoping that he might discover something that would give him cause to hope, perhaps some new information he could take to Lhvunsa that would convince her it would be safe to go back. Instead, all he discovered is that the planet's name was actually Earth, not Irt, and that even though the inhabitants were of a single species, humans, as they called themselves, they were divided into hundreds of different factions, most of which were at violent odds with one another. In many ways, it was even more primitive than Gsefx had initially thought.

He supposed it didn't matter, he was so far behind on his work, he wasn't sure he could catch up if he worked straight through until the GTCA audit, much less if he tried to take time off to go back to Earth. Still, he couldn't help but wonder what had happened to the friend he'd left behind.

There was a knock on his door, just before it opened to reveal his best friend in this part of the galaxy, Planvc.

"Gsefx, where is file Z7163? You said you would have it done two sars ago and I need it ... two sars ago."

"What?" asked Gsefx, his thoughts still everywhere but where they needed to be: on his work.

"File Z7163, you know, the Pigawitts account? The one we're nearly seven rotations behind on?"

"Yes, of course, Planvc. Sorry. I'm almost finished with it. I'll have it for you shortly."

"Gsefx, what's going on with you? You haven't been yourself lately, and in all the turns we've worked together, we've never been this far behind. I'm starting to worry about you?"

Gsefx smiled at his friend. They had started at Galacticount together nearly ten turns ago and became close friends right from the very beginning. Planvc was a Nerrillian, which meant he wasn't native to the Galactic Community. It wasn't unheard of for beings to live in galaxies not their own, but it was a rarity. For that fact alone, Gsefx went out of his way to make friends with his new co-worker. As the turns went by, he also took it upon himself to stand up for Planvc when others around them were ready to push the foreigner out completely, as much because of his heritage as for his lack of interpersonal skills. Gsefx simply reminded those in charge of his friend's superior abilities with numbers, and that usually ended the conversation.

"It's nothing, Planvc," said Gsefx, returning the smile. "I've just been a bit distracted lately. I'm fine and we will catch up, I promise. Give me thirty ebyts and I'll bring the file over to you."

Planvc seemed less than convinced, but didn't push it any further.

"Okay, but you know you can always talk to me if you need to."

"I know and I appreciate it. There may come a time when I take you up on that offer. But for now, let's get back to work."

Planvc left the office and Gsefx turned back to his files.

"I have to focus," he whispered aloud. "If I don't get caught up, Xtlar's never going to forgive me." He took a deep breath, then let it out slowly. "Better to not think about that for now, Gsefx. Just shut up and get to work."

He reached over and turned the vidcon off completely, got up, shut his office door, and locked it. He dove into his work with a zeal that, while it lacked the passion normally present when he was as deep in his element as he was now, was as efficient as ever. He finished Planvc's file in the promised thirty ebyts, but continued on without the slightest hesitation. He was on a roll and didn't want to break his concentration. At one point, he heard a knock on the door, grabbed file Z7163 and slid it under the door, then turned back to his work. Eventually, his stomach began to growl and his eyes started to cross, and he knew it was time for a break. He finished the file he was working on and sat back satisfied. Without the constant interruptions that had become a normal part of his work day, he'd been able to complete nearly a full rotation's work in half the time. If he could keep up this pace, he could, theoretically, be caught up in no time.

Theoretically.

He let out a deep sigh and turned the vidcon back on. Ten messages, all from Lhvunsa, except one, which was from Qilzar. He started to the play the one from his boss, thought better of it and played Lhvunsa's most recent message.

"Gsefx, I don't know what's going on or why you're not answering," said the image of his lovely wife, "but please call me back as soon as you get this. I think Qilzar is in serious trouble."

Gsefx entered the code to his home vidcon and pressed the send button.

"Oh, thank the Gods," said a clearly relieved Lhvunsa when she answered. "I was afraid something ... never mind ... you're okay, aren't you?"

"Yes, of course. I'm fine. I was just working, trying to catch up. I'm so far behind, I needed to focus and work for a while without any distractions. What's going on? What's this about Qilzar?"

"He called and left a message for me, but it makes no sense. I don't know Qilzar all that well, but from what I do know of him, the message seemed very strange. He appeared calm, but it was like he was trying to hide how frightened he was. Here, let me play it for you."

She pushed a few buttons on her side and the vidcon screen split down the middle, with Gsefx's boss appearing on one side, while Lhvunsa's image shrunk to the other half.

"My dear, Lhvunsa," began Qilzar, "I'm just calling to let you know that I'll be away for a while. Should you need to contact me for any reason, my traveling code is 1391441112. I will contact you again upon my return. Farewell, dear Lhvunsa."

Gsefx sat staring at the screen, feeling something between puzzlement, shock, and a slight twinge of jealousy. That was a rather intimate message for his boss to leave his wife.

"That is strange," he managed finally, trying not to give away his feelings.

"I'm scared, Gsefx. I'm afraid it has to do with ..."

"I know exactly what it has to do with," said Gsefx, anger now pushing away all of his other emotions. "He swore to us that he wouldn't go back after the paintings, or even discuss it any further."

"Yes, I know. Do you think he's broken his promise?"

"I don't know. Has he talked to you about going back?"

"He tried to bring it up on a couple of occasions, but I shut him down quickly each time. I told him under no circumstances would we be a part of such a risky adventure, and that I would tell you if I found out he was planning anything."

"Thank you," said Gsefx, doing his best to keep in check the sudden swell of emotions that threatened to overwhelm him. Lhvunsa had that kind of effect on him—she always had. "That means more to me than you know. My guess is that he planned something and didn't tell you. Have you tried calling the traveling code he gave you?"

"Yes, of course. That's where it gets even weirder. The code is not even in service. Have you heard from him?"

"No, I haven't ... wait ... yes, I have a message from him that I haven't watched yet. I called you back first. Here, let me play it."

Gsefx pushed the appropriate buttons on the vidcon and they both watched as Qilzar's image appeared on their respective screens.

"My dear Gsefx, I'm calling to let you know that I've decided to take a vacation and so I'll be away for a while. I'm leaving you in charge while I'm out. If you need to contact me, my traveling code is 1893141518. I will contact you again upon my return. Farewell, my dear Gsefx."

"He's done it," said Lhvunsa, "he's gone after the paintings. This is his way of telling us it's too late. He's even given us phony traveling codes so we can't reach him."

"I'm not so sure," said Gsefx as he furiously scribbled notes on his desk. "I've known Qilzar for ten turns and worked directly for him for the last six. In the first place, he's not nearly brave enough to try something like this on his own. He'd need help and since we wouldn't provide it, he'd have to look elsewhere ..."

"Oh Gods!" said Lhvunsa.

"What?" said Gsefx, looking up from his desk.

"He swore to me he wouldn't go after the paintings, but he did mention that it would be the kind of job worthy of ..."

"The Ricnor Gang," they said in unison.

"How did you know?" asked Lhvunsa.

"Not only do I know he's involved with the Ricnor Gang," said Gsefx, "I also know they've taken him to Mindaal."

"Mindaal? Where's that? And how do you know that?"

"I have no idea where Mindaal is, but the codes he gave aren't traveling codes at all. They're a type of code we use internally at Galacticount to pass messages during meetings when we don't want a client to know what we're discussing. They come in very handy. Qilzar must have known he was being watched. Probably told whoever was watching that it would be strange if he just disappeared without a message, and even stranger if he didn't leave a traveling code in the message. They probably didn't pay close enough attention to realize he gave us each different codes. Your code translated to Mindaal, my code translated to Ricnor."

"Gsefx, we've got to do something. The Ricnor Gang is ruthless. They'll steal the paintings and kill him, and they probably don't care what order they do it in."

It wasn't that long ago that Gsefx was staring at an open plain full of heavily armed humans all ready to open fire on him. He thought that had been his defining moment, the point in his life where he truly became the being he was meant to be. Now, as he sat across the vidcon from his lovely wife, he knew the life-and-death situation he encountered on Earth was an adventure, and nothing more. Here, in the comfort of his everyday life, faced with the kind of choice he now had to make, was where his life would truly be defined. Who was Gsefx, really? Who would he be? He hesitated, but only for a moment.

"Lhvunsa, find out where Mindaal is and program it into your vehicle. Then pack up with everything we might need and get together as much money as you can. I'll square things here and be on my way to you as soon as I can leave here without raising suspicion."

"Gsefx ..." she was nearly in tears.

"I know, me too ... but there's no time for that now. I'll need to wait until the end of my rotation, and then I'll be home as fast as I can. I love you, my darling."

"I love you too, Gsefx."

As planned, Gsefx timed his departure from work to coincide with the rest of his team, so as to not arouse suspicion, and he gave no hint to anyone, not even Planvc, that anything was amiss. If necessary, he'd miss work by pretending to be sick, but he'd wait until the last moment before making that decision.

As he piloted his way through the evening traffic, his normally loud music turned completely off, he tried to understand what could have driven Qilzar to do such an incredibly stupid thing. Granted, he himself had very recently done a very stupid thing by going to Earth all alone without having his ship checked out first, but at least he didn't involve anyone else. Qilzar actually invited the Ricnor gang into something he promised he wouldn't even get involved with in the first place. He should have known he couldn't trust Qilzar, from the way he'd looked at the painting.

And now, Qilzar had brought the Ricnor Gang into the situation and was very likely being held prisoner by them. Like it or not, Gsefx was pretty certain another trip to Earth was in his near future, that is if they all survived long enough to make the trip. When he finally arrived at his home, he pulled his vehicle into its parking spot next to Lhvunsa's, locked it up, and went inside.

"Lhvunsa, I'm home."

No answer.

"Lhvunsa?"

No answer.

"Lhvunsa?" A shout this time.

Still no answer.

The vidcon lit up with an incoming call. It was from an unknown number. Gsefx pushed the answer button. An image of his beautiful wife, with a hand over her mouth and a large, very sharp spike held against her neck, filled the screen.

"Don't speak, Et Gsefx, just listen carefully. Clearly, we have your wife. We also have your friend, Et Qilzar. We want just one thing in exchange for both of them. The painting from Irt. If you'd had it hanging in your home, like one would have expected, especially considering that it was such a special gift, or so I've been told, we wouldn't have had to take your wife. But, since you decided you had to hide it from us ... well ... you know the rest. Coordinates are on the desk in front of the vidcon. You have two sars. Don't be late."

The image of Lhvunsa disappeared as the vidcon went dark.

Chapter 35

Are You Going to Talk Tonight?

O ver the previous six nights (Henry assumed they were nights, although he couldn't be sure, as he hadn't seen the sun since the day in the clearing when this little adventure first began), the guards had gone to great lengths to ensure any signs of their handiwork would be hidden under his clothes, away from the prying eyes of anyone who might be looking for signs of prisoner abuse. The guards never seem concerned that Henry would rat them out, although he gave them no reason to believe one way or the other.

But last night something had changed. From the moment they busted into his cell, Henry felt a tension that hadn't been there before, and it concerned him immediately.

"Prisoner two-one-seven-three-three-nine-seven-six-three, you are hereby charged with ..." Sergeant Hickam stopped and looked around. Henry could see sweat rolling down his temples, even though it was actually rather chilly in the day room where they held their mock court. The man was nervous about something.

Is he ... are we, being watched?

Henry forced himself to not look around for a hidden camera, but instead kept his focus on Hickam himself. The more he studied the Sergeant, the clearer it became that it wasn't just nerves. Hickam was flat-out scared.

"Enough of this," said Hickam, suddenly breaking the silence. "Are you going to talk tonight or not, Backus?"

Backus? He's never called me that.

For the first time since they'd locked him up, Henry was more than a little frightened himself. But he wasn't about to let anyone see his fear, Hickam least of all.

"I should think you'd know the answer to that by now, Sergeant," he said, using bravado to hide his fear. The guards hadn't attached Henry to the wall yet, so perhaps his play on the Sergeant's apprehensiveness would force a quick retreat and Henry would be taken back to his cell.

To Henry's dismay, Hickam went the opposite way and charged him. He let out a yell as he connected with Henry, knocking him over, along with the two guards who were holding him. They fell in a heap, but Hickam immediately jumped up and pounced on the defenseless artist and unleashed a barrage of blows to his face that nearly knocked him unconscious, all the while screaming obscenities at the top of his lungs. Just before he lost consciousness, Henry felt the other guards pull Hickam off him in an effort to try and salvage what was left of their careers.

"It doesn't matter! It doesn't matter!" was all Henry could hear coming from Hickam over the din of other commotion in the room. "It doesn't matter. We're all screwed anyway, and it's all his fault."

The room quieted momentarily as Hickam's last statement sunk in throughout the rest of the guards. Then someone threw water in Henry's face to snap him back to total consciousness. After that, the unbridled mayhem began again, with Hickam leading the way and the others matching their comrade's fierceness blow-by-blow. At one point, Henry thought they would kill him, and he welcomed it.

Just before he blacked out completely, he felt, just barely, the hands of his destruction being pulled away from him, while at the same time a voice was shouting, louder than the others, to break it up, before they all ended up behind bars.

I know that voice ...

He woke the next morning, bandaged as best his captors could manage without taking him to a hospital. Without a word, he was led to his daily interview with General Alcorn. Henry did his best to walk into the interrogation room under his own power, but he could barely stand upright, much less walk. He couldn't move his right arm at all, his left eye was completely swollen shut and he was pretty certain a couple of his ribs were broken. How they thought Alcorn wasn't going to notice was beyond anything Henry could imagine. Maybe they no longer cared.

"What in God's name happened to you, son?" said the General, as Henry was helped into his chair.

Henry didn't respond. He wasn't sure he could.

"Guard! What the hell happened to this prisoner?"

"Sir!" said the guard, snapping to attention. "He was like this when we found him in his cell this morning, sir."

"Bullshit!"

Henry did his best to keep up with the interaction between the General and the guard with his right eye, but all he could see was the General glaring at the guard for what seemed like an eternity. Henry had to give the guard credit for standing strong and not shrinking under that glare. In his former life, before he met Zef, Henry was certain he wouldn't have held up as well.

"Don't even think about moving your ass," Alcorn finally said to the guard.

He walked over, opened the door, called for his officers, and then sat back down in front of Henry.

"Son, I think you know pretty clearly how much I think of you ..." said Alcorn.

Henry nodded and watched the General's eyes as he was thoroughly examined by his captor, but he said nothing.

"... but, I do not condone this type of behavior in my men. Torture is never a solution, and ... what's been done to you isn't even torture, it's mindless brutality, done in the name of sport."

Two men entered the room, one with a silver bar on his collar and the other a gold leaf. Henry knew them as Major Wellston and Lieutenant Skinner. They both stood at attention and in one voice said "Sir!"

"Lieutenant," said Alcorn, in a voice that made it clear to Henry the effort he was making to contain his displeasure. "Please take our prisoner to the infirmary and make sure he is provided the very best in medical care."

"Yes, sir!"

The general stood up.

"Lieutenant."

"Sir?"

"The very best care, son. I mean it. Do you understand me?"

"Yes sir!"

He reached down and helped Henry to his feet.

"Come on, let me help you up."

As they left the room, Henry heard the General say something to the Major about "rounding them up" just before the door shut behind them.

"Yes sir," the Major replied.

Henry stopped.

"I know that voice," he said, half under his breath.

It was Wellston! He's been behind these beatings the whole time.

"Of course you do," said the Lieutenant, "Major Wellston has been in all of your interrogations."

Henry stared at the Lieutenant for a second, then caught himself. He shook off the feeling as best he could in his condition.

"Of course, you're right," he said, trying to quickly change the subject. "I'm not thinking clearly. What did the General mean by "rounding them up?""

The lieutenant smiled at that.

"He means that as bad of shape as you're in, you're better off than the guys who did this to you are gonna be. Come on, let's go."

Henry spent the next nine days in the infirmary, recovering from three broken ribs, a badly swollen eye, and numerous bruises, lacerations, contusions and other wounds he couldn't pronounce, but that hurt just as badly. In the end, he was informed by his doctor that he'd been quite fortunate, as none of the injuries were severe enough to cause any permanent damage. Henry had never believed, nor disbelieved, in God, but after this, he was beginning to think someone, or something, had to be watching out for him.

By the fourth day, he'd recovered enough to spend more time awake than asleep. He took advantage of that time by reflecting on all that had happened since that day in the clearing.

General Alcorn had wanted to know everything that had taken place that day, from the time Henry first saw Zef's ship begin its descent, to the time the General and his troops showed up. He didn't know why the General was so interested in hearing the whole story. It wasn't like there was much to tell. He also wasn't all that sure as to why he hadn't just told Alcorn everything from the very beginning. He supposed he was just being obstinate, being uncooperative because of the way they had treated him, and the way they had treated Zef. But then, after a while, it became more a test of wills, a contest to see who could hold out the longest. More recently, when the beatings began, it somehow seemed a moral imperative not to say anything, as if his very soul would be lost if he gave in. The more he thought about it, lying there in that hospital bed, the more he believed that part, at least, to be true.

But he also knew that Alcorn wasn't behind the beatings. Even before witnessing the General's reaction to his condition, Henry knew Alcorn would never condone such actions. He didn't know exactly how he knew it, he just did. It was something he could sense about the man. Alcorn was as tough as nails, and he was pretty sure they would never like one another very much, but the General was also a fair man, even to those who disagreed with him. Now that he knew Major Wellston was involved, he had to let the General know somehow. He had to get him alone, without Wellston or any of the other officers who seemed to cling to Alcorn like a fungus.

"The doctors tell me you're healing well," said a voice from the doorway, interrupting his train of thought. Henry looked up from his bed and standing there, as if on cue, was General Theodore Eustace Alcorn.

Chapter 36

I Want to Hear Her Voice

Gsefx stood frozen, staring at the screen where the image of his beloved Lhvunsa had appeared just moments before, with a razor sharp spike at her throat and terror in her eyes. He couldn't move. He knew what he had to do and that he didn't have much time to do it, but he couldn't seem to make any of his limbs move, even just a little. After what felt like an eternity, the vidcon buzzed again with the same unknown number. He answered, but this time no image appeared, just the same cold, threatening voice.

"The clock is ticking," it said, "and you're wasting time."

"I want to speak to her," Gsefx said suddenly. "I want to hear her voice."

"A reasonable request."

"Gsefx!" It was Lhvunsa. "Help me, Gsefx!"

"I'm afraid that's all you have time for," said the voice. "Now get moving."

The vidcon went silent.

This time Gsefx moved without hesitation. He grabbed the coordinates from the table, stuffed them in his pocket, and headed for the door. He stopped before reaching it. Something inside him insisted he slow down and think through what he was about to do, regardless of the urgency. That something was Lhvunsa herself. It was her voice inside his head, the one she always used whenever she tried to convince him how unproductive it was to act rashly. If he had listened to that voice the day Qilzar had fired him, she wouldn't be a prisoner right now. None of them would be in this mess.

He pulled the coordinates out of his pocket and quickly pulled them up on his computer. As he suspected, they were for Mindaal, which meant the Ricnor Gang now had both Lhvunsa and Qilzar.

It also meant that, since it would take Gsefx much longer than two sars to reach Mindaal—at least five by his calculations—there was no way he could deliver the painting to them on time. Of course, they knew that was the case, which meant they had no intention of letting any of them live and he was walking into a trap. Gsefx was likely being watched right now. As soon as he led them to the painting, their lives would be over, his, Lhvunsa's, and Qilzar's.

Qilzar, that miserable little womble. If we all get out of this in one piece, I might just kill him myself. He looked around his house. *Until then, I need a plan, and I need it now.*

He ran into the bedroom and flipped the bed over. On the floor near where he usually slept was the scrambler he kept within arm's reach. It wasn't meant to be a deadly weapon, although at a close enough range, and if used for an extended period of time, a scrambler could potentially kill. Rather, a scrambler was meant to render an intruder unconscious long enough for the authorities to arrive. Gsefx hadn't had the occasion to use it yet, but Lhvunsa had been so shaken up by the break-in, he felt he needed something to help him defend her if something like that ever happened again. He wasn't sure if she knew that he'd purchased the scrambler, or if she would approve, but he was sure glad he had it now. He stuffed it in his pocket and ran out the door.

Gsefx piloted his way in silence to the storage facility where he kept the painting. Since his return from Earth, he no longer listened to the music that had once played such a large part in his life, especially the albalan music native to Earth. Its once pleasurable effect now gone, he found it more distracting than anything else, especially as he focused on more pressing matters, like his work and what was going to happen with the painting.

As beautiful as the painting was, and as moved as he was when Henree had given it to him, he'd lost count of how many times he'd wished he'd never laid eyes on it. It had brought nothing but grief and misery since he brought it back with him. When Henree first handed it to him, after he recovered from his initial shock, he remembered thinking how great it would look in the main living area of their home. But seeing Qilzar and Lhvunsa's reaction to it changed everything, and he knew he'd have to lock the painting away, safely out of sight. He'd not even told Lhvunsa where it was, not because he didn't trust her, but because she didn't want to know. He briefly considered destroying it, but couldn't bring himself to do that to Henree's work. Even if they could never display it, he had to keep it safe.

So he decided to lock it away in the storage facility he'd rented to hold all of the stuff he couldn't bear to part with, but didn't have room for in their home. He first started renting the facility when Lhvunsa threatened to throw away the military spacecraft models he had scattered about. Model building had been his latest hobby at the time and, combined with several of his previous hobbies, his "junk was taking over their home" as his wife had so eloquently put it to him. He rented the storage facility to ensure the models and all of the other treasures he couldn't part with would not mysteriously disappear when he wasn't paying attention. There were times Gsefx believed that renting the storage facility was perhaps the single best financial investment he'd ever made in their marriage. He knew better than to ask Lhvunsa, but he was pretty certain she would agree.

Gsefx reached the facility and parked his vehicle, being careful not to show that he was aware of the dark-gray, multi-passenger vehicle that had been following him, and was now parked just around the corner behind him. Gsefx went inside, but instead of going to his private storage unit, he went to the other end of the building and back out the other side. Working his way back around to the front as quietly as possible, Gsefx crept back to the corner where his vehicle was parked and waited in the shadows for something to happen. He wasn't sure what, but he hoped he would know it when he saw it. He didn't have to wait long.

It was difficult to see who or what it was at first, it moved very quickly and blended in with the environment—an eye less trained for detail might have missed it. It helped that one of Gsefx's Galacticount co-workers was also a Yelton. He'd been scared enough times in the break room by that little prankster to know how to watch for him. So when he saw the ever-so-slight rippling motion slide by his vehicle, he raised his scrambler and fired.

A brief high-pitched shriek pierced the otherwise still Clangdorian night air, followed by the sound of his stalker falling to the ground unconscious and fully visible. Gsefx took a step from behind the building, froze suddenly, and then jumped back into the shadows. Were there more of them? Surely they wouldn't send just one? But, then again, Gsefx was just an accountant, hardly one to be feared. Why send a whole army after him? He waited a few ebyts more, then slowly made his way out to the unconscious thug lying next to his vehicle.

"I wonder how long he'll be out?" he said quietly to himself.

"About another ten ebyts," said a deep voice behind him, "if that's a standard, over-the-counter scrambler. I told him to watch out, but he said not to worry, you're just an accountant. Now look at him. What an idiot. He'll never live this one down."

Without moving his body, and as gently as he could, Gsefx moved his hand so the scrambler was pointed back toward this new enemy and fired. Nothing seemed to happen.

"Don't bother, it won't work on me," said the voice, "I'm protected. You'll have to do better than that if you want to knock me out. Now, toss it over, then put your hands up. All four of 'em."

Gsefx did as he was told.

"Now, turn around very slowly, and face me."

Gsefx turned around, wondering how, or if, he was going to be able to get out of this. When he was face-to-face with his captor, he found himself staring at a Jikian, a being from one of the inner worlds, who wasn't particularly large or intimidating, but whose race had a reputation for being malicious, mean-spirited creatures. Perhaps it was because Jik was one of the more over-crowded and economically depressed worlds, or perhaps it was because the

Jikians as a race were just nasty little beings. In any case, what Gsefx did know for sure was that Jikians were also notoriously big talkers, usually without much to back it up with. If this one hadn't been pointing an obliterator at his head, Gsefx knew he could easily outmatch him. Without the weapon, all this inner world loudmouth had going for him was attitude and a deep voice. For now, since the obliterator kept things heavily in the Jikian's favor, he would bide his time and wait for the right opportunity.

"Well," said Gsefx, "I clearly only have a short time left to live, but I'm guessing you're on some sort of schedule, so, shall we get on with it?"

"By all means, if you're in that big of a hurry to die, I don't mind obliging you. Lead the way. But don't try anything ... understand?"

He said the last by shoving Gsefx around and putting the obliterator against the back of Gsefx's neck.

"Yes," said Gsefx. "I understand."

"Good. Now pick up my partner and let's get the painting."

Gsefx bent down and picked up the unconscious body. It was not particularly heavy, but its skin was very rough, prickly almost, and uncomfortable to the touch. He grimaced as he walked toward the front door.

"Don't complain to me," said the Jikian. "You're the one who knocked him out."

When they reached the door, Gsefx had to shift the body around a bit while he opened it, but it wasn't enough to be able to get at his captor. Not yet.

They went down several corridors until they found his storage unit. Gsefx dropped his burden unceremoniously, then stepped over the body to the lock.

"Hey, no funny business," said the Jikian.

"No funny business," said Gsefx, hands raised. "I'm just opening the lock. It requires a DNA sample, just like almost any other lock in the galaxy."

"Okay, just stay where I can see you."

"Sure thing."

As Gsefx put his hand up to the lock, his mind raced.

What in the galaxy am I going to do? Once the lock is open, the door will rise and the painting will be visible. As soon as that happens, this goon is going to kill me. Then Lhvunsa and Qilzar are next. Gods, what can I do?

He hesitated, but only for a moment before the deep voice behind him reminded him of the precariousness of his situation.

"What's the hold up? Not trying to think of some way out of this are you?" he said. "Because you know there isn't one. Now open the lock and let's get on with it."

Gsefx nodded his head, unable to speak with his heart stuck in his throat. Then, just before he activated the lock, just when he didn't think it could get any worse, he heard the lump of unconscious flesh laying on the ground behind him begin to stir. His heart fell from his throat down through his stomach, broke into four equal parts and sank into all four of his knees.

"It's about time you woke up, you useless pile of sludge," said the Jikian to his waking partner in crime.

"Whoa, what in the galaxy ..."

"You got hit with a scrambler, you idiot. Wait 'till the boys hear about this—the great Klarnus getting taken out by an over-the-counter child's toy."

Gsefx remained with his hand above the lock, waiting to see what happened next, knowing his time was almost up, as was Lhvunsa's.

"A scrambler? Why you little ..."

Klarnus tried to get up, but finding his body uncooperative, fell immediately back to the floor. At this, the Jikian burst into laughter. Not just any laughter, but the kind usually reserved only for those who themselves have been the victim of someone else's jokes for far too long.

"Quit laughing, Dilnch, you Jikian welt, and help me up," said Klarnus, still trying to get to his feet.

As Dilnch laughed even harder and Klarnus continued his struggle to stand upright, Gsefx took a chance, reacting more on instinct than anything else. He activated the lock, sending the door to the storage unit sliding noisily upward, momentarily startling his preoccupied captors. In that split second of confusion, Gsefx whipped around and grabbed the still dazed Yelton by what passed for his shoulders and pulled him up, just in time to deflect the shot that came from Dilnch's obliterator.

While Dilnch's weapon recharged, Gsefx threw the limp body of Klarnus at what was now nothing more than a glass-jawed, inner world loudmouth, knocking him over and sprawling both of Ricnor's thugs in a pile on the floor. Gsefx ran over and stepped on the arm that was still holding the obliterator.

"I figured you had it programmed with the entire gang's DNA, so I didn't think it would permanently damage you," said Gsefx to the Yelton, who was still struggling to get up. "Klarnus, is it? But I was hoping you would make a good deflector. Thankfully, I was right."

He reached down, pulled the obliterator away from the Jikian, and tossed it aside. Then he reached into Dilnch's pocket and retrieved his scrambler.

"But, I am going to have to put you down again."

"No! Wait!"

Gsefx pushed the button and Klarnus went completely limp for a second time.

"And you," he said to the Jikian, "Dilnch, I believe I heard him call you, the one drawback to obliterators, or so I've heard, is the recycle time in-between firings. It can seem to take forever when you need to take more than one shot quickly."

He leveled his scrambler at Dilnch. The Jikian sneered at him in a most unbecoming way.

"I told you, accountant, it won't work on me. I'm protected."

"So you did," said Gsefx, grinding his foot on his captive's wrist a bit harder as the deep voice turned into a high-pitched whine. "Too bad for you. I guess we'll have to do this the hard way."

Gsefx grabbed him by the collar of his jacket with one hand, then punched him three times in the face, once with each free hand, rendering the defenseless thug unconscious. Gsefx dropped him to the floor on top of his buddy, took a deep breath, and looked around for something to tie them up with. Fortunately, one of Gsefx's ongoing hobbies involved electronic gadgets, so he had plenty of spare parts and extra wires lying around. He drug both limp bodies into the storage unit, found some wire strong enough to hold them, and tied them up tight. Reaching into Dilnch's pockets, he found the controller to the Ricnor vehicle, grabbed the painting, and left. He watched the two unconscious criminals leaning against one another as the door closed just as noisily as it had opened. When it was about halfway down, Gsefx reached over and stopped the door. A thought entered his mind. He didn't know exactly how, but he was quite certain that these two were going to be useful somewhere down the line. He raised the door again and for the first time in what seemed like forever, Gsefx smiled.

Chapter 37

An Urge to Scream

"General Alcorn, I wasn't expecting you. Please come in."

As Alcorn walked over and sat next to his bed, Henry tried to shape his thoughts so this fortuitous time alone with the General could be put to good use.

"What can I do for you, General?" he asked once Alcorn was seated.

"What? No small talk first?" Asked the General. "Fair enough. Let's get to it then, shall we? Henry, the men who did this to you are in custody and have provided a full confession. All you have to do is press charges and we can proceed with their court martial."

Henry paused for a moment, looking for something in the General's expression, some hint at the game he was playing. In the limited time he'd interacted with Alcorn, he'd come to find that nothing was ever quite as it seemed with this man. This time, however, he couldn't be sure. Alcorn had made his disapproval of what had happened to Henry quite clear. He supposed Alcorn could simply be looking to punish those responsible.

"They're your men, General," said Henry, looking away. "Discipline them as you see fit, but don't involve me. I want no part of it."

"So you're not pressing charges?"

"No, sir, I'm not."

"Somehow, I didn't think you would," said Alcorn, standing up and preparing to leave. "No matter, as you said, they're my men. I will take care of the matter, even if you won't stand up for yourself. That's what the military has been doing for more than two hundred years, taking care of the dirty work so liberal, hippie, flower-children, peace-at-all-costs, hypocrites like you can sleep at night with clear consciences."

"Well, now we're finally getting somewhere, aren't we?" said Henry, looking back at Alcorn and pulling himself up into a sitting position. "It's about time we injected some honesty into our conversations, don't you think? I'd say I'm surprised to hear that's what you really think of me, but I don't suppose I am. Just because I got in the way of you capturing your alien—pardon me, your non-terrestrial, as you call them—because I got in the way of you getting your prize, your trophy, now suddenly I'm a liberal, peace-at-all-costs hippie? Well, for the record, I do believe peace is preferable to war, as I believe you do as well, but you don't know the first thing about me or my reason for not pressing charges."

"Okay Backus, why don't you explain your reasons to me," said Alcorn, sitting back down and returning Henry's smile with one of his own. "I can't wait to hear this."

"General, I'm not pressing charges, not because I'm some peace-loving hippie, but because those men don't know any better. They are intellectual imbeciles, which is why they are in the jobs they are in. Even an elite force like yours has needs that can only be filled by a particular type of individual. They can't be faulted too badly for acting in accordance with their instincts, training, and level of intelligence, can they?

"Those sound more like insults than reasons to me. Is that all you've got, Backus? If so, you're not saying much to change my mind about you."

"Not insults, General, facts. If it was you, or someone of your caliber who did this to me, I wouldn't hesitate to prosecute them to the fullest extent of the law, because you would know better and would deserve the severest of punishments. The poor dumb bastards who did this are not of your caliber or mine, and their training revolves around finding, fighting, and destroying the enemy at all costs, with almost no critical thinking needed. They depend on their leaders for that part of their mission. No, I won't hold them accountable for their actions, but rather the one who forced them into taking the action they did."

"And who might that be?"

Henry closed his eyes and took a deep breath, attempting to calm his nerves over revealing this information. Alcorn would not accept it easily, nor should he.

"Major Wellston," said Henry, opening his eyes and looking directly at the General.

"Wellston?" said Alcorn, his eyes showing clear surprise at the accusation. "What in the hell does Major Wellston have to do with this?"

"He was behind the beatings," said Henry.

Alcorn stiffened and leaned in close to Henry.

"That's quite an accusation, young man," he said, his tone very dangerous. "I've known Ben Wellston for more than ten years. He's one of the finest officers I've ever known, and is in line for promotion to Lieutenant Colonel. I hope you have some proof to back up your claim."

"No solid proof, General, except for the bruises and broken bones you see before you. But, before you say anything else, I challenge you to think about this for a minute. This group of guards, all of them privates except for Hickam, ran a very delicate and rather sophisticated operation for a full week, without you or anyone else knowing about it. You say you've known Major Wellston for ten years. How long have you known Terrance Hickam, and more importantly, do you really think him capable of such an elaborate plan?"

Alcorn didn't answer, but looked away.

"I knew from the very first night, that someone else was pulling the strings on Hickam's little operation, but couldn't get a fix on who it was. Then, the night they did this to me, the night they lost control and would have killed me, someone stopped them. I couldn't see who it was, but I heard their voice. It was Major Wellston."

Alcorn looked up, a glimmer of hope in his eyes.

"So Major Wellston discovered what was going on, stepped in and saved you. Seems to me that makes him a hero rather than a criminal."

"Perhaps, but ..." Henry looked away as he searched for the right words. "... I can't explain how I know he's behind it, I just do."

Alcorn opened his mouth to speak, but Henry held him off with a wave of his hand.

"Look General," he said, turning back to lock eyes with Alcorn, "it's not even about pressing charges against Wellston. What happens to me is inconsequential. It's about you protecting yourself. Whether you want to believe it or not, Wellston is not the man you think he is, and you need to watch your back."

Alcorn held Henry's look for a moment, then broke away.

"Why the sudden interest in my welfare?" he asked. "Don't think that, just because I disapprove of what my men did to you, it changes anything. You're still going to remain in custody, and you will eventually tell me everything that happened in the clearing that day. Have no illusions about that."

"Yes, of course. I understand."

Henry closed his eyes and fought down an urge to scream. This was getting neither of them anywhere. It was clear to Henry that, while he believed Alcorn to be a good man, they were on such different wavelengths, he wasn't sure if they would ever be able to truly communicate. The only thing Henry knew for sure was that this stalemate had to end. He had to try and make Alcorn understand, not just as an attempt to be released from prison, but because there was something much larger at stake, even though he didn't know what that was exactly. Just like he couldn't prove Wellston was behind the beatings, Henry couldn't put his finger on what was going on, or why it was important, or even why Alcorn was important, he just knew that the General needed to have all of the information he could provide.

"Look General," he said when he'd regained his composure, "we don't have to like each other to respect one another, and believe it or not, I do respect you and the work you do."

Alcorn scoffed.

"You could've fooled me," he said.

"Well, it's true. I understand the need for a strong military as much as anyone. I just don't like being held prisoner by it, nor do I like it when it oversteps its bounds, like it did in the clearing." Henry held up a hand to stop Alcorn from interrupting. "To prove myself, let me give you what you want. Let me tell you why I helped the non-terrestrial escape."

Alcorn straightened up and met Henry's eyes once again.

"You're a strange one, Backus, that's for damn sure. That's about the only thing I know for certain. And you're right, I suppose, I don't have to like you to respect you, which is a good thing, because I really don't like you."

Henry smiled.

"I'd say I get that a lot, but mainly just from my wife. Well, my ex-wife or soon-to-be ex-wife, I guess."

"I can't imagine why it didn't work out between you."

"Different reasons than you might think, but that's another story."

"Yes, I believe you're about to tell me something a lot more important."

"I am," said Henry. "I helped Zef, the non-terrestrial as you call it. His name is Zef. I think Zef's a male, so I'll refer to it as him, although I can't really be sure. But I do know his name is Zef. And he knows my name is Henry."

"I'll be a son-of-a-bitch," said Alcorn, half under his breath. "Why didn't you say anything about this before?"

Henry thought for a minute before he answered.

"Part of it was just simple defiance, I think, just not wanting to let you win. But there was more to it than that. I think it was because it was you, a big, powerful Army general, with the full weight of the government behind him on one side, and me, a small, powerless civilian sitting across the table in an uncomfortable, straight-backed chair, in a closed, badly ventilated interrogation room. It was like a scene straight out of some badly written spy movie. It couldn't have been any more cliché. General, the whole thing was a joke, a travesty, especially for two intelligent adults like us. There was no way I was going to play a part in such a poorly executed scenario like that."

Alcorn looked confused. "You're not making any sense, son. You're telling me that you didn't like the room you were in, and that's why you wouldn't talk?"

"What I'm saying, General, is that if you want to find out what a person knows, you need to first know the person. I'm an artist, as you probably guessed by all of the paintings you confiscated when you arrested me."

Henry suddenly looked concerned.

"You did get my paintings, didn't you?"

Alcorn nodded. "Yes, they're secure."

"Good. Well General, the one thing an artist seeks, above all else, is truth. Truth in beauty if we can find it, but if not, then truth in whatever condition it happens to be in. That is why I couldn't hold a job in the 'real' world, being forced to bastardize my artistic talent in a vain attempt to sell things people don't need to people who can't afford them. That's also why my marriage failed, because there was no truth in it. That, General, is why I couldn't be a part of that sham you called an interrogation."

Alcorn nodded slowly, at least pretending to understand what Henry was saying, but he remained silent.

"Before my encounter with Zef," said Henry, "I probably would have tried to answer your questions in the interrogation room. I was so cowed, so intimidated by life, and so disillusioned by it all, I would have probably done everything possible to try and fit in to make you like me. But it wouldn't have worked. At some point I would have gone over the edge, created such an outburst that I likely would have ended up in here anyway, only your men would have been justified in putting me here."

The General sat quietly for a few more minutes before finally speaking.

"Okay Backus, I get it, I think. I think you're a bit of a loon, but I get it. Tell me the rest of the story about your encounter with Zef and why you protected him."

"Okay, but before I do, may I ask one favor? Would you mind calling me Henry? You don't have to read anything into it. I just prefer it, that's all."

Alcorn frowned. "Fine. Henry it is."

"Thank you, General. Now, let me ask you a couple of questions. What country, aside from the United States, is you and your family's favorite place to visit?"

"Good God, son, what does that have to do with anything?"

"Please General, bear with me."

"Oh, all right," said the General. He thought for a moment before continuing on. "Greece, I suppose. My wife and I vacation there regularly. Great food, and the people are warm and friendly. Of course, the beaches aren't too shabby either."

"Great. Now, what one country, in your opinion, represents the single most dangerous threat to American citizens right now?"

"Well, there are several, actually," said Alcorn. "North Korea, several Middle Eastern countries, as well as several places in the former Soviet Bloc. It's difficult to pick just one."

"Okay, no problem," said Henry. "Here's the situation. Your entire family is in Greece on vacation, except you. You had some special mission to take care of, then you were to fly your private jet there and meet them. The mission went well, but on your way to Greece, the plane malfunctions. It's nothing serious, but you can't make it all the way, so you have to land and fix it. It's a simple repair, one you can do yourself, you just need a couple of hours in a safe, private spot. Here's the problem, the only place available to land is in one of those Middle Eastern or former Soviet Bloc countries that are none too safe for Americans.

"That wouldn't happen, you know. I'd file flight plans that would only route me through friendly airspace."

"My scenario, my rules, General. Besides, let's say the malfunction you had was your navigation system and you didn't realize where you were until it was too late."

"Your scenario, your rules, but for someone so hung up on truth, I'm telling you it wouldn't happen."

"Facts often get in the way of deeper truths, General."

"Perhaps," sighed Alcorn. "Are we anywhere close to the truth about your encounter with Zef, because I'm just about out of patience."

"Yes, General, we're getting close. Realizing you're in unfriendly territory, you try to get below radar coverage and find as isolated of an area as possible to make your repairs. As you make your landing and get out of your plane, you see a single local approaching. He's armed, but clearly scared. You try to make it clear that your intentions are friendly, but since you don't speak the same language, it's impossible to communicate."

Henry paused for a moment, thinking back to that moment in

the clearing when he and Zef stared at each other, not knowing what to think or do.

"Well, then what?" Asked the General.

"You reach into your cockpit and turn on your radio."

Chapter 38

Don't Call me "Accountant"

As Gsefx sat comfortably admiring the large cockpit of Ricnor's vehicle, he was struck by how quickly the situation had changed. Just thirty ebyts ago, he thought he was dead for sure, along with Lhvunsa and Qilzar. Now he was, quite literally, in the pilot's seat, and it was rather a plush pilot's seat at that.

The ship was a Klurdine Remlin, the galaxy's top of the line multi-passenger vehicle. Apparently, the Ricnor gang flew nothing but the best. He'd connected his ship to the Remlin, effectively increasing the ship's size and power, even if it wasn't by much. It was either that or leave his vehicle behind and Gsefx had a feeling he might need his own transportation again before this was all over.

Gsefx's captives were once again conscious, but securely locked into two of the passenger seats behind him. Klarnus wasn't much in the mood for talking, but Dilnch wouldn't shut up. He finally had to be threatened with another beating, only this time with the butt of the obliterator instead of Gsefx's fists, before he would quiet down.

"Fifteen ebyts before the deadline," said Gsefx. "Time to call your boss and make a new deal."

"Good luck with that," said Dilnch. "You're gonna need it."

"Remember our agreement," said Gsefx, "you two behave and I allow you to remain conscious. Otherwise, I'll turn the lights out again." He waved the scrambler at Klarnus, who was still fuzzy from his first two encounters with the device. "And you know I will."

"Just keep your mouth shut, Dilnch," said Klarnus to his partner. "I've been stunned enough to last me for a good long while."

Dilnch looked as though he was about to say something, but thought better of it and nodded his head in compliance.

Reaching for the vidcon, Gsefx entered the code Klarnus had provided and waited for their boss to answer.

The screen lit up and was filled with the dark red face of a very unhappy Alvarian.

"What in the galaxy has taken ... wait a ... what are you ... where are ..."

"Go ahead, get it out of your system, then we'll talk," said Gsefx, hoping flippancy would hide his fear.

The unhappy face turned an even darker shade of red, followed by a sinister smile and the revelation of razor sharp teeth.

"Don't forget who you're dealing with, accountant. I've got your wife and Qilzar, and you're out of time."

"Trust me, I haven't forgotten who I'm dealing with, Et Ricnor, and I'm keenly aware of the time. But, and this is important, I'm also quite aware that I was out of time the moment you took Lhvunsa, so let's not pretend that I'm the one who's failed here."

Ricnor's face softened, but only slightly.

"Fair enough," he said. "But the fact remains that I still have your wife and Qilzar and I won't hesitate to kill them. If you think I won't, you're sadly mistaken."

"I believe you will," said Gsefx. "In fact I'm certain that you will kill me as well. But not yet, not when you still have so much to gain by keeping us alive."

"Go on, I'm listening."

"I have the painting, which is all you say you want. But, I also have two of your associates, one of your vehicles, and several of your weapons."

Gsefx switched viewpoints on the vidcon as he went through the list to show Ricnor that all he said was true.

"Now, we could set up an exchange, where we swap what I have and you want for what you have and I want, but I don't see that as playing out very well in my favor."

At this, Ricnor actually smiled. "But what other choice do you have?" he said.

Now it was Gsefx's turn to smile. "What other choice indeed? Et Ricnor, I may only be a lowly accountant and not a criminal mastermind like yourself, but I'm not a complete idiot. We both know that the painting in the cargo hold, while quite valuable in and of itself, is nothing more than a map to a larger haul of paintings, each worth at least as much as this one, some probably worth much more. Am I right?"

As Gsefx spoke, Ricnor's smile disappeared and was replaced by a more neutral expression.

"It's been my experience that a little knowledge can sometimes be a good thing," he said, "but too much knowledge can be hazardous to one's health. What do you think, accountant?"

Gsefx's stomach was in knots and he felt sweat trickling down his back, but this was not a time to show weakness. Gamesmanship was the key to all successful negotiations and he had to prove he was up to the task or he, Lhvunsa, and Qilzar were all as good as dead.

"I agree, of course," said Gsefx, "that sometimes too much knowledge can be a dangerous thing. Like, for instance, when I shared too much information with Qilzar about my trip to Irt, which is actually pronounced Earth, by the way, and my encounter with the artist who painted these magnificent works. Had I known the fool couldn't keep his mouth shut, I would never have told him. Look at all the trouble he's caused."

That evoked a round of laughter from Ricnor and those around him. Gsefx pretended to laugh with them.

"Ah yes, Qilzar, the poor sap, led us right to you. I imagine you're none too happy with him for putting you and your lovely wife in the spot you're in."

Ricnor paused for a moment, as if in thought.

"You know, now that you mention it, Qilzar really is no longer necessary. We can dispatch him for you if you'd like."

He motioned to one of his men.

"No!" said Gsefx, a little too quickly, "I assure you, that's unnecessary. He may be a fool, but he's still a friend."

"Then listen closely, accountant," said Ricnor, all trace of humor gone from his voice. "Stop playing games and get to the point. I don't like games or complications, and as you've provided way too much of both, I don't much like you, either."

"All right, all right, I understand" said Gsefx, swallowing hard. "Here it is. Give me six rotations, the use of this vehicle, the weapons on board, and the cooperation of your two associates and I'll deliver all thirty-one paintings to you. In exchange, you agree to release my wife, Qilzar and me, and stay out of our lives for good."

If Ricnor was surprised, he didn't show it. But he also didn't respond immediately either. After a few ebyts, during which he looked at Gsefx appraisingly, he finally replied.

"An interesting proposal, accountant. My first question is an obvious one. Why? I mean, I understand that you don't trust me to exchange the one painting for your wife and Qilzar, but how does your trust improve, simply because we're exchanging more paintings?"

"You said it yourself, too much knowledge is a dangerous thing. With one painting, we know too much about your plans for you to allow us to live. But, if the job is already complete and your involvement is virtually non-existent, then what reason do you have for harming us?"

"You still have knowledge of us and our whereabouts."

"But no knowledge or proof of any crime."

Ricnor eyed Gsefx warily.

"Okay, we'll assume that's good enough—for now at least," he said. "But what makes you think you're any more qualified to obtain the paintings than I am, or any of my crew? After all, we've actually done this type of job before and I'm assuming you haven't."

"True enough, I haven't done anything like this before. But I have been to Earth before. I've actually seen the paintings and I have a pretty good idea who I'll be dealing with when I arrive. I can't say for sure, but I'm guessing that neither you nor any of your associates can say the same."

Ricnor said nothing.

"Oh, and one other thing, Et Ricnor, instead of currently being dead like you expected, I'm quite alive, with the two associates you sent to kill me subdued and restrained. I'm in control of your vehicle and your weapons stash. So, no, I don't think you need to worry about the criminal part of the plan."

At this, Ricnor actually started to laugh—a genuine laugh of mirthful amusement.

"All right accountant, you win. Well, you have my blessing, at least, except for two things. First, you have three rotations, not six. This is no luxury vacation on the beach. You're on my time, which means you have three rotations to get the job done and deliver the paintings into my hands. Secondly, my associates, as you call them, are free to make their own choices. In our organization, nobody goes on an assignment unless they agree to it. So, if you'd be so kind as to patch them into the conversation, we can ask if they are willing to accompany you to Irt, or Earth, or whatever you call it, and perhaps regain some of their lost self-respect." Ricnor's mirthful smile reappearing.

"Not only will I patch them in, I'll go a step further and unbind them completely," said Gsefx as he got up from his seat to set his captives free. "But I must have at least five rotations. The job can't be done properly in less time than that."

"Do you think I give a clelchin's fart about proper? Just bring the paintings back and everyone is happy."

"Let me guess. Your way is to locate the paintings, go in with your obliterators set on maximum, take the paintings, and kill anyone who happens to get in the way, right?"

"Of course. What's wrong with that?"

"Nothing, I suppose," said Gsefx as he sat back down in his seat and patched Dilnch and Klarnus into the conversation, "if you don't mind starting an intergalactic incident and bringing the heat of the Galactic Community Police down on your heads. I suppose that's no big deal for you and your gang, but for me and mine, it is a much bigger deal."

"You're the one who wants in."

"Only as a means for getting out. Even if I wasn't involved in any of this, if you had the paintings and let Lhvunsa, Qilzar, and I go on our way, who do you think the GCP would come after first? The last known visitor to Earth, that's who. Give me five rotations and I'll slip in and out with the paintings and nobody will even know I was there. You'll get your paintings and I'll be free and clear of this entire mess."

"Four rotations. That's forty sars and the clock starts now. That's my final offer, take it or leave it. But we haven't asked what they think. Klarnus, Dilnch, do you want to go with him, or would you rather just kill him now?"

Both Klarnus and Dilnch's eyes lit up at the prospect, but it was short lived as Gsefx tossed Dilnch an obliterator.

"Go ahead, give it a try. While you were napping, I added my DNA to all of your weapons. If you're going to kill me, you're going to have to find another way, and honestly, I don't think either of you are up to it. So, what do you say, wanna take a trip to Earth?"

Dilnch tried to fire the obliterator just to make sure Gsefx wasn't bluffing, then dropped the weapon when it was clear he wasn't. Both of Ricnor's thugs nodded glumly, but affirmatively.

Gsefx turned back around to face the vidcon screen, his face set hard toward Ricnor, who seemed even more amused now than before.

"Looks like it's settled then," he said. "forty sars from now you'll have your paintings and I'll have my wife and boss back. But I have a couple of conditions of my own, first."

"I'm listening," said Ricnor.

"I want to see Lhvunsa and Qilzar, now, before the clock starts."

"And the second?"

"After I see my wife."

Ricnor paused, but just for a moment.

"I thought you might ask to see them. To show that I'm not entirely unreasonable, here they are."

Ricnor's image moved out of sight and was replaced by Lhvunsa's. She was a bit disheveled, but did not appear to have been harmed. To Gsefx, she was even more beautiful than the day they'd met.

"Lhvunsa, my love! How are you holding up?"

"Gsefx! I'm okay, but I'm worried about you. They've let me listen to the conversation ... I know what you're planning to do ... I don't want you to do it. Just give them the painting. I don't want you to go back to Earth."

"Lhvunsa, please try not to worry. You have to be strong for a while longer. I will be back for you. Nothing will stop me from coming back for you. That is my promise. You do you believe me, don't you? Lhvunsa, say you believe me."

She nodded her head, but couldn't speak. At this, Qilzar moved into view and, despite himself, Gsefx felt all of the love and compassion he felt for his wife vanish, replaced with cold outrage.

"Gsefx, I assure you ..."

"Save it, Qilzar. You have only one job and that is to make sure nothing happens to her. Do you understand?"

Qilzar started to speak, but apparently thought better of it once he saw the look on Gsefx's face.

"Yes, I understand," he said. "If it makes any difference, I am sorry Gsefx."

"I'll let you know if it makes a difference in about forty sars. In the meantime, take care of her ... and take care of yourself, too."

Qilzar nodded in acknowledgement and moved away. Ricnor appeared back on the screen.

"Touching, especially your concern for Qilzar," said Ricnor.

Gsefx said nothing.

"I'm anxiously awaiting your second condition, accountant."

Gsefx looked back at his former captives, now shipmates, who were sitting uneasily in their chairs. They didn't appear to be interested in starting a mutiny just yet. He reached over and pushed the button marked privacy and gestured for Ricnor to do the same. When they had both locked their channels into privacy mode, Gsefx spoke very directly and very clearly.

"Ricnor, as you've been fond of pointing out, I'm just an accountant. As such, life is, for the most part, little more than a series of business transactions. This arrangement between you and I is currently a business transaction and nothing more. But let me be very clear about one thing. Accounting is just my day job and I'm much more than a simple number cruncher. I'm smarter and more resourceful than you. If anything happens to either my wife or to Qilzar, anything at all, you will find out just how much meaner I am than you or anyone in your entire organization ever thought an accountant from Clangdor could be. When I get back with the paintings, be ready to conclude our transaction by handing them over unharmed."

"Or?"

"Trust me, Ricnor, you don't want this to stray outside the confines of a business arrangement and into the personal. That wouldn't go well for you."

"Is that supposed to scare me? The idle threats of a being so far out of his league he has no idea I could have him killed while he's talking to me."

It was now Gsefx's turn to laugh.

"I'm assuming you're referring to Dilnch and Klarnus? Unlikely. You see, in addition to adding my DNA to all of the weapons on board, I also modified my scrambler so that it works on all species, even those who are supposedly "protected.""

Gsefx took his vidcon out of privacy mode long enough to turn on his companion's screens. As he claimed, both were out cold.

"I put your boys out as soon as you went into privacy mode. They won't be giving me any trouble and neither will you if you know what's good for you."

He flipped his vidcon back to privacy mode.

"If I were you I'd keep that in mind as you plot to double-cross me—that and how I've been one step ahead of you, and the thugs you sent to kill me, this entire night. Just let this play out my way, Ricnor. It will be better for everyone that way. Oh, and one last thing. Don't call me accountant. My name is Gsefx. You'd do well to remember that."

Gsefx turned off the vidcon, fired up the ship and set course for planet Earth.

Chapter 39

Zef Isn't Coming Back

" do what?" asked General Alcorn, who, as far as Henry could tell, was very close to losing his patience.

"You reach into your cockpit and turn on your radio," said Henry, using a combination of his voice and hand gestures in an attempt to get the General to catch on by himself. When Alcorn still look confused, Henry forged on.

"Look, never mind. Do you know the song *Rock On My Children* by Ogilvy?"

"Of course," said Alcorn, throwing Henry a condescending frown. "Unlike some people, I remember when it first came out."

"Well ... Zef played it for me as a way to communicate."

That got the General's attention.

"He did what?" cried Alcorn, leaping to his feet. "Dear God! That means they've probably been listening to us for some time, monitoring our communications and who knows what else. I'll bet they know all about us by now. It's only a matter ..."

"General please," said Henry, interrupting Alcorn before he could weave together too many wild scenarios. "Stop thinking like a military man for a second and go back to the story we're weaving."

Alcorn paused for a moment, then shook his head.

"All right Henry," he said with a grimace. "For the sake of argument, we'll play it your way, for now at least. What makes you think he was just a traveler with engine trouble and not a scout on a fact-finding mission of some sort?"

"Well, first off, if they have, in fact, been monitoring us for any length of time, why in the world would they use a mid-70s rock song to say 'Hello'? I mean, I like *Rock On, My Children* as much as anyone, but really?"

The General rubbed his chin. "You may have a point there."

"Secondly, I watched the ship land. It was bucking and lurching from side-to-side so badly, I'm not sure how he even got it on the ground in one piece."

Alcorn conceded that point with a nod.

"Fair enough," he said.

"And finally, General, and this is key, he only played the song as an afterthought, a last resort after we had both tried to communicate in other ways. He spoke the lyrics first, before he played the music. It really freaked me out at first. He'd been spouting out what sounded to me like gibberish, which I'm sure is what English sounded like to him, then wham, all of the sudden he started quoting lyrics to 'Rock On My Children.' It was so surreal. Hey, are you even listening to me?"

Alcorn seemed to have drifted off in his own thoughts, but came quickly back without missing a beat. "What was his demeanor through all of this?"

"He was scared, General," said Henry. "Just like you or I would be if our plane had landed or our car had broken down somewhere we weren't expecting."

"What about weapons? Did he have anything?"

"Nothing I could see. I was the only one with a gun."

"Yes, about that, what exactly were you doing with a gun out in the middle of nowhere, with all of those paintings?"

Henry closed his good eye and exhaled. *Dammit,* he thought. *I meant to skip over that part.*

"Let's leave that alone for now," he replied. He raised his hand to deflect Alcorn's imminent objection. "I'm not hiding anything relevant, General, and I promise not to hold anything back at all, but please, let's stay focused for now."

"Fine, but we will be coming back to this," said Alcorn.

"Of that I'm certain."

"Okay Henry, you've convinced me. Zef was nothing more than a wayward traveler. But that still doesn't explain or excuse your interference in my operation, and in helping him escape."

"If I had stepped aside, General, what would you have done? What would have happened to Zef?"

"We would have taken him into custody and ..."

"Would he still be in custody today?"

"Well, that's difficult to say."

"Not really, it's actually quite simple. Would Zef still be in custody? Yes or no?"

"You have to understand ..."

"Yes or no, General?"

"Yes, Henry. He would very likely still be in custody today."

"In reality, General, chances are that Zef would never have been released, isn't that right? Why would we release a captured non-terrestrial, when we could keep it and study it, poke it and prod it, all in the name of scientific research and national security?"

"Now Henry, I wouldn't go that far."

"I would. I'm just calling it as I see it, General."

"All right Henry, I've been patient with you and played your little bullshit games, but I've had just about enough. You have no idea what you're talking about and you have absolutely no right to judge."

"And you, sir, have no right to capture and hold a being who's just trying to join his family on vacation in Greece!"

The two sat in silence for several minutes, Henry quietly daring the General to defend himself and his country's policies. The General finally broke the stalemate.

"So," he said softly, "as the artist, the self-proclaimed seeker of truth, is that the best you could come up with?"

"That's just reality, General, not truth. But there is a truth, my truth at least, if you'd like to hear it."

"Sure, why not? We've come this far, haven't we?"

"After Zef finished playing the song, and we were both left wondering what came next in our effort to communicate, he noticed my paintings on the other side of the clearing. He seemed mesmerized and went over to them. We stood together and looked at each of the pieces together. I've never seen anyone look at my work as he did. As we reached the last one, I noticed tears in his eyes, and it was then that I discovered my essential truth. That even if I never painted another stroke, I had moved the heart of another being. It may not have been a being of my own species, but it didn't matter, something I created touched someone, which means that I have lived and my time on this planet hasn't been for nothing. That is my truth. And that, General, even more than just protecting a wayward traveler, is why I willingly risked my physical well-being to protect Zef. And that is why I am unwilling to press charges against those poor fools who did this to me."

Henry noticed that Alcorn was looking at him differently, as if he didn't recognize him.

"I guess that makes a certain kind of sense," said Alcorn.

"I'm glad you see that," said Henry. "Because it's also why I'm going to ask you for one final favor. I'm going to ask you to solve a riddle. After that, you may do with me as you will. I will answer any question, I will do any task, and I will happily accept any punishment."

"What's the riddle?"

"The one you asked me earlier. Why was I in that clearing? The answer lies within my paintings. Look at them and then you tell me why I was there."

"I've looked at those paintings," said Alcorn. "All they are is a bunch of paintings of some guy in various poses and settings. They don't make any sense to me. I've never been able to understand art—or artists, for that matter."

"Try it again," said Henry. "But this time don't look at them as General Theodore Eustace Alcorn. Look at them as Teddy, the man, the husband, and father. Look at them, by yourself and be completely honest with yourself. No preconceptions, no illusions, nothing to prove and nothing to hide. Find your own truth. If there is beauty to go with it, great. But if it's an ugly truth, embrace that as well. Find your truth, General, and you will find the answer to my riddle."

"Dammit Henry, I don't have time for this nonsense."

"Why, what else do you have to do? Zef isn't coming back. At least, I wouldn't if I were him."

"Don't be so sure about that," said Alcorn. "You helped him escape, and if he thinks you made the kind of connection you think you did, he has got to know that you'd pay the price for what you did. He may come back to try and rescue you, and he may bring friends. That's the contingency I have to be prepared for. Wayward traveler or not, Henry the artist, my job is to ensure the safety of this country, and perhaps even the planet, which means I have to be prepared for whatever possible outcome might occur. As part of that preparation, I not only have to prepare my troops, which, thanks to our little encounter with Zef, I found are woefully unprepared, but I also have to keep those above me in my chain of command informed."

Alcorn stopped and looked away. Henry could tell something was bothering him, something more than the weight of his military responsibilities.

"What is it General?" he asked.

Alcorn sighed heavily and turned back to face Henry.

"You probably noticed that the interrogations stopped for a few days, right?" he said.

"Yes," said Henry. "During which time Wellston began his own interrogations, using Hickam and the other guards as pawns."

"Right. Well, about Hickam anyway. I'll reserve judgment on Wellston until I know more, but that's neither here nor there. What you don't know, Henry, is that I was in Washington D.C. briefing my superiors. One of my mandates upon my return was to get you to talk, by whatever means necessary."

"Go on," said Henry, doing his best to keep his voice steady.

"You have to believe me, Henry, I had nothing to do with this," said Alcorn, gesturing to Henry's condition. "I would have increased the pressure of my interrogations, perhaps used other tactics like sleep deprivation and nutritional manipulation, but I do not condone torture. I never have and never will. Aside from the moral and ethical issues, it simply isn't an effective means of obtaining reliable information."

"I believe you, General," said Henry softly. "In fact, I never believed you had anything to do with it in the first place. I may not have liked you, or even trusted you, but I never doubted your integrity, General."

Alcorn, looked away again.

"Thank you, Henry," he said. "I'm not sure I'm deserving of such high praise, but thank you for it anyway."

"So, can I take it as a yes then, that you'll do me this favor and look over my paintings one more time? That you'll try to find your truth?"

"Henry," said Alcorn, "I meet with the Secretary of Defense in less than three weeks, then the entire Security Council a week later. I don't have time to go on some damned truth journey right now. I need to know all of the details now, so I can provide an accurate report to my superiors."

"First of all, just because they outrank you, doesn't mean they're your superiors," said Henry. "I heard that in a movie once, but it's true, especially in your case. And secondly, you need a truth journey now more than ever, General. Don't let the facts get in the way of your truth."

"Well, thank you for the compliment, I think. But you don't understand the military, son. Things don't work the way we want just because we want them to. I can't just make up a report to fit the story I want to tell, that's not the way it's done. It's certainly not the way I do things. Especially when the decisions that are being made can affect everyone on the entire planet."

"Fair enough, and I'm not asking you to lie. All I'm asking is that you take some time for yourself to gain some perspective, a little clarity, perhaps. That's all. General, right now, you and I both know, beyond any doubt, that there is highly intelligent life beyond the boundaries of this planet. The decisions that will be made in the coming days, weeks, and months will be critical to the future of our country, our planet, and our people. These decisions must be made by the right people, for the right reasons. As much as I've wanted to despise you, General, I see a truth in you, deeper and stronger than I've seen in anyone I've ever known. But I also see someone who has lost their way, and that, General is something I'm a bit of an expert on. Spend some time with my art, see if it has any effect on you, any at all. If not, come back and I'll keep my end of the bargain and tell you everything. Deal?"

Henry held out his hand. The General hesitated for a moment, then reached out and shook it.

"You're a strange one, Henry, but I dislike you less than I did an hour ago, so I guess that's something. I'll be back in a few days and I expect to hear the rest of the details then."

"Yes, sir."

But Alcorn never came back. Five days later, Henry was released from the infirmary and sent to a minimum security facility where he had the freedom and supplies to draw, sketch, and paint as much as he wanted. When he first arrived in his cell he found a note on his bunk that said simply:

"I found the truth. I'm glad Zef arrived when he did. The world would have been a darker place without Henry Backus in it."

Chapter 40

It's All Your Fault

Lhvunsa laid facing the wall, on what passed for a bed in the small cell she shared with Qilzar. While he relentlessly paced back and forth—three paces one way, then three the other—she laid on the cold, stone slab and did her best to remain calm. Her best wasn't very good.

"Qilzar!" she said, sitting up when she could no longer take it. "By the Gods, if you don't stop that incessant pacing and sit still, I swear I will make you wish Ricnor had finished you off long before I ever got a hold of you!"

Qilzar, who'd become a haggard, broken creature at the hands of Ricnor and his gang, stopped and looked at her.

"Apologies," he said quietly, and sat down with his back to her.

In no mood to deal with his pouts or neurosis, Lhvunsa laid down again, her back to him and her face to the wall. She closed her eyes and tried to will herself to sleep. She couldn't remember when she'd last slept, but it had been quite some time. It had been nearly a full rotation since she'd last spoken to Gsefx on Ricnor's vidcon before he'd left for Earth on that foolish mission of his. He was going to get himself killed and she would never see him again. Of that much, she was certain. But, then again, what choice did he have? If Ricnor had his way, they'd all be dead by now.

"And it's all your fault!" she said aloud.

"I know it's my fault," said Qilzar without moving, his back still to her. "Don't you think I know it's all my fault?"

Without warning, he jumped to his feet and turned to confront her.

"By the Gods, madam, I've been locked up here longer than you have," his voice rising, "and during this entire time, even though I know it somehow has to be my fault, I've been unable to figure out just exactly how."

Lhvunsa rolled over to face him.

"What do you mean by that?" she asked. "Of course you know how it's your fault. You contacted the Ricnor gang, after you promised both Gsefx and I that you wouldn't make any attempt to return to Earth and acquire the paintings. And now, unless Gsefx can somehow figure a way out of this, we're all going to die, and ..."

"Yes, we are all likely to die, you are correct," said Qilzar, interrupting before she could finish. He moved to her side and knelt down, his face inches from hers.

"Lhvunsa," he said, his voice barely above a whisper, "I'm flattered you think me capable of such a feat as being able to contact a group as notorious as the Ricnor's, but I assure you, I did not. I'm as much in the dark about what happened as you are."

Lhvunsa sat up, her eyes never leaving Qilzar.

"How could it not have been you? I know it wasn't me and we both know it wasn't Gsefx. The three of us are the only ones who knew about the painting."

"Apparently not," said Qilzar. "Are you sure you or Gsefx haven't said anything to anyone else?"

Lhvunsa frowned at the Dremin and his ridiculous question.

"I'm sure, Qilzar. I'm sure about us, that is. I'm still less than convinced about you."

"Quite understandable," said Qilzar, looking away. "I would be less convinced about me too, if I were you. But I know I didn't tell anyone, which leaves me more than just a bit confused. What about when Gsefx hid the painting? Is it possible anyone could have seen him?"

Lhvunsa thought for a moment.

"Anything is possible, I suppose, but very unlikely. He kept the windows in his vehicle darkened after we left the restaurant, and even then covered the painting with an extra coat he keeps in his vehicle. He dropped me off at our home, then went straight to hide it. I told him not to tell me where he was taking it. I didn't want to know. Maybe someone saw the painting when he hid it, but as careful as he was being with me, I can't imagine him being that careless."

"Nor I. But someone found out, not only about the one painting, but the fact that there were thirty more on Earth, and alerted Ricnor about it. Someone who was not me."

Lhvunsa leaned back against the wall. These last several rotations had been one long horrendous nightmare, but until this moment, she'd been able to stand firm in the knowledge that it was all Qilzar's fault. If what he was now telling her was true, and she had no reason to doubt him, then she had nothing at all to stand on. Someone had set all three of them up, and they didn't have the first clue as to who it could be. How could they even think of finding a way out of this when they had no idea who or what they were even up against? They were lost, with no hope of escape. And what about Gsefx? He still thought Qilzar was the one who told Ricnor, which meant he was acting under the belief that Ricnor was ...

"Oh Gods!" said Lhvunsa. "We have to warn Gsefx. What if Ricnor isn't the one who is really in charge? What if whoever else is involved is actually the one pulling the strings? Gsefx could be flying into a trap."

Qilzar's expression didn't change. In fact, he didn't react at all to Lhvunsa's revelation. His face retained the same haggard look it had before, his body the same rote emotionless movements. She was at first taken aback at his apparent lack of sensitivity and even started to get angry before noticing that, mixed in with his obvious despair, was a deeper thoughtfulness. A moment later she came to another, more startling realization.

Qilzar has actually looked this way since I first arrived, I just haven't noticed it before. I guess I've been too busy being furious with him to see it. He's not being insensitive, he's already figured it out. He knows Ricnor isn't the one in charge. Even as Gsefx was making his deal, Qilzar knew what he was getting himself into, but the poor dear couldn't say or do anything, and it's tearing him apart.

Lhvunsa reached out and put a soft, green hand on Qilzar's ashen cheek. He flinched, but didn't pull away.

"Qilzar, I'm sorry. You've been as much a victim as Gsefx and I, even more so because we've been against you too."

She pulled her hand from his cheek and motioned for him to sit down next to her.

"Sit down and tell me what's happened to you. You've been struggling with this by yourself for too long. Perhaps together we can figure something out."

Qilzar's face softened ever-so-slightly, the haggardness dissipating just enough for Lhvunsa to see a bit of her friend in the creature who now knelt before her.

"You believe me, then?"

"I do, and I'm ashamed of myself for ever doubting you."

"Don't be," said Qilzar, as he moved to sit next to her. "I know for a fact that I didn't tell Ricnor a thing and I still doubt myself."

"Even so, Qilzar, I shouldn't have ..."

He stopped her with a wave of his hand.

"No more," he said, "we have more pressing matters. We have to figure out what to do from here. We're only alive because of Gsefx's quick thinking and over-the-top bravado. We have to do something to help him or it will all be for naught."

Lhvunsa shook her head in agreement.

"Yes, of course, you're right."

She took a deep breath and let it out slowly to settle herself. When she was steady again, she looked at Qilzar.

"Tell me all that has happened to you," she said, "and don't leave out a single detail. That might give us some insight as to what to do next."

Qilzar looked her in the eyes, the haggardness returning to his face. His momentary resolve dissipating like smoke in the wind. It was clear that he'd relived this part of his nightmare more times than he cared to think about and now she was asking him to do so again. But this time he wouldn't be alone. She took his hand and held it tight.

"Go on, Qilzar, tell me," she said. "I'm right here. We'll relive it together and perhaps together we'll discover something you couldn't see by yourself."

He turned his head away and pulled his hand back to his lap.

"It was a couple of rotations ago when I was on my way home from the office and someone took control of my vehicle. I ..."

"Wait, what do you mean someone took control of your vehicle? That's impossible. Especially with a high end ship like yours. It's simply not possible."

"Yes, I know. However, since it did happen, it clearly is possible. I just don't know how. Now, shall I continue?"

"Not just yet," said Lhvunsa, her eyes out of focus as her mind raced with possibilities. "Let's talk this through a bit further. What would you have to do in order to remotely take control of another vehicle?"

"Since, as you said, it's completely impossible, I have no idea," said Qilzar. "If it was possible, vehicle theft would be rampant, yet I've never heard of a vehicle ever being stolen. Have you?"

"No, I haven't, but clearly it is possible, just not very easy or lucrative for the criminal, I suppose. My guess is that they probably can't just break into the vehicle's computer system remotely. They would need physical access to the vehicle in order to reroute commands or attach a device or do something that would then allow them to access it remotely whenever they wanted to."

"How do you know so much about vehicular electronics?"

"Not vehicular, specifically, but, as you know, Gsefx is somewhat of a hobbyist and I guess I've picked up a few things."

"If you're right, then how would they get to my vehicle? When I'm not in it, it's locked securely in parking structures either at my home or at Galacticount. Nobody gets in or out of either of those places without credentials, and we both know those cannot be counterfeited."

"Exactly. Which means that someone physically tampered with your vehicle, Qilzar, and they had access to either your home parking structure or Galacticount's.

Qilzar's head snapped back as if he'd been slapped.

"By the Gods! The thought had never crossed my mind." He paused for a moment, as if in shock, then shook his head. "It wouldn't have been anyone in my parking structure. There are only ten of us and none have ever shown the slightest interest in me. And none of them know you or Gsefx."

"Which means someone at Galacticount is in league with the Ricnor gang," they said together.

Chapter 41

Don't Go Away Mad

The only truth I've found is that Henry Backus is no longer needed in this investigation," said General Alcorn to his wife during breakfast. "Keeping the poor fool locked up in maximum security won't do us any good, and it's likely to get him killed."

Over the years Alcorn found talking to Janice about his work to often be beneficial in helping him see things from a new perspective. Early on in his career he had to be careful what he said to her, especially when it came to classified material. As he progressed through the ranks, gaining more clout along the way, he worried less about what would happen if someone found out he was sharing classified material with his wife, and more about what would happen to those under his command if he didn't. By the time he pinned on his first star, Janice Marie Alcorn was an official Pentagon consultant, with a security clearance equal to his own and a need to know that was based fully on his discretion. In other words, after nearly forty years of service to his country, Janny, as he called her, was the only person on the entire planet he trusted without reservation.

"I understand not keeping him in max-sec," said Janny, "but why go to the trouble to lie to him like that? Seems kinda silly, not to mention completely unnecessary to tell him you "found your truth" when you didn't." She made little air quotes with her hands as she said the last, emphasizing her point.

Alcorn mumbled something while suddenly becoming very interested in the last piece of bacon on his plate.

"What was that, Teddy?"

He looked up at his wife, certain that he looked as much the old fool as he felt.

"I said, I didn't want to disappoint the poor bastard, he's been through enough."

Janny reached over and put her hand on his.

"Why Teddy, if I didn't know any better, I'd think you'd actually grown fond of this young man."

"Maybe. I don't know, Janny. I think maybe it's just a combination of feeling sorry for him and not wanting to deal with him anymore. Telling him I found my truth gets me off the hook from having to deal with him again. He's safe enough for now. I'll get him transferred into a psych facility when I get back from Washington. They'll be able to make sure he doesn't try to hurt himself again, and it will keep him out of my hair for good."

Janny quietly sipped her tea while her husband ate his final piece of bacon and washed it down with the last of his coffee.

"What if he's right, Teddy? What if your truth really is in those paintings and you need to find it? What if this planet needs you to find it?"

"Good God Janny, not you too?"

Janny went on, as if she hadn't heard him. Alcorn noted that she did this quite often.

"Henry told you that, since we now know for certain that we're not alone in the universe, we needed someone to lead the discussion and decision-making about where and how mankind is going to fit into the grand scheme of things. He seemed to think you were that someone."

Alcorn took a deep breath and tried not to lose his composure. That was a guaranteed way to lose an argument with his wife.

"Janny," he said as gently as he possibly could, "that boy is a nutcase who was about to blow his own brains out until that spaceship practically landed on top of him. What exactly do you think he knows?"

"I've seen his paintings, Teddy, and I've seen enough in them to know that yes, he was depressed enough to want to take his own life, but he's far from a nutcase. I can also tell you there's a whole lot more to those paintings than I can see."

That took a little of the wind from his sails. Alcorn looked at his wife, suddenly very intent on listening to what she had to say.

"Like what, Janny? Tell me."

"I wish I could," she said. "I can see that there is a certain kind of truth in them, but I can't see what it is. I don't know how to look any deeper."

Teddy shook his head. "I don't know how you see anything at all. It's just a bunch of damn gobbledygook to me. I wouldn't even know about his intention to commit suicide if you hadn't figured it out." He paused. "Are you sure there's more?"

Janice nodded. "A lot more. But if you want to know what it is, you're going to have to do something you don't want to do."

"No," he said, a bit too loudly. He got up from the table and took his dishes to the sink. "No, that's out of the question."

"I thought you might say that," said Janny, as she calmly sipped her tea. "That's why I called him. He should be here by three."

Alcorn cursed under his breath as he looked down at dirty plates in the sink. As many times as he and Janice had danced this dance, he should have seen this coming.

Dammit, she was good.

All he wanted was to have a quiet conversation with his wife this morning, without any games. it was too late for that now. He caught his breath and turned around to face her.

"Did you now?" he said. "I suppose that's reasonable enough; a mother inviting her son for a visit from his home in New York, to hers in Virginia. I mean, it's been at least six months since ..."

"Eight months."

"Eight months since he's been here."

He was stalling, trying to get his bearings. He wasn't going to win this one, that much was certain, but he might be able to ...

"Why thank you, General," said Janice, interrupting his internal tap dance. "I didn't think I needed your approval, but it's nice to know I have it." She took another sip of her tea as Alcorn watched her closely. "Oh for the love of God, Teddy, aren't you the least bit interested in seeing your own son?"

He turned back toward the sink, unable to face her, and looked out of the window to the large gray barn where Henry's paintings were currently being stored.

"Of course I am," he said, his voice strained. "You know how much I miss him. But you also know what's gone on between us. Theo and I have never had an easy relationship, and with what's going on right now, I'm not sure this is the best time to try and resolve our differences."

"And I disagree, Teddy. This is the perfect time. Whether you like it or not, whether you accept it or not, Theo is one of the foremost art experts in the country, certainly on the entire east coast, and he will be here, at your disposal, later today. Now, before you puff up and tell me that I'm not allowed to bring up the artwork or Henry Backus or aliens, that it is a matter of national security, let me set your mind at ease by reassuring you that I am well aware of my responsibilities. I've been in this game almost as long as you have and I know the rules just as well as you do. But let me go one step further, General, by telling you that you are a damn fool if you do not put your personal situation aside and take advantage of his expertise on this matter."

Alcorn sighed. The game was over and he not only didn't win, he didn't even get a chance to play.

"Is that all, Ms. Alcorn?" he asked as he straightened his uniform and turned to face his wife.

"Yes, General, I think that about sums it up."

"Very well. I'll take your recommendation under advisement." He walked over and kissed her on the top of the head. "I've got some phone calls to make."

"Don't go away mad," said Janice, a sly smile on her face.

"Wouldn't dream of it," said Alcorn as he left the room.

He walked across the house, doing his level best to keep from exploding. One of the benefits of his rank was the option to work from home when the time and situation allowed. This situation not only allowed, it practically demanded it. He couldn't think of anywhere else where the paintings would be safer than his barn, which, in truth, was no more a place for cows, horses, and hay than was the rest of his so-called farm. While he and Janny referred to their ten-acre spread as *the farm*, and the large building near their house, *the barn*, the entire property was more like one giant safe, a place where they could store all of the things they needed to keep secure. The barn was particularly well-protected, as its walls and roof were formed from steel reinforced concrete, three feet thick. The single entrance was secured with the highest tech locking system available and the entire structure was wired to detect even the most minute movement. A team of highly trained soldiers were on standby to swarm the building if even the slightest unauthorized movement was detected.

Now that Backus was of no more practical use, but safely confined, Alcorn needed some time to think and a peaceful place in which to do so. His meeting with Secretary Langhorne was just ten days away, and there wasn't a more perfect combination of security and solitude than the Virginia countryside. Besides, between the secure phones, computers, and other techno-toys at his disposal, he might as well be sitting in his office at the Pentagon. The only difference is that he didn't have to put on his uniform, which he did on most days anyway.

He reached the other side of his house, went into his office, shut the door, and fell back against it, struggling between his nearly uncontrollable desire to scream at the top of his lungs and the certainty that he had no other choice but to maintain control. The effort left him shaking and gasping for air.

When he finally regained his composure, he sat and stared out the window for what seemed an eternity, unwilling to move. He wasn't mad, he decided, not really. Certainly not at Janny, anyway. She was just doing what she always did. Prodding and poking at him, forcing him to think through his decisions more clearly, while engaging the parts of his psyche he would rather leave quietly dormant. In other words, all of those maddening things that had caused him to fall in love with her in the first place. No, as much as he might want to be at times, he couldn't be mad at her.

If forced to admit it, however, he was mad. More than that, he was furious. He just wasn't quite certain where to direct his anger. Perhaps, if he could figure that out, maybe he'd know this "truth" Henry seemed to be all fired up about. It was possible that he was just mad at himself. God knew he had a right to be. He'd made enough mistakes in his life to justify plenty of self-rage. Even so, he didn't really believe that was all there was to it.

Regardless of his own failings, he didn't think he was the sole target of his inner hostility. The one thing he knew for sure was that it had to do with his son, Theo, and their relationship. Like many father/son relationships, theirs was a complicated one. No, that wasn't right. It wasn't all that complicated, it was just difficult. Difficult beyond measure—and completely his fault.

He remembered when Theo was first born. Good God, could a man have been any prouder?

A son, he'd thought then, *this is my son. The continuation of the life I started. The one who will take over where I leave off.*

Never in his life, before or since, had Teddy been so happy or proud. So much so that he convinced Janice right then and there to name the boy Theodore Eustace Alcorn, Junior.

The happiness and pride remained for a while, but as the infant grew into a toddler, and then into a little boy, Alcorn began to notice that Theo was much more like his mother than he would ever be like him. It wasn't supposed to matter, of course. He loved Janny dearly, and he certainly didn't love little Theo any less. It was just, well, disappointing, if a word had to be assigned to the feeling. He so wanted Theo to follow in his footsteps, but the more he tried to interest Theo in the things that interested him, like hunting, fishing, and athletics, the more the boy turned away. As if to compound the problem, the more disappointed Alcorn felt, the more ashamed of it he became, which, in turn, caused him to withdraw from Theo and throw himself further into his career.

He knew it was wrong. Why the hell should he care if Theo was more like his mother? Janny was beautiful, intelligent, and great with people. On top of that, she could sing. God, could she sing. Theo had all of that and more. All except the singing part. His gift was painting and, even though Alcorn could tell he would never be on the level of a Henry Backus, he was pretty damn good. Even so, Alcorn just couldn't seem to accept the fact that, no matter what he did, his son would follow in his wife's footsteps and not his own.

Things between father and son worsened as Alcorn focused on his career, which often meant months at a time away from home. By the time Theo was ten, and Alcorn was off to Iraq for Desert Storm, the two barely spoke.

Major Alcorn spent twelve months in the Iraqi desert, with very little time to do much of anything except command his troops and send the occasional letter home. The only thing he did a lot of was miss his wife and son. With all that had happened, he was surprised how much he missed the boy. There was no doubt about his love for Janny, but as terrible as his relationship had been with Theo, he didn't expect the absence of his son to weigh on him like it did. On more than one occasion, he vowed to himself that once he made it home, he'd change things with Theo. He'd make it right, whatever it took. But by the time he finally made it home, Theo had changed. He'd grown harder, more distant, and try as he might, Alcorn couldn't get through; Theo was lost to him. Finally, Alcorn gave up and decided Theo's life would be better if he just stayed out of it altogether.

Over the years since, he and Theo had come to an uneasy truce. They acknowledged one another, even granted each other the occasional small talk, but there was no relationship, no bond, and no trust. Teddy still loved his son, more than life itself, but at this point in their lives, he didn't see any chance of their relationship ever changing.

Alcorn looked at the clock, then took a deep breath and let it out. He had a few hours to get some work done before Theo arrived. He punched Lieutenant Skinner's number into the phone and waited for the answer.

"Yes, Lieutenant, good morning. Report please."

Chapter 42

I'm Ricnor, By the Gods!

icnor tried to calm his nerves as he entered the numbers into the vidcon. The Master had said this was going to be a simple job. Kidnap a couple of accountants, one of whom was supposed to be some weak, pathetic coward, the other smart and capable, but not terribly heroic, along with his wife. After kidnapping them, obtain the painting, eliminate them, and then go to some out-of-the-way planet named Irt and get the rest of the paintings from its pitifully primitive inhabitants. Simple, or so he had said. The reality, however, had been much less so.

Capturing the first accountant, Qilzar, the supposedly cowardly one, had been as easy as promised. The Master had fixed his vehicle so that Ricnor's team took control of it without any issues. But, as it turned out, Qilzar wasn't nearly the coward he'd been made out to be. Even after being held prisoner in his own vehicle for almost half a rotation, and then several sars of torture after his arrival at Mindaal (mild though it may have been), he still insisted he knew nothing about the painting. As much as Ricnor hated to admit such things, he'd been as impressed by the Dremin's defiance as he was annoyed by it. The Dremin race had never been known for having principles, much less standing by them, which made Qilzar's display all the more impressive.

The wife, Lhvunsa, hadn't been much of a problem either, at least not yet. But then again, Ricnor's only demand of her so far was to serve as leverage, a frightened beauty to keep her husband in line. An easy task, considering the razor sharp spike he'd been holding against her striking green throat.

No, it was her husband, this Clangdorian nobody who fancied himself a hero, that was the real problem. He didn't seem to realize who he was dealing with.

"I'm Ricnor, by the Gods," he said in a nearly inaudible mutter, "where in the galaxy does this accountant get off thinking he can cross me?"

It simply wasn't done. In the early days there had been a few who had tried, and who were promptly made into examples. Terrible, gruesome examples. But that was before the Master had come into the picture, unbidden, holding leverage over Ricnor that couldn't be ignored. The Master had forced him to change his ways, refine them in order to become more discreet in his dealings with those who attempted to oppose him. At first Ricnor had resented and resisted the Master's meddling. But when he found he could not break free of the Master's grip without cutting his own throat in the process, he stopped fighting and gave his unwanted overlord the respect he demanded. In the process, Ricnor became more prosperous, and more feared than he ever dreamt possible. He and his gang also became virtually untouchable by any form of law enforcement.

The Master remained discretely hidden behind the scenes. No one, aside from Ricnor, even knew of his existence, not even the rest of Ricnor's gang. It was the way the Master wanted it. His only demands were a cut of the profits and final say on all major decisions. The respect Ricnor once gave begrudgingly to the Master, only because he had to, soon began to come naturally, as did his fear of failing him.

Now he had to call the Master and tell him how this simple plan he'd been given had been thrown into chaos because of what that overzealous accountant, Gsefx, had done. Worse yet, the prisoners, Qilzar and Lhvunsa, who were being monitored, of course, were starting to piece things together. As much as Ricnor feared the Master's wrath, he had to be told of these developments.

Ricnor took a deep breath and pressed "Connect." The vidcon dialed, connected, made three short clicking noises, and then disconnected. That was the signal that his call had been received. The Master would call him back when he deemed it appropriate to grant Ricnor an audience. Ricnor no longer questioned the process, or even gave it a second thought. That's just the way it worked.

A light flashed on the vidcon, but it was too soon for the Master; this was an internal signal.

Ricnor pressed the button and Gruleg's face, disgusting as it was, filled the screen.

"I thought I made it clear I wasn't to be disturbed," said Ricnor, showing his razor sharp teeth and making it clear he was in no mood for his orders to be questioned.

"Yes sir," said Gruleg, "but I thought you might want to know that the prisoners have figured out that whoever tampered with the vehicle works at Galacticount."

"It's not your place to think, Gruleg," said Ricnor with a snarl.

"Interrupt me again and what's left of you will be Clelchin snack food. Now do as you were told, record their every word and movement, and don't interrupt me again."

He turned off the vidcon before the befuddled Gruleg could say another word. His second-in-command had done the right thing by passing on this information, it was something the Master was sure to want to know, but he couldn't allow Gruleg, or anyone else, to blatantly disobey an order of his. Discipline had to be maintained or the gang's entire structure would collapse. Gruleg would understand. Too bad if he didn't.

Another light flashed on the vidcon. This time it was the Master. Ricnor steadied himself, bowed his head, and answered. It didn't matter that the Master used audio only, he knew when he was being given the proper respect and when he wasn't, regardless of whether he could see Ricnor or not.

"Master," he said, face to the table, not daring to speak directly into the vidcon.

"Ricnor," said a voice the gang leader knew only as the Master, even though it was clearly an electronic manipulation of his true voice, "you have news for me?"

"Yes, Master. Qilzar and Lhvunsa are captive, but ..."

"But Gsefx is causing you problems. Is that your news?"

"Yes, Master." By now, Ricnor was no longer surprised when the Master knew things he couldn't possibly know.

"Go on, tell me everything."

"Yes, Master."

Ricnor told him everything. How Gsefx had bested Klarnus and Dilnch, and had then taken them captive along with one of his vehicles, complete with a full cache of weapons. How he'd negotiated a new deal and was now on his way to Earth to collect the paintings. As much as he despised showing weakness, he also admitted to the Master that he was unsure about what to expect when they met to make the exchange. His preference would be to have Klarnus and Dilnch simply kill him, but he didn't believe they were capable. He believed Gsefx would be too much for them.

While he was clear about the things that had gone wrong, he wasn't ready to take responsibility for them.

"With respect, Master, this job was never going to be as simple as I was originally told, was it?"

"Why Ricnor, if I didn't know better, I'd say you were questioning my judgment," said the Master, a touch of humor coming through the electronic voice.

"I would never question your judgment, Master. I simply asked if you provided me with all of the information I required to carry out this job."

"Very well," said the Master, the humor gone from his voice, "you are correct, Ricnor. I did not tell you everything. My hope was that you'd be able to handle it anyway. Unfortunately, I was wrong. No matter. We are no worse off than if you had known the details, and I have every faith in your ability to control the situation."

"Thank you, Master. Can you provide any further details that may be of assistance?"

There was a brief silence as the Master contemplated his answer.

"You said that Gsefx programmed his own DNA into the weapons on your ship and also increased the power output of his own scrambler, correct?"

"Yes Master."

"And what does that tell you, Ricnor?"

"That he knows his way around weaponry. But, why would an accountant be that familiar with weapons? It doesn't make sense, unless it's just a hobby."

"Or, that his expertise isn't specific to weapons, but to electronics in general."

Ricnor looked up at the blank screen, a startled look on his face.

"Yes, of course, that makes sense."

"Is there anything else? I have other business to attend to."

"Yes, Master, one other thing. We have been monitoring Qilzar and Lhvunsa in their cell, and they have been retracing Qilzar's abduction."

"Go on."

"They believe they've tracked down an accomplice to his abduction to someone inside Galacticount."

Another brief silence.

"Have they mentioned any names?"

"Not yet, Master."

"Cease all monitoring immediately. Do you understand? Immediately!"

"Yes, Master."

"And separate them. Why in the galaxy did you ever put them in the same cell to begin with?"

"They weren't on speaking terms at the time, so it didn't seem to matter."

"Clearly they've patched things up, haven't they? Get the paintings, Ricnor. Get the paintings, then kill them. Kill them all."

The vidcon went dead. The Master was gone.

"Yes, Master," snarled Ricnor to the blank screen, the earlier subservience gone now as his lips curled into a most unattractive sneer. Something had just changed in his relationship with the Master, something Ricnor liked.

The Master was more than angry, he thought, *he was scared. Scared his identity might be revealed.*

Ricnor dialed up Gruleg.

"Yes, Boss?" said his second-in-command as he appeared on the vidcon screen.

"Gruleg, don't you take your eyes or ears away from the prisoners, not even for a byt."

"Yes, Boss!"

"No one else but you or I will monitor them, and you will report what you see and hear only to me. Are we clear?"

"Yes, Boss!"

Ricnor switched off the vidcon and allowed himself to do something that had been unthinkable for countless turns. He dreamed of the time, perhaps not far from now, when he would take back control of his gang and be rid of the precious Master.

Chapter 43

Thanks Dad ... I Think

"No Senator, that won't be necessary," said Alcorn with a sigh. This was his tenth and most tedious call of the day. He'd been on with Senator Jasper from Montana for nearly an hour and, for the life of him, Alcorn still didn't know why they were speaking at all, other than it apparently made the Senator feel particularly powerful to have a four-star general at his beck and call. Alcorn didn't care much for the game of politics, though he played it well enough. You didn't climb as high as he had on merit alone.

"I assure you Senator, we have the situation well in hand. I've already briefed Secretary Langhorne and the Joint Chiefs."

He noticed the blue light over his office door begin to flash. That was Janny's gentle way of telling him dinner was ready and it was time to excuse himself from his duties for a while.

"Senator, I apologize, but I have another call coming in and I do have to take it. I've enjoyed our conversation immensely and look forward to speaking with you again, soon."

A brief pause as he waited for the senator to respond.

"Yes, and to you as well, sir. Give my best to Caroline. Yes sir, I will. Goodbye, now."

He hung up the phone, exhausted and hungry, but hesitant. He knew Theo would be at the dinner table. He missed his son and longed to see him, but he didn't miss the anger and awkwardness that always dominated their relationship. Now, more than ever, he needed to think clearly in order to assess the potential non-terrestrial threat to the U.S., perhaps even the entire planet, and develop an action plan to present to Langhorne and the Security Council. If the work he'd done this day, all of the phone calls, briefings, and glad-handing had helped clarify anything for him, it was that he couldn't let his relationship with Theo cloud his thinking and his judgment, which was exactly what it would do if he wasn't careful. He took a few deep breaths to gather himself, then stood up and walked to the dining room.

Janny and Theo were already seated when Alcorn walked in to join them.

"Well, well, something smells delicious," he said, doing his best to put on an air of joviality as he made his way to the table.

"Lasagna," said Janny. "Theo's favorite, and yours too, if I'm not mistaken."

"It most certainly is," he said. He put his hands on Theo's shoulders. "You're looking well, Theo. It's good to see you."

"You too, Dad. I see you're still working as hard as ever; even wearing camos in the house. I guess some things never change."

That didn't take long, thought Alcorn, unsurprised.

"The Army's still paying me son," he said before he could stop himself. "They still expect me to put in a full day—in uniform. That doesn't change just because I'm getting close to retirement."

"That's not what I meant," said Theo. "Dammit Dad, why do you twist everything I say into something else."

"Well maybe if ..."

"Enough you two," said Janny. "Let's eat before the food gets cold."

"Your mother is right, Theo," said Alcorn. "Let's not fight."

"Fine with me," said the boy, who Alcorn realized was rapidly approaching thirty, and no longer a boy. Theo held his plate out while Janny filled it with lasagna. "Thanks Mom," he said.

"Of course," said Janny, with the ever-present smile she used when she was trying to reunite the two of them. "Why don't you tell your father about your news?"

"I already told you, Mom," said Theo, "Dad isn't interested in that kind of stuff."

"Go ahead and tell him," insisted Janny, "you might be surprised."

"You know, I'm sitting right here," said Alcorn, holding out his plate.

"Go on, Theo," said Janny, "tell him."

"Okay," said Theo, with a shrug of his shoulders, "but don't say I didn't warn you."

"You shall remain blameless," said Alcorn. "Now let's hear it."

"Well, the University recently received a collection of paintings on loan from the Louvre. That's in Paris, Dad."

"Thanks, Theo, I know where the Louvre is," said Alcorn dryly. "Believe it or not, I even know what the Louvre is." He took a bite of lasagna before continuing. "Congratulations son, that's quite a coup. What are the paintings?"

"It's not so much about the actual paintings themselves," said Theo, the excitement in his voice unmistakable. "It's about the artist. It's a collection of works by Raffaello Sanzio, who's better known as Raphael. It's an opportunity to study the works of one of the greatest artists in history, up close, and with no restrictions. It's the chance of a lifetime."

Alcorn watched his son's enthusiasm grow with every word he spoke. He watched the young man's eyes sparkle at the prospect of examining the paintings of some guy who'd been dead for five hundred years. He didn't understand what it was that drew his son toward the arts, but he understood the compulsion, a desire that is so strong it overrides everything else in your life. That's what led him into the Army. How could he deny his son that same joy, even if his pursuit was something he himself couldn't understand?

"That's amazing son," he said quietly. He reached out and squeezed Theo's shoulder. "Congratulations."

"Thanks Dad," said Theo, a confused look on his face. "I think."

"What's that supposed to mean?"

"It means, Dad, that throughout my entire life, you've never shown any interest in me or the things I love, so forgive me if I'm a little confused when you suddenly get all excited about my work."

Alcorn looked down at his mostly uneaten plate of lasagna, trying to keep it together. This is where things always seemed to go south between them. After a moment, he set his fork down looked back up at his son.

"Theo, you hold a Ph.D. in Art History and have gained a level of respect within your field that is unheard of your age. You're not even thirty yet and are considered one of the foremost art experts on the entire eastern seaboard, if not the whole U.S. of A. And now, you have an opportunity to examine the paintings of Raphael? Now, I don't know about you, but those sound like pretty damn good credentials to me. So what confuses the hell out of me ... what I can't seem to put my finger on, is why you continue to worry, even one little bit, about what I think. Clearly, I wasn't the father you think I should have been. Hell, I wasn't the father I think I should have been, but right now, that's neither here nor there. You have to stop living in the past, son, and start looking ahead. Theo, you have a bright future ahead of you. Don't screw it up by letting memories of a past, which neither of us can do anything about, get the better of you."

He held his son's eyes for a moment longer, then went back to eating his dinner.

"Now, what's the latest with you and Cheryl?" said Alcorn, in between bites of lasagna. "The last I heard, the two of you were getting pretty serious."

"We broke up," said Theo quietly, not looking up from his plate.

"I'm sorry to hear that," said Alcorn. "What happened?"

"I'd rather not talk about it."

The rest of the meal went on, more or less, in silence, broken up by the occasional attempt by Alcorn or Janny to start a conversation, only to have it quickly and quietly rebuffed by their only son.

"Very good meal, Janny," said Alcorn finally, pushing away from the table when the last of his plate was clean. "I'm headed out to the barn for a while. Don't wait up. No telling how long I'll be out there."

"No dessert?" asked Janny. "I made bread pudding."

"No thank you," said Alcorn, standing up. "I couldn't eat another bite. I'll bet Theo will have some though. Your bread pudding was always his favorite."

Theo didn't say a word, but remained quietly looking down. Alcorn walked out of the room, grabbing his jacket on the way outside. The cold night air felt good after the stuffiness of the dining room.

What the hell was that? He thought as he walked toward the barn. *What were you thinking? You're supposed to be trying to fix things with Theo, not make things worse.*

"What the hell was that?" came a voice from behind, echoing his own thoughts. If he hadn't known his wife so well, the voice might have startled him. He turned back to see Janny standing by the back door, hands on her hips. "I thought you were going to talk to him, not give him one of your standard lectures and then clam up."

"Janny, I'm not in the mood," he said. He turned and started back toward the barn.

"Don't you walk away from me, Teddy," said Janny, coming closer. "I want to know just what in the hell you plan to do to make things right with your son?"

Alcorn turned back to face his wife, a flood of emotions threatening to erupt from where they boiled incessantly, just below the surface of his well-practiced façade.

"Janny, I meant what I said in there. As much as I might want to, I can't change the past. I can't go back in time and become a better father to that little boy. He's gone. But the man he's become has so much potential, I can't even imagine. But he has to let go of his anger toward me and everything he blames me for. It's time for him to start realizing that what he's already accomplished, he did in spite of my poor parenting and that he can do so much more, if only he will let go."

Janny frowned back at her husband.

"That sounds like nothing but a big cop-out, if you ask me," she said. She immediately held her hands up to ward off any response. "Be that as it may, I'm not going to argue that point with you right now. We've gone down that road too many times to spend any more energy on it tonight. What I am wondering, though, is why you didn't ask him to take a look at Henry's paintings while he's here? I thought you were at least smart enough to get his help on that?"

"He has his new project at the University, the Raphael study. Did you see how excited he was? I don't want to take him away from that."

"I saw," she said, giving him a look that made him think he might be more in the clear with her than she was letting on. "But how would you be taking him away from that project if he looks at Henry's paintings while he's here? It's not like he'd be giving up one for the other."

Now it was Alcorn's turn to give his wife a look.

"I may not know much about art, but I do know you, and Theo, better than you might think. I watched you while you were examining Henry's paintings and I know for a fact you did more than just glance over them for a few minutes before going back into the house to work on something else."

Janny looked away.

"Janny, look at me. How many hours did you spend looking at Henry's paintings?"

Janny turned back and met Alcorn's eyes.

"I don't know ... maybe ten or so."

Alcorn frowned and tilted his head, but didn't break eye contact.

"Okay, okay, it was probably more like twenty ... five ... or thirty ... maybe more."

"There you have it," said Alcorn. "If you spent that much time, how much more do you think Theo would? One project would, in fact, force him to give up the other. I won't put him in that position ... and neither will you."

Janny reached up and put her arms around her husband.

"I love you, Teddy."

"I mean it, Janny. Do not say anything to Theo about the paintings."

"I won't, I promise. Now kiss me before I freeze to death out here."

Chapter 44

Only One Way to Fix This

Theo watched his mom leave the room, chasing after his dad, just as she'd done countless times throughout his childhood. Without knowing how it happened, he was suddenly that helpless ten-year-old boy again, distraught over disappointing his father, yet again, and angry for having to try and live up to standards he knew he could never meet.

He shook the thoughts from his head and pushed his chair back. For once, the old bastard was right. It was time to stop living in the past and start looking ahead.

If I leave right now, he thought as he stood up and turned toward the door, *I can be back in the city by midnight.* He tossed his napkin on the table and started for the door.

"Theo, where are you going?"

Dammit.

He turned back to face his mother, who was setting a large baking dish of bread pudding on the table.

"Mom, I'm sorry, but I can't stay," he said. "Something's come up and I have to get back tonight."

"Theo, sit down and have some dessert with me ..." she said as if she hadn't heard a word he'd said.

"Mom ... look, I'm sorry. I know how much you want Dad and me to ... connect, or whatever, but it's not gonna happen. For once, I happen to agree with him. It's time to start looking forward instead of back, and that means I need to go. I'm sorry, Mom, I really am."

"Are you finished?" She was giving him one of her 'you may be finished, but I'm just getting started' kinda looks.

"Umm ... yeah, I guess so."

"Good, now sit down and have some dessert. Another ten minutes with your mother before you leave isn't going to kill you."

Theo did as he was told and sat back down, while his mother dished up her famous bread pudding.

"Thanks," he said quietly when she'd handed him a serving.

"You're welcome. Now, would you mind explaining why you're in such a big hurry to leave that you weren't even going to tell me goodbye?"

Theo ducked his head as he was being scolded, but it lasted only for a moment when he realized he was no longer that ten-year-old boy.

"Tonight, this whole meal, it's like nothing has changed" he said, looking up at his mother, defiant tears forming in his eyes. "Dad with the lecture first, followed by the cold silent disregard right before he leaves, then you running out after him. It's just like it was when I was a kid."

His mom started to interrupt, but he kept going.

"Dad was right. I don't need this crap anymore. I love you, Mom. You know that I do and I always will. But you don't need to chase after him anymore on my account. He's part of my past, and like he said, I need to look forward. I can't do that if I'm constantly seeking his approval. I'm never going to get it, so I need to stop chasing after it. I'm done with him."

"Theo, I wish you wouldn't say that."

"I know that's not what you want to hear, Mom, but it just can't go on like it has. I can't go on like that."

"No, I don't suppose you can. But, your father wasn't right about everything, or at least your interpretation of what he said wasn't right."

"What's that supposed to mean?"

"Theo ..." His mom stopped and rubbed her forehead, while she took in a deep breath and let it out. He'd seen her do this before, usually when she was worried about something very important.

"Mom? What is it?"

She looked up at him and smiled.

"Theo, I don't know if you realize this or not, but as much as you take after me, you are just as much your father's son as you are mine. You are two of the most stubborn men I have ever known."

Theo ducked his head again.

"Hey, I stayed for dessert," he said, a small grin on his face. "There's no need to be rude."

He looked up at her again. She wasn't smiling.

"Mom, seriously, what's going on?"

"Your father was right, in the sense that to continue dwelling on the past does you no good. But, if you interpreted that as meaning that he wants you to move on with your life without him in it, then you missed the point."

"So, he just expects me to forgive and forget? I'm not sure I can do that, Mom."

"I don't know about forgiving and forgetting, but at least cut him enough slack for the two of you to figure out how to move forward."

Theo thought for a moment.

"I'm willing to do that," he said finally, "but I doubt he is. I mean, how am I supposed to go forward when he doesn't approve of anything in my life?"

His mom stared at him with her mouth agape. He'd stepped into something this time, he just wasn't sure what.

"Theodore Eustace Alcorn, Junior!" she said. "Were you not at the same dinner table I was at this evening? Did you not hear your father talk about his son with the doctorate in art history? His son, who was one of the foremost art experts on the entire east coast? His son who was going to have the rare chance to examine some of Raphael's paintings up close? I don't know who you were listening to, but the man I heard speaking not only approved of what you do, but seemed pretty damned proud."

Theo stared at his mother as he processed all she'd just said. As he thought about it, he did say all of those things, that's just not how he'd heard them. His father hadn't really meant them like that, had he?

"Theo? Theo, are you still with me?"

"Why'd you go running after him?" he said suddenly, coming out of his daze.

At this, his mom looked down and ate another bite of dessert.

"Mom? Clearly there's more to this than you're telling me. What the hell is going on?"

"Theo, I've watched you and your father struggle for nearly thirty years and I know just how much both of you hurt. Yes, both of you. He hurts too, Theo. More than he'd ever want you to know. More than that, though, I also know a lot more about what your father does for a living than you might guess, a lot that's classified and I can't talk about. About the only thing I can say, is that he needs your help, Theo. He's struggling with something big, really big, and it involves your area of expertise." She looked around the room. "That's all I can say ... it's probably more than I should have said."

"Why didn't he ask me himself? No wait, I know ... because he either didn't want me around or didn't think I could be of any help. Maybe he's not all that proud of me after all. All of what you just said about him has been one big manipulation to try and get us together, hasn't it. I'm sorry Mom, I truly am, for your sake, but it won't work. I have to go."

He stood up and started to leave the room.

"So be it," said his mom, tossing her fork down onto her plate. She stood up and started clearing the dishes from the table. "Go on back to New York ... and Raphael."

"Mom, look ... I'm ..."

"Goodbye Theo," she said as she took an armload of dishes into the kitchen without another look in his direction.

Dammit! You really screwed that up.

He stood in the dining room for a moment waiting for his mother to come back out, but silently hoping she wouldn't. He didn't know what he would say to her if she did.

There's only one way to fix this, you know. You're going to have to go out to the barn and square things with the old man.

Dammit!

Chapter 45

What is Your Mission, Zef?

lcorn went through the security steps to open the door to the barn as if in a daze, his body functioning but his mind still on Theo. Had he gotten through to his son? As much as he wanted a relationship with Theo, he wanted his son to find happiness even more.

Maybe the boy will pack up and go back to New York and Raphael, he thought. *Ultimately, that's probably what's best for everyone.*

As he played out the various scenarios in his head about what might or might not happen with his son, the one thing he wasn't doing was the one thing he'd preached for nearly all of his years in the Army, and that was to be in tune with his surroundings and be ready for any contingency. Had he been more focused on the task at hand, he might not have been so ill-prepared for the scene that unfolded before him as he walked into the barn.

The cold in the room immediately alerted him that something was wrong, even before he had a chance to look up. When he did look, the first thing that caught his attention was the gaping hole eight feet high and twenty feet wide that had been cut out of the far wall. As shocked as he was by that, he was equally taken aback by the fact that where thirty paintings had once been displayed on easels across the main floor, there was now nothing but empty floor. Empty, except for a familiar pale blue creature with four arms and four legs, who was staring directly at him.

"Come in, General Alcorn," said the creature in near perfect English. "We have much to discuss, and little time to discuss it."

Alcorn hesitated briefly, then walked toward the blue being from another planet, moving at a pace that was slow enough to allow his thoughts to catch up with him and assess the danger of his situation.

"I see you've learned our language and who I am, Zef," said Alcorn, when he got close enough to the intruder. "That is your name, isn't it?"

"You've spoken with Henry, then," said Zef, his tone changing from the previous melodramatic welcome to one of genuine concern. "Tell me, is he okay?"

Alcorn looked closer at Zef, looked into the non-terrestrial's eyes. At that moment he knew that this creature, this being from outer space, truly cared about Henry and what had happened to him. Alcorn realized he did too.

He was about to answer Zef's question and tell him that Henry was okay, when he caught movement in the shadows of the far corner of the room. He looked over just in time to see another non-terrestrial moving quickly toward him. This one wasn't like Zef. It was short and mean-looking, and was carrying a rather large device that couldn't be mistaken for anything other than what it was: a weapon. As it got closer, it started shouting at him in a language he recognized, but didn't understand. It was the same language Zef spoke during his last visit. His linguistics team had been trying to translate it, albeit unsuccessfully, ever since.

Though weaponless, Alcorn prepared himself as best he could for an attack from this new quarter. He'd faced armed opponents before and came out in one piece. And there was something about this creature that didn't feel particularly threatening. Even amidst the chaos and questions swirling in his head, and with this new creature pointing a weapon at him, he somehow didn't feel all that concerned. Alcorn thought it strange, but as the being moved closer and its snarls grew louder, the menace it presented actually seemed to diminish by the same proportion.

The alien stopped its approach two feet away from Alcorn, closed its mouth and stared as menacingly as it could, yet the yelling continued. That's when Alcorn realized it was Zef who was shouting, but he was yelling at the other non-terrestrial.

The creature ignored Zef's commands, raised its weapon, and pointed it at Alcorn's head. Before he could react, Zef came over, pushed the weapon aside, and said something quietly into the being's ear. Alcorn saw it flash what could only be considered an uneasy grimace, which quickly turned into a smirk. It gave Alcorn a nasty look, then turned around and walked back into the shadows of the far corner.

"My apologies, General," said Zef. "My associate, Dilnch is ... well, let's just say he's a very unhappy creature."

"I'd say that's an understatement," said Alcorn. "I think your friend needs a rabies shot and a straightjacket."

"I'm sorry, I don't understand."

"Never mind, it's not important. What do you want, Zef? Why did you destroy my barn and take all of Henry's paintings? And how did you do it without setting off any of the alarms? And what do you want from me?"

"First, you must tell me about Henry. Is he okay?"

"Yes, Henry is fine, now. He had some rough times after you left, but he's recovered and doing well."

For some reason he couldn't explain, Alcorn seemed to feel it necessary to make sure Zef knew that Henry's life wasn't all wine and roses after his last visit.

"I'm very sorry to hear that Henry has suffered because of me," said Zef, lowering his head. "He had no reason to help me, but he did. I owe him everything."

"What's your mission, Zef? Why did you come to Earth the first time and why are you back now?"

"I know what you are thinking, General. I think I must put your mind at ease. I am not here to invade. There is no fleet of ships coming to attack your planet. Exactly the opposite, in fact."

"What do you mean, by that?" asked Alcorn.

"Well, it's embarrassing, General Alcorn, but to be perfectly honest, this planet of yours is not of much interest to anyone. The only reason anyone even knows about it at all is because of your music. We call it Albalan, but you refer to it as rock-and-roll. It's become quite popular in some sections of the galaxy. That is why I came here last time. I wanted to add some of this music to my collection. As I entered orbit, my vehicle broke down and I was forced to land. Henry helped rescue me. He helped rescue me from you. And now, here I am again, asking you to help me rescue him."

"You want me to do what?"

"As I said, General, we don't have a lot of time. I will explain everything back on the ship."

"On the ship? I'm not going on any damn ship. I'm not going anywhere and neither are you. You're coming with me ..."

Before he could finish his sentence, the barn door opened and Theo walked in.

"Dad? What the hell is ...?"

"Theo! Don't ..."

Alcorn turned to warn his son, but a sharp pain shot through his body and darkness overtook him.

Chapter 46

Where's Henree?

Gsefx sat in the ridiculously comfortable pilot's seat of Ricnor's ship, and used the solitude he'd been given to collect his thoughts and reflect for a moment on just how in the name of the Gods he'd ended up here. Klarnus had taken Dilnch into the separate compartment formed by Gsefx's ship, where they were most certainly up to no good.

No matter, he thought, *I'll deal with them later.*

He glanced over at his new passengers—he still considered them passengers, even though they were unconscious and bound—and wondered how long they'd remain knocked out. To Gsefx's knowledge, no scrambler, certainly not one enhanced like his, had ever been used on a primitive before and he couldn't be certain of the lasting effect it might have. He regretted having to knock them out, but it couldn't be helped.

He regretted a lot of the things he'd done lately. Including coming to Earth the first time. If he hadn't, if he'd just gone home like he should have, none of the things that were happening now would be taking place. He regretted not destroying the painting when he had the chance, right after he first saw the look of pure lust on Qilzar's face, and then again on Lhvunsa's. If he were being honest, though, he wasn't sure he would have been able to destroy the painting. It was a gift from Henree. Destroying it would have been a cruel, callous thing to do. He regretted not being more forceful with Qilzar, knowing his boss could not be trusted.

While Gsefx regretted much, he also knew that his regrets were useless. He and those around him, friend and foe alike, were now on the same path, and they must see it through to the end. He just hoped that when General Alcorn, and the other Earthling he called Theo, awoke, they would be friends, not adversaries. He looked at them again, and while he regretted using the scrambler on them, he knew if he hadn't they'd both be dead.

All had been going well with his meeting with Alcorn, when, without warning, the second Earthling came through what was supposed to be a locked door, and called the General "Dad." Fortunately, Gsefx had become quite adept at reacting quickly recently, and so right about the time the General turned and said "Theo! Don't ..." Gsefx recovered enough of his senses to remove the scrambler from his pocket and fire it on the General, rendering him unconscious and out of the way. Without hesitation, he turned to aim the scrambler at the other Earthling, a younger version of the General, in hopes of limiting the exposure of their presence so they could clear out as quickly as possible. As he did so, out of the corner of his eye he caught Dilnch raising his obliterator at the boy as well. Gsefx fired the scrambler in an attempt to knock the younger Earthling to the ground before Dilnch's blast turned his body into ashes, but he was too slow. The boom of the obliterator sounded just as Gsefx pressed the button on the scrambler. A moment later, the explosion of the obliterator's shot hitting its target shook the building.

Gsefx screamed and took two steps forward before realizing the younger Alcorn was still there, lying on the ground in one piece, a large hole smoldering high in the wall behind where he once stood. Dilnch had missed and Gsefx hadn't. The one the General had called "Theo" was unconscious and alive.

Perhaps everything will be all right after all, he had thought, breathing a sigh of relief, *after I deal with Dilnch. That Jikian welt will pay for this.*

He turned to confront the traitor, only to find him lying unconscious, his former partner, Klarnus, standing over him holding the obliterator.

"I tried to reason with him earlier, boss," said Klarnus, looking up at Gsefx. "I told him that we work for you now, at least as long as we are on this job together."

The Yelton looked back down at Dilnch and shook his head disapprovingly.

"But he wouldn't listen. And now, here he is trying to kill the Earthlings you're trying to protect."

Klarnus turned back to Gsefx and flashed a large, toothy grin.

"That just won't do, will it boss?"

As Gsefx now sat comfortably in the pilot's seat of the ship, he remembered how that smile had turned his stomach and made him feel as though the ground was washing away from beneath his feet. He also remembered seeing how Klarnus' grin actually got bigger when he saw Gsefx's reaction, and how realizing that little fact was all he needed to get his feet back under him again.

"Thank you, Klarnus," Gsefx had told the Yelton, looking him directly in the eyes. "You're a team player and you'll be rewarded for it. I'll make sure of it."

At that, the toothy grin evaporated.

"Now let's get everyone on board and we'll get out of here."

"Yes boss," said Klarnus, his tone much less friendly than before, "whatever you say."

They loaded everyone onto the ship, Klarnus dragging Dilnch none too gently, while Gsefx carried Theo, then both of them teaming up to carry the much larger General. When everyone was secure, they headed up into a high orbit. Klarnus had taken Dilnch to the secondary compartment, and as soon as they were both out of sight, Gsefx took DNA samples from both of the Earthlings and loaded them into Ricnor's weapon filtering system. Once that was done, the Alcorns were as protected from any inadvertent weapons fire as he was. Now it was just a matter of waiting for them to regain consciousness.

Gsefx looked over his console to make sure everything was running like it should be.

Navigation: high orbit around Earth, check.

Communication: everything quiet, check.

Storage: thirty-one paintings accounted for, check.

Wait a minute. Communication?

Gsefx looked at the time, and then glanced at the General and his son. Both were still unconscious. A quick glance toward the doorway connecting Ricnor's vehicle to his showed no sign of Klarnus or Dilnch. He turned to the vidcon and punched in a complicated combination of several numbers and waited. A few byts later, the screen lit up and Planvc's face filled the screen.

"Gsefx?" said his friend in a hushed voice. "Wait, I'll switch to privacy mode."

Gsefx sat quietly while Planvc adjusted the vidcon on his end.

"There, no one can hear us now. Are you all right? Is everything okay?"

"Yes," said Gsefx, "everything is as good as it can be, at least for the moment. I just called to check in and see how you were doing. Have I missed anything? Has Xtlar been snooping around?"

Planvc smiled in the simple, friendly way of his that always comforted Gsefx.

"Nothing much has changed since you checked in last time. We're all working away, just trying to keep up. I know you can't tell me what's going on, but when this is all over, you owe me an explanation and the rest of the team a big thank you."

"I owe you more than that, Planvc, and you know me, I'm good for it."

"Yes, I know you are. One thing I should mention, while I have the chance. Remember that file you were working on for me, number Z7163?"

"Yes, I think so. What about it?"

"Well, when I incorporated it back into the other sections I was working on, it led to a small, almost unnoticeable, discrepancy, which I followed to another file that didn't make sense to me."

"How so?"

"I don't really know, just yet. I'm still investigating, but something seems very odd to me."

"Do you think Pigawitts is trying to hide something?"

"I don't know. Possibly."

"Okay, let me ask a different way. Do you think it's anything the GTCA investigators would find?"

Planvc paused for a minute. "Hmmm ... good question. They're very good, you know."

"As good as us?"

Planvc smiled. "Not even close. There's no chance the GTCA finds this."

Gsefx heard a moan from behind, signaling that one of the Alcorns was waking.

"I have to go. I'll check in again as soon as I can. Keep digging on this, it could be important. And watch out for Xtlar, don't get into any trouble on my account. Thanks Planvc!"

Gsefx clicked off the vidcon before Planvc could answer and turned around to see a dazed and very unhappy General looking at him.

"So, General Alcorn," he said, "enough of the small talk. Where's Henree?"

Chapter 47

A Prisoner In My Own Vehicle

Qilzar was puzzled.

"By the Gods, do you think it possible that someone at Galacticount is really collaborating with the Ricnor gang?" he said to Lhvunsa. "It seems rather far-fetched to me."

"As far-fetched as someone remotely taking control of your vehicle?" Lhvunsa replied, without hesitation.

"Fair enough," said Qilzar, conceding her point. Having never heard of a vehicle being taken over, as his had been, it now seemed that anything was possible. "It's just a lot to take in, I suppose. What do we do now?"

"What happened next, after they took control of your vehicle?"

He hesitated briefly as he pondered her question.

This isn't the right approach, he thought. *I know she means well, and is clearly very bright, but Lhvunsa is going in the wrong direction.*

"Lhvunsa," he said aloud, "you know how highly I regard you, and how much I trust your judgement, but since we know, or at least believe it's someone at Galacticount, shouldn't we go back to earlier in the rotation instead of going forward with my kidnapping? If we recount everyone I interacted with, we should be able to narrow the pool of suspects down considerably."

"Perhaps," said Lhvunsa, again without hesitation. "But you may not have interacted with them at all on that particular rotation. Hearing what the kidnappers said after they took you will help us narrow the list down even faster, I think."

Qilzar thought for a moment, then nodded his head slowly. He still wasn't sure, but he wasn't about to argue. He'd learned quickly enough that when Gsefx's wife had her mind set on something, it was best just to go along with whatever she wanted.

"Very well, my dear, I trust your judgment," he said, even though he didn't. "When they took control of the vehicle, I had no idea what was happening or what to do about it. I was trying to steer, press pedals, push buttons, and do whatever I could to try and regain control, all to no avail. My vehicle was taking me somewhere, but I had no idea where, certainly not to my home. I tried calling the GCP on the vidcon but that wasn't working either, or so I thought. Eventually, I gave up fighting and let the vehicle take me where it would."

"And where was that?"

"That's the strange thing, it didn't take me anywhere, it just flew me around. I tried watching the route we were taking, but the ship just flew in seemingly random patterns. Sometimes I backtracked on myself, sometimes I went far beyond any civilized areas only to come back around and re-enter heavily populated sections again. One time, I came within a few parsecs of Galacticount before being whisked back out again."

"How long did you fly around like that?"

"I was a prisoner in my own vehicle the entire break between working shifts," said Qilzar. "I actually fell asleep at one point, but was awoken by my vidcon not long before I was supposed to be back at Galacticount."

"I thought you said it wasn't working," said Lhvunsa.

"I didn't think it was. I certainly couldn't make any outward calls on it."

"What did you do?"

"I answered it, of course," said Qilzar. "There was no video, only a voice. A voice, I would find out later, belonged to Ricnor."

'Greetings, Et Qilzar,' he said in that mocking way of his. 'I trust you had a pleasant stay as our guest.'

'Who is this?' I asked.

'No one to trifle with, I assure you,' he said.

'What do you want?' I asked.

'Nothing much. A very simple task really. All I want is the painting. Deliver that to me and your life will go back to normal,' he said.

'Painting? What painting?' I asked

'I see,' he replied, a hint of disgust in his voice. 'Are you sure you want to play it that way? I thought you were smarter than that, or more cowardly. Ah well, have it your way,' he said.

'Apparently you misjudged me, in more ways than one,' I said, which I probably shouldn't have, because his voice immediately turned cold and dangerous.

'The painting from Irt,' he said, 'I want it and you know how to get it for me. Let me be very clear, Et Qilzar, from this point forward, everything you say and do is a choice, so think very carefully before making your next move.'

"I won't deny it, Lhvunsa," said Qilzar, "I did think about it. I thought about telling him everything, if for no other reason than to save my own pathetic skin. I wish, for all of our sakes, that I had. Perhaps then he'd have the painting and would have left us all alone."

"If, in fact, that's what he would have done," said Lhvunsa, "then I agree with you and wish you would have told him everything. But he wouldn't have, you know. That's not the way Ricnor operates, at least not as far as his reputation goes. He would have killed us all as soon as he had the painting anyway, so we're no better or worse off, and you still have your honor, Qilzar, which means more to Gsefx and I than you can ever know."

Qilzar smiled, comforted by his friend's reassuring words.

"Thank you for that, but I'm not sure it matters because as it turns out, they didn't need me for information at all. They already knew everything I could have told them. I don't even know why they took me, other than as an additional hostage."

"Finish telling your story and perhaps we'll figure it out."

Qilzar took another deep breath and went on.

"As I said, I thought about Ricnor's proposal for a moment, then gave my reply."

'I have no idea what you're talking about,' I said. 'I know of no such painting. And where is this Irt you're talking about?'

'Well then,' he said, 'I see you've made your choice. It was the wrong one, but I must give you credit for standing by your friends. Not that it will mean anything when you're all dead, which will be very soon, now. Goodbye, Et Qilzar.'

"I started to say something but the line went cold," said Qilzar. "I looked out the window and realized that we were not far from my home. I tried the vidcon again, to call out, but no luck, it was completely dead, as I feared I would soon be as well. It wasn't long before my vehicle pulled quietly into my very own garage and straight into my spot. The vehicle turned itself off and the doors opened, all without me touching a thing.

"Before I could get out, or even turn around, hands grabbed me, pulled me out of my seat, and slammed me against the outside of my vehicle. A disgusting face pushed in close to mine. The disgusting face of a Palquistian."

'You're coming with us,' he said, 'orders from above.'

"Another set of Palquistian hands grabbed me and together they dragged me toward another vehicle."

'Wait!' I said, grasping at anything that would delay the inevitable. 'I can't just disappear without any kind of notice or warning, my colleagues will start looking for me.'

'So, why should we care if anyone looks for you? They won't find you.' he said.

'Maybe, but my colleagues are rather smart and quite tenacious. They might be better at looking than you think and are likely to involve organizations you may not want involved, like the GCP perhaps.

Besides, a couple of quick calls and nobody will even think of looking for me for several rotations,' I said.

'I don't know, I don't think the boss would like it,' he said.

'Give him a call and ask if you'd like. I'm sure he won't mind. Surely he doesn't expect you to be able to make decisions like this on your own,' I said.

'What do you mean by that? Of course we can make decisions on our own and I'm telling you we're leaving now, no calls and no more talking,' he said.

'Suit yourself,' I said, 'I'm just trying to help you out. I've got nothing to lose after all, since your boss has already declared me dead. I just thought I'd try to help your careers along, but clearly you don't need my help.'

"We started moving toward their vehicle again, but didn't get far before they stopped and stood me up."

'Wait here,' the first one said, 'my colleague and I need to confer on this matter.'

"They moved away from me and briefly talked back and forth in low voices, then came back as if they'd reached some kind of monumental decision."

'All right, one call," said the first one again, 'and you'd better make it a good one. You can use the vidcon in our vehicle.'

'Oh no, that won't do.' I said. 'They'll see where the code is coming from when I call. If they see it's coming from your vehicle, they'll start asking questions and that won't be good for anyone. I must call from my home. We're right here, it will only take a few ebyts.'

'Hmm ... that makes sense, I suppose, but we need to make it quick. We're expected back on time. Let's move,' he said.

"We went inside and they watched as I called Xtlar, who wasn't available, of course. I left a message, but convinced them it was still necessary to speak to a live being, and they allowed me to connect to the operator, who connected me to Gsefx."

"And that's when you left him the first traveling code, which you knew he would translate into the word, 'Ricnor,'" said Lhvunsa.

"That was my hope," said Qilzar.

"How were you able to call me?"

"Well, my dear, as you know, Palquistians are not known for their brainpower, I assure you. I'm pretty certain I could have talked them into almost anything, short of letting me go. I simply told them that you were a news reporter friend of mine and that we had a lunch appointment scheduled for later. If I failed to show with no warning, you would know something was wrong and wouldn't stop until you found out what it was. But if they wanted to take me back to their boss with a snoopy reporter on their tail, it was okay with me. They practically entered your code for me."

"While part of me hoped you would answer, I was, in truth, greatly relieved when you didn't. I wanted to warn you, without dragging you any further into this mess than absolutely necessary. So, I left you the message with the second code. I'd overheard one of them mention Mindaal, and hoped that between you and Gsefx, you'd figure it out. Little did I know that Ricnor had already set traps for you both, which made my efforts worthless."

"Not worthless at all, Qilzar, at least not to me," said Lhvunsa. "You tried to protect and save us when you knew it would be dangerous, and perhaps even deadly to yourself to do so, and that is worth more than you can know. Besides, I can't help but believe that Gsefx knowing the information that you passed along to him made a difference in his getting the upper hand from the two Ricnor sent to take care of him. You may very well have saved his life, and ours along with it."

At this, Qilzar brightened considerably.

"I hadn't thought of that," he said.

"Well, you may just have to start giving yourself a bit more credit, Et Qilzar."

"Perhaps," said Qilzar, who still felt as if they were missing the big piece, even as it was staring them right in the face, "but none of this explains how Ricnor knew about the painting, or any of the other paintings, or even about our trip to Irt—or Earth—in the first place. I tell you, I haven't told anyone. Not even Xtlar, who for some reason has been trying to get me to talk about what happened that rotation."

At the mention of Xtlar, Lhvunsa's eyes opened wide, as if she just realized something horrible.

"Oh Gods!" she said.

"What? What is it?"

"I told Xtlar."

"What?" said Qilzar. "What did you tell Xtlar?"

"I told Xtlar that we were going to Earth to rescue Gsefx."

"When would you have told him that?"

"When you first called and told me that you fired Gsefx. I hung up on you and called him. He confirmed what had happened and told me that he'd ordered you to bring him back. I told him then that I knew Gsefx was on Earth, and that I was going to make you take me there to bring him back. It's Xtlar. Qilzar, he knows. Xtlar is the one behind all of this."

Chapter 48

That's Not What Ricnor Wants

"Wake up!" said Klarnus, as he reached across from his seat and smacked Dilnch along the side of his head. "Wake up, you fool!"

"Huh ...? What ...?"

"I said, wake up!"

Klarnus slapped his Jikian partner a second time and Dilnch jerked up, then looked around at the inside of Gsefx's vehicle, which was now acting as a secondary section to the larger ship. He seemed to find the economy-sized portions of this section rather cramped in comparison to the luxurious spaciousness he was used to inside the larger area they used to occupy all by themselves.

"Where are we?" he asked, still trying to get his bearings. "What in the gralt happened? Wait, I remember now, you knocked me out, you piece of Flingorium flotsam. What'd you do that for? I was about to take care of that juricking Earthling and the next thing I know, your ridiculous head pops up in my line of sight, followed immediately by your fists. What in the galaxy is wrong with you?"

Rather than kill Dilnch right then and there with his bare hands, which is what he wished to do more than anything, Klarnus instead glared silently at his partner, waiting patiently for him to finish his incessant rambling.

"I knocked you out," he said, when Dilnch finally fell silent, "because I didn't have the time to explain how completely incompetent you are, or how you nearly ruined Ricnor's plan. If I hadn't stopped you, you would have destroyed his plan beyond the point where I could have fixed it. You do know what happens to those who mess with Ricnor's plans don't you? Or are you even more ignorant than I thought?"

Dilnch bowed his head without saying a word. It was such a rare oddity that Klarnus took it to mean he actually understood the severity of the trouble he was in.

"Personally, I could care less if he were to discipline you," said Klarnus. "However, since he made the two of us partners, your screw-ups spill over on to me, and that is something that does concern me ... a great deal, as a matter of fact. So, I took care of the problem by taking care of you."

"I ... I ... I'm sorry, Klarnus," said Dilnch. "But how was I supposed to know, I mean, how do you even know what Ricnor's plans are? We haven't been in contact with him since we left Clangdor."

"You mean YOU haven't been in contact with him since we left Clangdor. I spoke with him while you and the accountant were waiting in the barn. He told me exactly what he wants us to do."

Dilnch's eyes grew wide.

"How? I mean, how were you able to contact him without the accountant seeing or hearing you?"

Klarnus smiled. This little drama of his was having the effect he wanted. His idiot partner was in awe of him and on the defensive for his own skin. This was nice, for a change.

"The accountant isn't nearly as smart as he thinks he is," snarled Klarnus, "and he certainly doesn't know this ship like we know it, and I know it even better than you. While the two of you were waiting for the first Earthling to show, I went invisible, and came back in here and made a call on an untraceable line."

"An untraceable line?" asked Dilnch, clearly not believing his partner. "There's no such thing."

"That's what you think, which is why I'm in charge and you're not. Maybe someday, if you straighten up and start pulling your weight around here, I'll show you how, but right now we have more important things to do."

"Like what?"

"Like keeping the accountant on track with his mission and getting him back to Mindaal with the paintings."

"We already have the paintings," said Dilnch, "why don't we just kill him now? We'll be heroes back at Mindaal."

"Because that's not what Ricnor wants, you idiot." He smacked Dilnch again, in the same spot on the side of the head. "This Gsefx character has gotten the boss riled up and Ricnor's cooked up something special for him back at headquarters. Our job is to play along with Gsefx, like we're really helping him, but also make sure he gets back to Mindaal with the paintings as soon as possible.

"Do you think you can do that, Dilnch? Do you think you can do it without making Gsefx angry enough to knock us out again, or worse? I don't know about you, but I've been knocked unconscious quite enough lately. And you'll want me in a good mood when I report to Ricnor, because my report will have a lot to do with your next assignment. If you ever have another one. Do you understand me, Dilnch?"

"Yeah, sure thing, Klarnus. I'll do whatever you want me to do. Just say the word."

"Good. Now, let's get out of this juricking piece of gralt and back into our ship."

Dilnch got up and reached for the latch to open the door that led back into the main cabin. Before he could unlatch it, Klarnus grabbed his shoulder.

"Remember Dilnch, do whatever the accountant tells you to do, and if he doesn't tell you to do anything, then don't do anything. Got it?"

Dilnch smiled.

"I've got it, Klarnus," said the Jikian. "There's nothing to worry about."

"That's what worries me," said Klarnus.

Dilnch unlatched the door and stepped into the main cabin. Klarnus was about to follow his partner through when he heard Dilnch let out a brief yell, then drop to the floor. He leaped through the door, only to find the accountant pointing that juricking scrambler at him.

"Sorry Klarnus," said the accountant, "but my plans have changed and I don't have time to explain them to you."

"You'll pay for this, accountant," fumed Klarnus.

"Very likely, but it can't be helped."

The pain, now as familiar as a Yelton sunset, shot through Klarnus' body and he dropped to the floor. As darkness overtook him once again, his mind raged with thoughts of revenge against the Clangdorian accountant. The one who was supposed to have been such an easy mark, but had instead become his incessant tormentor. He, Klarnus, would exact revenge for all that had been done to him and even as he fell into the dark abyss of unconsciousness, his lips curled into an evil, if innocuous, smile.

Chapter 49

I Should Be Happy

Henry sat in his room, brush in hand, staring at the canvas in front of him. It was blank, just as it had been for the past two days.

"This is madness," he said aloud as he set the brush back onto the easel, stood up, and stretched carefully before walking across the room to the sink. He had healed well, but he was still tender in places.

For a prison cell, Henry's room was actually quite spacious, especially compared to his previous accommodations. The only way in or out was the solid metal door located in the far right corner, unless you counted the two-foot-by-two-foot window covered by a steel mesh grate, located on the wall opposite the door. That was fine, Henry had no intention of trying to escape.

Aside from Henry's bunk, sink, and private toilet (a blessing for which he was eternally grateful), his cell also boasted its own personal art studio, courtesy of General Alcorn. It came complete with a chair, easel, and enough canvasses, brushes, paints, and other accessories to last a very long time. It seemed he'd made an impression on the General, after all.

He also had the other, more mundane things, like food, water, and shelter—things that Henry used to spend most of his time and energy trying to acquire. So much so, that he had given up on his art altogether. More than anything else, though, Henry had peace and quiet. No more interrogations, or psychotic guards trying to torture or kill him. No more demanding wives or parents, insisting he live and act a certain way.

I should be happy, he thought as he splashed water on his face. *Sure, I'm locked up, with no chance of ever getting out but I also don't have any worries. In truth, I'm freer than I ever have been. So why can't I paint anything? I had all of these ideas while I was in the other prison, with no outlet for them. Now that I'm here, I've got nothing.*

He splashed his face again, and with his eyes still closed, reached for the towel hanging by the sink and began drying himself. When he turned around and opened his eyes, he jumped nearly a foot in the air and let a short yell that was immediately cut short when the four-armed, four-legged, blue-skinned alien that had come up behind him reached out and covered his mouth.

"Henry," the alien said in a whispered voice, "you must be quiet, or I won't be able to rescue you."

Henry nodded and the alien uncovered his mouth.

"Zef!" said Henry in a whispered shout, "what are you doing here? I never thought I'd see you again. Wait ... you speak English?"

Gsefx smiled. "Yes, I learned your language shortly after I departed the last time I was here. It's actually quite a simple language. But no time for talking now. We have to get out of here before we're caught."

Henry was not ready to move on just yet.

"But, how did you get in here?" he asked, looking around the room and not seeing any sign of forced entry.

"Shhhh ... lower your voice," said Gsefx as he turned Henry around and gently pushed him toward the easel and his art supplies. "You must grab whatever items you need to take with you, and then we must go."

"Go? Where are we going?" asked Henry defiantly, although he wasn't exactly sure why he was acting that way. "I'm not going anywhere. I'm finally in a place where I'm safe and comfortable. I can't leave here. I mean, why would I want to leave?"

"I do not understand, Henry," said the clearly puzzled non-terrestrial. "Do you mean you would rather stay here, locked in a cage, than come with me and be free?"

Henry frowned, turned away from his alien friend and went to sit on his bed.

"It's not that I would choose to stay here over going with you," said Henry, "but look around ... for the first time in my life, all of my needs are being met. I now have the freedom to draw and paint whenever and whatever I want. I'm not sure I can just walk away from that."

Henry watched as his blue-skinned friend did as he was asked and looked around. After a few minutes Zef walked over and picked up the blank canvas sitting on the easel and held it up.

"I won't pretend to understand Earthlings or what motivates you to do the things you do. I can't even tell you why I do some of the things I do. But I can tell you, Henry, you are not someone who should be caged up like a criminal, because that is not what you are. They may be meeting some of your needs here, but not all of them. You are an artist, Henry, and from where I come from, artists must actually experience life to be able to express it in their work."

Henry sat for a moment, dumbfounded. He always assumed Zef was very advanced technologically, considering how he'd traveled to Earth in a spaceship and all, but clearly he'd underestimated his non-terrestrial friend.

"But, there's another reason you must come with me, Henry," continued Zef. "The last time I was here, you saved my life and I am forever indebted to you for that."

"And now you want to save my life by freeing me from prison," said Henry, interrupting his friend. "I understand, Zef."

"No, I don't think you do. I'm not here to repay you, Henry. I need your help again. My wife has been kidnapped and I need your help to get her back."

At once, dozens of questions jumped to the tip of Henry's tongue, waiting for the chance to burst forth. *Why me? What can I do? Your wife?* Instead of verbalizing his questions, Henry looked his friend in the eyes, and there saw everything he needed to know. For his eyes couldn't lie, and they told Henry that Zef was tired, exhausted even. But, he was also desperate, as if he'd run out of options and had nowhere left to turn, which made sense if he'd come back to Earth seeking help from an imprisoned artist who had absolutely no idea how to help. But none of that mattered. His friend needed him, and Henry wasn't about to turn his back on the only being in the entire galaxy who seemed to actually care about his well-being.

"There's nothing here I need," said Henry, standing up. For some reason, he felt stronger than he had in a long time. He seemed to stand a bit taller, too. "I don't know what your plan is for getting us out of here, but whatever it is, let's go."

Zef smiled and reached out his hand.

"I believe it's customary in your culture to shake hands in moments like this," he said.

"Only if we were going into business together or something ridiculously mundane like that," said Henry. He stepped in and wrapped his arms around his friend from beyond the stars. "This requires a hug."

Henry felt four arms wrap around him, which was an odd enough sensation in and of itself, but then he was squeezed harder than he'd ever been squeezed in his life. He wouldn't have guessed it, but, in addition to being much smarter than he looked, Zef was also much stronger. When Zef finally released him, and he could breathe again, Henry decided he wouldn't underestimate his alien friend ever again.

"Okay, now that that's out of the way, how do we get out of here?"

"Simple physics. Allow me to show you."

Zef reached into his jacket, and pulled out a square device with several buttons and a dial on it. He pointed the device at the outside wall, just below the window, and pressed one of the buttons. He then began turning the dial. Henry looked up at the wall and saw a faint red outline begin to form. It grew larger as Zef turned the dial. He stopped when the outline reached about three feet square.

"What are you doing?" asked Henry.

"Patience, my friend, patience."

Zef pressed more buttons and, without a sound, without so much as a chip in the paint, the steel reinforced concrete, that had been outlined in red, began to shrink, and was suspended in midair by a second, blue beam. Zef moved the block out of the way so they could escape through the newly created hole in the wall.

"Unbelievable," said Henry as he walked over and looked outside. "No alarms went off—not a sound at all. We can walk right out of here. Well, we could if we weren't on the third floor. Any thoughts on that?"

Zef simply smiled and pressed another button. A moment later, a ship floated down from where it had clearly been hiding somewhere high above.

"I recognize this baby," said Henry as the ship stopped right next to the freshly made opening in the wall. "I hope she's in better shape than the last time you flew her here."

"Yes, I've had her completely checked out," said Zef. "She's in as good of condition as possible." He clicked another button and the ship's doors retracted. "Now, we really should go."

"Yes, of course," said Henry, "we wouldn't want someone to see the ship and notify General Alcorn. He's been red hot over your escape. He said you'd be back for me and I wouldn't want to see what he'd do if he ever caught you."

Zef smiled that damn smile of his again.

"What is it with you?" asked Henry. "You're always smiling, like you know something I don't. What is it this time?"

"Don't worry about General Alcorn," said Zef, walking past Henry and climbing into his ship. "I've taken care of him. Now, let's get out of here."

"What exactly does that mean?" asked Henry, as he climbed into the ship after his friend. "Zef ... what did you do to General Alcorn?"

Chapter 50

By the Gods, You Are Entertaining

lcorn paid no attention to Dilnch, as the little creature led him and Theo, both with hands bound behind their backs, into Ricnor's grand chamber. Like any well-trained soldier, he was too busy performing reconnaissance: scanning for exits, determining strategically stronger vantage points, and most importantly, sizing up and counting the opposition. In this case, he and his son were badly outsized as well as outnumbered. Even if Gsefx managed to neutralize their weapons, as he promised he would (which Alcorn wasn't sure he believed), there were several hundred aliens in here and some of these monstrosities could easily tear him and Theo apart with their bare hands, or paws, or whatever the hell they might have at the end of their arms. They were lined up all around the outer wall of the chamber, which was itself another matter entirely. It was a huge, almost cavern-like round room with a domed ceiling at least fifty feet high. It was all white, with no adornment, and no strategic vantage points.

It's nothing but a giant arena, thought Alcorn. *An arena for fighting—sport fighting to be more precise. They're all lined up around the outer wall, keeping the arena floor clear ... while ensuring no possibility of escape.*

Aside from the way they had just come in, Alcorn could only find one other doorway, a heavily-guarded archway, near where a three-foot riser had been built into the wall. On the riser were six rather ornate chairs, all of which were currently empty. In the middle of the chairs, an elaborate throne towered above the others. On the throne, looking rather relaxed, jovial even, sat a very nasty looking creature with dark red skin, long blonde hair, and long straight facial hair. Though he'd never seen this being before, it was abundantly clear to Alcorn that this was the infamous Ricnor everyone seemed to be so concerned about.

As they reached the middle of the room, Ricnor halted them and told Dilnch to approach the throne alone. In the process, the gang's leader flashed several rows of razor sharp teeth and Alcorn suddenly understood what all the fuss was about. It was almost hard to believe that it had only been a few hours, or sars as they called them out here, since he had first heard the name Ricnor.

After being knocked out in his barn, Alcorn had awakened, only to find himself and his son on board a spaceship, bound and unable to move. Gsefx was there and, at first, Alcorn suspected that everything Henry thought about this alien he'd befriended had been wrong. That, instead of being the wayward traveler stopping on Earth to fix his vehicle, Gsefx's intentions were significantly more nefarious. But then the blue-skinned non-terrestrial began talking—first about Henry, but only briefly—it was Ricnor he really wanted to discuss.

"Ricnor is the head of the most notorious criminal gang in the entire galaxy," Gsefx had said. "It's infuriating that Qilzar would sell us out over these paintings."

"Are you sure it was him?" asked Alcorn.

"Who else could it have been?" replied Gsefx.

"I've been thinking about that as you've been talking," said Alcorn. "It's been my experience that criminal organizations like your Ricnor gang don't usually last over the long term, unless they have some sort of protection."

"What do you mean by protection?"

"What I mean," Alcorn explained, "is that someone high up, someone powerful, someone with connections, who can keep the authorities off the backs of the gang, is helping them so they can focus on their criminal activities. This person will not seem to be connected to the gang in any way, but their money and power will protect the criminals, and in return the gang will provide their protector a cut of the profits or will simply be on retainer for specific jobs they need done. Often it's both. At least, that's the way it's done on Earth."

"And you would know this, how exactly, Dad?" Theo asked, looking at his father even more harshly than usual.

"I've been around the block a few times, Theo. But don't worry, I've never been involved with criminals ... I just know how it works."

"That would actually explain a lot of things," said Gsefx, spinning his chair around to look at the ship's console. "I have to think for a moment."

Alcorn took the opportunity to have a private conversation with his son.

"Are you okay, Theo?" he asked.

"Sure thing, Dad, I'm fine ..." said Theo, who was clearly anything but fine, "... except for the fact that I find out you're involved with criminals ... and aliens ... and ... and ... I have no idea what the hell is going on."

Alcorn had been heartbroken by the pain and accusation in his son's voice.

"I know, Theo," he said, "I would have told you all about it, in fact, I planned to, but when I saw how excited you were about your Raphael project ... well, I just couldn't bring myself to say anything. I sure didn't expect you to come out to the barn on your own."

Theo paused for a moment, before answering.

"Okay, I suppose I get that," he said, finally. "But now can you tell me what is going on? Who the hell is this? And where are we?"

"This is Gsefx, we met him about a month ago when he had engine troubles and had to land on Earth to make repairs."

"Who's this Henry he keeps talking about and what's this about a painting?"

Gsefx turned back around before Alcorn had a chance to answer.

"I know who is behind it," he said as he got up from his chair. "I'll be leaving you, which means you'll be on your own with Ricnor's henchmen. They won't be able to hurt you, but they are going to take you back to their headquarters."

"Whoa, wait a minute," said Theo, "that doesn't sound like a good plan to me."

Gsefx walked over and placed something around Alcorn's neck.

"This is a translator. It's always on, so be careful what you say. You'll be able to understand anyone talking in Galactine Standard, which should be pretty much everyone, and they will be able to understand you, as long as you speak North American English."

"Gsefx, what about ..." began Alcorn, but he was interrupted when a door between the ship's two sections opened before he was able to finish. The squatty, mean-looking alien Gsefx had earlier called Dilnch hopped through.

Without a word Gsefx pointed a device at Dilnch, pressed a button, and the short little creature screamed and dropped to the floor, unconscious. Another alien came through the door, one that Alcorn had not yet seen, but assumed from what Gsefx had said, was named Klarnus. He and Gsefx exchanged a few words before Gsefx rendered him as unconscious as his partner.

"Where's Gsefx?" roared Ricnor, loud enough for the whole room to hear, snapping Alcorn back into the moment. "And where are my paintings?"

Dilnch dropped to his knees, his head bowed.

"Sir, we couldn't stop him. He knocked us unconscious with that enhanced scrambler of his, and then took off."

Ricnor stood up, baring all of his teeth.

Impressive display, thought Alcorn. *Very impressive.*

"Dilnch! Get up and tell me where my paintings are!"

Dilnch stood up, but couldn't meet Ricnor's harsh gaze.

"Sir, he took half of the paintings, but left the other half—they're being unloaded as we speak. He said that he would return with the other half within the agreed upon time limit, and that, as a gesture of his good faith, you could have these two hostages to do with as you wish."

Ricnor smiled and looked at the General and his son.

"He did, did he? How nice."

"Sir, he did add one other thing," said a trembling Dilnch.

Ricnor's smile disappeared.

"Careful Dilnch, your next words could have a very profound effect on your future."

"Yes, sir. He said that you could do whatever you wished with these hostages, but that he expected you to maintain your part of the agreement regarding his wife and boss, Lhvunsa and Qilzar. He said they are not to be harmed."

Ricnor stepped down from his perch and approached Dilnch, his teeth shining in their full glory. What Alcorn found most interesting about his newest adversary was that the more he watched Ricnor, the less dangerous he became. It was all showmanship. Ricnor was a dangerous creature, no doubt, but Alcorn had dealt with his type before, people who depended more on the emotion of fear than the actual terrifying follow-through. The fact that he wasn't human meant little in this equation. Ricnor was an adversary to be wary of, to be sure, but he was far from unbeatable.

Ricnor stood face-to-face with Dilnch, who was clearly on the verge of collapse. Then Ricnor smiled.

"Is that all?" he asked. "I hadn't planned on killing them until after the deadline anyway."

He laughed and grabbed Dilnch by the shoulders.

"Now, let's have some fun with these Earth creatures, shall we?"

Ricnor snapped his fingers and someone tossed a large weapon to him. It was one that Alcorn recognized as an obliterator. He handed it to Dilnch.

"Let's see what one looks like when it explodes."

Alcorn remained expressionless as he watched Dilnch's eyes light up with pent-up joy as he took the weapon from his leader. Clearly the little psychopath was going to enjoy this. He turned toward Alcorn and started walking toward him, picking up speed with every step. When he was just a few feet away he slowed and started to lift the weapon toward Alcorn's head. That's when the General made his move.

Surprising everyone, including Theo, Alcorn freed his hands, slid to the ground, and swept Dilnch's legs out from underneath him, taking him to the ground while at the same time grabbing the weapon away from the befuddled Jikian.

"Whoa!" said Theo, loud enough for everyone to hear. "Who knew the old man had moves like that?"

Alcorn smiled inwardly at his son's remarks, but didn't have time to engage in idle banter. He jumped up quickly, popped Dilnch in the jaw with the butt of the obliterator, then flipped the weapon lengthwise and slammed it down across his knee, shattering the weapon into hundreds of tiny pieces.

"Space junk," he said as he put his foot on Dilnch's throat.

Alcorn looked over at Theo just in time to see his son free himself and grab hold of an ever-so-slight rippling motion that had slid up silently beside him. In one fluid motion, Theo reached into his inside vest pocket and drew out the curved dagger Gsefx had slipped there before leaving them. He held it dangerously close to the rippling motion.

"Funny thing about sticking a knife into something that may or may not really be there," said Theo, "you never know what you might actually cut into."

The rippling motion solidified into the form of Klarnus.

"Be careful, boy," said the Yelton. "You can cut yourself playing with knives."

Theo took the knife and held the tip right to the edge of Klarnus' eye. Klarnus let out a long, low growl, but his body went completely still.

"You were saying?" said Theo.

Alcorn smiled at his son. He'd been proud of Theo before, but at this moment in time, if they died right now, which was a distinct possibility, he didn't think he could be prouder of the man his boy had become. Not because he was holding a knife at an alien criminal's vulnerable spot, but because he was strong under pressure. He was the best of both his mother and him, which is all anyone could ever want for their children. The sound of clapping interrupted his moment of pride. It was the sound of a single individual clapping. It was the sound of sarcastic clapping. It was the sound of Ricnor clapping.

"Very good," said the gang's leader, his face the picture of sheer rapture as he moved toward them. "Glorious, in fact!"

Alcorn looked around. None of the other aliens had moved. They should have come in to take them down. To either kill or at least detain them, but they hadn't moved.

Dammit. Ricnor had expected this.

"I was expecting something," said Ricnor, "but nothing quite this entertaining. You are splendid, absolutely splendid. What is your name?"

"Don't come any closer or we'll kill your men, or whatever they are," said Alcorn. "We mean it. We'll kill 'em." He knew it was cliché, as Henry would call it, even as he said the words, but what else was he to do? He also knew they couldn't kill Dilnch or Klarnus, if, for no other reason, that once they were dead, he'd have no protection at all."

Ricnor did stop at least, if only to laugh.

"By the Gods, you are entertaining," he said. "Here, let me take care of that for you."

Ricnor motioned once and immediately two high pitched pinging sounds rang out. Dilnch's body, already limp from Alcorn's knockout punch, went completely flat as the Jikian's body literally melted beneath the General's boot. At the same time, Alcorn heard his son gasp and looked up to see Theo let loose of what remained of Klarnus.

"Those two were dead no matter what you did or didn't do, Earthling," said Ricnor, all trace of humor gone as quickly as it had appeared. "They screwed this assignment up from the very beginning and I do not tolerate failure. Your little show here was entertaining, but nothing more."

He turned to walk away, then stopped as if considering something, then turned back to Alcorn.

"Because you were entertaining, I will let you live until Gsefx returns with the rest of the paintings. After that, your fate will rest with him."

He turned and left the room.

Well now ... that went better than expected, thought Alcorn, as several hands, claws, and other assorted appendages grabbed a hold of him and his son.

Chapter 51

All of This Over My Art?

"Y ou did what?" said Henry, his voice rising somewhere past incredulity, but not quite reaching the level of full-on hysteria. "You took General Alcorn and his son hostage and then turned them over to the same gang of ... what ... intergalactic terrorists that took your wife?"

Henry was shocked beyond what he thought he could handle. Granted, he didn't really know the blue-skinned being sitting next to him, using two of his hands to pilot the spaceship they were currently flying in, while using the other two to calmly explain how he'd sent the General to his untimely demise. He looked around him, as the realization of where he was and what was happening to him suddenly, and fully, sunk in.

Holy crap! He thought. *I'm flying in a spaceship! In outer-freaking-space! To a totally unknown destination with a creature I barely know. Perhaps I've misjudged this entire situation, including Gsefx. I mean, what do I really know about him anyway?*

"Gsefx, I realize General Alcorn tried to capture you the last time you were here," he said, taking a deep breath in an effort to keep panic from overtaking him completely, "but he was just doing his job. He didn't mean you any real harm. You didn't have to ..."

He was interrupted by laughter coming from the pilot's seat. Loud, jovial, raucous laughter. The being sitting there may not have been human, but there was no mistaking the sound. A joke had clearly been played, and it had been at Henry's expense.

"Hey, what's so damn funny?" asked Henry.

"I am sorry, Henry," said Gsefx, when he was finally able to control himself. "I couldn't keep it in any longer. Please forgive me, I haven't slept in a very long time and this," he waved two of his arms around wildly, "has all been so difficult. It seemed like a harmless joke to let you think the worst for a little while. It was actually the General's idea, but it was all meant to be taken as good fun."

Henry glared at the alien. *Harmless joke? General's idea? Good fun?*

"Gsefx, for the love of everything holy, would you please tell me what in the hell is going on?"

"Yes, of course," said Gsefx. "But first, let me say that I'm glad to see you think as highly of General Alcorn as I'd hoped you would. I wasn't sure what to expect when I first encountered him, but he appears to be a capable being with both honor and courage and it is good to see that you seem to think so as well."

Gsefx paused for a moment, his expression turning serious once more.

"He will need to live up to our expectations, and more, if we are all to come through this in one piece," he said finally.

"General Alcorn is a good man," said Henry. "Although he's a little old to be going out on a combat mission. But I suppose he's capable enough."

"Let's hope you're right. Now, let's see if I can catch you up on 'what in the hell is going on' as you put it. It began shortly after I left you the last time, after my boss and friend, a being named Qilzar, and my wife, Lhvunsa, first saw your painting in the back seat of my vehicle."

Gsefx went on to recount Lhvunsa's and Qilzar's reaction to Henry's painting and how valuable they both considered it to be. He also told Henry of how Qilzar wanted to go back to Earth right then and there, to get the rest of Henry's paintings, whether Henry was willing to give them up or not.

"Wait a minute," said Henry, "you wanted to steal the rest of my paintings from me after I gave you my favorite one?"

"No Henry, not me," said Gsefx, "and not Lhvunsa either. We wouldn't even allow Qilzar to discuss it any further. In fact, I forced him to swear to me that he would never bring the subject up again, to anyone, ever."

Henry sat quietly for a moment, taking in all he had just heard.

"Thank you for that," he said finally. "Although, I have to admit, it's rather complimentary for him to make such a fuss over my work."

"If you find that complimentary, wait until you hear the rest."

Gsefx then told Henry how he believed Qilzar had betrayed them to the Ricnor gang, leading to Lhvunsa's abduction. How he'd nearly been killed himself trying to get Henry's painting from its hiding place, but that he'd overcome his attackers and in the process had gained some small bit of control over the situation.

"It wasn't much, but it was enough to negotiate my way into leading Ricnor's expedition to steal your artwork, which gave me a chance to warn you and keep you safe. My hope is that I'd be able to find a way to save my Lhvunsa, and even Qilzar too."

"All of this over my art," said Henry, more than a little dumbfounded. "That's crazy. No one has ever even given my work a second glance before, well, no one on Earth anyway."

"It's often the case that an artist's own people are the last to see their worth. Or perhaps it was just a matter of not being seen by the right people. Whatever the case, Henry, your art is truly masterful. I wasn't paying close enough attention when you first gave me the painting because I was so touched by the gesture, but your paintings are worth a fortune. Ricnor will stop at nothing to get his hands on them."

"Unbelievable," said Henry, half under his breath. "Too bad Lucy can't see me now."

"Who is Lucy?"

"Huh? Oh, nobody really. She used to be my wife. I guess she still is, technically, although our marriage had been over long before you came to Earth the first time."

"I'm sorry to hear that, Henry."

"I'm not," said Henry. He paused for a moment, then continued. "That sounded harsher than I meant it to. I don't have any ill-will toward Lucy. Not really. Well, not any more, at least. We were just never very good together. I could never be the solid, dependable breadwinner she wanted me to be, and she could never be the free-spirited soul mate who supported my artistic search for truth. We were like oil and water; we just didn't mix. All we did was disappoint one another."

Gsefx looked even more tired than he had just minutes before.

"I think I understand," he said. "Still, I find it sad when those who were once together find that they must part ways."

"Yeah, it's sad, I suppose," said Henry, "even if it was the right thing for both of us."

Henry sat up straighter in his chair and forced a smile, then reached over and hit Gsefx's shoulder lightly with the back of his hand.

"On the other hand," he said, "I wouldn't have painted any of those paintings if we hadn't split, and then you and I would never have met."

"Then I am glad for that, at least," said Gsefx, his tired look unchanged, "even though it is the paintings that are at the heart of all this trouble."

"Speaking of that," said Henry, "how did Alcorn get wrapped up into all of this?"

Gsefx didn't answer right away, but seemed to be considering how to answer Henry's question.

"The easiest way to explain it," he said, at last, "is that I used the painting you gave me as a guide, kind of like a map, and with it was able to track down the location of your other paintings. They were in General Alcorn's possession."

"That makes sense," said Henry, nodding his head, "about Alcorn anyway. I asked him to examine my paintings closely to see if he could find some of the answers he was looking for. That must have been why he had them."

"Once I realized he had them, I made sure that I not only got the paintings but that I was able to speak with him as well. I had to know you were safe."

"That was very kind. But it still doesn't explain why he and his son are now on their way to Ricnor's headquarters. Clearly you spoke to him, but how did they end up as hostages?"

"Well, that's where things went off-plan a little," said Gsefx. "The General and I were discussing how he was going to assist me in freeing you from captivity, when young Theo came in. At that point, I had no choice but to render them both unconscious and take them along, hoping that, with enough time, I could persuade them to help me."

"What do you mean you had no choice?" Henry suddenly seemed less certain of his friend's motivations.

"I mean my companions, Klarnus and Dilnch, the two from Ricnor's gang, would have been just as happy to kill both of the Alcorns and be done with them. In fact, they came very close to killing Theo, as it was. Ricnor's weapons wouldn't work on me, so I was safe from them, and I could even exert some control over them, but the General and his son didn't have that kind of protection, at least not at that point. I didn't have time to think. I just reacted, and rendering them unconscious and taking them with us was the only solution I could come up with in the short amount of time I had."

"I understand," said Henry. He didn't really, but he was willing to let it go for now, in order to hear the rest of the story. Perhaps by hearing more, it would all come together and make sense. "But then, why did you leave them alone to be taken to Ricnor's headquarters?"

At this, Gsefx smiled and turned back to the ship's controls.

"I didn't. General Alcorn chose to go with them."

"He did what?" Now Henry was really confused. "Why would he do such a thing? And why put his son in such terrible danger?"

"I can't say for sure why he chose to help me by going with them, but if I had to guess, I would say that it was because of you, Henry."

"I don't understand."

"He said you told him to find his truth and that he intended to do just that, by helping me rescue Lhvunsa."

"He told me that he'd already found his truth."

"Yes," said Gsefx, "he asked me to tell you that he is sorry for lying. He was wrong to do so, even though he felt it was necessary at the time. But he also wanted you to know that even though he doesn't really understand art, it was your paintings that led him to this decision."

"How's that?"

"I don't know, Henry. Let's hope we meet up with him again so he can explain it to both of us. I can tell you that before we parted ways, Theo wanted to see your paintings. According to his father, he is some kind of expert on art."

"Did you show them to him?"

"Yes, but only briefly. We didn't have much time. We couldn't keep Klarnus and Dilnch knocked out indefinitely, and we still had a lot left to do."

Gsefx turned toward Henry, ensuring he had his full attention.

"Henry," he said, "Theo was astonished at what he saw in your paintings. Though, I'm unfamiliar with your people, I've never seen anyone react like that to art before. It was almost as if he were seeing inside of it, and reading it, like it was a book or something. It was like he could see you in your paintings. Even in the short time he had."

Henry listened intently to his friend, but could not find the words to speak.

"After that," said Gsefx, "no amount of arguments by his father could persuade Theo to return to Earth with me. He had made his decision to accompany the General to Ricnor's headquarters, and that was final."

"So what happened next?" asked Henry. "Why are you here and not there with them?"

Gsefx looked back at the ship's console.

"If I haven't said it already," he said as he nonchalantly turned a dial and pushed a couple of nondescript buttons, "I am truly grateful for the General's willingness to help, particularly since there is no real reason why he should put his life and that of his son's in danger on my behalf."

He turned his attention to Henry again.

"But I am more indebted to him for his insight, and that of his son's. They have put me on a track that might make all the difference to the whole situation."

"What do you mean by that?"

"The more I told Alcorn about Ricnor and the whole situation, the more curious he became about Ricnor himself; what he was like, how long he'd been a "high profile criminal" as he called him, and things like that. I told him all I knew, but he wanted more, so I pulled up more data on the computer for him. Again, time was a factor, so he didn't get much, but it seemed to be enough."

"Enough for what? Gsefx, stop beating around the bush and tell me what the hell is going on!"

"Ricnor isn't the boss. At least not the ultimate boss. He's working for someone and I think I know who that someone is. That's where we're headed now."

"Terrific," said Henry, "and just what am I supposed to do when we get there?"

"You're going to help me find out if he is, in fact, the one responsible for kidnapping my wife."

Chapter 52

I Was Just Doing My Job

Alcorn struggled to break free from the hideous creatures who held him tight as they carried him out of Ricnor's main hall.

"Let go of me, you ugly bastards," he screamed at them, knowing his efforts would be of no use. There was no possible escape from the vice-like grip with which he and Theo were being held. Nor was he actually trying to escape. Not yet anyway. But he needed to keep up appearances, and, truth be told, it made him feel somehow more valiant to struggle, like he and his son might actually pull this rescue mission off somehow.

The very fact that they were still alive meant things were going better than any of them could have hoped, and that the plan was still intact. It also meant that things were only going to get more dangerous from here. They were no longer safe from Ricnor's weapons, which Gsefx had previously inoculated them from somehow, and Alcorn figured the best way to stay out of the line of fire was to act like the primitive beings this rabble believed them to be. That meant playing it to the hilt.

I just wish Theo could get the hang of it, he thought, when he was able to glance ahead and see that his son was struggling all right, but he wasn't being nearly vocal enough. *Apparently, he saves his verbal outbursts for family squabbles.*

"You bastards will be sorry you ever tangled with me," said Alcorn, with a sudden, renewed sense of vigor.

"I like this one," said a voice in the crowd that followed his captors, "he has spirit. He will be fun to kill."

"Too bad we have to wait!" said another voice.

"Who says you have to wait," said Alcorn, egging them on, "put me down and I'll show you how much fun it will be."

The crowd roared at that and several hands, claws, and other assorted appendages grabbed at him, only to be beaten back by those who carried him.

"ENOUGH!" Came a voice from above. A loud, commanding voice. A voice that silenced the crowd at once. "I said the prisoners would not be harmed," said Ricnor looking down on his gang, "and they won't be. Now, unless I'm mistaken, the rest of you have work to do. I suggest you get to it."

The crowd dispersed immediately, and the guards carrying Alcorn and Theo continued on their way.

"Too bad," said Alcorn, in a voice loud enough to be heard by everyone, including Ricnor, "it was just starting to get interesting around here."

There was no response, no sound other than the shuffling noise of Ricnor's dispersing troops and the tromp of the guard's boots as they marched on, carrying Alcorn and his son to their cells. He hoped they would end up somewhere close to where Gsefx's wife was being held.

Alcorn continued struggling, but less enthusiastically. Now that the audience was gone, it seemed somehow less worthwhile, although he was certain Ricnor was still watching from his perch up above.

A few minutes later, the guards stopped and Alcorn looked ahead to Theo's entourage. They had stopped as well, in front of a large, iron-looking door, which one of them was now unlocking. Once the door was open, they threw Theo into the room without a word. He heard Theo yelp in pain when he hit the floor, but Alcorn had no time to object, as he was moved into position and thrown in on top of his son before he knew what had happened.

"Ooof ... oh my God!" he heard Theo yell. "Get off of me, Dad, you're smashing my leg!"

"For the love of ... I'm trying Theo," he replied. "I'm not exactly in the best position ..."

Alcorn was interrupted by the sight of the most stunning female he'd ever laid eyes on before, and that included his beloved Janny, although he would certainly never admit such a thing to her. The creature before him had emerald green skin that was perfection itself and her black, silken hair glistened like water in the moonlight, even in the low light of the prison cell. As for her eyes, Alcorn could find no words to describe them.

As it turned out, he didn't need any words, because while he was lost in wonder at the sight of her, Theo found the energy to clear himself of his father's weight, knocking Alcorn onto his backside in the process.

"For crying out loud, Dad," said the boy hotly, "grow up, will ya, you're married!"

The green-skinned beauty laughed at Alcorn as he lay awkwardly on the floor of the cell, and as quickly as it had taken hold of him, her spell was broken.

"Okay, okay, I deserved that, I suppose," said Alcorn as he pushed himself to his feet. "Don't worry, Theo, she's married too."

He held his hand out to the lady.

"Lhvunsa, I presume?"

"Why yes," she said. "How did you know my name? You must know Gsefx!"

"Yes, ma'am, as a matter of fact, I've just come ..."

"Just come from locking him up on Earth, or worse, I presume," said a nasty whine of a voice from the shadows on the other side of the small cell. "Probably experimenting on him as we speak."

"Qilzar! That's no way to speak to someone who has information about my husband."

"My dear Lhvunsa," said the voice, not bothering to come forward from the shadows. "I never forget a face. I only saw it briefly as we flew by, but it's one I won't forget. This is the Earthling who was trying to capture Gsefx when we flew by and rescued him. He was leading their militia. He was the one who began shooting at us as we flew away."

Alcorn walked over and examined the thin, chalky-gray being looking back at him with venom spewing from his eyes.

"Qilzar? Yes, Gsefx told me of you as well. In fact, he asked me to give you a message."

"Indeed," said Qilzar, "was that before, during, or after you tortured him?"

Alcorn resisted the urge to look away in shame for the things he might have done, probably would have done, if things had gone differently that afternoon. An afternoon that now seemed so long ago. Instead, he held Qilzar's eyes with his own.

"I'm afraid you have it wrong, sir," he said. "As wrong as I was about Gsefx. As for shooting at you as you flew by, well, I was just doing my job."

Alcorn hesitated for a moment, then looked around to include Gsefx's wife in what he needed to say next.

"But doing my job doesn't justify everything," he said raising his hands in a sign of surrender. "I've been wrong about a lot of things in my life." He glanced at Theo. "A lot of things. It took your husband, ma'am, and a man named Henry, a fellow Earthling, to get me to start looking at things differently."

He paused again, looking at Qilzar first, then Lhvunsa.

"For my part in what happened to Gsefx when he came to Earth, I offer my sincerest apologies, and I offer my services in this current situation as a token of my good faith."

"Wait," said Qilzar.

"I understand that it will take more than just a few words to convince you of my ..."

"That's not it," said Qilzar, interrupting the General, "although, since you ask, no, I'm not convinced." He pointed to the translator around Alcorn's neck. "What's that?"

"This? It's a translator. Gsefx gave it to me, which, I might add, should be proof enough that we're working together and not ..."

"Oh, by the Gods," said Qilzar, "would you please stop talking and listen to me."

Alcorn went silent.

"Did they try to take it from you?" asked Qilzar.

"Who?"

"Who else? Ricnor or his guards?"

"No."

"Did they search you?"

"No, come to think of it, they didn't, but I see what you're getting at," said Alcorn looking around the cell, focusing particularly on the ceiling. He turned and shook his finger slowly at Qilzar. "Very good, Et Qilzar. Again, I apologize. I'm truly living up to the primitive reputation of my people."

"Dad, what are you talking about?" asked Theo, clearly confused. "And what are you looking for?"

Alcorn continued looking around at the ceiling and the corners, as he answered his son.

"I'm talking, Theo, about your old man trying too hard to be some damn superhero, and not paying enough attention to the basic tenets of good soldiering. As our good friend Qilzar has just pointed out to us, we're being watched and listened to, and I'm currently looking for the camera."

Lhvunsa gasped.

"What? He's been watching us this whole time? How can you be sure?"

"If he's not watching himself, he's having someone else do it," said Alcorn. "That's what I would be doing if I were in his place." He stopped searching for the camera and grabbed the translator that hung around his neck and looked at Lhvunsa. "Why else would he let me keep this, unless he wanted to hear what we had to talk about?"

"I'm afraid he's right," said Qilzar as Alcorn resumed his search for the hidden camera. "It's very likely that Ricnor has heard every word we've said since we've been in here."

"Then he knows that we know," said Lhvunsa.

"What do you mean he knows that you know?" asked Alcorn.

"What do you know?"

"I guess it doesn't matter if we talk about it now," said Lhvunsa, "since he's already seen and heard us talk about it before. We believe that Ricnor reports to someone else and we think we know who it is."

"That's funny," said Theo, "so do we."

"Theo!" said Alcorn, moving quickly to cover his son's mouth. "Not another word!"

Alcorn looked around at everyone in the cell.

"Not another word from anyone."

Chapter 53

We're Under Attack

icnor walked through the room examining each of the prisoners as they stood or sat silently looking back and forth at one another; all four afraid to speak. First Qilzar, the Dremin, who had recently—and quite inconveniently—found his conscience, then Lhvunsa, the accountant's wife, and finally the two Earthlings, who were far more entertaining than he'd thought a primitive could be.

"I don't think we're going to get anything else out of 'em boss," said a voice from beyond the room.

"For once in your life, Gruleg, I believe you are correct," said Ricnor with an uncharacteristically pleasant smile as he stopped directly in front of Alcorn. "But I have all I need. This one—the one in uniform—thinks he's clever, and in comparison to the rest of his primitive species, he probably is. Even so, he was much too careless and gave away more than he realized."

"What was that, Boss?"

"Nothing that concerns you, Gruleg. Shut down the recording, it's no longer necessary."

"Yes Boss."

The cell and its prisoners disappeared and Ricnor stood in an empty, black-walled room. The narrow strip of light that encircled the room near the top of the wall and had, moments before, generated the holographic image of the prison cell, gave off a pale blue glow as it cooled down.

"Go and join the others, Gruleg," said Ricnor. "You've done well and you will be rewarded."

Gruleg bowed low and left the room without speaking. Ricnor waited until he was gone, then departed the room by a different exit, one known only to him. He walked down a short hallway, turned left, walked exactly six paces, then stopped and looked around to ensure he was alone. He was about to make contact with the Master again, and, as always, secrecy was his utmost concern. This time perhaps even more so, now that he had a lead on who the mysterious Master might actually be.

Convinced of his privacy, he reached out with his left hand and pressed a small, barely discernible contact on the wall. A door appeared that hadn't been there a moment before. Ricnor opened it, walked into the room, and secured it behind him. He wasted no time in punching the Master's code into the vidcon and pressing the "Connect" button. Following their usual procedure, it could be anywhere between a few ebyts and several sars before the Master called him back.

While he waited, he contemplated the possibilities of knowing the identity of the one who'd been pulling his strings for so long. Granted, he'd prospered mightily under the Master's command, and his reputation throughout the galaxy had become almost legendary. The Ricnor Gang had become the most powerful criminal force in the galaxy. Powerful enough that the GCP didn't bother messing in his business. But, while Ricnor received the credit and glory, it had been the Master's doing all along. It was high time Ricnor stood on his own. He'd learned a lot from the Master, but now it was time to get out from under his tutelage, and his thumb. He never liked submitting to anyone, especially the way Master had blackmailed him into doing so. Now he finally had the chance to get his freedom back.

Beyond that, however, there was a more practical reason to do away with the Master. That blasted accountant, Gsefx, along with his family and friends, including the Earthlings, seemed to have more insight into the Master and his doings than he ever did. And, more importantly, Gsefx was on his way to the Master right now. If, by chance, he was successful in exposing the Master, that could lead them right back to Ricnor and all of his operations.

Still, Ricnor was having difficulty making sense of it all. The Master was smarter than this. He'd proven that many times over. There was simply no way this nobody of an accountant and his rag-tag crew could have come up with all of this on their own so quickly. Unless they were wrong. Or, unless they only knew what the Master wanted them to know. Perhaps he was baiting them, leading them into a trap. If that were the case, Ricnor had best be careful himself. He'd seen firsthand what happened to victims of the Master's traps. If this was indeed one, he had to ensure he stayed clear.

A light flashed on the vidcon; the Master was prompt this time. Ricnor bowed his head and answered.

"Master," he said.

"What is it, Ricnor?" asked the Master, the digital manipulator unable to hide the irritation in his voice. "I don't have time to hold your hand any longer on this job—you're going to have to figure things out on your own this time."

"Of course, Master," said Ricnor, fighting down the words he longed to tell the Master, opting instead to keep his cool and wait to see how this all played out. "I simply wanted to warn you that Gsefx slipped away from his guards and is on his way to Galacticount headquarters now. Apparently someone has convinced him that I answer to someone, and he believes he knows who."

"I see," said the Master, his electronic voice conveying a much different tone than before. "And who does he think I am, Ricnor?"

"That I do not know, my Master."

"Nor would you tell me if you did. Of that much I am certain. No matter. What Gsefx knows, or thinks he knows, is of little concern. How long ago did he leave for Galacticount?"

"I cannot say for certain, Master. His guards returned just over a sar ago, and he'd escaped from them at least two sars prior, perhaps longer."

"Incompetent clelchin fodder. They should be disintegrated for their failure!"

"It has already been taken care of, my Master."

"Well, at least you've done one thing right. What about the paintings? I suppose Gsefx still has them as well?"

"Not all of them, Master. He ..."

Before Ricnor could finish, the vidcon went dead and darkness filled the room.

"Master ...? Are you there ...? Master ...? By the Gods!"

Ricnor was cut off again by the sound of weapons fire and shouting throughout the compound.

"We're under attack," said Ricnor as he stood up and felt his way toward the door. "Who in the galaxy would be so bold?"

He carried no weapon other than his hand spike, but it was all he needed. The spike was made of brushed metal, shaped into a long, thin cone that reached a razor sharp point at the end. The handle was made of bone, some say of one of his earliest victims, and near the top was a button that, when pressed, released several miniature blades along the length of the spike itself. Ricnor touched the bone-handle reassuringly, but left it sheathed.

Power was restored as he reached the door and light returned to the room. He pressed the contact and the door opened, but as he stepped into the hallway, the weapon blasts and shouting abruptly stopped, and everything went eerily quiet.

Ricnor moved carefully down the corridor toward the main areas of the compound—his compound—listening for any sound or movement, but hearing none. He decided to work his way to the dining hall; it was the closest room and would be the most heavily populated right about now. He moved slow and steadily, being careful to not make a sound.

When he finally arrived at the dining hall, he was dismayed at what he found. Everyone was down on the floor, dead, with their weapons flung everywhere. What in the galaxy had happened? If they were attacked, where were the attackers? And if they were dead, where was the blood? He reached down and checked the pulse of one closest to him, Jelnit was her name. She was alive, but unconscious.

"Wake up," he said, shaking her limp body. "Wake up I said!"

"They're not getting up anytime soon, Ricnor," said a voice from the other side of the room.

Ricnor dropped Jelnit's limp body and stood up to face his attacker, only to find his former prisoners: the Dremin, the accountant's wife, and those two ridiculous Earthlings staring back at him. It had been the large one, Alcorn, who had spoken.

"Is that so?" said Ricnor looking around. He talked slowly, trying to get his bearings. "Nice trick, especially for a primitive. I'm guessing you had help."

"You'd be guessing correctly," said Alcorn, smugness oozing from every pore. Ricnor couldn't wait to turn the tables and wipe that look from the primitive's face. "This was all compliments of our mutual friend, Gsefx. He really is something with computers and electronics." The Earthling looked around the room at all of Ricnor's associates unconscious on the floor.

"Enough of this," said Ricnor with a growl. He grabbed an obliterator from the floor, aimed it at the Earthling and attempted to fire, but nothing happened. He threw the weapon down and picked up a different one, an annihilator this time. Same result.

"They won't work," said the Earthling. "None of them will. As I said, that Gsefx is really something with electronics. I, on the other hand, don't know all that much, but it seems that one of the drawbacks with having all of your weapons networked like you do, is that it makes it easier to hack your entire system. When I busted Dilnch's obliterator, it set off a chain reaction that shut everything down, including all of your weapons."

"Isn't he the clever little accountant," said Ricnor, pulling his spike and moving toward Alcorn and the others. He stopped when the Earthling pulled a different type of weapon from behind him and pointed it at Ricnor.

"But here's one that does work," said the Alcorn. "Nothing electronic about it. It's a primitive Earth weapon called a .357 Magnum. Gsefx used it to fix his ship the first time he came to Earth. After he repaired his ship, he put it back together, tossed it in a storage compartment and forgot about it. Lucky for me. Also lucky that you didn't search me. I guess you were too busy hoping I would share some vital information to worry about whether or not I was armed."

"Well, well, well," said Ricnor with a smile, although he found little humor in his situation, "it seems Gsefx isn't the only clever one in your little gang, is he? Now that you have me at a disadvantage, what would you have me do?"

"For starters, I would have you toss that pretty little stick of yours over this way, nice and easy."

Ricnor maintained his smile and bowed low.

"But of course," he said, "we're all friends here. I would be most happy to grant your request. But first, before I give up my only means of defense, might I inquire about your longer term plans. More specifically, what do you plan to do with me?"

"I think you should kill him now," said a different voice. It came from the Dremin, Qilzar.

"What do you think, Ricnor?" said Alcorn. "Qilzar here thinks I ought to shoot you now and be done with it."

"I think Qilzar should stick to accounting," growled Ricnor, "and leave battlefield tactics to the ones who know what they're doing. You haven't answered my question. Do you even know what you plan to do with me, beyond getting me to drop my weapon, that is?"

Alcorn laughed.

"Oh yes," he said, "the Galactic Community Police are already on their way. They'll be here long before any of your people regain consciousness and before you can talk your way out of anything. So, for the last time, put down your weapon."

The Earthling did something with his weapon that made it seem distinctly more menacing.

Ricnor was beaten and he knew it, but what he couldn't figure out, was how. He leaned over and dropped his spike onto the floor, but as he did, the entire wall to his right burst open knocking him, and more importantly his attackers, to the ground. When he was able to look up, Gruleg was there in one of their short-range scout vehicles. He'd turned it to shield them from the Earthling and his crew.

"Get in, Boss!" said Gruleg, as he opened the passenger door. "Hurry!"

Ricnor didn't have to be told twice. He grabbed his spike and dove into the vehicle head first, just as projectiles, presumably from the Earthling's primitive weapon, flew by his head.

"I'm in! I'm in! Get us out of here."

Gruleg did just that, flying through the hole he'd created on his way in.

Ricnor looked back just in time to see the Earthling aim his weapon uselessly at them as they made their escape.

"Gruleg, I owe you my life. I told you once already that you've done well and you'd be rewarded. Now, doubly so."

"I'm just glad we got out of there with our skins, boss. I don't know what happened, but someone hit us hard."

"I know who hit us and they will pay, I promise you that, Gruleg. Take us to the main bay. We're going to need a bigger ship."

"Yes Boss."

Chapter 54

You're Going to
Have to Trust Me

enry sat up in his seat and rubbed his eyes.

"Ohhh ... maaaann," he said, as he stretched his arms and looked around. "I must have dozed off. Where are we ...?" A glance out of the side window woke him up immediately. "Holy crap! Where'd all of these other ships come from?"

"You've been asleep for just over one of your hours," said Gsefx with a smile. "As for where we are, we're in the Neljim Quadrant, but that probably doesn't mean much to you. Let's just say you're not in Kansas anymore."

"Cute," replied Henry with a deadpan nod, "but for the record, I'm from Oklahoma."

Gsefx started to respond, but Henry interrupted, he was too fascinated by all of the other ships outside.

"This is unbelievable," he said, looking first out of the side window, then the front, then the side again.

Henry had watched his share of sci-fi movies, but they paled in comparison to his current reality. There were ships everywhere, literally thousands of them, no, tens of thousands, of all shapes and sizes, and going in all different directions. But there was no haphazardness about their movements, no recklessness. It was chaotic, but there was a harmony to the chaos, as if orchestrated by an all-seeing, all-knowing conductor.

Henry looked at his friend as he piloted their ship along their route, as if it were simply another ordinary day, and he was once again filled with a renewed sense of wonder and respect for this four-armed, blue-skinned being from ... well, not from Earth.

"Why are you looking at me like that?" said Gsefx, a puzzled look on his face.

Henry looked back out of his window again, then suddenly turned back toward Gsefx.

"Wait ... how fast are we going?" he said, his calm disappearing, replaced with a concern he felt growing stronger with each passing second.

"How fast are we going?" repeated Gsefx. "Why do you care how fast we're going?"

Henry waved his hand around, pointing at the other ships flying near them.

"Because there are ships, Gsefx, a lot of ships, all of them very close to one another, and all traveling at, what I'm guessing, are really, really high speeds ... " As the words tumbled out of his mouth, Henry felt the pace at which they flowed begin to increase correspondingly with the rise in the pitch at which they were spoken. He could feel his heart beating faster, too. "I'm wondering what happens if someone makes a mistake and bumps into someone else. It seems like it would be bad, Gsefx, really, really bad."

Gsefx smiled again, this time it was a kind, if condescending, smile, the kind a parent gives when they find humor in the unfounded fears of their child.

"You have nothing to worry about, Henry," he said. "We are perfectly safe."

"Are you sure?" asked Henry, feeling himself creeping ever closer to the edge of hysteria.

"Of course I'm sure, Henry. Please try and calm down and I'll try to explain it in a way that you will be able understand. I'm not sure how successful I will be, but I will try."

Henry held up his hand.

"Just make it simple enough so I won't feel as if we're about to die an imminent fiery death at any minute."

"Of course." Gsefx took a deep breath, pressed several buttons on the console in front of him, and looked over at Henry. "I just put us on auto-pilot, so we can talk without any concerns. The ship will take care of everything. Now, I could tell you that we're traveling at 4.7 Vrax, but, like our location, that wouldn't mean anything to you."

"Auto-pilot? Is that supposed to make me feel better?"

"Henry, you're going to have to trust me."

Henry closed his eyes and took a deep breath.

"Okay," he said. "Tell me about this Vrax. Is it some variation of light speed ... um ... traveling at the speed of light? Because that, I can kind of understand."

"No, I'm afraid not," said Gsefx. "Light speed is ... well ... it's a rather primitive concept, I'm afraid. Theories based on anything as antiquated as 'speed-of-light travel' are simply of no real value out here. The distances we must regularly travel are too vast and must be covered more efficiently."

"Hmmm, light speed is primitive. Okay, so what is a Vrax?"

"Vrax isn't a what, it's a who. She was the engineer who developed our current mode of travel and so it was named in her honor. I'm not an engineer, so I can't tell you a lot about it, any more than most humans can probably tell you about their automobiles, but Vraxian technology allows us to travel, what would otherwise be unfathomable distances relatively quickly, using very little fuel and with no tangible effects to the organic life forms inside."

Henry thought about this for several minutes as he watched all of the other ships flying in all directions around them. As he did so, and could see how smoothly all of the ships interacted with one another, he felt his fears of dying in a fiery crash begin to subside, only to be replaced by another, equally pressing concern.

"When you say unfathomable distances, what do you mean, exactly? Gsefx, how far away from Earth are we?"

"About three-and-a-half-hours, in Earth-time," said Gsefx calmly, clearly not perceiving Henry's concern.

"That's not what I meant and you know it," said Henry. "How many miles?"

"I don't know the exact distance in Earth miles and honestly Henry, why is exact distance of more importance than the time it takes to travel it?"

"I don't know," said Henry, after thinking about it, but not being able to come up with a good answer. "It just is."

"Henry, I know this is all pretty overwhelming to you and that I'm asking you to accept a lot of new information quickly, but you must trust me when I tell you that we are perfectly safe and that you will be able to return home whenever you want."

Henry sighed and nodded his head. He was trying to understand and accept all of this, it just wasn't working very well. He had always been able to adapt pretty easily to new situations, but this was too much. He looked out the window and found the chaos of the other ships threatening to overwhelm him once again. He was finding it hard to breath.

"All of these ships, all of this chaos," he said, trying to catch his breath, "how can you be so calm? I just don't see how this is all working without ships crashing into one another?"

"As I said, I know this is all very difficult," said Gsefx, "but I need you, Henry. My life, the way it once was, is over, I know that. I can never go back to just being an accountant and having a normal life. I've accepted that and I'm okay with it. But, to have any chance of getting my wife back, I need you."

"I know that, Gsefx, and I'm trying, but ..."

"Please let me finish. What you need to understand is that what you're seeing right now, all of this traffic, this is not busy right now. Nor is this even remotely chaotic, compared to what you're about to experience in just a few minutes."

At Gsefx's words Henry's stomach sunk and his heart skipped a beat. He started to object but Gsefx stopped him before he could respond.

"Henry, let me try to make an analogy as best I can. We are traveling on, what would be comparable to an interstate highway on Earth, which, out here, links the long stretches of space in between planets."

Henry took a deep breath and tried to focus on Gsefx's voice.

"Okay, that seems to make sense," he said, "but I have to tell you, Earth's highways are not all that safe, so if you're trying to make me feel better, it's not working."

"Well, be that as it may, we're on the highway, but we're just ebyts ... err ... minutes away from exiting the highway and entering what you might think of as city streets. Because we're traveling so fast, we're not able to see our destination planet, Laxor, but we're not far from it. When we exit the "highway" we're on, in favor of the "city streets," the planet will not only be visible but it will fill most of our field of vision. Moreover, the number of vehicles is going to increase exponentially."

"This is still not making me feel any better," said Henry.

"Perhaps not, but think about your highways and city streets for a moment. Now, think about how those highways and streets might appear to someone who you would consider a primitive from Earth's past."

Henry thought about it for a moment, and as he did so, something clicked in his mind, as if a door he didn't even know existed had been flung wide open, revealing an entirely new way to look at his situation.

"You mean like a caveman or something?" he asked as a feeling of serenity flowed out from this new-found door and he began breathing easier.

"I haven't done that much research on Earth's history," said Gsefx, "but I trust you know who to choose."

"Yes, the caveman was, to us, the first form of humankind. They literally lived in caves, hunted with spears, and walked everywhere they went. For them to see our highways and city streets would be overwhelming and terrifying."

"And yet," said Gsefx, "you feel perfectly safe traveling on them every day, right?"

"Well, I wouldn't say that," said Henry. "They're not perfectly safe. We still have accidents, and people die on them every day."

"That's where things differ out here. We have accidents, there's no way to avoid them. However, regardless of how bad the accident is, occupant safety is the mandated first priority of every Vrax-Vehicle. If, for some reason, we were to be in the worst possible accident we could be in, you and I would be encased in individual ejection pods, and moved to a safe distance from the accident scene."

As Henry let this new information sink in, he gave his friend an irritated look.

"Why didn't you just say that from the beginning?" he asked. "We could have saved a lot of time if you'd have just jumped to the punch line and skipped all of the explanation,"

"We could have saved even more time if you'd simply have trusted me when I told you there was nothing to worry about," said Gsefx, who somehow seemed ready for Henry's reaction. "Henry, I'm going to need you to trust me even more as we move forward. Having an accident is the least of our concerns. It's the chaos you're about to experience that worries me. It's going to be overwhelming and very disconcerting. I can close the shades and keep them closed until we reach our destination, if that will help."

"No," said Henry, without hesitation. "That would just make it worse. I'll be fine."

"Okay, if you say so," said Gsefx. "We're going to make the transition in about thirty byts ... err ... seconds."

Henry nodded and silently counted down from thirty, his heartbeat picking up speed as the number approached zero.

"Here we go," said Gsefx as Henry passed five ... four ... three ... two ... one ...

Henry felt the ship change speeds, noticeably slowing down, then suddenly where there was once nothing but dark space, void of anything except other ships, there was a planet. A huge, bright green planet. And where, a moment earlier, there were just tens of thousands of ships, there were now easily hundreds of thousands of them. As before, going in all different directions, all choreographed in a massive, hysterical, and chaotic, yet mesmerizing dance. If anything, Gsefx had undersold the vision.

Henry cried out, in spite of himself.

"Are you all right?" asked Gsefx. "Shall I close the shades?"

"No!" said Henry. "No, I'll be okay ... just ... just give me a minute to get my bearings." He looked from window to window trying to take it all in. "There are just so many different kinds of ships ... and ... and ... beings flying them."

"Yes, and thankfully for us it's not a busy, high-traffic, commuting time. If it were, you might see one of the accidents I mentioned, and then we'd be stuck, crawling along. Then it would take us too long to reach our destination."

"This ... this is not that busy?" Henry looked out of the front window again. "I think I'm beginning to get a feel for what a caveman would have felt like if he'd suddenly appeared in time for rush hour traffic in L.A. or New York."

Henry paused for a moment, not looking out either window. Not looking anywhere, but thinking about where he actually was. He sat this way, motionless, for several minutes until Gsefx finally broke the silence.

"Henry, are you still with me?"

"You know, people on Earth have no idea this is out here," said Henry, softly, without moving. "They just go about their daily lives like they're the center of the universe. They have no idea."

"No, and that's as it should be, Henry. I made a terrible mistake coming to Earth like I did, and my wife and friends are now paying the price. We have to hope we can fix my mistake before the consequences get any worse."

"I'm not sure exactly what you need me to do," said Henry, "but we will fix it, Gsefx, and we will get your wife back, I promise you we will."

"Thank you, Henry. No matter what happens, I know how difficult all of this is and I want to thank you for at least trying."

Henry smiled and looked back out the window. For all of the fear and near hysteria he had felt just minutes before, knowing he was a part of something bigger than himself helped him feel remarkably calm and serene.

"I think a part of me knew there was something more to life than what I was living," he said. "I just didn't know what it was. Now, I'm seeing just how much more. Our tiny little planet seems pretty inconsequential when looking at all of this."

The cockpit was silent for a few minutes as Henry took it all in. He finally turned toward Gsefx, who seemed to be waiting for him.

"Inconsequential? Earth?" said Gsefx. "I don't think so." He pushed a few buttons on his console, and then looked at Henry and smiled. A moment later the cockpit filled with the sweet sounds of a late '70s rock song. Henry smiled and they both sang along to the music at the top of their lungs.

Night is day and day is night
Don't say I won't 'cause you know I might.

You are wrong and I am right
Don't cross my path 'less ya wanna fight.

Rock on my children!
Rock on my love!
Rock all day and rock all night,
Roll in the sounds from heaven above.

Chapter 55

Our Enemy Waits for Us Above

Rock on my children!
Rock on my love!
Rock all day and rock all night,
Roll in the sounds from heaven above

Even as Gsefx sang along with Henry, he marveled at the Earthling's ability to adapt so quickly to this new, strange, and fast-moving environment. When Henry had first fallen asleep, Gsefx hoped he'd remain that way until they reached the Galacticount offices. He'd even adjusted the temperature and oxygen levels in the cockpit slightly in order to help him remain asleep. But this was better. Henry was awake, aware, and, after a brief bout of fully understandable panic, in complete control of himself.

Aside from the relief he felt for his friend's well-being, Gsefx was also pleased by the fact that Henry's current state of mind also made him much more capable of assisting him in his attempt to uncover the identity of Ricnor's boss.

"Woooo-hooooo!" shouted Henry as the song came to an end. "You are absolutely right, my friend, whatever else may happen in planet Earth's future they can never take rock-n-roll away from us! Woooo-hooooo!"

Gsefx laughed aloud, in spite of the seriousness of the situation. The music, combined with Henry's infectious enthusiasm, was hard to resist. Throughout most of the song, he'd been "playing the air git-arr," which made very little sense to Gsefx, but seemed fun nonetheless. When the lightheartedness of the moment was over, Gsefx reached into the back seat and grabbed one of Henry's smaller paintings, and handed it to his friend.

Henry looked confused.

"What's this?" he asked. He immediately held up his hand. "Wait, obviously I know what it is. Why are you handing it to me?"

"Henry, no one can say what will happen in your planet's future," said Gsefx, "whether Earth will ever become a planet of consequence within the Galactic Community is a complete unknown at this point in your history. But what is known, what nobody can deny, is that the music you call rock-n-roll and we call albalan, has found a place within the galactic culture."

He then put a hand on Henry's painting.

"And, should you choose to share your art with a larger audience, I have no doubt that it, too, would find favor throughout the galaxy. Look at the lengths Ricnor and his gang have taken in order to steal it away from you."

Henry nodded, but didn't speak.

"No matter what happens, Henry, Earth will never be inconsequential, not only because of rock-n-roll, but because of you as well."

Henry looked at Gsefx, a solemn look on his face. "But mostly because of rock-n-roll!" he said suddenly smiling, and broke into playing his air git-arr again.

"At some point you're going to have to explain to me what that's all about," laughed Gsefx, as he returned the painting to the back seat with the rest and covered them up. "But it will have to wait because we're here."

"Huh ... I guess we are," said Henry, looking out his windows. "It's a good thing too, 'cause I really gotta go, if you know what I mean."

Gsefx was puzzled.

"I don't have any idea what you mean," he said. "Where do you have to go?"

Henry smiled.

"It's just an expression. I have to ... um ... you know ... use the restroom."

Gsefx thought for a moment, recalling his study of the English language and American pop culture. Then he understood.

"Ahhh, I see. You have to eliminate your bodily wastes. Is that correct?"

Henry looked away. Was he embarrassed?

"Well, yes, I guess that's one way to put it." He turned back to Gsefx. "What do you say when you have to 'eliminate your bodily waste?'"

"Oh, that's not an issue," said Gsefx, "at least not for most species. We don't have any. There are a few species who ... oh ... sorry Henry. Let's go inside and get you to a ... what did you call it?

"A restroom."

"Yes, of course."

As they exited the vehicle and walked into the Galacticount lobby, Henry still seemed to have something on his mind.

"What exactly do you mean when you say you don't have any, well, you know, waste?" he asked as Gsefx closed the lobby door behind him.

"I mean," said Gsefx, lowering his voice so as not to be overheard by anyone, "we eat only what our bodies' need and nothing more. Over the millennia, we've evolved quite efficiently."

"Huh," said Henry, an expression on his face that somehow managed to convey his bewilderment, while also showing he was rather impressed. "Maybe there's hope for us someday."

"Perhaps. Now, the room you need is right over there ... you might want to ... oh never mind, you'll figure it out. I'm going to get the files I need and I will meet you right back here. It will only take a few ebyts ... err ... minutes."

"So, I'm supposed to just hang out in the restroom? What if someone asks what I'm doing here?"

"No one will bother you. Trust me, Henry. I'll be right back."

"Okay, if you say so."

Gsefx made sure Henry was headed in the right direction, then went to the lift and the 327th floor. He needed to get those files, collect Henry, and leave before Xtlar found out he was here. When the lift stopped at his floor, Gsefx went straight to Planvc's office, walked in, and closed the door behind him.

"Gsefx!" said Planvc, looking up from the enormous stack of files surrounding him on all sides. "By the Gods, I was beginning to lose hope. Where have you been?"

Before Gsefx could answer, Planvc stood up, extricated himself from his work and embraced his friend. "It's good to see you again."

"And you, as well," said Gsefx, smiling back at the one individual he knew he could trust and who wasn't currently being held prisoner by the galaxy's most ruthless criminal. "I'm sorry I haven't been in touch, and that this will only be a brief visit. I'm afraid things are ... not yet resolved ... is the best way to put it, I suppose."

Planvc's smile evaporated quickly.

"Then why are you here, if you're not back for good? Gsefx, Xtlar knows you've been gone. He's out for your blood."

Gsefx fell silent for a moment. He knew this was the case, of course, but even so, hearing it said out loud made betraying Xtlar's trust all the more real. Galacticount's Chief Financial Officer had always looked after him and had treated him well, and Gsefx knew he was letting him down. He also knew that his days at Galacticount and as an accountant were over, no matter how this little adventure ended. It was too bad, really. He'd always enjoyed his work, but if rescuing Lhvunsa and Qilzar meant that it was over now, then so be it.

"That can't be helped," he said, a look of staunch resolution on his face. "I need to know more about the Pigawitts files you were working on, the ones where you found the discrepancies."

"What about them?"

"The last time we talked, you were still looking into them. What did you find out? Did they lead anywhere?"

"Yes, they did and it's big, Gsefx, really big," said Planvc, as he turned back and began rifling through the stacks of files on his desk.

"Let me guess, Pigawitts has been hiding money, lots of it, for a long time."

Planvc stopped and looked back at Gsefx.

"How did you ...?"

Gsefx stopped his friend with a wave of a hand.

"It doesn't matter," he said. "Planvc, I need those files. They're all the proof I need to ... wait ... you haven't told anyone else, have you?"

Planvc turned back to his files.

"No, of course not. I was getting a little nervous not hearing from you but I would have waited as long as I could before showing anyone else."

"Good," said Gsefx. He let out a sigh. "That's very good. Let me have them and I'll be on my way."

"Gsefx, what do you need the files for? What are they proof of, other than Pigawitts being a crook and all."

"I can't tell you much, Planvc, for your own protection. All I can say is that I'm taking this proof straight to Pigawitts himself. He's going to answer for what he's done. And then he's going to undo what he's done to me, and to Lhvunsa."

Planvc looked horrified. All of the color had drained from his features. Clearly he saw something reflected in Gsefx's face he didn't recognize, and didn't much care for.

"Gsefx, I don't know what's going on, but you're not the same Clangdorian I knew a few rotations ago."

"No, I'm not. And the less you know, the better. You don't need to be mixed up in any of this if you can help it."

"I won't argue with that. I'm certainly no hero. But Gsefx, Pigawitts is here, at Galacticount. He's in the Pinnacle right now, meeting with Xtlar and Tsedle."

A grim smiled crawled slowly across Gsefx's face.

"Perfect. They can be my witnesses."

Planvc handed Gsefx the files.

"Gsefx, are you sure you know what you're doing?"

Gsefx took them, then reached over and took his friend by the shoulder.

"Planvc," he said with a sigh, "I haven't been sure of anything for quite some time now. But there's too much at stake. I have to take action now, before it's too late."

Gsefx paused for a moment, as if in deep thought, then took a step back.

"Planvc, I think it would be best if you weren't here when all of this goes down. I'm not exactly sure what's going to happen, but it's almost certain to be unpleasant. The further removed from it you are, the better. Go home, Planvc. That's a directive from your supervisor, though I may not be your supervisor for much longer. Go home, now."

"Gsefx, are you sure?" asked Planvc. "I can stick around, just in case you need ..."

"No," said Gsefx. "If not for your own sake, then for mine. Please, just go."

"Okay, Gsefx, if you say so."

"Thank you. I'm not sure when or if I'll see you again, so please understand how much I appreciate all of your help and support and friendship. You have always been my best friend. I will be forever in your debt."

"What are you talking about?" asked Planvc, his confusion evident. "Of course we'll see each other again. But hey, you're my best friend, too. Take care of yourself, Gsefx. I mean it."

"You too."

Without another word or a second glance, Gsefx turned and walked out of the office, and went straight to the lift. When he reached the lobby, he found Henry waiting for him.

"Whoa, you look grim," said Henry.

"The time has come to face the one who has been pulling our strings," said Gsefx.

"What are we waiting for? Let's go."

Henry turned toward the door.

"Not that way," said Gsefx. "Our enemy waits for us above."

Chapter 56

I Speak Your Language

Lhvunsa stood staring at the scene in front of her, watching it all unfold as if she were seeing it through someone else's eyes. It seemed as though she were outside of her own body taking it all in, but paying very little attention to the events that should have been of utmost importance to her, as if she had been transported into someone else's surreal dream—or nightmare. The only thing she was certain of was that the vulgar Earthling, named Alcorn, was going on about something he seemed rather passionate about.

"Would someone explain to me what in the hell just happened?" he was saying in what she had come to recognize as his typical loud and obnoxious voice. "They were supposed to be knocked out! All of 'em, even Ricnor. And then, out of nowhere, boom! Not only is he up and running around, here comes another one of 'em busting through the damn wall to rescue him. How in the hell does that happen?"

He continued on like that, but Lhvunsa had no interest in his inane babbling. Nothing that was happening around her seemed important any longer. Everything she once held dear, her husband, her home, and her career was now lost, as was she. Her knees buckled and she dropped to the ground.

As her body hit the floor, a memory flashed through her mind. It was a memory of her career. It seemed odd that at this moment, when all was lost, her mind should go to this and not her beloved Gsefx, but the mind isn't always a predictable thing. She knew that she had once had a career, an important one, or at least a highly respectable one, but what was it? It had something to do with buildings. Perhaps she had been an engineer. No, that wasn't it. An architect? Yes, that was it. She had once been an architect, and a highly respected one at that. Moreover, she had recently been awarded a very prestigious contract, but the nature of it eluded her. She fought to remember the contract because it somehow seemed important that she try, but even as she did so, she observed, seemingly from a distance, her friend Qilzar approach her.

"Lhvunsa?" he was saying. "Lhvunsa, are you okay? Talk to me, Lhvunsa!"

When she wouldn't respond, he began shaking her and talking louder.

"Lhvunsa, snap out of it! We need to get moving. Lhvunsa! Come back to me, Lhvunsa!"

She pitied him, really. Qilzar was a good-hearted soul and she actually cared for him in her own way, but she wasn't going back. There was no reason to go back now.

Then Qilzar stopped. The Earthling, Alcorn, had approached and quietly asked him to move aside. *This is an interesting development,* she thought, as she distantly wondered what this beastly primitive would do. *Perhaps he will hit me or throw me up against the wall until I respond.*

"Lhvunsa," she heard him say in a voice so gentle and soft, she wasn't sure it was the same being that had been ranting just a few ebyts before. "Lhvunsa, I know what you must be thinking. You must believe that all is lost, even though we're free from our prison cell and the authorities are on their way. Ricnor has escaped and your husband, who isn't here, has left your fate in the hands of some obnoxious lout, who has done very little except make a lot of noise since he arrived.

Very true, thought Lhvunsa, drifting in a little closer.

"Lhvunsa," said Alcorn, "I know that's what you're thinking, but here's what you don't know. Among my people, in my profession I am a very high-ranking man. I don't say that as a matter of pride but only to make the point that there are very few people I take orders from, and then only because I'm required to, not because it's something I choose."

"I don't doubt that." She heard Qilzar say, in a voice that was none too polite. "So far, you haven't struck me as the type to take orders from anyone."

Alcorn didn't move, not even the slightest flicker, but kept his eyes locked on Lhvunsa.

"That's right," he said, "I don't take orders well, not unless they come from someone I respect, someone who I believe has the intellectual capacity and mental fortitude to give orders on my level, or better yet, on a level higher than my own. Call it hubris, simple arrogance, or whatever you want, but when lives are on the line, the one giving the orders has to know what they're doing. Until a few hours ago, I'd yet to meet anyone who I believed worthy of that respect."

Lhvunsa didn't know what the Earthling was trying to tell her, and though she was not ready to rejoin the waking world just yet, she remained intrigued and listened as Alcorn continued.

"From what I've gathered in my limited conversations with your husband, Gsefx spends his days, or whatever you call them out here, working as an accountant, but he is so much more than that, Lhvunsa. I'm not exactly sure how to put it, but he is perhaps the most brilliant individual I've ever met. It's not just intelligence either. I mean, clearly, by Earth standards, all of you are much more advanced than we are. It's his innate grasp of tactics and strategy that caught my attention. When we were talking and mapping out a rescue plan, I would barely begin a sentence before he not only knew what I was going to say, but then had a plan to address the situation."

Alcorn was talking about her Gsefx, but not about how much danger he was in. He was telling her how much he admired him.

This is unexpected.

Without realizing how or when it happened, Lhvunsa had reassumed her own body and was hanging on every word this vulgar creature was saying.

"Gsefx didn't ask me to come on this mission, Lhvunsa, I insisted. I've always dreamed of being a leader like him. But, after just a few minutes, it was clear to me I could never achieve his level, so I decided the next best thing was to serve under him."

He sighed and took her hand in his and she looked down at it.

"Lhvunsa, even the most perfectly run mission experiences some bumps along the way. And while I may yell and scream and jump up and down, all is not lost. I will also tell you that while Gsefx is by no means out of danger, he's far from helpless, nor is he alone. As for us, we're not out of danger yet either and we need you to come back to us now."

"The Klarock," said Lhvunsa with a slight shake of her head. "It was the Klarock Museum."

"I'm sorry, what did you say?" asked Alcorn.

Lhvunsa smiled and squeezed the Earthling's hand gently with one hand, patted it with another, and reached up to caress his cheek with her third.

"Nothing important, just something I had been trying to remember. Thank you, General Alcorn. I believe I've misjudged you, and perhaps the whole situation. It seems you have things more under control than I gave you credit. I'm sorry. Everything just became a little overwhelming."

"Please, no need for apologies. I understand, ma'am, I truly do."

He started to get up, but Lhvunsa stopped him.

"Did you really mean all of that? The things you said about Gsefx?"

Alcorn smiled at her.

"Ma'am, I'm not above lying if I think it will give me a tactical advantage," said Alcorn. "However, in this regard, I'll let your friend, Qilzar, who I deem to be an outstanding judge of character, be my judge and jury. I am indeed an arrogant man, who not only finds it difficult to humble himself in front of others, but finds it just as difficult to lie about doing so, regardless of the tactical advantage. I would never willingly admit to serving under the leadership of an inferior."

Alcorn got to his feet and reached down to help Lhvunsa up.

"And if Qilzar's testimony isn't enough," he continued, "I'll offer my son's. He's known me a lot longer and knows exactly what a son-of-a-bitch I can be."

Lhvunsa smiled.

"I don't know if all that will be necessary," she said. "I'd hate to stir up any family trouble in the midst of everything else we're dealing with."

"Well, I have no problem testifying to his arrogance," said Qilzar, who, from what Lhvunsa could see, appeared to be trying to maintain his dislike for the Earthling, even through his gratefulness at seeing her come back to herself.

"Theo, anything to add?" asked Alcorn.

"No comment," said Theo with a weak smile.

"There you go," said Alcorn. "Guilty on all counts."

"Okay, okay," said Lhvunsa, who, inconceivably, actually found herself trying not to laugh. "I thought we were in some kind of hurry or something. So what's next?"

"I don't know if it's possible," said Alcorn, "but we need to stop Ricnor from leaving. It would also be great if we can find the paintings before the police get here and collect them as evidence. They belong to Henry, and Gsefx would like to ensure they are returned to him."

"That was a short-range vehicle Ricnor and his companion were using," said Qilzar. "They won't be able to get off-planet with it. They'll have to find another ship. If we can get to their main bay before they're able to leave, we might be able to catch them."

"Great," said Alcorn. "I can get us to the main bay, let's just hope it's in time."

"This place is a maze of twists and turns," said Lhvunsa. "What makes you think you can get us there?"

"I've been mapping out the place since we first arrived. I have it all in my head. It may not be the most direct route, but I know how to get back to every place we've been."

"It's good they didn't drug you when they brought you in," she said, trying not to seem impressed by the increasingly more impressive Earthling. "Ricnor's thugs hid inside my home, then ambushed me before I had a chance to react. After Ricnor held his spike to my throat in order to get Gsefx to do his bidding, they knocked me out. I was unconscious when I arrived and I simply woke up in my cell."

"As did I," said Qilzar, who also seemed to be trying not to look impressed, but was failing miserably.

"I think I know the way pretty well, too," said Theo.

"Good," said Alcorn. "Theo, you and Lhvunsa look for the paintings. If you find them, bring them to the main bay. Qilzar and I will go there and try to stop Ricnor. While we're there, we'll see if we can secure a vehicle for ourselves. We'll meet back in the Grand Chamber."

"Wait," said Qilzar. "I'm not sure splitting up is the best plan. For one thing, we only have one weapon. What if we run into someone else who wasn't knocked out?"

"Good point," said Alcorn, while Lhvunsa and he made eye contact. He took the primitive Earth weapon from his belt and handed it to his son. "You only have three shots left, Theo, so use them carefully."

"Yes, sir."

"Any other objections?"

"Yes, as a matter of fact," said Qilzar, "a rather important one. We have to remain together if we want to continue communicating. You have the only translator."

"Huh, another good point," said Alcorn. "Well, I suppose we could ..."

"I speak your language," said Lhvunsa, in near-perfect English. "Gsefx believed he was being secretive when he was learning English. I believe that's what you call it. I let him keep his secret but thought it might be a good idea to learn it for myself. It appears I was right."

"Well, I guess that takes care of that," said Alcorn with a smile. "Anything else?"

"You're missing the point," said Qilzar, "I don't ..."

Lhvunsa reached over and put a slim green finger over Qilzar's mouth.

"Qilzar, my dear friend, we need to trust, if not in them, then in Gsefx, who sent them."

Qilzar started to object again, but Lhvunsa shook her head.

"No more," she said. "We're wasting time." She kissed the Dremin on the forehead. "Take care of the General, and take care of yourself. We'll be together again soon enough. Come, Theo, let's go."

She gave Alcorn one last look, then turned abruptly and walked away.

Chapter 57

This Isn't Earth, You Know

Alcorn watched Lhvunsa walk away, his expression never betraying the emotion he felt inside. In all his years with Janny, no woman had ever so much as turned his head, but then again, he'd never left planet Earth before, either. Marital statuses aside, both his and hers, it wasn't that he was interested in Lhvunsa in any kind of romantic sense, though she was strikingly beautiful. It was something else about her, something that was more intriguing than anything else. With every thought she expressed aloud, he knew there were at least a dozen others she kept hidden. She and Gsefx were alike in that regard.

Probably why they're such a good match for one another.

Gsefx seemed to be more of an extrovert, preferring to lay all of his cards on the table, whereas Lhvunsa was more introverted, more mysterious than her husband. At least that was the impression he'd gotten so far. But aside from that difference, which was more complimentary than anything else, they seemed to be very much alike in the way they were several steps ahead of everyone else around them. In any case, Alcorn liked her as much as he liked Gsefx, and swore to himself he would go to whatever lengths necessary to protect and serve both of them.

Theo turned to follow Lhvunsa, and Alcorn snapped out of his reverie to reach out and touch his son on the shoulder.

"Theo ..."

Theo turned and locked eyes with his father. Alcorn's throat closed up unexpectedly and, without warning, he found that no words could escape. He gave his son the best smile he could muster and nodded, hoping that would be enough to show Theo how proud he was of him. He also hoped that he would get the chance to actually tell him someday. Theo smiled weakly, and then went on to catch up with Lhvunsa.

Alcorn afforded himself another moment to look at them both, and then turned to Qilzar, who was watching Lhvunsa, with much the same look of dedication to her that Alcorn felt. He pretended not to notice and walked on in the direction of the cafeteria.

"We'll need to go this way," he said in a soft voice as he walked by.

Qilzar cleared his throat and turned to follow.

"Yes, of course," said the gray-skinned non-terrestrial. "I do hope you know what you're doing. This isn't Earth, you know, and these aren't primitive criminals we're dealing with."

Alcorn looked away and smiled. As annoying as Qilzar had already proven himself to be, he was also extremely sharp and had, on more than one occasion, thought of things he, the four-star general, hadn't. If there was one thing Alcorn had learned over the years, is that often the people who were the most difficult to deal with personally, could also have the most to offer, if you knew how to treat them. Gsefx had said Qilzar could be an asset if he could be trusted, and he was right.

"That's why I wanted you with me," said Alcorn, turning back to Qilzar. "I know strategy and tactics, and those things don't vary too much, regardless of how primitive or advanced a culture becomes. You know a lot more about what goes on out here than I do, and have already saved our bacon more than once. Together, we should do pretty well."

"Saved our bacon? What, in the name of the Gods, does that mean?"

"It's just a primitive Earth expression, meaning you've saved us by thinking of things I haven't," said Alcorn, turning and walking on. "You're a good man, Qilzar."

"I am no such thing," said Qilzar, in his most offended voice, but following along, nonetheless. "I am a Dremin, and to call me a man is to equate me with the likes of you, which, no offense, is beneath me by several millennia."

"No offense taken," laughed Alcorn. "You're a good Dremin, then. How's that?"

"Better, although other Dremins might disagree on that point. General, there is still one thing that bothers me."

"Hold that thought," said Alcorn, lowering his voice to a whisper as he moved them both against the wall. "We're about to enter the Great Hall again, and even though it was quiet the last time we came through, there's no sense in taking any chances."

"Yes," said Qilzar, "I quite agree."

Alcorn peaked around the corner and slowly worked his way until he had a full view of the room. He took a few more steps, carefully examining the room before motioning the 'all clear' to Qilzar.

They walked steadily, but warily, through the Great Hall, remaining alert while in such a wide open space, only relaxing when they made it to the other side without incident, and the walkways became closer and easier to navigate. There were no bodies here, unconscious or otherwise, which was fine with Alcorn. They continued making their way toward the main bay, balancing caution with speed.

"What was it you wanted to ask me back there?" said Alcorn, when they were in a passageway safe enough for conversation.

"What do you mean?" said Qilzar.

"Back there, before the Great Hall, you said there was still one thing that bothered you. What is it?"

"Oh yes, that. When Lhvunsa was first put into the cell with me, she accused me of telling Ricnor about the paintings and of bringing him into all of this in the first place. She said that she and Gsefx would never forgive me."

"Yes, but apparently, that's not the case," said Alcorn. "You didn't bring Ricnor into this. Someone else did."

"That's correct," said Qilzar. "But Lhvunsa and I figured that out by ourselves, alone in a cell. How did Gsefx figure it out?"

Alcorn stopped and looked at Qilzar appraisingly.

"You and Lhvunsa figured it out by yourselves, while locked alone in a cell?"

"Yes, that's right."

"Qilzar," said Alcorn as he turned and continued on his way, "did I say you know a lot more about what goes on out here than I do? You simply know a lot, period. I'm not sure how you figured it out, but it's pretty damned impressive."

Qilzar's gray face flushed into a brighter shade of gray.

"Thank you, General," he said. "But, to be honest, it was more Lhvunsa's doing than it was mine. She had me recount my abduction, step-by-step, every last detail, which led me back to Galacticount, which led her straight to Xtlar, the one Ricnor reports to. He also happens to be my boss, as well."

"X-who? No ... no—Gsefx said it was someone named ... uh ... umm ... Piggy ... something-or-other."

"Pigawitts?"

"Yes, that's it."

"No, it couldn't be Pigawitts. Could it?" Qilzar seemed truly puzzled. "Why in the galaxy did he think it was Pigawitts?"

"Apparently Gsefx and his team found some discrepancies buried pretty deep in this guy's books when they were going through them. He thinks that's why they took both you and Lhvunsa hostage, instead of just one of you. They wanted to make sure they pulled him away from digging any deeper."

Qilzar seemed to consider the possibility for a moment.

"I can see the logic there, I suppose, but whoever kidnapped me had to have access to my vehicle, which means they had access to the Galacticount parking area."

"Would that include Pigawitts?"

"Not normally, although he did come into the offices for meetings on occasion. I'm trying to recall if he was there the rotation I was ... yes, yes he was there! I remember seeing him with Xtlar ... Oh Gods!"

Qilzar stopped and the brightness left his face, leaving him an ashen gray.

"What? Qilzar, what is it?"

"What if Xtlar and Pigawitts are working together? Gsefx could be walking into a trap."

Alcorn thought for a moment. He didn't know either of the

beings Qilzar was talking about, nor did he know the situation they all lived in. But he knew enough. He knew Gsefx.

"You bring up a fair point, Qilzar, to be sure, and even though I don't know either of them, I have to trust your judgment about the possibility of the two of them working together."

He raised his hand to ward off Qilzar's intended interruption.

"Be that as it may, I also have to trust in Gsefx. And in Henry. They are far from helpless. Think about it for a minute. Regardless of whether or not Xtlar and Pigawitts are working together, where would Gsefx confront either of them?"

"In their offices, I imagine," he said, after taking a moment to think about it. "For Xtlar, that would be Galacticount, where Gsefx and I both work, or worked. I don't suppose either of us will have a job any longer, even if we do find a way to get out this whole thing alive. For Pigawitts, it would be at his offices. They're both on the planet Laxor."

"And both are relatively public places, as well, I imagine. Right?"

"Yes, I suppose so," said Qilzar.

"Where it would be difficult, if not impossible, to make a move against Gsefx and Henry," said Alcorn. "Plus, Gsefx still has to get and then review the proof first, which should give him better insight as to who is really behind all of this."

"Perhaps, but ..."

"But nothing, Qilzar," said Alcorn, signaling that they needed to continue on their way to the main bay. "We have to trust that Gsefx can take care of himself, if for no other reason then there's nothing we can do to help him. Besides, he does have Henry with him."

"You keep saying that. What good is the artist going to be in this situation?"

Alcorn looked startled.

"I thought you'd seen his paintings."

"Well yes, I've seen one of them. It's exquisite, but what has that got to do with helping get Gsefx out of danger?"

Alcorn's startled look changed to disappointment.

"Here I was," he said shaking his head, "starting to actually believe how much further advanced you were than I, and yet after seeing Henry's works you have to ask that question."

"Just what is that supposed to mean?" said Qilzar, drawing himself up in a most offended way.

"It's not *supposed* to mean anything. It *actually* means that if you had looked at that painting, and really knew what you were seeing, you'd know what Henry has to offer. And you'd know that Gsefx is much safer with him than with any of us."

"Just what is it that he has to offer?"

"He sees the truth, Qilzar. He sees the truth in everything. In people, in situations, in ... hell, I don't even know, just everything. He will know if this Xtlar is lying, or if Pigawitts is, or if they're both telling the truth. He will be able to tell if they are in any danger well ahead of time."

Qilzar looked unconvinced.

"That seems unlikely," he said. "But even if it's true, what good does it do to know that Xtlar is lying to them if they're already trapped in the room with him?"

"That's where our trust has to come in, Qilzar. Trust in Gsefx's instincts."

Alcorn stopped and looked at Qilzar.

"How long have you known Gsefx?" he said.

Qilzar looked up, as if he was counting in his head.

"I've known him for nearly ten turns, and worked closely with him for the past six," he said, "why?"

"What is a turn?" asked Alcorn. "Is it anything like a year, the length of time it takes Earth to orbit our sun?"

"I suppose for our purposes, yes, consider them the same," said Qilzar with a sigh. "What are you getting at?"

"What I'm getting at, is that you've known Gsefx for a lot longer than I have. You know far better than I do what he's capable of, yet you have far less faith in him than I do; someone who's only known him for a few hours."

"Perhaps," said Qilzar, "or perhaps it's that, since you have only known him for a few hours, as you call them, you don't understand just how much he means to those of us who have known him for a lot longer. Perhaps if you did, you'd be trying harder to find a way out of here instead of bickering about how we should simply trust in his ability to survive."

"Perhaps we can do both," said Alcorn, "the main bay is just through those doors ahead of us."

Alcorn watched Qilzar's eyes as he looked at the doors, and saw a brief flicker of doubt, quickly followed by deep resolve. The kind of resolve that showed just how much Qilzar cared for his friend.

"Lead the way," said the Dremin.

While Alcorn didn't fully agree with Qilzar's assessment of Gsefx's situation, he did share his concern. Gsefx and Henry were both at risk, as they all were, and would continue to be until they could find and stop whoever was at the root of all of this. Of course, there was also the possibility that Qilzar was right and Gsefx was in over his head, but that was not something he wanted to think about. He squared his jaw and walked toward the door, ready to face whatever might be waiting on the other side.

Chapter 58

Stop Looking At Me Like That

Lhvunsa held her head high and walked away from Qilzar and the Earthling, Alcorn, as if she feared nothing. She had lost herself just moments before but she was back now. The General had brought her back and now she was expected to go on, as if everything was fine and her whole world hadn't just completely shattered. Perhaps Gsefx would be able to take care of himself, as Alcorn suggested, but it didn't make it any less difficult for her. She made it around the corner and through a set of doors before dropping to the floor again, this time in a pile of tears.

"Lhvunsa, are you okay? What's wrong?" It was Theo.

"Nothing," she said through her tears. She held up her hand to keep him back. The last thing she needed was to be rescued again. "Just ... give me a ..." the tears overtook her words.

"Sure," said Theo as he plopped down next to her.

Lhvunsa continued sobbing, all the while waiting for Theo to offer some words of comfort, or encouragement, or something else to get her to stop, but nothing came. He remained silent.

When she finally looked up at him, he was sitting there next to her, his knees pulled up and his arms folded across them, with his head resting comfortably and eyes closed. Was he asleep?

"Theo?" she asked tentatively. "Are you sleeping?"

"No, just waiting," he said. "As much as I would love to find Henry's paintings, I'm in no big hurry to blindly run around this complex hoping to stumble upon them. My dad is a brilliant man, but sometimes he doesn't really think things through very well."

Lhvunsa smiled.

"I hadn't thought of it that way, but I suppose you're right."

She paused for a moment and then continued.

"Thank you," she said.

"For what?"

"For letting me cry, and not trying to stop me or comfort me or do all of the things most males try to do when they encounter a weeping female."

"Sure thing," said the younger Alcorn with a smile. "My mother is a very strong woman. She's had to be to be married to my dad for all these years. But I learned early on that there were times when she just needed to sit and cry. She and my dad have always been very close, they're a team really. Actually, more so than I ever knew. But, with his position in the military, he wasn't always around, which meant my mom had to carry the load by herself a lot of the time. Sometimes it got to be too much and she'd break down and cry. I'd try to comfort her, and sometimes she'd let me, but most of the time she'd tell me that she was okay, just like you did, and that she just needed some time to herself to let out some of the things inside of her."

"Later on, she would explain to me that when she cried it wasn't always because she was sad or upset or having a breakdown. Sometimes she just needed to let things out so they wouldn't hold her down any longer, and that it was okay for her to do that."

Lhvunsa was stunned. She tried to say something, anything, but found that she could do nothing but stare at the General's son.

"What?" asked Theo. "Stop looking at me like that. You're kinda creeping me out."

Lhvunsa shook herself free and looked away as well.

"I'm sorry," she said. "It's just that ... I would never have expected ... your world and your people are still in very primitive stages of development, yet you and your father show incredible signs of maturity."

"Umm ... thank you ... I think."

"It is a great testament to you that you are so advanced. Are all of your race similarly mature?"

Theo scoffed. "Hardly. And don't be so quick to lump the General and me into the overly mature category, either. We have our moments, but we also have our moments when we're not all that advanced either."

"The General, you mean your father, right?"

"My father, the General, Sir-Yes-Sir, they're all interchangeable. It makes no difference."

"I see," said Lhvunsa, and she did. She thought of the trials she had with her mother and the way they often fought. It made her sad for Theo, but it also made her feel less distant from Earthlings as a whole. "Would you like to talk about it?"

"About what? My daddy issues? No thanks. I gave you your space, I'll ask that you do the same."

"Fair enough," said Lhvunsa, getting to her feet. "We should probably start looking for the paintings."

"Would you mind if we didn't?

"Excuse me?"

"Look, don't get me wrong, art is my specialty, paintings in particular. In fact, on Earth, I am probably one of the top twenty or so experts on the entire planet. I've actually seen some of Henry's work, the ones that Gsefx held on to. They are ... well, they're beyond words. In just the few minutes I had to examine his paintings, it was clear to me that Henry Backus is one of the greatest artists our planet has ever known and I would love nothing more than to spend hours analyzing his work ..."

"But ..."

"But, running around this maze of a place, like we actually know what we're doing, is not what I had in mind. Not to mention the fact that it's a completely idiotic idea."

"It was your father's idea," said Lhvunsa. "You think he's an idiot?"

"No, my father is a genius, and I mean that in all seriousness," said Theo. "But like I said before, he doesn't always think things through. Besides, he really doesn't care if we look for the paintings or not, he just didn't want us along while he chases after Ricnor."

Lhvunsa was surprised by the accusation and wondered how true it was. It did make a certain amount of sense.

"Are you sure?"

"I've known the man all my life," said Theo, "and I can tell when he wants me out of the way. I'm his biggest disappointment, you know."

"I doubt that very much," said Lhvunsa.

"It's true, but I've learned to live with ... hey ... we're not talking about this, remember?"

"You're the one who brought it up," said Lhvunsa, smiling.

Lhvunsa sat back down, this time across from Theo, so she could see his face.

"But, as you wish," she said, once she got situated, "we won't talk about it. Let's talk about my husband instead."

"Gsefx? Sure, what do you want to know?"

"You were with him at the same time as your father, correct?"

"Yes. Why?"

"Because I want to know what you think of him," said Lhvunsa. "The General was certain that Gsefx can take care of himself, that he is somehow this strong, intelligent hero who is capable of anything. I want to believe that. I want to see my husband again, but I'm not sure I share your father's confidence."

"Sure, I get that," said Theo. "Let me think of the best way to put it. I guess I would agree with the General, in that Gsefx is very capable. He is strong, smart, and he's able to see and understand the big picture quickly."

"Why do I feel you're about to add something that I'm not going to like?" said Lhvunsa.

"Because, as much as I agree with my father about your husband's abilities, Gsefx doesn't see it in himself. He thinks he's just another accountant, just an everyday guy trying to rescue his wife. He thinks everything he's done has been out of desperation and doesn't even realize all that he's accomplishing, much less how he's doing it. He lacks confidence in himself, at least in the larger sense. And that lack of confidence, a feeling like he's always winging it, will end up hurting him, and maybe all of us, if he doesn't start believing in his ability to lead."

Lhvunsa was silent for a while, as she mulled Theo's words over in her head. She could see that what he said was true. Gsefx was, in his own way, quite brilliant, but aside from accounting, he'd always been unfocused, bouncing from one hobby to another, never landing on anything that really spoke to him the way architecture had always spoken to her. And the part about his confidence made her heart ache for her husband, because that, above all else, she knew to be true. Even when all of the evidence pointed to his extraordinary talents and strengths, he still questioned his own abilities all too often, and she had no idea what to do about it.

"Lhvunsa, are you still with me?" asked Theo. "Did I say something wrong?"

"No," she said. "You are exactly right. I just don't know how to help him. How to help him find the confidence your father has, preferably without the arrogance."

"You may not believe this," said Theo with a smile, "but the General is not nearly as arrogant as you might think. In fact, he's actually rather humble."

"You're right, I don't believe it."

"Given what you know about me and my relationship with him, do you think I'd say it if I didn't believe it to be true?"

"What makes you so sure?"

"It's an act. General Theodore Eustace Alcorn is a phenomenal actor. It's how he gets what he wants out of other people, and he's able to pull it off because he has the one thing Gsefx lacks—confidence."

"So, as far as you're concerned, everything's an act with him. Is that it?"

"No, not everything," said Theo. "In fact, the people he's closest to mostly see the genuine thing. Now, he and I have never been all that close, but, like I said earlier, he and my mom are, and since I'm close to my mom, I've had enough chances to see them together. I've also been able to see him work the people he didn't know, when he wanted something from them, and he pulls out all kinds of personality traits when the situation calls for it."

"Has he ever worked you before?" asked Lhvunsa.

"He's tried, but it's never really gotten him anywhere," said Theo. "He wanted me to be a soldier, to follow in his footsteps, so to speak. But you can only hustle someone for what they have, and soldiering just wasn't in me. In the end, all he did was push us further apart."

"What brought you back together?" asked Lhvunsa.

"What makes you think we've come back together?"

Lhvunsa stumbled for a moment, looking for something to say. When nothing presented itself, she decided silence was best.

"Look, don't get me wrong, I love my dad, and I have a lot more respect for him than he thinks I do. And for the most part, I really don't harbor that much resentment for him, especially after what we've been through over the past day or so. But, no matter how you slice it, we're just not that close and I don't see that changing any time soon."

"I think I understand," said Lhvunsa, rising to her feet and thinking of her up-and-down relationship with her mother, hoping she would get a chance to see her again and deciding that if they got out of here in one piece, she would make it a priority to make things right. "We should get going. I'm not sure how far it is to the Grand Chamber, but it's almost time to meet up with your dad and Qilzar."

"Agreed," said Theo, also standing up. "Hey, shouldn't the police, or whatever you call them, be here by now?"

Lhvunsa stopped. Her dealings with the GCP had been limited to her one experience during the break-in, but they'd certainly been prompt then.

"Yes, as a matter of fact, they should have," she said. "Something must have gone wrong. We'd best hurry so we can resend the signal."

Theo led as they picked their way through a maze of corridors and rooms, both large and small. Scattered in various places throughout their path, they came across the bodies of several of Ricnor's gang, still unconscious. When they finally reached the entrance to the Grand Chamber, they stopped to survey the path ahead of them before charging on through. All appeared to be clear, so they entered the chamber and began working their way across.

When they reached the half-way point, they heard a loud shriek and turned just in time to see what Lhvunsa recognized as a Lildrinial fire a blast from an obliterator.

"Theo! Look out!" she screamed.

Chapter 59

All This Time, It's Been You!

There were exactly thirty-seven steps between the lift and the conference room door. In Gsefx's ten turns at Galacticount, he'd walked them often enough to know precisely how far he had before he committed career suicide, and possibly much worse. As he walked, he fought down the multitude of thoughts running through his mind, all of which led back to his beloved Lhvunsa. When they reached the door, he gave Henry a look he hoped was more reassuring then he felt, and took a deep breath. He reached for the door, but was stopped before he could open it.

"Gsefx? I'm just checking to make sure you're okay before we go in. You haven't said a word since we left the lobby."

"Yes Henry, I'm okay." He paused for a moment before continuing. "What we're about to do is going to be very difficult. Fortunately, they haven't revoked my access yet, so we should be able to get into this room. This is where Pigawitts is. He's the one we're after, the one who's behind Lhvunsa's kidnapping."

"Then it's good we're here, right?"

"Yes, except that once we're in the room, they're likely to call security right away, and Galacticount security is both fast and none too gentle. We're probably not going to be in the room very long. Are you sure you're ready for this, Henry?"

"Hey, I've been thrown out of nicer places than this," said Henry holding up his fist toward Gsefx. "Let's do this."

Gsefx looked at the fist, confused. "What is that?"

"It's a fist bump. It's normally a greeting like a handshake or something, but for you and me, it's a sign of solidarity; it's a sign that we are in this thing together, win or lose. We will live to fight another day or we will die trying, but we will do it together, as a team. Make a fist and bump mine, and we'll go in and find the truth behind all of this."

Gsefx made a fist, and with a smile on his face, bumped it with Henry's. Then they both walked into the conference room.

As soon as he stepped inside, Gsefx knew he'd made a terrible mistake. The conversation that had been taking place inside abruptly stopped and three sets of eyes turned on him. Two pairs of those eyes belonged to the most powerful figures at Galacticount, while the third was the namesake of one the company's oldest and most prestigious clients.

"What is the meaning of this interruption?" said Xtlar, who rose to intercept the intruders. "Gsefx, have you lost your mind? You know better than to interrupt a private meeting. Aren't you in enough trouble as it is?"

Gsefx almost faltered at Xtlar's scolding. His mouth went dry and he suddenly forgot why he was here.

What was so important that he needed to interrupt a meeting of this magnitude?

The beginnings of an apology formed in his mind and on his lips, but then Henry cleared his throat and nudged him, which seemed to knock something loose, because suddenly all of the events of the last several rotations flooded back into his mind, followed by the image of Lhvunsa with Ricnor's spike at her throat. The realization that the client his bosses were meeting with was wholly responsible for Lhvunsa's imprisonment, and Qilzar's too, steeled his nerve. The apology that had formed in his mind remained, but now it came with renewed clarity and an entirely different direction behind it.

"I apologize for the intrusion, Et Xtlar, Et Tsedle ... Et Pigawitts," he said as he nodded to each in turn, hesitating slightly before the last. "My team found some discrepancies in the Pigawitts files that could not wait to be presented."

"Discrepancies?" said Pigawitts as he rose to his feet. "What kind of discrepancies?"

"Stop right there, Gsefx," said Xtlar. "We have channels for these types of matters, built specifically to avoid alarming our clients unnecessarily ... channels of which you are well aware."

"Yes, Xtlar, I am aware of the proper channels, and as you know, Qilzar, is ... ah ... on vacation ... and therefore unavailable, so I'm bringing this to you and to the client, now. As I said, it's not something that can wait."

"Oh, for the love of the Gods, Xtlar," said Pigawitts, sitting back down, "let him speak. He's talking about my company and I want to hear what he's found."

Xtlar was far from satisfied, but he acquiesced. "Very well," he said. "Let's hear it Gsefx, and for your sake I hope it's worth it."

"Before you begin, perhaps you should introduce us to your friend," said another voice, this one belonging to Tsedle, Galacticount's President and Chief Executive Officer.

"Yes, sir, of course." He held his hand up in Henry's direction. "This is Henry. He's from a planet called Earth, which is not currently a member of the Galactic Community. He doesn't understand Galactine Standard, but I speak his native language, so I will translate when necessary."

"Why is he here?" said Xtlar. "What possible reason could he have for being involved in our business?"

"His purpose will become clear soon enough, sir. Now, if I may?" Gsefx walked forward and laid the file on the conference table. "The discrepancies were buried deep within a myriad of connecting relationships spread across numerous sub-accounts. Once we tracked everything down, what we found was big."

"And what was it that you found, exactly?" asked Pigawitts. "I've always prided myself on running a clean company."

"What we found, sir, is that your company has, over the past several turns, laundered exorbitant amounts of dirty money, coming in from sources all over the galaxy."

"That's outrageous!" said Pigawitts, as he flew across the table at Gsefx. "I don't believe you. Show me."

Gsefx had expected some denial, but he was somewhat taken aback by the level of Pigawitts' outrage—and apparent sincerity.

"Of course," he said, opening the file and doing his best to maintain his resolve. "I'll walk you along the same path the money takes through your company; from the time it comes in until it leaves."

He began explaining the files and the discrepancies. About halfway through, Pigawitts stopped him.

"Enough, enough!" he said. "I can't understand a thing you're telling me. Accounting has never been my forté, and since I don't know you, I'm not just going to take you at your word. Xtlar, Tsedle, does this make any sense to you?"

"At first glance, I'm afraid it does," said Tsedle. "Xtlar, why don't you take a closer look at the file, while Gsefx here tells us more about his friend."

"Of course," said Xtlar, as he took the file and moved back into his chair.

Tsedle and Pigawitts were now looking at Gsefx, expecting him to explain exactly why Henry was there with him.

"Yes, sir. If I may speak to him briefly, explain to him what's going on."

"As you wish," said Tsedle, "but be quick about it, Gsefx, you may have brought important information to our attention, but it doesn't excuse the impertinent manner in which you've done so."

"Yes sir," said Gsefx, as he quickly turned to Henry. The Earthling's obvious distress caught him off guard. "Henry, what is it? What's wrong?"

"Everything. Gsefx, we have to get out of here."

Gsefx was about to ask why when he was interrupted.

"He's right, young Gsefx, you do need to get out of here," said an unexpected voice from the conference table. They both turned to see Xtlar looking up and speaking perfect English to them. "Except that it's too late, it was too late to get out of here as soon as you opened those doors."

Before Gsefx could say anything, the conference room doors burst open and Galacticount security grabbed both he and Henry.

"You disappoint me, Gsefx," said Xtlar, a condescending look on his face. "You didn't really expect to succeed, did you?"

Gsefx was in shock.

"By the Gods! It's you!" he said as they dragged him from the room. "All this time, it's been you."

Chapter 60

Cover You With What?

hvunsa grabbed Theo and threw him to the ground just as the obliterator blast flew past where their heads were moments before.

She looked at Theo as she got up to run, expecting him to be doing the same, but instead, he had taken the primitive Earth weapon and was aiming it toward their attacker. Before she had time to react, he fired, and the projectile from the weapon struck Ricnor's gang member in the head, dropping him to the ground, dead.

"Well done," said Lhvunsa rather amazed at what she had witnessed. "I didn't realize Earth weapons were so accurate, or that you were so well-versed with them."

Theo hadn't moved, he was frozen in place, the weapon still pointed straight ahead.

"Theo? Theo, are you okay?"

He slowly lowered the weapon and looked down.

"I'm the only son of a General in the United States Army. I really didn't have much of a choice but to become an expert with pretty much every weapon there is ... well, Earth weapon anyway. But this is the first time I've ever shot anything other than a paper target."

Lhvunsa knelt down and touched Theo gently on the arm.

"Theo," she said softly, "we need to go. If that one was awake, there are bound to be more. We need to find the others and get to the main bay."

Theo didn't move. Lhvunsa shook him less gently.

"Theo! We have to go!"

Theo stirred finally.

"Yeah ... sure ... you're right. Let's go."

They took off toward the far end of chamber, but got only a few feet before obliterator blasts went off around and above them. They froze and were immediately surrounded by three members of Ricnor's gang, all pointing different, but equally dangerous looking weapons at them.

"That's far enough," said the one in front, who Lhvunsa recognized as one Ricnor had called Cindror. "I don't know exactly what happened, but your pathetic attempt to escape is over. Now, tell your friend to drop his little toy, because the both of you are going back to your cell."

"What did he say?" asked Theo.

Before she could respond they heard the sound of another obliterator blast and the captor to Theo's right exploded into tiny bits of flesh, bone, and goo.

Lhvunsa took advantage of the ensuing chaos by grabbing Cindror's obliterator and pushing it upward, while drawing herself close enough to knee him, quite forcefully, in his most sensitive of areas. As he buckled, she heard Theo's Earth weapon fire again, but she had no time to check on him. She ripped the weapon from Cindror's hand, flipped it around, and used the butt of it against his head, knocking him unconscious.

"What the hell?" she heard Theo and Alcorn say simultaneously, as they each stared at her in disbelief.

"What?" said Lhvunsa.

"Where did you learn to do that?" asked Theo, while the General continued to stare with a dumbfounded look on his face.

Lhvunsa looked at each of them and shrugged her shoulders.

"I don't know," she replied hastily as she ran past them for the doorway Alcorn had just come through. When she got to the door, she turned back to them. "Are you coming or are you going to just stand there?"

Lhvunsa didn't wait for an answer, but turned and ran until she reached cover. Alcorn and Theo were close behind. Both were carrying obliterators.

"Do we have a clear path to the main bay?" asked Lhvunsa, not giving either of the Alcorn men a chance to bring up her fighting skills again.

"Yes, it should be clear, but we can't go just yet," said the General. "We have to give Qilzar some time."

"Time for what?" she asked.

"Qilzar has a ship for us, but he needs some time to disable the other ships so we won't be followed."

"I'll go and help," suggested Theo. "Maybe it will go faster."

Lhvunsa saw the conflict flash across the General's face. Clearly he didn't want his son going alone into danger, but he also knew it was the right thing to do, for all of their sakes. Fortunately, the General was one who knew how to make difficult decisions quickly.

"Good idea, Theo," he said, "We'll hold them off for as long as we can. Be safe, son."

The concern in the General's eyes was clear as he sent his son on his way. She glanced at Theo and saw the same look in his eyes, as he nodded his head and took off for the main bay. In that instant she knew what she had to do—if they survived their escape attempt, that is. Before she could do anything, an obliterator blast sent them both to the floor. More blasts followed.

"How did they get working weapons?" said Lhvunsa, yelling to be heard over the sound of blasts. "I thought my genius husband was supposed to have knocked them all out. And where in the Galaxy is the GCP?"

"If I knew that, we wouldn't be here."

They both took turns returning fire and taking cover.

"I count six of them," yelled Alcorn.

Lhvunsa stood up, fired, and then dropped back down under cover.

"Five," she said, "but there will be more coming."

Alcorn looked impressed.

"Agreed," he said. "We need to move forward. I'll go first, cover me."

Obliterator blasts continued exploding above their heads.

"Cover you with what?" she asked, confused by the Earthling's command.

"Sorry, 'cover' means that you fire as many shots as you can at the enemy, while I advance. Then I'll do the same, so you can advance."

More obliterator blasts, mixed with other types of weapons fire were landing all around them.

"I'm not sure this is such a great idea, General. Why don't we just stay here?"

"Look, there's no time to explain right now. You have to trust that I know what I'm doing."

The weapons' fire seemed to be getting more intense.

"But, I don't ..."

"Look, Lhvunsa, there's no time for this! Just cover me, dammit!"

Alcorn popped up and fired, then took off. Lhvunsa put her shock—and anger at his arrogance, real or not—aside, popped up and began firing. She saw Alcorn reach cover and she dropped back down.

The attacking fire seemed a bit less now, perhaps her 'cover' fire landed once or twice.

"Okay," yelled Alcorn over the din, "when you're ready, you fire once, then start running and I'll cover you."

Lhvunsa took a deep breath, stood up, and fired as she took off for Alcorn's location, firing as often as possible. When she'd covered the space, she dove in next to Alcorn, where he was firing as well.

Their attackers stopped firing.

"Okay General," she said, catching her breath, "now what?"

"Now, we keep them from getting any closer for about ten minutes or so, then we make a break for the main bay."

"They've stopped firing. That's a good sign, isn't it?"

Alcorn looked concerned.

"Not usually," he said. "Stay down."

She watched as he checked his weapon to make sure it had fully recharged before popping up again to fire. He dropped back down immediately as they were bombarded by more weapons fire than Lhvunsa had thought possible. It continued steadily for some time.

"That's what I was afraid of," said Alcorn over the roar of surrounding explosions. "Their reinforcements have arrived."

"So now what, General?"

"We wait."

"We wait? Shouldn't we shoot back?"

"Not now, it's too dangerous. We're safe enough here. Whatever this is made of," he banged on the wall they were hiding behind, "it seems to be strong enough to withstand their weapons."

Lhvunsa wasn't convinced, but she wasn't about to argue.

"If you say so, General."

Weapons fire continued to blast all around them, but Lhvunsa decided it was time to say something anyway.

"General," she said, doing her best to be heard over the blasts, "while we have the time, we need to talk about Theo."

"What about Theo?" asked Alcorn distractedly.

"We need to talk about your relationship with him and how to repair it."

Alcorn stopped what he was doing and looked at Lhvunsa. It wasn't a kind look.

"This is hardly the time ... besides, what do you know about my relationship with my son?"

"Quite a bit, actually. I know that the two of you are a lot more alike than either of you want to admit, and ..."

A particularly large burst battered the wall in front of them, knocking them backward.

"Perhaps we should discuss this later," said Alcorn a sour expression on his face as he moved back to the wall.

"Perhaps, General," said Lhvunsa, following suit, "but I will tell you one more thing first. Theo doesn't think you're nearly as bad of a person as you seem to think you are. But, he won't make the first move. It will be up to you."

Alcorn looked as if he wanted to throw an angry retort her way but couldn't think of one, so he closed his mouth and tried to act as if he was ignoring her.

"Ignoring me won't do you any ..."

"Shhh ...," said Alcorn, hushing her into silence. "They've stopped firing."

They listened to the silence briefly before the General spoke again.

"Follow my lead," he said in as soft a voice as he could manage. "Do exactly as I do."

She nodded her understanding.

Alcorn, jumped to his feet and fired toward the enemy line, then dropped back down.

Lhvunsa did the same, which immediately drew fire back from their adversaries.

"Why, in the name of the Gods, did we do that?" asked Lhvunsa when they dropped back down below the barricade.

"As long as they're firing at us, they're not advancing. When it gets quiet, we're in trouble."

"I see ... I think. How much longer before we can get out of here?"

"I'm ready now. It's just a matter of ..."

Before he could finish his sentence, the wall behind them exploded and a short-range scout, similar to the one that had rescued Ricnor, came flying through, this time with Qilzar at the helm. The ship flew around between them and Ricnor's gang and the door opened.

"Let's go," said Qilzar. "Theo's waiting!"

Lhvunsa and Alcorn jumped in and they were off.

"Thank God you showed up when you did," said Alcorn. "I wasn't sure how we were going to get out of there."

He looked at Lhvunsa.

"Don't say it," he said to her, "just don't."

"Why should I say anything?" said Lhvunsa, "We both know you had no idea what you were ..."

"Hold on," shouted Qilzar, "this part's going to be a bit bumpy."

They banged and bounced their way through a hole that was too small for their scout to fit through, but somehow made it through anyway.

"Whoa, that was close," said Alcorn.

"There wasn't enough time to make the opening any larger," said Qilzar. "We're almost there and it looks like the natives are not far behind us. When we stop, we're going to have to make a quick transition from this vehicle into the larger one. I'll go first since I'm piloting, but hurry in behind me."

"Right with you, boss," said Alcorn.

"Get ready," said Qilzar. "In three, two, one ... Go!"

The scout spun around and stopped, its doors lined up directly with the doors of a Klurdine Remlin. The door popped open, and Qilzar flew out and jumped into the larger ship.

"Lhvunsa, go!" said Alcorn.

Without hesitating, Lhvunsa jumped out of the scout and into the Remlin, with Alcorn close behind.

"Dad, get down!" said Theo, as the younger Alcorn pointed a large weapon that Lhvunsa had never seen before at the scout. Alcorn dove down to the floor and Theo fired, destroying the scout, and, more importantly, blowing the bulk of its wreckage back into the entrance from whence they came, completely blocking the way.

"I hope everyone is in," said Qilzar, as the door closed and the ship lifted off.

"We're in!" came the response from Lhvunsa, Alcorn and Theo all at once.

"Go!" yelled Alcorn.

"Get us out of here!" said Lhvunsa, taking the seat next to Qilzar.

"As you wish, my dear," said Qilzar. "I cannot tell you how glad I am to see you again."

"And you, dear friend," said Lhvunsa, touching his cheek.

"Where shall we go?" asked Qilzar.

"Right now, anywhere but here sounds good to me," said Alcorn, coming up behind them.

"Agreed," said Lhvunsa. "But for now, let's head for Laxor. General, you and Theo had better strap in."

"Right," said Alcorn. "What about the rest of Ricnor's gang? Clearly the cops aren't coming. Are we just going to let them go? Shouldn't we call the police again?"

"Not now, not from this vehicle fleeing the scene," said Lhvunsa. "But, we're not doing nothing General. We're contacting the one you said is the only leader you would ever agree to serve. We're contacting my husband, Gsefx."

Chapter 61

We're Not Out
of the Woods Yet

Gsefx focused on looking straight ahead as they rode the lift back down to the lobby and not at the four Galacticount guards surrounding him. He'd warned Henry not to say a word, as the Earthling's escorts had forced him onto the previous lift. They were probably already in the lobby by now.

Gsefx had really screwed up this time and he knew it. No amount of fast talking or deal making was going to get him out of it, either. The GCP would be waiting for them just outside Galacticount's doors and they would both be arrested for trespassing, slander, and whatever other charges Xtlar, Tsedle, and Pigawitts could come up with. He'd seen it before and had, in fact, participated in it as well, with other former Galacticount employees.

If it were just a disgruntled ex-employee looking to give the boss a piece of their mind, the charges were usually nothing more than a way for the company to flex their muscles and scare the individual into silent submission. But, if Xtlar was truly the one behind all of this, as it now seemed certain, there was little doubt that he and Henry would spend the rest of their lives rotting in a GCP prison on Elnor Prime, or worse.

They reached the lobby and exited the lift. Henry and his guards were waiting by the main doors. Henry looked as if he was about to say something as he approached but Gsefx shook his head to silence him. The less said the better. The guards opened the doors and escorted them outside. At that point, all but one of the guards, an Ilvian named Risplin, turned around and went back inside. Gsefx looked around, but there were no GCP vehicles anywhere in sight.

"My instructions are to escort you to your vehicle and watch you leave Galacticount property," said Risplin, in response to Gsefx's unasked question. "Should you decide not to cooperate in this request, or return to Galacticount property, you will be held by security until the GCP arrives, at which time you will be prosecuted to the full extent of galactic law."

Gsefx was stunned, so much so that he had no idea what to say.

"What are we waiting for?" said Henry, who didn't seem to suffer from the same problem. "Let's get the hell out of here."

As Henry started walking toward the ship, Gsefx snapped out of his daze and hurried to catch up.

"I don't understand this," he said to Henry in a whisper when they were walking side-by-side again. "I expected the GCP to be here to arrest us and take us off to jail."

"Don't question it," said Henry. "Just be thankful and let's get out of here."

"Yes, I think you're right."

They got to Gsefx's vehicle, with Risplin right behind them, watching their every move.

"I need to reach into my pocket so I can unlock my vehicle," said Gsefx, turning back to the guard. "I don't want you to think I'm reaching for anything else."

Risplin nodded. "Proceed."

Gsefx reached into his pocket, touched his control, opened his vehicle, and moved to get in. As he did so, Risplin moved toward him and reached out his hand.

"On a personal note, Et Gsefx, I've taken no pleasure in my duties today. I've always enjoyed working with you and I wish you great fortune ahead."

Gsefx looked at the guard's hand, then shook it.

"Thank you, Risplin. I've enjoyed working with you as well. I will miss Galacticount and all of you who have made it such a great place to be. May great fortune find you as well."

Gsefx climbed into his vehicle and buckled himself in. Henry was already in and ready to go.

"What is it, Gsefx? What's wrong now?"

"Nothing," said Gsefx. "Not here, at least. Let's go."

He fired up his vehicle, gave Risplin a final wave, and flew off. When they were safely off Galacticount property and far enough away to be well out of sight, Gsefx held up a tiny piece of metal and showed it to Henry.

"What is that?" asked Henry.

"You remember how I said it was odd that the GCP wasn't there waiting to haul us away?"

"Yes, but ..."

"Well, it was odder still that Risplin would say goodbye like that," said Gsefx.

"Oh, I don't know," said Henry. "I've had a lot of jobs, and have been escorted off the premises more than once. Just because the head honchos don't like you any more doesn't mean everybody hates you. The security guard is just ..."

"Henry, for someone who sees the truth in things, you're completely missing the point. He wasn't actually saying goodbye. He was giving me this."

"Oh, I see," said Henry, whose face was turning a bright shade of red. "Sorry, I was just trying to help you feel better about losing your job. I know how much it meant to you. That's all."

"Thank you, Henry, I appreciate that," said Gsefx, who now felt bad for mocking his friend. "But right now, I care more about getting my wife and our friends back alive than I do about that job. Let's see what this is all about."

He stuck the metal fragment into a tiny slot on the ship's console and a string of numbers popped up on the vidcon.

"What does that mean?" asked Henry.

"Hmmm ... it's code." said Gsefx, "But not the standard internal Galacticount code. This is different, somehow."

"Can you break it?"

"Break it? Oh, you mean decipher it? Yes, I think so."

Gsefx looked at it, then used the keys on his console to tinker with the numbers before finally leaning back in his seat with a puzzled look on his face.

"I've deciphered it, but it doesn't make any sense."

"What does it say?"

"Wait 30 ebyts, then call. Xtlar."

"Xtlar?" asked Henry. "Isn't he the one who just had us thrown out? The one who was most definitely lying about or hiding something?"

"Yes, the very same."

"So what are we going to do?"

Gsefx checked the time.

"It's already been nearly ten ebyts," he said. "We're going to wait another twenty and then call him. In the meantime ..."

He was interrupted by an incoming call on the vidcon.

"Is that him calling you?" said Henry. "I thought he wanted us to wait."

"He does," said Gsefx. "This isn't him. I don't recognize the number." He looked at Henry. "Sit back, out of view and stay quiet. If this is someone who doesn't know about you, I'd like to keep it that way.

Henry nodded in agreement and moved as far away from the vidcon as he could. Once his friend was out of range, Gsefx pressed the answer key.

"Hello," he said.

"Hello to you, my love," replied his beautiful Lhvunsa, who appeared to be doing all she could to contain herself.

"Lhvunsa! You're safe! Thank the Gods!"

"Yes, thank the Gods, and you, General Alcorn, his son Theo, and, of course, our dear friend Qilzar."

"You're all there? And everyone is okay? So the plan worked? Tell me everything."

"Yes, my darling, I will, but let me just look at you for a moment. The General told me that you'd be okay, that you were better prepared than I might have thought, but I still worried for you. Did you find out who is behind it all? Was it Xtlar, as Qilzar and I suspected?"

Gsefx's joy at seeing his wife slipped away suddenly.

"What? You suspected all along it was Xtlar? How did you ... what made you ... what do you mean?"

Lhvunsa held her hand up to silence him.

"Explanations can wait until we are together again. Things did not go completely as planned, and while we're safe for the moment, we won't be for long unless we take immediate action."

Gsefx set his jaw and steeled himself for what was to come next.

"Tell me," he said.

"The GCP never showed and Ricnor's gang regained consciousness before we realized it. They also found a stash of weapons that were unaffected by what you did. We barely escaped but we managed to disable all of their vehicles. At least the ones in the local area. But unless the GCP arrives soon, they will escape."

"I'll take care of it," said Gsefx, "just as soon as we finish here."

"There's one more thing," said Lhvunsa. "Ricnor escaped."

Gsefx tried not to react, but it was too much to keep in.

"By the Gods, how? He should have been rendered unconscious like everyone else."

"Yes, my love, he should have but he wasn't. We almost had him but he had help, and, well, there wasn't anything we could do to stop him."

This isn't Lhvunsa's fault, he thought. *If anything, it's yours. The whole plan had been a long shot anyway, so don't go blaming her just because things didn't go as planned.*

"No, of course there wasn't," he said aloud, trying not to let his wife see his disappointment and unease. "I'm just happy that you're all safe. We'll figure a way out of this, I'm sure of that. We still have half the paintings, which means we still have negotiating power. Now, in the meantime, we must figure out a safe place to meet."

"I've been thinking about that," said Lhvunsa. "How about where we met after our last visit to Earth?"

"Yes, excellent choice. We can be there in about three sars. I can't wait to hold you in my arms again."

Lhvunsa smiled at him. "I will see you soon, my love."

Gsefx watched as she reached toward her screen, pressed a button, and then disappeared from view. He sat motionless, thinking of how long it had been since he'd last held her in his arms. His thoughts scattered when a hand touched his shoulder.

"Hey, are you still with me?" asked Henry. "We're not out of the woods yet. You still need to call that Xtlar guy."

Gsefx shook off the daydream of his beautiful wife and of holding her in his arms once again. Henry was right, there was still a lot to be done.

"Yes, but first I need to call the GCP."

"The police? Are you nuts? We just got thrown out of your building, and you said yourself that you were surprised they weren't waiting there to haul us away."

"But they weren't and we need to make sure Ricnor's gang doesn't escape."

"Call this Xtlar guy first. Find out what his involvement is in all of this. It won't take long to figure out, then we'll call the cops."

Gsefx thought about it, but couldn't decide what to do. His instincts told him to trust Henry and call Xtlar, but his logical side told him the clock was ticking and that he needed to call the GCP now or Ricnor's gang would get away, and they would all be doomed.

"Gsefx," said Henry softly, "you brought me on this little adventure of yours for a reason. For some strange reason, you trust my ability to see the truth in people, or beings, for lack of a better word, even though it's an ability I've never claimed to have. But now that I'm here, trust my instincts, not just about people or beings, but about situations too. Call Xtlar, it's the right move."

Gsefx nodded in agreement, reached over to the vidcon and punched in the number to Xtlar's direct line. It took only a moment before Xtlar's image appeared on the screen.

"You're late," said the Fweurlian. "I wasn't sure you'd call at all, but I'm glad you did."

"I wasn't sure I was going to call either, knowing what I know," said Gsefx. "Tell me, sir, how long have you been working with Ricnor and his gang?"

"Ricnor? You mean the Ricnor, of the Ricnor Criminal Gang? Gsefx, have you completely lost your mind?"

"Don't play dumb with me, Xtlar, you've been in on this from the beginning, otherwise you wouldn't have had Galacticount security throw us out before I could get to the source, which as it turns out was you all along."

"Gsefx, what in the name of the Gods are you talking about? I had you thrown out because it appeared you had falsified those files in an attempt to frame Pigawitts for something he clearly hadn't done. I was trying to save you from yourself, and get you out of there before things went too far and you found yourself in a corner with no way out."

Gsefx started to say something, but Henry grabbed his arm.

"Gsefx, he's telling the truth," he said. "He's not involved with Ricnor."

"Gsefx, what in the name of the Gods is going on with you?" said Xtlar.

Gsefx rubbed his eyes and let out a long, deep sigh.

"It's a long story, sir, but the short version is that Ricnor kidnapped my wife, and Qilzar and someone at Galacticount is involved."

"By the Gods!" said Xtlar, a look of shock on his face, which turned to horror as the depth of the situation sunk in. "Oh Gods, Gsefx, I am sorry. Lhvunsa and Qilzar both? And you thought I was involved ... no ... you thought Pigawitts ... but surely you could tell that the files had been falsified? A cursory look wouldn't reveal anything, but anyone with your skills would have looked deeper and easily found the ..."

"I didn't look at the files at all," said Gsefx, his heart sinking as he realized who had betrayed him. "I trusted the one who gave them to me, and he knew it. He knew I wouldn't look at them."

"Who?" asked Xtlar. "Who gave you those files, Gsefx?"

Gsefx felt his heart breaking as he revealed the name of the traitor.

"It was Planvc. It's been Planvc all along."

"Planvc?" said Xtlar. "I find that hard to believe. I can't imagine he'd even have a job if you hadn't been watching out for him all of these turns."

"I've watched out for him, Xtlar, because he has always been unfairly discriminated against simply for not being a native of our galaxy. Add to that his lack of social graces or political savvy, and yes, he was someone who needed a friend. Put all that aside and you'll find that Planvc is a brilliant accountant, and certainly intellectually sharp enough to pull this off.

Especially when it's the last thing his best friend would ever suspect of him."

If Xtlar still had his doubts, he didn't voice them. His reply was, instead, much softer and more compassionate.

"I'm sorry, Gsefx," he said. "I know you valued his friendship. Even so, I must send security to pick him up."

"He's already gone," replied Gsefx. "I told him to go before I came up and interrupted your meeting."

Xtlar let out what seemed to be an exasperated sigh. "Very well, I'll contact the GCP and have them start looking for him."

"Thank you, Xtlar," said Gsefx. "And, I'd like to apologize for accusing you of being in league with Ricnor. I won't make any excuses, except to say that the last several rotations have been more than a bit stressful."

"No need to apologize, my dear boy. Is there any word on Lhvunsa and Qilzar? Is there anything I can do to help?"

"Oh yes, it seems I left the best part of the story out. With some assistance from our Earthing friends, they've managed to escape. We're on our way to meet up with them now."

"Thank the Gods," said Xtlar. "That is good news."

"Have him tell the cops about Ricnor's gang," said Henry softly as he nudged Gsefx.

"What was that?" said Xtlar.

"Oh yes," said Gsefx. "I don't seem to be thinking very clearly at the moment. Perhaps because I haven't slept in several rotations. All that aside, during the escape, Lhvunsa, Qilzar, and our Earthling friends managed to trap most of Ricnor's gang in their headquarters on the planet Mindaal. Unfortunately, the call that was supposed to go to the GCP never made it. Since you're calling them anyway, can you have the GCP dispatch some units to Mindaal to pick up Ricnor's gang before they find a way to escape?"

Xtlar stared back at the screen with a dumbfounded look on his face.

"Gsefx," he said, "you're telling me that over the past few rotations, rather than come to work as you were supposed to, you conspired with a handful of beings from a primitive planet, a planet that's not even part of the Galactic Community, to not only rescue your wife and supervisor, but to also capture the most notorious criminal gang in the entire galaxy. Is that about right?"

"Well," said Gsefx, "yes sir, that's about right. Although, we still haven't captured Ricnor yet. Sir, I know I'm out of a job, but if you give me another chance, I know we can still meet the deadline on the Pigawitts account."

Xtlar could do nothing but laugh at this. The more he tried to stop, the harder he laughed. Soon, Gsefx and Henry had joined him, until all three were laughing, although while Xtlar's was a jovial, laugh of pleasure, Gsefx and Henry were laughing more out of general hysteria than anything else.

"Gsefx, my dear boy," said Xtlar when he'd finally gained the ability to speak again, "in the first place, you've never lost your job. If you recall, I may have had you escorted from the building, but I never fired you. Secondly, anyone who can do what you've just done is someone I want to work with for as long as I possibly can. Go and see your wife and Qilzar, and come back when you're ready. In the meantime, I'll make sure the GCP gets out to Mindaal and starts looking for Planvc."

"Thank you, sir, for everything," said Gsefx, breathing a sigh of relief for the first time in a very long while."

Xtlar nodded, then reached forward and disconnected from his vidcon.

Gsefx took a deep breath, stretched as best he could within the confines of his cramped vehicle and looked over at Henry.

"Thank you for insisting we call Xtlar," he said. "I haven't felt this much at peace in a long time."

"Hey, that's what I'm here for," said Henry with a smile.

"I'm going to put us on auto-pilot and go to sleep for a while, if that's okay with you. It's been a very long time."

"Of course. I can't think of anyone who deserves some rest more than you do."

"Thank you, Henry."

"Gsefx?"

"Yes?"

"I'm sorry about your friend."

"Yeah, me too."

Chapter 62

Our Business is Unfinished

Lhvunsa scanned the horizon for her husband's vehicle from the front seat of the ship that, up until a few sars ago, belonged to the most infamous criminal in the galaxy. They had been parked for the past thirty ebyts at the refueling hub and restaurant where they were to meet Gsefx and the Earthling artist, Henry. Lhvunsa was excited to see her husband again, to hold him in her arms and feel his lips against hers, but she was also a bit apprehensive. A lot had happened over these past few rotations, and neither of them were the same as they were when they were last together.

Will we be okay? She thought. *Will our relationship be as good as it was before? How do we pick up and go forward after so much has happened?*

And there was still the secret she had kept from him. The violence she never thought herself capable of had now become second nature. Since her capture and rescue by General Alcorn, she had become as much a soldier as she had ever been an architect. Moreover, she was shocked by how quickly she had made the transformation. The self-defense training had been more about helping her feel better about the break-in than anything else. She'd never really expected to put what she'd learned into practice. But circumstances had changed and here she was, someone who was just as comfortable with an obliterator in her hand as she was with any of her drawing tools.

But there was a larger issue than all of that. She had taken life from the universe, which meant she could never bring life into it. While that bothered her, she had no regrets over the lives she'd taken. From the moment she had first held an obliterator in her hands at the start of her weapons training, she knew this outcome was a possibility. Whether or not she was aware of it, she had prepared herself for this eventuality. Had she not taken the action she had at Ricnor's headquarters, they would all be dead or still imprisoned in Ricnor's cells—herself, Qilzar, General Alcorn and Theo. It had taken all of them, working together, to escape, and she would not mourn the deaths of a few violent criminals, even though the personal cost she had to pay was high.

I just hope Gsefx will ... well ... in truth, I'm not sure what I'm hoping for, she thought, *other than that we will find a way to be okay.*

A noise from the rear seat shook her from her thoughts. It was the General. Apparently some Earthlings didn't breathe properly when they slept and made sounds unlike anything she'd ever heard before.

"What a horrible sound he makes, don't you think?" said Qilzar, who sat next to her in the pilot's seat. "I can't imagine how anyone gets any sleep around someone who makes that kind of noise."

"It's called snoring, and it's not so bad," said Lhvunsa, concealing her true feelings about the horrific sounds. "The General and his son are good souls. We wouldn't be here without them."

"True enough," said Qilzar, an uncharacteristic smile on his face. "I like them both as well. And he's right, you know. The General, I mean."

Lhvunsa gave Qilzar a curious look. "About what, exactly?"

"About Gsefx. About him being the kind of natural leader everyone wants to follow. If you remember, I said as much not so long ago, which is why I was always so jealous of him. But all of that's behind us now. Lhvunsa, after what we've been through, you need to know that while I may be his supervisor at work, I would follow him anywhere—and I would follow you, as well."

Lhvunsa reached over and took Qilzar's hand. "Thank you, Qilzar. That means more than you know."

Qilzar squeezed her hand and smiled, then seemed to catch something out of the corner of his eye.

"Ah, they're here," he said, turning fully toward the front. "Shall I wake our friends?"

"Not just yet," said Lhvunsa, standing and moving toward the door. She bent down and gave Qilzar a kiss on the cheek. "Give me a moment with my husband, first."

"Of course, my dear."

Lhvunsa opened the vehicle door and stepped outside just in time to watch Gsefx and his Earthling companion land their ship. In a span of time that at once seemed to pass by in a flash and last forever, Gsefx was in her arms and all that had happened over the past several rotations just melted away, for they were together once again. Later, when she would reflect back on this moment, Lhvunsa would try to recall how long they embraced, but the only memory that would ever be clear to her was how the entire galaxy paused, as she and Gsefx stood at its center. As they held one another, she knew, beyond any doubt, that their relationship would be just fine, no matter what the galaxy might throw at them. She could have stayed in that moment forever, and would have, gladly, but they were interrupted by the sound of someone shuffling around close by.

"As much as I hate to break up your reunion," said the voice attached to the shuffling, "I think we're being waved in."

Against her every desire, Lhvunsa pulled her body away from Gsefx, kissed him one last time, then looked toward the speaker.

"And you must be Henry," she said, reaching out her hand, "my husband's newest best friend, and the galaxy's foremost artist."

"At your service, ma'am," said Henry gently taking her hand and nodding. He released her hand and pointed at Lhvunsa's ship. "But I really think they want us to get inside."

Lhvunsa looked back up to see Qilzar, Alcorn, and Theo motioning for them to come back inside the ship.

"I guess we'd better go," said Lhvunsa, a conspiratorial smile forming on her lips.

"After you, my darling," said Gsefx.

Lhvunsa climbed back up into the ship first and looked around.

"What's going on?" she asked. "Why the rush for us to get back into the ship?"

"Shhh ... listen," said Qilzar, working some controls on the console, as the others followed close behind and began reuniting with one another. "I was checking to see if there had been any news reports and, well, see for yourself ..."

The vidcon lit up with a news broadcast.

> *Repeating the breaking news out of Mindaal, the GCP is reporting that in a daring raid on what was*

believed to be the headquarters of the infamous Ricnor Gang, it has apprehended more than three hundred suspects. Along with the suspects, the GCP has also discovered an unspecified number of warehouses of merchandise believed to be stolen, as well as an untold number of weapons and vehicles. Said one GCP official, "We are just scratching the surface of what's here. It could be several rotations before we have a total of just how much stolen merchandise and other items we're going to find." Officials said this raid came after nearly a full turn of deep undercover work. They also would not comment on if Ricnor himself was among the suspects apprehended.

"Bastards!" spat a clearly disgusted Alcorn. "I guess it doesn't matter how evolved you get, politicians never change. They let someone else do the work and then they take the credit."

"Now, General," said Lhvunsa, attempting to articulate the voice of reason, "would you prefer they had told the truth? That an accountant, his wife, his boss, and three Earthlings, who, in the course of fighting for their lives, also just happened to bring down the Ricnor Gang?"

"I don't know," said Henry, "sounds like a pretty compelling story to me. The truth usually is."

"It makes no difference," said Qilzar with a wave of his hand. "What's done is done and we need to plan our next step."

"As usual, Qilzar, you are correct," said Alcorn. "I will let it go. But before we plan our next step, how about something to eat. I'm famished, and even though I don't speak your language,

I'm pretty sure that's a restaurant over there. So what do you say we go and grab a bite?"

"We should probably stay out of sight," said Qilzar. "Ricnor is still out there somewhere and who knows what kind of spy network he has. We still don't know who his boss is."

"Actually we do," said Gsefx quietly.

"We do?" Asked said Qilzar, turning toward Gsefx. "Who is it?"

"Was it that Pigawitts fella, like you thought?" asked Alcorn.

Lhvunsa watched the pained look on her husband's face grow deeper as he struggled to answer.

"Gsefx, what's wrong?" she asked. "Who is Ricnor's boss?"

"It's Planvc," he said in a voice barely above a whisper. "It's been Planvc all along. All this time, he's acted as though he was my best friend, all the while betraying me, betraying us, and we had no idea what he was doing."

"Planvc?" said Qilzar. "That can't be. He's not ..."

Lhvunsa, never taking her eyes from her husband, reached over and silenced the Dremin with a gentle touch to his arm.

"It was him, Qilzar," said Gsefx, "there's no room for doubt ... and I will say no more about it for now, except that we needn't worry about hiding from him. Xtlar has the GCP looking for him and I doubt he'll be too concerned with us."

Gsefx looked over at Qilzar.

"However, Qilzar is correct that we should keep a low profile. Would you and Theo mind going into the restaurant and bringing back some food for us?"

Qilzar seemed surprised, first by the support and second by the request. He quickly glanced at Lhvunsa, who smiled at him and nodded her approval.

"Yes, Gsefx, of course," he said, rising from the pilot's seat and moving toward the door. "Come along, Theo. I apologize that this will be your first introduction to intergalactic cuisine, as it's far from the best we have to offer, but I'm sure we can find something everyone will enjoy."

As Qilzar and Theo left the ship, Gsefx took the pilot's seat. Lhvunsa sat down next to him and overheard Henry ask Alcorn something about 'finding his truth' as they settled in toward the rear of the ship, but she gave them little attention. She was too concerned about her husband.

"I can't believe Planvc could do this to us, to you," said Gsefx, as she took his hand. "He wasn't just my friend, he was my closest friend. I trusted him. I just can't believe he could betray us like this. More than that, I can't believe he fooled me so thoroughly. I didn't see any of it coming."

"I know how hard this must be for you, my love," said Lhvunsa. "You were always so close to him, but it wasn't your fault. He fooled everyone. He fooled all of us."

"That's no excuse, and you of all people, Lhvunsa, should know it. But that doesn't even matter. What I really don't understand is why. Why would he do this to us? To me?"

Lhvunsa took a deep breath and squeezed his hand. She hated what she was going to have to say next, but Gsefx needed to hear it, and she was the only one who could say it to him.

"Gsefx, you must listen to me very carefully now," she said. "You are a kind, wonderful, caring soul who wants to see the best in everyone around you. That's one of the things I love about you, but it also tends to blind you to the faults in others."

Gsefx started to speak, but Lhvunsa silenced him with a gentle, green finger to his lips.

"Please, let me finish. Planvc would have never been a suspect in my mind, had I been given a thousand turns to consider all of the possibilities. But looking back in hindsight, it does make a certain kind of sense. Gsefx, even though you have chosen not to see it, Planvc has a jealous streak within him and you have certain innate abilities he will never possess. I can see how that would send him spiraling in the direction it did."

Lhvunsa put her arms around her husband.

"I know you're upset, my love, but there's also another possibility for his actions that you may not want to consider. Even so, we cannot overlook anything at this point."

"What does that mean?" asked Gsefx, pulling away from her embrace.

"I know this sounds prejudiced, but Planvc is originally from the Nerrill Galaxy, which has never been on what we'd consider friendly terms with the Galactic Community."

"Oh, by the Gods, Lhvunsa, don't tell me you think this is politically motivated, because it's not. Planvc is a criminal, plain and simple, and he betrayed both of us."

Lhvunsa started to respond, but Gsefx raised his hand to stop her. Clearly she'd hit a sensitive point. If Planvc's motives were political, then he'd been deceiving Gsefx from the very beginning, and that would be more difficult to accept than any mere betrayal. Her husband turned away from her to look out the window. After some time, Lhvunsa reached over and squeezed his arm.

"Gsefx, tell me what you're thinking ..."

He turned to face her.

"What abilities?" he asked.

"What? What do you mean?"

"You said I had certain 'innate abilities.' What does that mean?"

Lhvunsa smiled at her husband and squeezed his arm again.

"One of your great charms, my love, is your naiveté, although I wouldn't classify that, specifically, as an ability."

"What does that mean, exactly?"

"It means that you don't even see how amazing you truly are," she said as she leaned over and kissed him.

"Why don't you enlighten me," said Gsefx, his face as serious as she'd ever seen him. She could tell he wasn't angry with her, but he wasn't exactly seeing the lighter side of it as she was.

Lhvunsa removed her hands and sat back in her chair.

"The last several rotations, we've both experienced some pretty extreme circumstances, wouldn't you agree?" she asked.

"Yes," said Gsefx with a slight nod of his head.

"In my case," continued Lhvunsa, "I've spent them with three individuals who would follow you anywhere and do anything you asked of them, just because you are who you are. Gsefx, you are a natural leader who gains the trust of others with barely more than a word or two. Moreover, you are brilliant in ways most others can't even fathom. You're able to look at something, hear something, or read about something and you automatically understand it."

"That's not true, I don't understand everything that easily. And that whole leadership thing isn't true at all. You're just over-exaggerating because you love me."

Lhvunsa frowned and looked away.

"I do love you, my darling," she said when she turned back to face him, "but when have you ever known me to over-exaggerate?

Stop. Don't answer, I'm not finished. Gsefx, think about it. Look back there at General Alcorn and Henry. Do you think they'd be here at all if they weren't ready to follow wherever you lead? What about Theo, Qilzar, or even Xtlar? Gsefx, they are all with you. Just think about that. And while you're at it, think about what you've accomplished over the past several rotations. You stood up to the galaxy's most dangerous criminal and won. Gsefx, you took down his whole organization. You did that."

"I had some help. Besides, I was just trying to rescue my wife and take care of my family."

"Yes, you had help, but it was your plan, Gsefx. You stood up to Ricnor, and using your intellect and leadership abilities, you beat him. You are our leader, Gsefx, and at some point you have to start believing in yourself the same way everyone around you believes in you."

Gsefx didn't answer, but looked back out the window.

"It's a lot to think about," he said finally.

"I know it is, my darling."

Now is as good a time as any, I suppose, she thought, taking a deep breath to steel herself for what she had to do next.

"Gsefx, as much as I hate to add more to the list of things for you to deal with, there's one more thing we need to discuss ..."

Lhvunsa was interrupted by an incoming call on the vidcon.

"I don't recognize that number, do you?" she asked.

"No." he said. "Sit back away from the screen."

Lhvunsa moved back and Gsefx answered the call. Ricnor's image appeared on the screen.

"Ahhh ... my friend, the Accountant," he said, being sure to show all of his teeth in the process. "It's good to see you again. I believe we still have some unfinished business."

"Yes, I believe our business is unfinished," said Gsefx. "You have half of my paintings and I want them back."

"Half of your paintings? I see you're still misinterpreting things, as you've been doing from the start. But, before we go much further, is General Alcorn with you? I believe he might be interested in what we have to say to one another."

"I'm here," said Alcorn, who'd come up from behind without Lhvunsa noticing. "What do you want?"

"It's not what I want, General," said Ricnor, "it's what you want ..."

He stepped out of view of the vidcon. When he came back, he wasn't alone. He had a female hostage and was holding his spike to her throat.

"Janny!" cried Alcorn.

"It's very simple, really," said Ricnor. "I tried it once with the accountant, and that didn't work out so well. So, we're going to try this again. You bring the other half of the paintings and I'll give you your wife back, General. An effortless exchange. We each get what we want and then we'll go our separate ways."

Gsefx started to say something, but Alcorn stopped him.

"When and where?" he said.

"Dolnarma. In three sars."

"Wait," said Gsefx. "I don't trust your calculations. I'm checking the distance."

"As you wish," said Ricnor.

Lhvunsa was already calculating the time it would take to reach Dolnarma.

"We can be there in two-and-a-half," she said.

"We'll be there," said Gsefx.

"Call when you get within thirty ebyts and I'll give you instructions on how to reach the exchange location."

Ricnor disconnected before Alcorn could talk to Janny, or get any further information from him.

Lhvunsa squeezed Gsefx's hand and nodded to him in confirmation when he looked her way.

Gsefx stood up and took the General by the arm.

"I promise you, General, we will get her back safely," he said.

"Thank you, Gsefx, I appreciate it, but it's not necessary ..."

"General, there's no time for discussion. Henry, go and get Qilzar and Theo. We'll connect the vehicles and make ready to go. Quickly now, we've no time to waste."

Chapter 63

I've Made a Mess of Things

In the back of his mind, it had always been one of Alcorn's greatest fears that someone would endanger his family, and then attempt to use them to compromise his position. His fear of this happening increased proportionately with his climb up through the ranks. His only miscalculation was in assuming the coward behind such an act would actually be from somewhere on planet Earth.

Janny.

She had always been his greatest strength. Whenever he needed someone to turn to, to lean on, or more often than not, someone to stand up to him and tell him when he was wrong, she was the one who was always there for him. She was the strength behind the four stars on his shoulders.

Now, in this critical moment, he would not allow her to become his weakness—for her sake, not for his. She would never be able to bear it, knowing that she caused his downfall, even if it were beyond her control, as it was now. No, for her sake, he couldn't relent, nor let his guard down, not even for a second. But there was someone else to think about. He and Janny weren't the only family members involved.

"General, may I have a word with you?" It was Lhvunsa. He was so deep in his thoughts he hadn't heard her approach.

"Of course," he said, as she took the seat next to him. "What's on your mind?"

"Reconciliation, General, reconciliation between you and your son."

Alcorn looked at Lhvunsa, then looked away.

"Yeah, after what you said back at Ricnor's headquarters, I kinda thought that might be the case. You wanna hear something funny? I've been thinking about it too."

"That's wonderful," said Lhvunsa. "So you'll talk to Theo, then?"

"I didn't say that."

Alcorn sighed. It was the sigh of a man carrying a heavy load, one he'd carried for far too long a time, but couldn't yet put down. He looked back at Lhvunsa, even though the sight of her expectations pained him even more.

"There's too much you don't understand, Lhvunsa. I've caused too much pain and resentment in Theo for one conversation to magically make it all better."

"You're wrong about that General," said the green-skinned beauty. "I may not understand everything, but I do know that much."

Alcorn shook his head.

"You may be right, but even so, it wouldn't matter. Janny's kidnapping is my fault. Whether it was Ricnor or someone on Earth, it was bound to happen at some point and when it did, it was always going to be my fault. But that's not the worst of it. What I have to do next is something Theo will never forgive me for. It's better he think badly of me now, then to think well of me, possibly even forgive me, and then have it all ripped away."

Lhvunsa nodded her head slowly, then without a word, stood up and started to walk away. Alcorn turned back to his thoughts and didn't notice when she turned right back around and was now standing right next to him. She bent over and spoke into his ear in a voice as soft as it was scornful.

"You may be right about some things, General," she said, "but here's something you don't know. Something you can't know, and that's what it feels like to have Ricnor squeezing you so tight with one arm that you can barely breathe, while he's holding that spike of his at your throat with the other. All the while, using you to threaten the people you love into doing things they otherwise wouldn't even consider. That's what your Janny is feeling right now, General. That's what I know."

Alcorn turned around to look at the striking female, whose face was inches from his own. Her face a frozen glare, daring him to challenge her. Physically, she looked nothing like the woman he loved, but he clearly recognized his wife in the scolding he'd just received. He also recognized when he was on the wrong side of a losing argument.

"Oh for love of God," he said, "sit down before you make a scene and Theo sees you."

"If you think that's making a scene," said Lhvunsa, "you have no idea what I'm capable of, General."

"Of that, I have no doubt," said Alcorn, his face a full-on frown. He looked away for a moment, then turned back to Lhvunsa, this time examining her much more closely, as if he were trying to analyze her right down to her DNA.

"What in the galaxy are you looking at?" she asked, even more irritation in her voice.

"I'm trying to figure out whether or not you're really a non-terrestrial," said Alcorn, "because you sound an awful lot like a certain Earth woman I'm married to."

Lhvunsa didn't flinch, nor even hesitate.

"I don't care what you think of me, General, nor do I care about all that has gone on between you and Theo. What I do care about is what your wife is going to see and feel when we show up to face Ricnor. Will she see a father and son divided or united? As someone who has been where she is now, I promise you, it will make all the difference." She stood up, as if to leave, but looked at him with eyes that pierced straight into his soul. "Now, go and talk to your son."

"Is that an order, ma'am?"

"General, I'm not sure whether or not you noticed just how good my English is ..."

"Yes, as a matter of fact, I have," said Alcorn. "But what does that have to do with anything?"

"In order to properly speak a language, one must understand the culture in which it's spoken. To that end, I've studied your culture as well as your language, and in so doing, I found that when a woman gives a man a directive, such as I've just given you, there are only two words that are considered to be an acceptable answer."

"I'm all ears," said the General.

"I believe the response you're looking for General, is 'Yes, dear.'"

Alcorn laughed out loud in spite of himself and the horrific situation he and his family were in.

He stood up and bowed deeply to the lady with three arms and green skin who, despite their obvious physical differences, still, somehow, reminded him of his beloved Janny.

"Yes, dear," he said, with a smile.

As Lhvunsa made her way back to her husband's side, Alcorn straightened back up and watched, catching Gsefx watching him. Alcorn could feel the empathy radiating from the gaze of the being he'd given his allegiance to. Gsefx knew what he was going through because he'd experienced it himself. Alcorn silently nodded his acknowledgement, then turned to find his son.

Theo was as far back in the corner of the ship as you could get, hunched over with his back to everyone. Alcorn didn't acknowledge Henry and Qilzar as he made his way past them, but instead kept his gaze focused straight ahead. He overheard Henry, who was now wearing the translator, tell the Dremin that the General and his son needed some privacy. Apparently the gulf between he and Theo was more obvious than he thought. Even so, he was grateful to Henry for the consideration.

He stood and looked at Theo for a minute, his heart beating so fast he felt it might explode from his chest at any moment. A part of him hoped it would and save him from what he knew he had to do. Knowing all too well that's not how life worked, he finally moved forward and sat down next to his son. There was no acknowledgement. No sign that Theo even knew he was there.

"Theo?" said Alcorn, putting his hand on his son's shoulder.

"Don't worry, Dad, I'll pull myself together and be the good soldier you want me to be by the time we get there."

Dear God, thought Alcorn, *what have I done to my child?*

"No, Theo," he said, pulling his hand back as if he'd been bitten, "that's not what I came to say." He took a deep breath and then let it out. "It's not at all what I came to say."

"Then say whatever it is you have to say and get it over with."

Alcorn looked again at his son, suddenly unable to speak. The words he'd prepared had all left his mind. There was nothing he could say that would make things right. He wished with everything in him that he was somewhere else.

"Well," said Theo, "are you going to say anything, or just give me that dumb stare of yours? Because, honestly Dad, if that's all you've got, then I'd just as soon you leave now."

Alcorn stood up and started to walk away. *It's better this way,* he told himself. It's what he always told himself.

"Yep, that's what I thought," said Theo, the scorn in his voice unmistakable.

Alcorn stopped. *What am I doing? Right or wrong, good or bad, this boy needs to hear the truth. For his own sake, he needs to know.* He turned back to his son.

"Theo, I'd like to tell you that I'm sorry for everything I've done. That all of this is my fault. I'd like to ask if there's any way that you could forgive me. But, true as all of it may be, that's too simple, too much of a trivialization of everything that's happened between us, and I won't insult you by going there."

Theo remained hunched over and silent. Alcorn stepped back over to the seat next to his son and sat down.

"So what I will tell you is this, a story I don't think I've ever had the guts to tell you. We all have certain memories burned into our brains, certain events, both good and bad, that we will never, ever forget. My greatest memory, the best moment of my life, is the moment you were born and holding you in my arms, realizing you were my son and just how much I loved you."

"I guess it's pretty much been all downhill from there, hasn't it, Dad?" Theo emphasized the 'Dad,' twisting the dagger just a little deeper.

He's not going to make this easy, thought Alcorn. *That's okay, I don't deserve easy.*

"I've been disappointing you ever since," said Theo.

"I'll agree that it's been downhill with us, all right," said Alcorn, "but not because of anything you've done. Contrary to what I've led you to believe, Theo, you've never disappointed me. I'm the one who's been a disappointment."

Theo looked up finally.

"You sure could've fooled me."

He started to get up.

"Theo, don't go. Please? I know I don't deserve it, but please let me finish before you give up on me completely. After that, if you never speak to me again, I promise I'll understand and I won't bother you again."

Theo sat back down.

"I'll listen," he said, "but no matter what you say, if anything happens to Mom, we're through."

Alcorn nodded his understanding, but couldn't speak for the lump in his throat. If anything happened to Janny, he wasn't sure he could bear losing Theo too. But that would have to wait for now.

"As I was saying," he said, when he regained his composure, "as much as I tried in the beginning to make it about you, to get you to be more like me and less like your mother, the more

I realized it was my own insecurities rather than anything you'd done. Theo, you were a child for God's sake, how could it have been your fault?"

"You sure made me feel like it was my fault. I always seemed to fall short of your expectations somehow."

Alcorn's heart was breaking, because he knew it was true.

"I know," he choked out, tears falling down his cheek. "For that I'll be never stop being ashamed."

Theo wasn't finished, he was on a roll now and wasn't going to let the opportunity pass him by.

"But then after a while, as if being disappointed in me wasn't enough, you decided to simply ignore me, like I wasn't even worth your time."

No! Alcorn wanted to say. *No, that's not why I did what I did!* But he couldn't speak, not even a word, for he was openly crying now, the guilt and shame from the pain he'd inflicted on his son was too much to bear. This wasn't going at all as he'd planned.

"Don't expect any sympathy from me, old man. You don't know how many times I cried myself to sleep because of you."

Theo stood up to walk away, but paused to look down at what Alcorn knew had to be a pathetic sight.

"You know," said Theo, "I was telling Lhvunsa just a bit ago that I wasn't nearly as angry with you as I acted, that it had become more of a habit than anything. But once I heard what had happened to Mom, I realized that I was just kidding myself. She's the only one who has ever truly loved and accepted me for who I am. You've certainly never cared much for me, at least you've never shown it, and if there's one thing I've learned from you, it's how to return the feeling, or in your case, lack of feeling."

Alcorn grabbed at Theo's hand.

"Wait, Theo, wait."

"Why should I? Give me one good reason why I should give a damn whether you live or die or just fade away?"

"Because you're right," said Alcorn standing up to face his son, not bothering to wipe the tears away. "You're right to hate me. You're right not to give a damn about whether I live or die, but you're not right about the why, and that's important—not to me, it's important to you. And, it's important to your mother. So please, just sit down and listen."

Theo's glare seemed to diminish, but only by a degree or two. He was still hot and Alcorn knew he had every right to be, but he also knew that Theo had to understand the why behind the actions. Theo had to understand beyond the intellectual, that what Alcorn had done to him had nothing to do with anything Theo had or hadn't done. He had to fully grasp that everything Alcorn did, all of the mistakes he had made, were all of his own doing, and not because of any flaws or shortcomings in Theo's personality.

He also needed Theo to know that no matter how badly he'd screwed up, it was out of incompetency, not indifference. He had to know, but not for Alcorn's sake. He wasn't seeking redemption, nor was he attempting to salvage a relationship that was broken beyond repair. He knew that ship had long since sailed. This was for Theo's sake. His son had to truly understand his own value and worth or, successful as he may be, he would never escape the demons that haunted him. And Theo could never do that as long as he held on to his destructive bitterness toward dear ol' Dad.

"Okay Dad, tell me why that's so damn important."

Alcorn noticed that Theo hadn't sat back down. He nodded his head up and down slowly, trying to gather his thoughts.

"Theo, do you remember when you were eight and I tried to take you and your friends to the zoo?"

"When something leaves that deep of a scar, it's kind of hard to forget," said Theo.

"Do you remember other events that went similarly?"

Theo looked at Alcorn.

"That's kinda the central theme of what we're talking about here, isn't it?" Anger and resentment dripping from every word.

"Yes, but think about it, Theo. You said a minute ago, that when you stopped disappointing me, I simply ignored you and walked away. But, if you think about that trip to the zoo and the other disasters, you might remember that I tried. You may not have been able to see it at the time, but I was trying to figure out how to be in your life without hurting you."

"Don't try and justify yourself to me, now, after all these years. You don't get to do that."

"I'm not justifying myself, Theo. I know you and I are broken. I get that, but just stop and listen to me for a minute. I didn't just turn my back on you. I tried to be a part of your life, but I didn't know how. Theo, it wasn't your fault, it was mine. At first, I tried to change you, and it was wrong. When I realized what I was doing and how wrong it was, I tried to figure out how to be in your life, without trying to change you, but all I did was make things worse. In the end, I couldn't bear seeing how much I was hurting you, so I stepped back and just let your mother take over, hoping that she could fix what I'd broken. But, as we both know, that only made things worse."

Alcorn looked down at the floor and let out a deep sigh.

"Son, I've made a mess of things, I know I have, but you have to know, for your own sake, that none of this was your fault; none of this was about you. It was about me being completely incompetent and not having the first clue what to do about it."

Theo didn't respond, but sat down silently, head bowed, next to his dad. Alcorn waited, giving his son as much time as he needed.

"The great General Theodore Eustace Alcorn, incompetent," said Theo, head still down. "I like the sound of that."

Theo looked over at him, the beginnings of a smile on his face, and Alcorn knew that, even though not everything was resolved between them, the bridge was not completely destroyed. There was hope, which was more than he had expected, and more than he deserved.

"Yeah," said Alcorn, "me too."

"So, now what?" said Theo. "You're not gonna hug me or something corny like that are you?"

"I don't know, I'm the incompetent one, remember? Am I supposed to hug you?"

"Let's pass on that for now," said Theo, "and figure out what we're going to do about Mom."

"Works for me," said Alcorn. He took a deep breath and looked away.

Now we really come to it, he thought.

"How much has your mother told you about her and me, and our working relationship?"

"Not that much, just that sometimes she offers you advice on some of your missions."

Alcorn shook his head. "Yeah, she undersold that one, by quite a bit," he said.

Theo looked confused. "What's that mean?"

"The truth is, your mother actually holds the same security level I do, and has almost my entire career. She's the reason I've been as successful as I have been. I doubt I would have made it past Captain if it weren't for her. Your mother and I are partners and have been in everything we've ever done."

"Except in raising me," said Theo.

"Even partners have disagreements, Theo. Your mother has never stopped trying to get us together; trying to get me to overcome my incompetence, among other things. So, don't blame her for any of the problems between us."

Theo looked down and didn't respond.

"Anyway," continued Alcorn, "as my career progressed and I climbed the ranks, one of our topics of discussion was the possibility of this very scenario, an enemy using my family against me. We came up with a plan, but I don't think you're going to like it."

Theo looked up at Alcorn, a concerned look on his face. "What is it?"

"Come on," said Alcorn, standing up, "we should tell everyone so there won't be any confusion when we're face-to-face with Ricnor and your mother."

Chapter 64

What Were You Thinking?

ucy.

Wait, what? Lucy?

Henry shook his head in an attempt to expel the unwanted thought of his wife, or ex-wife, or whatever she was from his mind.

What exactly is she anyway? He thought. *And why in God's name am I thinking of her now, when we're just about to rescue the General's wife.*

He shook his head again and looked around at everyone else from his secluded spot in the back of the ship, where he'd quietly escaped while Alcorn was explaining his rescue plan to the others. He'd listened to the plan, of course, but after his one and only experience with a gun nearly killed Gsefx during their first encounter, Henry had decided his role would be to provide moral support and nothing more.

Qilzar was in the pilot's seat, focused solely on the task of flying and safely landing the ship at the location Ricnor had instructed in his communication just a few minutes ago. Alcorn was sitting next to Qilzar, looking as grim as Henry had ever seen him, and that included the many interrogations they'd been through together before they ended up on the same side. Behind them sat Gsefx, Lhvunsa, and Theo, all sitting in silence, all looking straight ahead, either too focused on the task at hand to speak, or, more likely, not knowing what to say to one another at this moment in time.

As he looked at them, his thoughts inexplicably leapt back to Lucy. He wondered where she was and how she was doing. Then he remembered it was Lucy he was thinking of; she was doing fine. Still, he hoped she really was doing okay and finding the life she was looking for. Henry caught himself again. Why was he thinking about her at all, and why now? He tried to concentrate for a moment, examining his feelings to determine if perhaps, he was still in love with her, after all. He shook his head. No, that wasn't it. He had no desire to ever see her again, much less spend any time with her—particularly after what she'd done to him the last time they were together. No, it was something else, he just couldn't figure out what it was.

Come on Henry, he thought, *you're supposed to be this amazing reader of truths, why can't you figure out your own?*

"Look sharp, everyone," said Alcorn, breaking Henry's concentration. "We're here. Is everybody clear on what we're doing?"

Everyone nodded their heads in affirmation. Everyone, except Henry.

"Henry," said Alcorn, "are you with us?"

Lucy, along with Henry's search for truth, would have to wait.

"Yes," said Henry. "I'm with you."

Alcorn nodded his head in curt acknowledgement as the ship touched down.

Qilzar powered down and opened the door. Alcorn led the way, followed by Theo, Gsefx, and Lhvunsa, all armed with annihilators, which, according to Gsefx, were more accurate than obliterators, although not as powerful. Qilzar and Henry came last, unarmed. They would transfer the paintings from their ship to Ricnor's. A price all, including Henry, were willing to pay if it meant saving the life of Janice Alcorn.

Henry stepped from the ship onto what felt like concrete, although considering where he was, he was pretty certain it wasn't. He hadn't been paying attention when they were descending or landing, but it appeared they were in some sort of airplane hangar, or spaceship hangar to be more precise. By Earth standards, it seemed enormous, large enough for at least two dozen large passenger jets. But judging from his recent experiences in galactic travel, Henry guessed that this hangar was probably considered relatively small, by non-terrestrial standards. Qilzar had landed close to another craft, identical to the one they'd arrived in, except that it didn't have Gsefx's smaller ship connected to it.

Henry's observations were interrupted by the confrontation taking place just a few yards in front of him. Ricnor was there, holding Janice Alcorn tightly around the chest with one arm, and a spike to her throat with another. He'd seen Ricnor and that spike on the vidcon, but the screen had not done either of them justice. Henry had never seen anything more terrifying in his life.

Ricnor wasn't the only one doing the threatening. Alcorn, Theo, Gsefx, and Lhvunsa had their annihilators trained on Ricnor's head. It was a standoff and Janny's life depended on who blinked first. If Alcorn hadn't prepared them for what he was planning, Henry would most certainly have thought that the General had lost his mind. As it was, he still wasn't certain.

Henry looked back at Ricnor and then at Janny for the first time, and immediately took comfort in the look of resolve on her face. If she was scared, she wasn't giving Ricnor the satisfaction of showing it. Apparently, after being married to the General for all these years, Janice Alcorn was more than a match for anything this scary-looking space bastard could throw at her.

"If you want your wife to die," said Ricnor, breaking the silence first, "by all means, continue to point those weapons at me. If you care about her, I'd suggest dropping them on the ground. Now!"

"You should know by now that's simply not going to happen, Ricnor," said Alcorn, his voice firm, but calm. "Here is what is going to happen, though. We're going to hold up our end of the bargain. Qilzar and Henry are going to take the paintings out of the cargo hold of our ship and load them into your cargo hold. While they're doing that, you're going to hold onto Janny, and we're going to keep our annihilators pointed straight at your ugly little head."

Ricnor smiled.

"Is that so?" he said, maintaining eye contact with Alcorn.

"It is," said Alcorn, matching Ricnor's eye contact without flinching, "and I swear, if I see even the tiniest hint of a scratch on her neck, I will blow your head into the next galaxy."

"That would be ... inadvisable, General," said Ricnor. "But enough of this tiresome banter. If Qilzar and, whoever else it was you mentioned, are going to move the paintings, let them get to it."

"Qilzar! Henry!" said the General. "You heard the man ... or whatever the hell he is. Let's get this over with."

Qilzar, who was standing right in front of Henry, turned around.

"Shall we?" he said, making no effort to hide his rapidly fraying nerves.

"Lead the way," said Henry, who felt more numb than anything.

Henry followed as Qilzar led him to the cargo bay's outer access panel. Qilzar opened it and began handing Henry's own paintings to him. It took them three trips each to transfer the paintings, and thoughts of Lucy kept returning to Henry's mind. What was it about her that he couldn't shake?

Henry looked at the last painting Qilzar handed him and saw that it was the one he'd called 'Sunset Over An Empty Life.' He'd given it to Gsefx the day he'd landed on Earth, the day he'd almost killed himself, and probably would have if Gsefx hadn't literally crashed his party. So much had happened since then that the events of that day no longer seemed real. None of this seemed real. As he looked at the canvas in his hands, the one thing he knew for certain was that he wasn't the same person who painted this painting.

"Henry, what's wrong with you?" asked Qilzar. "Come on, let's go."

Henry looked up at Qilzar, who was clearly terrified.

"What seems to be the hold up?" asked Ricnor. "You aren't trying to pull a fast one, are you, Qilzar, my old friend?"

"No!" said Qilzar, his voice wavering nervously. "No, of course not. It seems our artist friend here is having a hard time letting go of one of his works. But, all is well. We're bringing the last of the paintings over now."

"That's good," said Ricnor. "Everything has gone well this far, I'd hate for things to turn badly for you now."

"Henry, come on!" growled Qilzar.

Henry nodded and began walking behind Qilzar toward Ricnor's ship. As he walked, Henry looked at the painting again, then looked over at the blue-skinned alien who had befriended him when he had no one else. Gsefx had understood him when no one else did. Then he turned to Alcorn, the overbearing and intimidating General, who turned out to be the most fair-minded and honest man Henry had ever met. He then looked at Theo, Lhvunsa, and Qilzar, and it suddenly made sense. Henry knew why Lucy kept popping up in his thoughts. He also knew what he had to do. He took a deep breath to steel his nerves, turned, and walked directly toward Ricnor.

He stopped just out of arms reach of the galaxy's most wanted criminal.

"No," he said in a voice that was neither loud nor soft, but was strong with a confidence Henry had never felt before. "You can have all of the other paintings, but not this one. This one is non-negotiable."

Ricnor smiled, being sure to show all of his razor sharp teeth, but never breaking his eye contact with the General.

"Ahhh, the painter," said Ricnor, his voice sickly sweet with condescension. "You clearly don't understand the first thing about negotiating. When someone like me has a spike to the throat of someone like her, everything is negotiable. Now, be a good little boy and put the painting on my ship, or the General may just shoot you before I have the pleasure of doing you in myself."

Henry held fast. He'd been ready to kill himself over much less not that long ago. Now, he was ready to die and even risk the life of another over much more.

"You know, Ricnor," he said, never taking his eyes off his adversary, "for someone who used to be known as the most notorious criminal in the galaxy, you're not very bright, are you? I mean, you tell me that I don't understand anything about negotiating with someone like you, and perhaps there is some truth to that. But what is clear to me is that you don't have the slightest idea who you're dealing with. Have you even looked at your captive—I mean really looked into her eyes? I don't think you have, because if you had, you'd have realized she lacks the one thing you need, the one thing you depend on for your very survival."

"And what is that, painter?" snarled Ricnor.

"Fear," said Henry. "Look at her, Ricnor. She's not afraid of you."

Ricnor flinched at that. It was slight, almost imperceptible, but it was there and Henry saw it. He took the opportunity to push harder.

"That's right," he said, "for all the shiny, sharp, and scary objects you carry around with you, designed to inspire fear in your victims, this woman, this primitive Earth creature, isn't scared of you. And neither are the rest of us."

"I'm not sure what your game is, painter," said Ricnor, trying to maintain his facade of confidence, "but I grow weary of it. General, tell this creature to put the painting on my ship or I will end her life in a most unpleasant way, regardless of whether or not she is scared of me."

"I don't think so," said Alcorn. "Henry is leading our negotiations now. He speaks for me. He speaks for all of us."

"You're making a deadly mistake, General," said Ricnor.

"No, he's not," said Henry, noticing the sweat now trickling down the side of Ricnor's face. "As the good General pointed out earlier, at the first sign of a scratch on his wife's neck, he will kill you. You may succeed in killing her, but you will die as well, and how will you profit from that? You're much better off taking what you have now and leaving for good. There are thirty paintings on board your ship, which, judging from your desire to have them, ought to be more than enough to compensate you for your troubles. Simply leave now and everyone wins."

Ricnor smiled, baring all of his teeth once again, but it was a smile that lacked the swagger it once carried.

"Perhaps you're a better negotiator than I gave you credit for, painter. But it won't work. We had a deal and you will hold up your end, or she will die. Even if it means I die with her."

Ricnor broke his visual connection with Alcorn to look at Henry.

"You say she's not scared to die, well neither am I. It's not about the money, painter, it's about winning."

In that instant, Henry knew the truth, not just that Ricnor was lying about being scared, he was, in fact, terrified, but he knew his own truth as well; about Lucy, about his art, and about himself. It felt good. It felt right.

"Good," he said. "I'm glad to hear you're not scared. It will make your transition from this life into the next that much easier."

Henry briefly caught the look of confusion on Ricnor's face as he turned his back on the criminal and walked away. He didn't flinch when he heard the sound of Alcorn's annihilator fire once, nor did he slow when he heard Ricnor's body hit the ground just milliseconds later. Though he longed to turn and watch when he heard the joyful sounds of the Alcorn family reunion, Henry Backus kept walking until he was face-to-face with his best friend in the entire galaxy.

"I think this belongs to you," he said as he handed the painting to Gsefx. "Try to hang on to it a little better this time, will ya?"

"By the Gods, Henry," said Gsefx, taking the painting and immediately setting it down on the ground in order to embrace his friend. "You scared us nearly out of our minds. What were you thinking?"

"I was thinking that, as the artist, I have the option of changing the title of my work, right?" said Henry, pointing to the painting. "Instead of 'Sunset Over an Empty Life' I'd like to call it 'Dawn of Endless Beginnings.'"

Gsefx smiled. "That wasn't exactly what I meant, but yes, I like that title much better."

Henry smiled back at his friend.

"When Qilzar handed me that painting," he said, "I looked at it and then I looked at all of you, and realized the sacrifices all of you were willing to make for each other, including me. I remembered back to the day you and I met and I gave you that painting. I'm not the same person I was then, and it's because of you. It's because of all of you."

By now the others had gathered around and were listening.

"When things ended with Lucy, I was a mess. I was totally lost. When Gsefx landed on Earth the first time, I was within seconds of ending my own life. I look back on that time and I don't even know that person anymore. I have all of you to thank for that. General Alcorn, I've been hounding you to 'find your truth' yet I didn't even know my own."

"And what is your truth, Henry?" asked Alcorn, one arm around his wife, the other around his son, and an ear-to-ear grin on his face.

"Well, for one thing, I need to make things right with Lucy ... not that we're getting back together, but to fix the way we left things; give it proper closure. She deserves that much. When I get back ..."

"Gsefx! Lhvunsa!" Qilzar was shouting from over near Ricnor's hold. Apparently he hadn't come over with the others. "Come here, everyone! Come quickly! You need to see this."

"This was lodged in between two of Henry's paintings," said the Dremin quietly, as they all gathered around to see what he'd found. Henry saw that he was holding up a small gray box. "It's addressed to Gsefx."

"What is it?" Asked Henry.

"It's a message box," said Gsefx, taking it from Qilzar. He pushed a button on the top and set it on the ground. "Let's see who wants to talk to me."

Light began streaming up from the box until it formed into the shape of a being so life-like, if Henry hadn't watched it spring from the box with his own eyes, he wouldn't have been able to tell it wasn't real.

"Congratulations, my friends," said the being, looking around at them, with eyes that seemed to actually see them. "Defeating Ricnor was no easy task, but I had every confidence you would succeed."

"Who the hell is this?" Asked Alcorn, echoing Henry's thoughts.

"You're probably wondering who I am," said the being, as if in response to Alcorn's question. "For lack of any better explanation, call me Gruleg for now. And, in answer to your next question, I've been watching you for some time and believed you had at least a reasonable chance of beating him. If you had failed, I would have simply killed Ricnor myself, and wrote you off as not being worth my time."

Gruleg smiled a wicked smile.

"Can you pause that thing?" Asked Alcorn.

Gsefx bent down and pressed a button on the box. Gruleg's image froze.

"What are you thinking, General?"

"I recognize him from somewhere," said Alcorn. "Theo, did we ... "

"He works, or worked for Ricnor," said Lhvunsa, interrupting the General. "He's the one who helped Ricnor get away. I remember seeing him after he broke through the wall in that scout ship ... as Ricnor was getting in."

"Yeah, that's right," said Alcorn, clearly trying to piece something together in his mind. "Why would he help Ricnor escape, only for us to kill him later? We could have killed or had him arrested right then. It doesn't make any sense."

"Maybe he didn't want to see him arrested," said Lhvunsa. "Maybe he wanted to make sure we killed Ricnor."

"Perhaps we should play the rest of the message and see if we can find out," said Gsefx. He pressed the button on the box and Gruleg began again.

"But since you did beat Ricnor," said Gruleg's image, continuing on, as if it had never been paused, "it shows me you are capable of so much—even more than you realize. Gsefx, for example, you are far more than the simple accountant you once thought you were, as I'm sure you've come to realize by now. And my friends from Earth, a world virtually unknown, filled with beings like Henry and the Alcorns, with natural talents and abilities that are only just beginning to be revealed. I have a feeling this planet, this Earth, might be worth further investigation. A time will soon come when I will need each of you and your abilities, but not just yet."

Gruleg paused and looked around, eerily meeting each one of them eye-to-eye. Henry felt a surge of something when Gruleg's eyes met his. It felt like amusement.

"In the meantime, it's important for you to know that I'll be watching," said Gruleg, his gaze fixed on Henry.

The image disappeared.

"He's here," said Henry, looking around. "He's somewhere close by, I can feel him."

Without warning, laughter filled the hangar with a force that nearly knocked them all to the ground.

"Well done, Henry!" Gruleg's voice came out of the laughter from every direction. "Well done, indeed! Remember, I'll be watching!"

Chapter 65

My Home is Where My Friends Are

Gsefx sat next to Lhvunsa on a makeshift bench they pulled together from some old, leftover engine parts that had clearly seen better days. Nearly a sar had passed since they'd found Gruleg's message and were nearly knocked off their feet by his maniacal laughter. The GCP had arrived and were busy scurrying around the hangar, doing all the various things GCP officers do, completely ignoring Gsefx, Lhvunsa and the rest of their party. Gsefx leaned over to kiss his wife.

"It occurs to me, my darling," he said, "that I owe you a vacation to that resort on Alnost. Once we're finished up here, why don't we slip away for a while? I think we deserve it, don't you?"

"I can't think of anything I would enjoy better, my love," said Lhvunsa, returning her husband's kiss.

"Ahem," said Qilzar, coming up from behind them. "I do hate to interrupt this pleasant reunion, but you cannot go to Alnost, because you cannot take a break. Gsefx, my dear boy, the Pigawitts audit is not going away just because of our little adventure here, and now that we know of Planvc's malfeasance, we'll essentially have to start over..."

Lhvunsa silenced the Dremin with a single hand over his mouth.

"Qilzar," she said, getting to her feet, "if you think Gsefx is going straight back to work after all of this, you have lost your mind."

At this, Qilzar raised his hand, not to defend himself but to point, indicating that Lhvunsa and Gsefx should look behind them.

Gsefx and his wife turned around to see Henry, General Alcorn, his wife Janny, and Theo all laughing at what was, presumably, a joke on them.

"Just kidding," said Qilzar, when Lhvunsa released him. "Well, not about how much work we have to do, but about you returning right away. Please take as much time as you need."

Gsefx and Lhvunsa joined the laughter, enjoying this peaceful moment with their friends.

At that moment, the GCP Officer in Charge approached the group and addressed Gsefx.

"Et Gsefx," he said, "the GCP is wrapping things up here and you're all free to go."

"Excellent," said Gsefx. "Thank you, officer." He watched the officer return to his troops, then turned back to his friends.

"Well then, I suppose it's time for us to say our goodbyes and return to our homes. I will miss you all terribly, but, I suspect our absence from one another will be short, for we are bound together now and we will see each other again, soon."

"Gsefx," said Henry, smiling, "if you don't mind, I'd like to stay, that is, if you'll help me figure out how to live out here amongst the stars."

Gsefx was taken aback, but was also somewhat relieved at not having to part with his friend.

"Yes, of course, Henry, if you're certain that's what you want."

"My home is where my friends are," said Henry, "and while some of them are returning to Earth, my best friend lives on Clangdor. There is nothing for me on Earth. But out here … out here, there is a galaxy to conquer."

Gsefx smiled and nodded, then looked at Lhvunsa.

"What do you think, my dear? Do you think we can handle a visitor for a while?"

"We can, right after we get back from Alnost," she said, holding up a slender green hand to ward off any protest. "In the meantime, I'm sure Henry will be quite comfortable in our home while we're away."

"It's settled then," said Gsefx, leaning in to give his wife another kiss. "You'll stay with us."

"Thank you, both," said Henry. "I promise I won't be an unwelcome guest, and that I'll only stay long enough to sell a few of my paintings. Then I'll find a place of my own."

Gsefx looked around to ensure he would not be overheard by the GCP.

"Have you sensed any sign that our friend has returned?" He asked Henry.

Henry closed his eyes and lowered his head for a moment.

"No," he said, finally. "I haven't felt anything from Gruleg since that awful laugh of his. He's gone, for now at least."

"That's good news," said Gsefx. He turned to the Alcorns.

"I guess this is farewell, my Earth-bound friends," he said.

"It looks that way," said the General. "These GCP fellas look like they're ready for us to clear out of here. I have to admit, I'm ready for a good night's sleep in my own bed."

Gsefx stepped closer to the General. He tried to speak, but Alcorn beat him to it.

"Gsefx, please, no words," said the General, speaking in a low voice. "We are both leaders, and we both know that with this Gruleg in the picture, we'll need to be in touch again soon enough. In the meantime, keep an eye on Henry and make sure he gets into a little bit of trouble, but not too much."

Gsefx smiled and nodded, but said nothing.

They said the rest of their goodbyes, then Gsefx, Lhvunsa and Henry boarded their ship. As they did, Gsefx overheard the General make a comment about how he was fortunate that Janny and Lhvunsa didn't have time to get better acquainted, or he would be in real trouble. He mentioned it to Lhvunsa, who smiled sadly and said she'd explain it to him later.

Once aboard, Gsefx looked out the window to see the Alcorns boarding a GCP ship and wondered aloud when he would see them again.

"Don't worry, my friend," said Henry, a mischievous grin on his face. "Something tells me it won't be long."

Gsefx smiled back and began working the console in preparation for their return trip.

"Henry," said Lhvunsa, "what about Lucy? You were going to reconcile things with her when you went back to Earth. Now that you're not returning, you won't be able to make things right with her."

Gsefx turned away from the console to look at his friend. The mischievousness was gone from Henry's face, but in its place was a look of contentment.

"I've asked General Alcorn to contact her. He will see to it that she gets what she wants and she will be content. It's not the way I wanted to handle it, but it won't really matter to Lucy."

"You're a good soul, Henry Backus," said Lhvunsa. "I'm glad you are Gsefx's friend."

"As am I," said Henry.

"Me too," said Gsefx.

"Okay, enough with the mushy stuff," said Henry. "How about a little traveling music?"

"As you wish, my friend," said Gsefx.

"Oh, by the Gods, not that noise you call rock and roll," said Lhvunsa, but it was too late. Gsefx had already pressed play.

Night is day and day is night
Don't say I won't 'cause you know I might.
You are wrong and I am right
Don't cross my path 'less ya wanna fight.

Rock on my children!
Rock on my love!
Rock all day and rock all night,
Roll in the sounds from heaven above.

Appendix A

Proper Names of Non-Terrestrials

As one might imagine with the dizzying variation of planets, languages, and naming conventions represented by the approximately 1.2 million member worlds that currently make up the Galactic Community (GC), proper names can pose a particularly difficult challenge across all spectrums of everyday life. The following guide is offered in an effort to assist with pronunciation.

Gsefx:	Pronounced "Zef"
Lhvunsa:	Pronounced "Loon-sa"
Qilzar:	Pronounced "Kill-zar"
Xtlar:	Pronounced "Ex-lar"
Planvc:	Pronounced "Plank"
Tsedle:	Pronounced "Teedle"
Ricnor:	Pronounced "Rick-nor"
Klarnus:	Pronounced "Klar-nus"
Dilnch:	Pronounced "Diln-cha"
Gruleg:	Pronounced "Groo-leg"

Appendix B

Time Measurements

Each planet in the Galactic Community (GC) has their own way of measuring time, usually based upon their planet's movement around their system's sun. As representatives from planets across the GC sought to standardize time measurements across all populated systems, they ultimately devised a system that divides time into units with a standard length, rather than a length based upon an individual planet's rotation around a particular sun. The base unit of this system is a "byt," with all other units being multiples of 10 of that unit. The following chart provides the Standard terminology and its functional equivalency in Earth time.

Galactine Standard	Functional Earth Equivalent
byt	second
ebyt	minute (100 byts)
sar	hour (100 ebyts)
rotation	day (10 sars)
multi-rotation/"multi-rot"	week (10 rotations)
grouping	month (10 multi-rots)
Semi-Turn	6 months (5 groupings)
Turn	Year (10 groupings or 2 semi-turns)

About the Author

David Allen Kimmel is the only member of his family born in Oregon after the family escaped to the state's central Willamette Valley from the rapidly advancing urban sprawl that began enveloping the Concord, California area in the early sixties. Raised on a farm, but never one for the outdoors, Kimmel spent much of his youth traveling to the distant (and often magical) lands he found in his books. Among his favorite authors are J.R.R. Tolkien, Terry Brooks, Anne McCaffery, Robert Silverberg, Isaac Asimov, Ray Bradbury, Stephen R. Donaldson and Douglas Adams. Kimmel currently makes his home in the less wide open spaces of Yukon, Oklahoma with his wife, daughter, son-in-law and two grandchildren. Kimmel is still trying to convince his daughter and granddaughter that Star Trek doesn't suck.

Kimmel loves to hear from his readers and can be followed and/or reached via the following:

Web/Blog: www.davidallenkimmel.com
e-mail: davidallenkimmel@gmail.com
Facebook: facebook.com/davidallenkimmel
Twitter: @dak1963
Google+: google.com/+davidallenkimmel